Richard Morris

Legends of the holy rood

Symbols of the passion and cross-poems

Richard Morris

Legends of the holy rood
Symbols of the passion and cross-poems

ISBN/EAN: 9783337153724

Printed in Europe, USA, Canada, Australia, Japan

Cover: Foto ©Andreas Hilbeck / pixelio.de

More available books at **www.hansebooks.com**

Legends of the Holy Rood;

Symbols of the Passion

and

Cross-Poems.

In Old English of the Eleventh, Fourteenth,
and Fifteenth Centuries.

EDITED FROM MSS. IN THE BRITISH MUSEUM AND
BODLEIAN LIBRARIES;

WITH INTRODUCTION, TRANSLATIONS, AND GLOSSARIAL INDEX.

BY

RICHARD MORRIS, LL.D.,

*Editor of Hampole's 'Pricke of Conscience,' 'The Ayenbite of Inwyt,'
'Early English Homilies,' etc. etc.;
Member of the Council of the Philological and Early English Text Societies.*

LONDON

PUBLISHED FOR THE EARLY ENGLISH TEXT SOCIETY,

BY N. TRÜBNER & CO., 60, PATERNOSTER ROW.

MDCCCLXXI.

Agents for the sale of the Early English Text Society's Publications.

DUBLIN: WILLIAM McGEE, 18 Nassau Street.

EDINBURGH: T. G. STEVENSON, 22 South Frederick Street.

GLASGOW: OGLE & Co., 1 Royal Exchange Square.

BERLIN: ASHER & Co., Unter den Linden, 20.

NEW YORK: C. SCRIBNER & Co.; LEYPOLDT & HOLT.

PHILADELPHIA: J. B. LIPPINCOTT & Co.

46

OXFORD:
BY T. COMBE, M.A., E. B. GARDNER, AND E. PICKARD HALL,
PRINTERS TO THE UNIVERSITY.

CONTENTS.

APPENDIX.

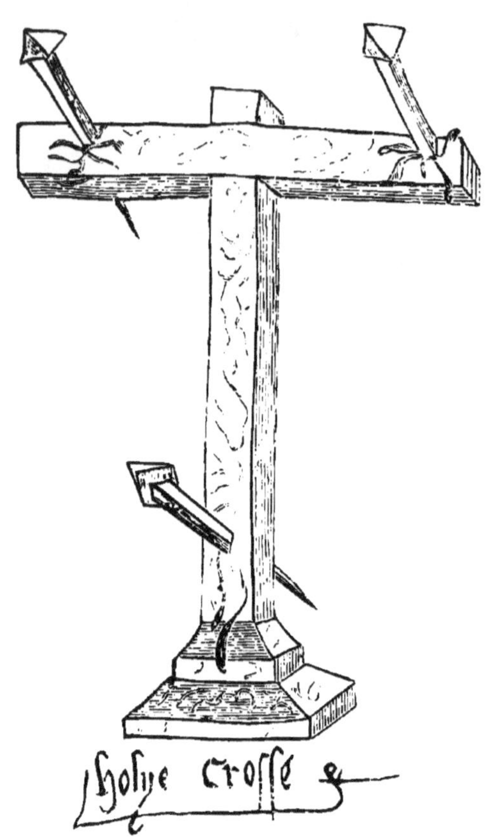
holye crosse

PREFACE.

WHILE consulting Hickes's *Thesaurus*, my attention was suddenly attracted by a reference to an Old English homily on the *Finding of the Cross*. Ascertaining that it had never been printed, and hoping that Old English students, who had read the beautiful legend of "Elene, or the Invention of the Cross," in Kemble's edition of the *Vercelli Poems*, might like to have a prose version of the story, I determined to edit it for the Early English Text Society. This homily is the first piece in our collection of Legends of the Holy Rood. It is printed from a MS. in the Bodleian Library, Auct. F. iv. 32.

While engaged upon this, I recollected that I had seen or heard of other Old English legends, and as soon as I could procure transcripts, I put them into print. Thus the work gradually grew larger and larger[1] while passing through the press, and a tolerably complete collection of legends, in an English form, concerning the Invention and Exposition of the Cross (celebrated by two festivals of the Christian Church) will be found in the present volume.

A few Cross-poems have been added, one of which deserves special mention, namely, the "Dispute between Mary and the Cross" (p. 131).

[1] This fact will account for the strange arrangement of some of the pieces.

After the version from the Vernon MS. was printed, another and rather longer copy turned up in Royal MS. 18 A x, with some additional verses on the "Festivals of the Church," in the same metre as the Cross-poem. These I have added in an Appendix.

Of the second poem, on the "Finding of the Cross" (p. 19), I have printed two versions—one from the Ashmolean MS. 43, Bodleian Library, of the latter part of the thirteenth century, which has been collated with an imperfect copy in Harl. MS. 2277, of the same date, which contains lives of the saints, &c.; the other from the Vernon MS., fourteenth century.

As the history of Cyriacus, the brother of Stephen the martyr, is included in the legends relating to the "Finding of the Cross," I have also added two versions of the saint's life.

The third legend (p. 62) contains the history of the material out of which the Rood was made, from the time it was a pippin until it was wrought into a cross[1]. It also relates the story "*De Fabrice Clavorum*," which I have not met with elsewhere in an English form.

This legend, as well as No. IV. (p. 87) and No. VII. (p. 122) are printed from Harleian MS. 4196, a bulky volume, containing metrical homilies and lives of saints in the Northumbrian dialect.

"The Uplifting of the Holy Rood," No. V. (p. 98), is taken from Ælfric's minster homilies in Cotton MS., Julius E vii. Ælfric's discourse on the "Finding of the Cross" will be found in Thorpe's edition of Ælfric's *Homilies*.

The sixth legend, "How the Holy Cross was found by St. Elene," is from the West-Midland version of the *Cursor Mundi*, Fairfax MS. 14, Bodleian Library[2].

The same story is found in the Northumbrian copy of the *Cursor Mundi*, in the British Museum, Cotton MS., Vespasian A iii, and in a MS. belonging to the University Library of Göttingen.

[1] A similar version of a portion of this story, but of an earlier date, is printed in my *Specimens of Early English* (p. 140).

[2] For the transcript of the pieces from the MSS. in the Bodleian Library, I am indebted to Mr. G. Parker.

This legend on the "Finding of the Cross" is very different from the others already noticed; and instead of the story of Judas or Cyriacus occupying a prominent place, it only comes in at the fag-end as an illustration of the diverse stories that are told of the Rood (p. 120). Instead of the ordinary legend, we get the story, so well known to us all in the *Merchant of Venice*, of the merchant and the pound of flesh[1].

All the pieces from I. to X. inclusive, are now for the first time printed.

The next two pieces (XI. and XII. p. 154–169) are from Caxton's *Golden Legend*, and these again supply a few particulars not found in the other legends.

The "Symbols of the Passion" are now for the first time edited from Royal MS. 17 A 27, and Addit. MS. 22,029, collated with another copy without the illustrations in Addit. MS. 11,748.

The curious illustrations are furnished by Professor de la Motte, who has kindly made the Society a present of those from the Addit. MS. 22,029.

R. M.

KING'S COLLEGE, LONDON,
Feb., 1871.

[1] Kemble seemed to think that this legend was only contained in the Göttingen MS. He has rightly noticed its absence from the Midland version of the *Cursor* in Trinity College Library.

INTRODUCTION.

§ 1. The Finding of the Cross.

"THe Inuencion of the holy crosse is sayd by cause that this daye the holy crosse was founden· for tofore it was founden of seth in paradyse terrestre / Lyke as it shall be sayde hereafter: and also it was founden of salamon in the monte of lybane and of the quene of saba / in the temple of salamon And of the Iewes in the water of pyseyne· And on this daye it was founden of Helayne in the mounte of caluarye /"

These prefatory remarks to the "Invention of the Cross" in the *Golden Legend* (see p. 154) suggest the order in which a summary of the legends contained in the following pages should be written.

§ 2. The Finding of the Cross by Seth in Paradise.

When Adam and Eve were driven out of Paradise for eating of the "apple tree," God promised to send them the *oil of mercy* (pp. 18, 19), wherewith they should be anointed and be healed of their sin-wounds which covered their bodies from "head to heel" to the number of "sixty and ten" (p. 64).

In the vale of Hebron Adam and Eve had passed more than

nine hundred years in sorrow and woe. They had lost during this interval their two sons, and as a kind of penance for their sins, they remained apart for more than two hundred years[1]. At our Lord's bidding Adam and Eve came together again, and after a time Seth was born. When Adam was nine hundred and thirty-two years old, he found himself enfeebled by toil, sickness, and old age, and he longed to die. But before his death he wished to be anointed with the oil of mercy. He calls Seth unto him and tells him of his ills (pp. 20, 21).

Seth has no idea what *pain and sorrow* mean, and thinks that his father's sickness arises from a longing for the fruits of Paradise (p. 62). But Adam tells Seth of God's promise to him on leaving Paradise, and bids him go to Paradise, and entreat the angel at the gate of Eden to send him the oil of mercy (p. 22)—the oil of life, "that medicine is to man and wife" (p. 65).

Seth being ignorant of the way thither, Adam gives him full instructions for his journey; and so Seth, starting from the head of the valley of Hebron, finds a green path which leads to the gate of Paradise (p. 22); then, turning eastward (p. 66[2]), he comes upon the way by which Adam and Eve had left Paradise, upon which, ever since the Fall, no grass had grown. Following this track, he reaches the gate of Paradise (made known to him by a great light, like that of a burning fire[3]), and with prayer and supplication he beseeches God to send his father the oil of mercy (pp. 22, 66, 154). While praying, St. Michael appears to Seth, and tells him that it is useless to pray for the oil of mercy, for it will not be sent upon earth until five thousand two hundred and twenty years shall have elapsed, when Christ shall come to die for man's sin[4] (p. 67).

The angel then commands Seth to put his head within the gate of Eden, and to note well whatever he sees therein. He did as he was bidden, and saw more marvels than tongue could tell. The

[1] Adam determined upon this penance because *woman* was the root of all his misfortunes (pp. 20, 21).

[2] See *Specimens of Early English*, p. 140.

[3] See *Specimens of Early English*, p. 141.

[4] The *Golden Legend* says 5550 years.

meads were decked with gay herbs and trees, diffusing all around most delightful perfumes; the trees were loaded with delicious fruits, and the birds sang joyously. In this land of delight and of joy Seth would fain dwell for ever.

In the middle of Paradise he saw a bright, shining well, out of which flowed four streams that watered all the world [1].

Above the well there stood a large tree with many branches, but without bark or leaves, like an aged tree (pp. 24, 68). Seth supposed that the tree stood thus bare on account of his parents' sin (p. 68; *Specimens*, p. 142).

A serpent, "all naked, without skin," was embracing the tree. This was the tree and the serpent that caused Adam first to commit sin (p. 24; *Specimens*, p. 142).

A second time Seth looked in, and to his amazement the tree was covered with bark and leaves, and appeared to reach unto heaven; and in the top of the tree he beheld a new-born bairn lapped in "small" (or swaddling) clothes [2].

The root of the tree went down into the uttermost ends of hell, and there he saw the soul of his brother Abel. Then the angel drove Seth from the gate, and he saw no more. These sights were afterwards explained to him. The babe in the top of the tree was God's Son, who in the fulness of time should bring mankind the oil of mercy (pp. 24, 69, 70).

When Seth took leave of the angel, he received three pippins or kernels of an apple, which he was bidden to put under Adam's tongue as soon as he was dead. Out of these three kernels three trees—cedar, cypress, and pine—would spring. These "wands" or rods betoken the Trinity: the cedar, "a tree of height," denotes the Father; the cypress, a tree of sweet savour, represents the Son; and the pine [3], a fruit-bearing tree, is a type of the Holy Ghost and His gifts (pp. 26, 70; *Specimens*, p. 144).

Seth returns home, and tells Adam of the oil of mercy that should come through the birth of a blissful Child, near the end of

[1] The *Cursor* names the four streams Tyson, Fison, Tigri, Eufrate (*Specimens*, p. 142, Genes.).

[2] The *Cursor* adds that the child lay squealing for Adam's sin (*Specimens*, p. 143).

[3] The *olive* seems to be the tree that is really meant.

the world, and of his death which should take place within three days. Great was Adam's joy when he heard of his approaching death, and for once in his life he laughed. He had endured so much sorrow and care, that he had rather dwell in hell than live any longer upon earth (pp. 26, 71; *Specimens*, pp. 144, 145).

When Adam died, his weeping wife and children tried to restore him to life, whereupon the archangel Michael appeared to them, and showed them what to do with the corpse. Under his direction, accompanied by angels "singing all full solemnly and making noble melody," they carried the dead body to the vale of Hebron, where it was laid in the earth; and they were told that for the future the dead must be buried "in earth or stone" (p. 72).

The pippins which had been placed under the root of Adam's tongue after a time began to grow, and three small wands or trees grew up, and stood in Adam's mouth until the time of Moses. Each grew separately by itself out of the same root, and was of an *ell* in length and no more.

§ 3. The Finding of the Rods by Moses.

After the Israelites crossed the Red Sea, they came unto the vale of Hebron; and one evening, as Moses was walking along, he came upon the place where the three trees were growing. Moses greeted these signs of the Trinity, and drew them out of the earth, from which issued "so noble a smell," that all the Israelites believed that they had at last reached the land of promise (pp. 26, 73).

By means of these wands Moses healed the sick, and performed numerous other miracles. When he knew that his end was near, he planted the wands beside a stream under Mount Tabor, in the land of Arabia (pp. 29, 75).

§ 4. The Finding of the Rods by David.

For a thousand years the wands continued in the same state, until King David, instructed by God, found them, and brought them to Jerusalem (pp. 28, 75)[1].

[1] The old Dutch legend, *Geschiedenis van het heylighe Cruys* (ed. Berjeau),

As it was eventide when he reached home, he planted the wands in a "dike," and set trusty men to see that no harm happened to them. On the morning, he found the wands grown into one tree with three branches springing from the top, so he did not attempt to remove it, but built around it a strong wall, and to mark its yearly growth he put around it a silver ring. For thirty years the tree stood in the same spot, and after that grew no more (pp. 28, 76, 77)[1].

Under the holy tree David did penance for his sins, and composed the whole of the Psalter (pp. 30, 78).

§ 5. The Rood-tree cut down by command of Solomon.

For fourteen years David was engaged in building the Temple, which after two and thirty years was completed by Solomon. When the work was almost finished, the carpenters found themselves in want of a large beam, but they could not find any tree of sufficient size to furnish it, except that which David had planted; whereupon Solomon ordered it to be cut down and taken into the Temple. The carpenters measure off thirty-one cubits, and after working it up, they find it one cubit too long. They take off the excess, and on measuring it again find it one cubit too short (pp. 30, 79, 80). Thrice they alter it to no purpose, so they inform the king of their extraordinary failure, and he commands them to make a bridge with it across an old ditch[2].

contains the following account of two miracles performed by David on his way to Jerusalem:—

XII.

"King David, here, as Scriptures say,
A great lord meets upon the way,
All leper-like, with sores and blains,
Till David cured him of his pains.

XIII.

And as he journeys with the trees,
Three black men coming soon he sees,
Who, touched with those three rods of might,
Became, in good sooth, pure and white."

[1] "To the west of Jerusalem is a fair church, where the tree of the Cross grew." Maundeville, in *Early Travels in Palestine*, ed. T. Wright, Bohn's series, p. 175.

[2] The brook over which the tree was placed is called Kedron in Norris's *Cornish*

§ 6. The Rood-tree discovered by the Queen of Sheba.

Here it remained until the Queen of Sheba, on her visit to Solomon, discovered it, and paid great honour to it. She advised Solomon not to allow the beam to remain, for a man should die thereon who should destroy the Mosaic Law; so he caused it to be removed, and buried deep and hidden from all men (pp. 32, 83)[1].

§ 7. The Rood-tree found in the Piscine.

Here, after some time, there sprang up a deep well, which, owing to the beam of the sacred tree, was endowed with miraculous powers of healing; so it was visited by the sick, who bathed therein and were healed (pp. 32, 82).

When Jesus came upon earth, the tree began to float; and when the Jews were in want of a "tree" on which to hang our Lord, they thought of the floating beam, and took it up and made thereof a cross (pp. 32, 84, 155).

§ 8. Of the Number of Pieces in the Cross.

The Cross was made out of two-thirds of the beam; and the part above ground was eight cubits long, the pieces on each side were of three cubits (p. 85).

In the *Golden Legend* (p. 155) the four pieces of the Cross are mentioned as consisting of four different kinds of wood:—

(1) The upright beam; (2) the over-thwart or cross-bar, upon which the arms were nailed; (3) the piece upon which was fixed the

Drama, i. 425. Maundeville speaks of the Rood-tree as having once been used as a bridge over the brook Cedron (*Early Travels in Palestine*, Bohn's edition, p. 176, *Notes and Queries*, vol. vii. p. 334, 1853).

[1] The old Dutch legend in Berjeau's *Holy Cross* says that after Solomon was rebuked by Queen Sheba for letting the tree serve for a bridge, he gave orders

> "To place it o'er the temple's door,
> Where men should bless it evermore."

Abias (Abijah) afterwards took the gold and silver from off it, that Solomon had placed around it, and the Jews removed it from the Temple.

table containing the superscription; (4) the socket, or mortise, in which the main beam stood.

The four kinds of wood were palm, cypress[1], cedar, and olive.

> "Quatuor ex lignis domini crux dicitur esse;—
> Pes crucis est cedrus; corpus tenet alta cupressus;
> Palma manus retinet; titula lætatur oliva."

§ 9. The Legend of Maximilla, the first Christian Martyr.

The Northumbrian version of the history of the Cross-beam (pp. 62–85) has a few variations from the Southern versions, and introduces a legend, probably of later origin, that I have not met with elsewhere in an English form[2]. Instead of the beam being turned into a bridge, Solomon is said to have caused it to be placed between two pillars of the Temple, and to have commanded that once a year every one should visit the "holy tree," and honour it "in their best manner." So it befell upon a year that all the country far and near went to Jerusalem to honour the sacred beam; and among the worshippers was an unbelieving woman (p. 80)—

> "She sought thither the sight to see,
> And trowed no virtue in the tree."

The woman, whose name was *Maximilla*, in unbelief sat upon the "tree," and forthwith her clothes took fire and burnt like tow. Then she began to prophesy,

> "And said, 'My Lord, mighty Jesu,
> Have mercy, and on me thou rue."

When the Jews heard her call upon Jesus, they were exceedingly angry, because she had slandered their God by the mention of

[1] Some say the stem was made of cypress, because it was a wood that did not easily decay.

[2] This legend is found in Arundel MS. 507: "Entre eux vient une femme Maximalla;" and in the Cornish play of "The Beginning of the World" (*The Cornish Drama*, ed. Norris).

a new one, so they turned her out of the town and stoned her to death—

"SHE WAS THE FIRST THAT SUFFERED SHAME,
FOR THE MENTIONING OF JESU'S NAME."

Many who had witnessed this sight honoured the "tree" more than any earthly thing (p. 82), whereat the Jews were grieved, and therefore secretly removed it, and cast it into a "dike," for they were afraid to burn or break it up. But God would not suffer the tree to be hid, but sent his angels between "undern and prime" to move the water in the dike; and all the sick and sore that got into the ditch when the water was moved, were healed "through virtue of the holy tree." Then the Jews took the beam out of the water, and turned it into a bridge "over a beck" (p. 82), hoping that it would soon be destroyed by the great wear and tear that it would be subjected to. Thus the tree lay until the sage queen "*Dame Sibell*[1]" came to Jerusalem, when she laid her clothes upon the bridge, and went over it barefooted, and "prophesied" that the "tree" was a true token of a "doomsman" who should judge all men. Here the tree was allowed to remain until Christ was about to suffer death (p. 83).

§ 10. The Making of the Nails of the Rood[2].

The Northern version of the history of the Rood contains also a legend on the making of the nails, which is as follows:—

The Cross is made, but three nails are wanting. The Jews go to a smith in the town, and bid him quickly

"Make three nails, stiff and good,
To nail the prophet on the rood."

[1] The Queen of Sheba is here confounded with Sibyl, as in the Arundel MS. 507: "La sage reyne Sibille vient a Jerusalem pour esprouuer le sauoir de Salomon." The old Dutch legend of the Cross does not make this confusion, but the story of the piscine goes before the story of the Queen of Sheba's visit; and as *Sibilla* is put to death, she is evidently confounded with the Maximilla of our English legend. The subject of chap. 49, bk. i. vol. i. of Gretser, is—"Crucem Domini apud Ethnicos per *Sibyllas* fuisse prænunciatam."

[2] This story is found in Norris's *Cornish Drama*, pp. 433–439.

When the "smith" heard that Jesus, whom he believed to be a prophet "true and good," was to be crucified, he was greatly grieved, and determined that he would not make any nails for this purpose (p. 84).

With boldness he answered the Jews, and said, "Ye shall get no nails from me. God has set his mark upon me, so that I cannot work." In his bosom he laid his hand, and said he had hurt it on a "brand," and had such pain in it that he expected to lose his hand.

The Jews would not believe him, but demanded to see his hand, which, when they saw it, appeared as though it were sore, but in reality was not so.

The Jews, being satisfied, were going about their business, when

> "Forth came then the smithës wife,
> A fell woman, and full of strife."

By the Jews she stood, and did not say much for her husband's good. "Sir," said she, "since when hast thou had such a malady? Yesterday evening your hands were uninjured. But since sickness is sent to thee, these men shall not be unserved, but shall have the nails ere they go, as soon, at least, as I myself can make them." So she set to work, blew fast the bellows, and at last made the iron hot. Then the Jews helped her to strike the iron, so that the three nails were soon made. Though they were very large, and roughly made, the Jews would not refuse them, but took them immediately, and with glad hearts hastily went their way until they came to "Sir Pilate."

§ 11. On the Number of the Nails.

The number of nails employed in the Crucifixion is a contested point. A writer in *Notes and Queries*, Series III. vol. iii. p. 315, in showing that *three* nails are depicted in the Crucifixion as early as the twelfth century, quotes the following from Labarte's *Handbook of the Arts of the Middle Ages*:—

"Fig. 14. Copper crucifix, twelfth century, Coll. Soltykoff. (No. 332, Debruge Labarte Coll.) Copper, enamelled and gilt. The

Saviour is not clothed in the long Byzantine robe of the eleventh century, but in a tunic descending to the knees, in which he is represented until the fourteenth century. His feet are not crossed or nailed, but rest on a tablet (*suppeditanum*), which a third nail fixes to the Cross. Before the thirteenth century, Jesus was attached to the Cross by four nails, one to each hand and foot. In consequence of some anterior discussions, the feet from this period were placed over each other, and attached by a single nail, it having been settled that three nails only were used at the Crucifixion. Cimabue is said to have been the first painter who adopted this arrangement. This crucifix (fig. 14) was made at the end of the twelfth century, when the four nails had been rejected, but the feet had not been superposed; so, to get rid of the difficulty, the third nail is here attached to the tablet which supports the feet."

"St. Gregory Nazianzen says of the taking down from the Cross, Γυμνὸν τριστήλῳ κείμενον ξύλῳ λαβών, clearly intimating that our Saviour was fixed to the Cross with *three* nails only.

"Nonnus, the Greek poet, in the fifth century describes the sacred feet of our Lord as placed one over the other, and fastened down with a single large nail.

"On the other hand, St. Cyprian, St. Augustine, St. Gregory of Tours, and Pope Innocent III, as also Rufinus and Theodoret, reckon *four* nails." (F. C. H. in *Notes and Queries*, Series III. vol. iii. p. 392.)

Ælfric speaks of *four* nails: "The Jews . . . . . fixed him [Jesus] on a Cross with *four* nails." (*The Homilies* of Ælfric, ed. Thorpe, vol. i. p. 217.)

The author of the *Ancren Riwle* notices the tradition of *three* nails: "His dear body, that was extended on the Cross, broad as a shield above, in his outstretched arms, and narrow beneath, because, as men suppose, the one foot was placed upon the other foot." (*Ancren Riwle*, p. 391.)

Curtius, in his treatise *De Clavis Dominicis* (seventeenth century), is in favour of four nails. See Gretser, vol. i. bk. i. cap. 93; Lipsius, lib. ii. cap. 9.

§ 12. The Finding of the Cross by St. Helena.

After the crucifixion the Jews tried to hide the Cross from Christians, so they buried it along with the two crosses whereon the thieves were hung, and for two hundred years they lay "under earth" (pp. 35, 108).

Adrian knew where the Cross was, but to prevent Christians from finding it out, he built a heathen temple on the spot; and so the place was forsaken, and finally neither pagan nor Christian knew where the Rood lay (p. 35).

After a time Constantine became emperor[1], pious and honourable, and a friend to Christians, although as yet he was unbaptized.

In the sixteenth year of his reign, a foreign but mighty nation assembled on the banks of the Danube to make war upon the Roman people[2]. Constantine, praying for divine assistance, marched against his foes; but, when he saw the hostile hosts, he was sad unto death, expecting that all his army would perish in the conflict. The night before the battle the emperor had a vision, in which he saw an angel, who bade him to be of good cheer, and to look up to heaven. On looking up he saw in the sky the sacred token of Christ's Cross, and above the Cross was written these words: "By this conquer" (p. 3).

On the morrow he commanded a cross to be made, after the pattern of that which he had seen in his vision, and caused it to be borne before him in battle, instead of a banner.

As soon as the enemy saw the sign of the holy Rood, they were seized with a panic, and fled; so Constantine won the victory through the power of the Cross (pp. 4, 36, 37, 88, 109).

When the emperor returned home, he made enquiry concerning the Cross, and whose token it was. Christians came and told him of the Trinity, and of the advent and death of Christ; so the emperor became a Christian, and was baptized by Pope Silvester (pp. 4, 36).

[1] The dates given in these legends are very incorrect. No. I. places Constantine's reign in the year 133 after the Passion; in the Vercelli poem (No. XI. Golden Legend) it is "an C yere and more."

[2] Eusebius, in his *Life of Constantine*, &c., speaks only of the war between the emperor and Maxentius.

Constantine, through reading holy books, learnt that the Cross was somewhere in Jerusalem; so he sent Helena his mother (who is said to have been seventy years old at this time) there to find, if possible, where it was hidden.

When Helena came to Jerusalem, she called together all the Jewish citizens, and bade them choose the wisest of their kin, who should come before her and tell her what she was desirous of knowing.

A thousand of the wisest of the Jewish people appeared before her, and she commanded them to select the wisest from among them to answer a question that she was about to propose to them (pp. 6, 38, 91).

After leaving the queen's presence in great fear, they discussed among themselves what the question might be. Then one Judas, the son of Simon, and brother of Stephen the martyr, said unto them: "I know what the question will be; for the queen will ask us where the Cross of Christ was laid. But beware that none of you tell her; for I know well that thereupon shall all the ordinances of our law be destroyed. For Zacheus my grandfather said to Simon my father, and my father at his death said to me, 'Inquiry shall be made concerning the Cross on which our elders hanged Jesus Christ; but beware, tell not[1], for any torment that thou shalt suffer, where the Cross of Jesus was laid; for after that it shall be found, the Jews shall reign no more, but Christian men shall have the sovereignty; and truly this Jesus was the Son of God'" (p. 8).

The Jews, having listened attentively to the discourse of Judas, unanimously declare that they will not reveal where the Cross is hid, and cautioned Judas to keep silent respecting it (p. 9).

Helena again summoned the Jews before her, and threatened them with fire unless they quickly made known where the Cross was to be found. Alarmed at the queen's threats, they presented Judas to her, saying, "Lady, this man is skilful and learned, and able to make known to you all the things that thou art desirous

[1] The first and second of our legends, agreeing with the Vercelli Cross poem, represent Simon as bidding Judas to reveal the place of the Cross before he is put to death.

of knowing." Then the queen let all the others go, but retained Judas, who, however, refused to give any information. Then the queen commanded Judas to be cast into a deep pit, where he was kept without meat or drink for seven days, at the end of which time he expressed his willingness to tell the truth concerning the Cross. When he was taken out of the pit, he brought Helena to the place of the crucifixion, and there offered up a prayer, beseeching God to disclose the place where the crosses were hidden (p. 10); whereupon the earth quaked, and there arose "the sweetest smell of all the most precious perfumes." Then Judas rejoiced and said, "Verily Jesus is the Saviour of the world." Having said these words, he began to dig, and at the depth of twenty feet he found three crosses, which were removed to Jerusalem. He could not say, however, which was the Cross of our Lord, so he awaited the manifestation of divine power. About noon the Jews brought in the dead body of a young man that was about to be buried. Judas retained the bier, and laid one of the crosses upon the dead body, and then the second; and when the third touched the corpse, it came to life, and blessed the name of the Lord. Then the devil was greatly enraged, and was heard crying in the air and saying, "Judas, what is this that thou hast done? Thou hast done the opposite what the other Judas did. Through him I won many souls, and through thee I shall lose many; through him I reigned over the people, through thee I have lost my realm" (p. 11).

Judas, being filled with the Holy Ghost, cursed the devil, and said, "May Christ sink thee into the deep abyss of hell;" whereupon the devil was no longer to be seen or heard. After this, Judas was baptized by the name of Cyriacus, and in time became bishop of Jerusalem (p. 12).

Helena longed to possess the nails of the Cross, and commanded Cyriacus to make search for them. He did so, and discovered them glistening in the earth like the purest gold. The queen, by a voice from heaven, was bidden to take the nails to set them in the bridle of her son Constantine[1] (p. 13). For three years he

[1] Some say that one nail was wrought as a bit, and fastened to the bridle of Constantine's horse, while two others were secured to the helmet. Other legends say

carried them about with him, and afterwards placed them beside the Cross. At St. Denis are the nails and the king's crown (p. 120). She gave also a part of the Cross to her son, and the other part she left enshrined in gold, silver, and precious stones, in a church which she caused to be built upon Mount Calvary (p. 96). Thus was the holy Rood found on the third of May, which we call Holy Rood Day.

§ 13. Another Legend concerning the Finding of the Cross (pp. 108–121).

Constantine, being desirous of finding the holy Cross upon which Jesus had suffered, sent two messengers, Benciras and Ansiers, to his mother Helena, bidding her without delay to make search for the holy Rood. The queen had with her at this time a skilful goldsmith, who owed a large sum of money to a Jew, under a bond to yield an equivalent in weight of his own flesh if the debt should not be paid when due. The day of payment came, and the goldsmith was unable to satisfy the Jew's claims. The case came before the queen's court, and was tried by Benciras and Ansiers, who ask the Jew how he proposes to take the penalty. He replies that he intends to put out the debtor's eyes, then to smite off his hands, and lastly to cut off his tongue and nose.

The judges bid him take the flesh, but beware to take no blood with it, for that was not included in the contract. The Jew says, "Methinks the worst part of the bargain is mine—

> To take the flesh if I assay,
> Then the blood will run away.

Ye have ruined me by your decision; a curse light upon you for it."

Then the judges declare the Christian man to be quit, and condemn the Jew to forfeit his goods to the queen, and to lose his tongue.

that one nail was thrown into the Adriatic Sea to quiet a whirlpool there, two nails were placed in the bridle of Constantine's horse, and one in Constantine's crown.

The Jew, aghast at this decision, offers to disclose where the Lord's holy Cross is to be found; whereupon Helena declares that if he can do so he shall receive a full pardon, but shall lose his eyes in case he does not perform his promise.

Then the Jew leads Helena to Calvary, and digs up three crosses, &c.

§ 14. How to make the Sign of the Cross.

Ælfric, in his instructions for making the sign of the Cross (p. 104), gives the Western mode as follows:—With three fingers must one make the sign of the cross, and bless himself, on account of the Holy Trinity. He seems to condemn the use of the open hand in making the sign of the Cross[1] (p. 104).

"The gesture of benediction is . . . . either Greek or Latin; it is always given with the right hand, the hand of power. In the Greek Church it is performed with the forefinger entirely open, the middle finger slightly bent, the thumb crossed upon the third finger, and the little finger bent. This movement and position of the five fingers form, more or less perfectly, the monogram of the Son of God." (Didron's *Christ. Iconog.* p. 407.)

"The Latin benediction is given with the thumb and two first fingers open, the third and little finger remaining closed." (*Ib.* p. 408.)

§ 15. The Exposition of the Cross[2].

There was, in the year of our Lord six hundred and fifteen, an impious king of Persia, named Chosroës, who commanded all his subjects to call him the King of kings and Lord of lords. With a great army he invaded Jerusalem, and destroyed the churches of the Christians. He went to the holy sepulchre with the intention of destroying it, but a great fear withheld him. Nevertheless, he

[1] "Make the sign of the cross on your mouth with the thumb, and say, 'God be our help;' then a large cross from above the forehead down to the breast, with the three fingers." (*Ancren Riwle*, p. 19.) See Gretser, vol. i. lib. iv. cap. 1, 2.

[2] See pp. 48–57; 87–107; 122–130; 161–169.

took possession of the holy Rood left there by Helena, and carried it away into his own country. Forthwith he raised a high tower of silver, ornamented with all kinds of precious stones; and therein he set a throne wrought of "red gold," in which was represented the sun, moon, and stars, so that it looked like heaven. By means of pipes perforated with small holes, he caused water to descend as rain; and causing horses to tramp constantly through hidden trenches, he imitated the noise of thunder. He even imitated the song of angels by means of "secret whistles." Here on his throne he sat, endeavouring to represent God himself; and beside him on his right side he placed one of his sons [1], feigning him to be God the Son; and a third person on his left hand represented the Holy Ghost. To his eldest son the impious king resigned his throne, and for many a day practised his cursed "maumetry." In those days there was an emperor named Heraclius, who was renowned far and wide as a brave, pious, and God-fearing sovereign. Chosroës' son was envious of the Christian king's renown, and determined to win from him his kingdom. The two armies met near the banks of the Danube, and the son of Chosroës proposed to the emperor to decide the contest by a single combat on the bridge of the river. Heraclius consented, and through the divine assistance won the victory, and slew his opponent. Then Heraclius came to Persia, and found the impious Chosroës, like a God, sitting on his throne. Because he had honoured the Cross, the emperor offered to spare his life, if he would forsake his "maumetry" and be baptized. On his refusal, Heraclius commanded his head to be struck off, and gave the kingdom to the son of the heathen king. The holy Rood he removed, intending to carry it back to Jerusalem. After he had descended from the Mount of Olives, he essayed to enter the gate of the city (by which the Saviour went to his Passion) on horseback, in royal array; but the stones lying

[1] Some legends say that the Cross placed on his right represented the Son, and a cock on his left represented the Holy Ghost. The Cross seems to have been a true representation of the Son. "The earliest Christian artists, when making a representation of the Trinity, placed a cross beside the Father and the Holy Spirit —a cross only, without our crucified Lord." (Didron's *Christian Iconography*, p. 369, Bohn's Illustrated Library.)

round the place suddenly closed about, and formed an impenetrable wall.

At the same time an angel appeared standing on the wall, with the sign of the cross in his hand, and reminded the emperor that Christ had entered by this gate in humble clothing, riding upon an ass. Heraclius, thus rebuked for his pride, dismounted, and stripped himself of his royal robes, and barefooted bore the Cross into the city, the obstacles to his entrance having suddenly disappeared. When the Cross entered the city, it gave forth a most delightful savour, and filled all places with its sweetness, and all assembled began to praise the Cross thus, saying, "O thou marvellous Cross, more luminous than the stars, greatly art thou to be honoured and loved by all the world; for thou alone wast worthy to bear the ransom of the world. Sweet tree, save thou this assembly that are here this day gathered together for thy honour and praise."

Thus was the precious tree re-established, and the ancient miracles were revived.

This took place on the fifteenth day of the month of September, and is still commemorated by the festival called The Exposition of the Holy Cross [1].

§ 16. Traces of the Cross before the Crucifixion.

The Cross is mentioned in the Old Law. It was planted in Paradise; Adam took shelter thereunder when he had sinned; the blood of Abel cried from under it.

It was the fact of Isaac's carrying the wood for his sacrifice in

[1] Many miracles are related in some of these legends as being connected with the Rood after its exposition (see pp. 103, 104, 130, 166–169). A few are mentioned in connection with the Invention (see pp. 115, 159, 160). Gretser has something on the oil of the Cross, vol. i. lib. i. cap. 91. See p. 115 of this volume.

In Harl. 2252 lf. 50 bk., mention is made of a great miracle of a knight called Sir Roger Wallysborow; how he in the Holy Land wanted to bring off a piece of the Cross; how his thigh opened marvellously, and received it; how he was carried to Cornwall, when his thigh opened and let the fragment of the Cross out. A piece of this he gave to his parish church, "Cross-parish," and the rest to St. Buryan's College.

the form of a cross upon his shoulders, that prompted God the Father to send an angel to arrest the arm of Abraham[1].

The four corners of Noah's ark were made of it[2] (p. 116).

Gretser (vol. i. lib. i. cap. 43–46), as figures of the Cross, mentions Jacob's ladder, Jacob's staff, the transposition of Jacob's hands in blessing the sons of Joseph, the scarlet cord in the window of Rahab, the nail with which Jael slew Sisera, the oak and rod of Gideon, &c.

Moses' wand came from this tree; and in Egypt the Israelites were saved by the sign of the cross. Moses raised a cross in the wilderness, by which those who were stung by serpents were healed. When he held up his own hands, it was in the form of a cross. The dispute concerning the priesthood was settled by Aaron's rod having a cross upon it (p. 117). (See Gretser, vol. i. lib. i. cap. 44.) When David went to fight with Goliath, he was armed with a staff like a cross (p. 118).

[1] Didron's *Christ. Iconog.*, Bohn's Illustrated Library, p. 370.

[2] For the following interesting note I am indebted to the kindness of the Rev. Dr. Barry:—

"The Scripture saith, 'Abraham circumcised 318 men of his household.*' Hear the meaning first of the 18, then of the 300. The ten and eight are represented, the ten by I, and the eight by H. There thou hast the beginning of the name ΙΗΣΟΥΣ. But because the Cross, in the form of the letter T, was to carry the grace (of salvation), therefore he adds the 300 (which is represented by T in Greek). So he shows forth Jesus in the first two letters, and the Cross in the third." (*Letter of Barnabas*, so called, c. ix.)

In c. xii. of the same Epistle, the Cross is spoken of as symbolized by the outstretching of the hands of Moses during the battle with Amalek (Exod. xvii. 8, &c.), which is assumed to have been a stretching out of both hands as on the Cross, though the mention of the "rod of God in my hand" (Exod. xvii. 9) suggests a different posture.

Then, "All day long I have stretched forth my hands," &c. So in Rom. x. 21, but Isa. lxv. 2 is 'I have spread out my hands all the day unto a rebellious people,' is explained as foreshadowing the Cross.

Next, the "pole" of the brazen serpent is explained as foreshadowing a cross. In fact, some old translators render ἐν δοκῷ by "in cruce."

On these passages Hefele refers to Justin. *Dial. c. Tryph.* n. 111, p. 204; Tertullian. *adv. Jud.* c. 10; *adv. Marc.* iii. 18; Justin. *Apol. I.* n. 35; *Dial. c. Tryph.* n. 97.

* This is not expressly in Holy Scripture, but in Gen. xiv. 14, 318 is given as the number of Abram's servants in the war against the kings; and in xvii. 26, 27, all the men of his house are circumcised.

When Elijah met the widow of Zarephath, that woman picked up two pieces of wood, which she held up in the form of a cross; and God, for that action, increased the quantity of meal and oil in her house, and afterwards permitted the prophet to restore her son to life[1].

The sign of Thau in the Old Law is a token of the cross[2] (p. 118).

"The Cross, made with beams put together, had the shape of the Samaritan Tau, says St. Jerome[3], whose words are these: 'In the oldest Hebrew letters, which the Samaritans now make use of, the last, which is Tau, had the form of a cross.' This Tau, like a cross, was like the T of the Greeks, according to Paulinus, who says that the shape of the Cross is expressed by the Greek letter Tau, which stands for three hundred. The Cross of our Lord was something different from the letter Tau; the beam that was fixed in the earth crossing that which was athwart it above, and made as it were a head by rising above it. . . . . . This is the form of the Cross which St. Jerome means, when he compares it to birds flying, to a man swimming, and to a man praying to God with his arms extended." (Humphrey's *Montfaucon*, vol. x. pt. ii. bk. iii. cap. 1, p. 158, quoted in *Notes and Queries*, 1853, vol. vii. p. 461.)

The paschal lamb seems to have been roasted in the form of a cross.

"This lamb, which was to be roasted whole, was a symbol of the punishment of the Cross, which was inflicted on Christ, Το γαρ οπτωμενον προβατον, κ.τ.λ. For the lamb which was roasted was so placed as to resemble the figure of a cross; with one spit it was pierced longitudinally, from the tail to the head; with another it was transfixed through the shoulders, so that the forelegs became

[1] Didron's *Christ. Iconog.*, Bohn's Illustrated Library, p. 37. "'Lord,' saith she [the woman of Zarephath] to Elijah the holy prophet, 'behold I am gathering two sticks.' These two sticks betoken that one stick which stood upright, and that other also of the precious Cross, which went athwart it." (*Ancren Riwle*, p. 403.)

[2] In Ezek. ix. 4, 6, the mark spoken of is the letter *Thau*.

[3] A certain Jew who had become a convert to Christianity, used to say that the Tau of the old alphabets resembled the sign of the Cross. (Origen, in *Notes and Queries*, Series II. vol. vii. p. 53.)

extended." (Vide Justini Martyri *Opera*, edit. Oberthür, vol. ii. p. 106, quoted in *Notes and Queries*, 1853, vol. viii. p. 545.) See also Gretser, vol. i. lib. i. cap. 44; Lipsius, bk. i. ch. 8.

§ 17. The Analogy of the Cross in Nature[1].

The first man and woman were made in the form of a cross (p. 118). The Cross is the head of Holy Writ, the foundation of clergy, and the rule of holy life.

It is made up of four notches and three woods, by which is understood the seven arts. Multiply three and four together, and it gives us the sum of the Old and of the New Laws—ten of the Old, and two of the New.

Man's form is like a cross, and he is composed of seven elements —the body of four, and the soul of three.

The Cross was made of wood, and not of stone, for very good reasons—through a tree man was lost, through a tree man was saved (p. 119).

The world is in the form of a cross; for the east shines above our heads, the north is on the right, the south at the left, and the west stretches out beneath our feet. Birds, that they may rise in the air, extend their wings in the form of a cross; men, when praying, or when beating aside the water while swimming, assume the form of a cross. Man differs from the inferior animals in his power of standing erect and extending his arms.

A vessel, flying upon the seas, displays her yard-arms in the form of a cross, and cannot cut the main unless her mast stands, cross-like, erect in the air; finally, the ground cannot be tilled without the secret sign, and the Tau, the crucifixion letter, is the letter of salvation. (Didron, p. 372.) See the curious plate to p. 42, bk. i. ch. 9 of Lipsius's *De Cruce*, Amsterdam, 1670. 12mo.

Thus we see that old writers found traces of the Cross throughout all nature, and in the words of one of our seventeenth century authors, poet and divine, are ever exclaiming—

[1] "The sign of the Cross is impressed upon the whole of nature." (*Apol.* i. § 72.)

[2] Rabanus Maurus (*De Laudibus Sanctæ Crucis*) detects the Cross everywhere. (Didron, p. 372.)

"Who can blot out the Cross, which th' instrument
Of God dewed on me in the sacrament?
Who can deny me power and liberty
To stretch mine arms, and mine own cross to be?
Swim, and at every stroke thou art thy cross!
The mast and yard make one when seas do toss.
Look down, thou spy'st ever crosses in small things;
Look up, thou seest birds raised on crossed wings.
All the globe's frame and sphere is nothing else
But the meridian's crossing parallels."

§ 18. The Story of Longinus.

There are two kindred subjects taken up in the present pages: (1) The story of *Longinus*, who, as usual, is confounded with the centurion that pierced the Saviour's side (see p. 106); (2) The uplifting of the Cross at the Crucifixion (p. 142).

On this subject, see Gretser, vol. i. lib. i. cap. 21: "Num Christus humi, an in sublimi sit suffixus cruci."

It is generally agreed that the Saviour was nailed to the Cross before it was fixed in the ground in an upright position.

For further information on the Cross, and the various legends connected with it, see—

History of the Holy Cross (Berjeau, J. P.), Lond. 1863.

The Ancient Cornish Drama (ed. Norris), Oxford, 1859.

Sacred and Legendary Art (Jameson, A.), Lond. 1848.

History of our Lord (Jameson, A.), Lond. 1864.

Didron's *Christian Iconography* (Bohn's Illustrated Library), Lond. 1851.

Works of Jacobus de Voragine and of Rabanus Maurus.

Hortus S. Crucis (Gretser, J.), Ingolstadt, 1610.

Gretser's *Works*, 17 vols. Ratisb. 1734–41; of which vols. 1–3 treat of the Cross.

De Cruce (Lipsius, J.), Amsterdam, 1670.

LEGENDS OF THE HOLY ROOD.

I.

DISCOVERY OF THE SACRED CROSS.

Hear ye now what I shall say to you concerning the holy rood (cross) upon which Christ suffered, how it was found on this day. When that one hundred and thirty-three years had elapsed after Christ's passion and ascension to heaven, then reigned Constantine the great, Kaiser in the city of Rome. He was pious in morals and honourable in actions, a supporter of Christian men, and, nevertheless, was not yet baptized. In the sixth year of Constantine's reign there was assembled a great foreign folk at the river which is called Danube, and they were ready to fight against the Kaiser and the Roman people. Then was it soon made known to the great Kaiser Constantine, and he immediately gathered together a great army, and marched against his foes with a sorrowful mood, and oft looked up heaven-wards, earnestly praying for divine assistance. When they came to the river then saw he the great and innumerable host of his enemies; then was he exceedingly sorrowful and sad even unto death, because he thought that they would all perish. Then on that same night, that Constantine slept and rested himself, there came to him an exceedingly beautiful (fair) angel in white shining garments, and he awoke him and said, "Constantine, be thou not sad, but look up now unto this heaven." And he immediately looked up unto heaven and there saw the sacred token of Christ's cross standing opposite him, and distinguished by the brightness of a great light, and these words were written above the cross: "Constantine, with this sign thou shalt overcome and subdue all thy enemies." He then awoke blithely (joyfully) because of the fair sight (vision) and for the great promised victory;

I.

[ÞǼRE HALGAN RODE GEMÉTNES.*]

*[Auct.F.iv. 32. (Bodleian Library) leaf 10.]

GEheraꝺ ge nu hwæt ic eow secgan wille ymbe þa halgan rode þe crist on þrowode. hu heo on þeosne dæg gefunden wæs. þaða wæs agán an hund[1] wintra ⁊ þri ⁊ þritti wintra æfter cristes þrowunge ⁊ úpstige to heofenum; þa rixode constantinus se mære casere on róma byrig. He wæs eawfæst on þeáwum. ⁊ arfæst on dædum. cristenra manna fultumend. ⁊ næs þeah þagyt gefullod. þa on þam sixtan gære þe constantinus rixode þa wæs gesamnod micel ælþeodig folc to þære ea. þe is gehaten danúbia. ⁊ wǽron gearwe to fihtane ongean þone kasere. ⁊ on[gean] þa romaniscan leode. þa wearð hit sona þam mæran constantine þam kasere gecyd. ⁊ he þa sone gegaderode micele fyrde. ⁊ ongæn his fiond ferde mid carfullum mode. ⁊ gelome beheold wiþ heofenas weard. biddende giorne godcundne fultum. þa hio to þære ea coman. þa geseah he ðær þa myeclan ⁊ þa ungerimed*lican ferde. þæra his fionda. þa wæs he swiðe sarig ⁊ geunrodsad oð deað. for þan þe he wende ꝥ hi calle scoldon sweltan; þa on þare ylcan nihte þe constantinus slép: ⁊ hine gereste. þa com him to sum swiðe fæger ænegel on hwitum scinendum reafe. ⁊ hine awehte. ⁊ cwæð. Constantinus ne beo þu na unrot. Ac beseoh nu up into þissere[2] heofenan. ⁊ he ða sona beseah up on þære heofenan. ⁊ þær geseah ꝥ halwænde tacen *Christes* rode on myceles liohtes brihtnesse ongean him geset. ⁊ gemearcod. ⁊ þas word bufen þare rode awritene wæron. Constantinus on þisum tacne ðu ofercymst ⁊ ofer-swiðest calle þine fiond; he awoc þa bliþelice for þære fægeran gesihðe. ⁊ for þære

Description of the Emperor Constantine.

His enemies prepare to fight against him.

* [leaf 10, back.]

Constantine's vision of the Cross.

[1] MS. nund.

[2] The letters *re* are added between the lines.

and he marked on his head and on his banner the sign of the holy rood in honour to God. Then immediately on the morrow the Kaiser commanded to be made a golden rood of the same form that he had seen so gloriously shining in the heavens, and he commanded it to be borne before him against the heathen. As soon as they looked upon the sign of the holy rood they immediately became terrified and turned to flight; and Constantine the great Kaiser had the victory, and his army slew the heathen, and some moreover were drowned in the river. On this day the Almighty God gave great victory to the noble King Constantine, through the great might of the illustrious cross of Christ. After that the great Kaiser again returned home to his own city. Then he commanded to be summoned before him all the elders and scribes of the Jewish folk, and asked them whose token that might be which he had seen shining so gloriously in the heavens. They then replied, "It is the great and the glorious heavenly token upon which the Son of the living God has suffered." When those that were Christians heard of this, then came they forthwith to the noble Kaiser Constantine, and with very joyful mood preached to him concerning the Holy Trinity, and the holy advent of the begotten Son of God, in what wise he was born of the human body of the holy woman Saint Mary; and they told him of the sufferings which our Saviour suffered on the cross, for the salvation and redemption of mankind, and how our Lord was buried in the tomb, and on the third day rose immortal from the dead; and harrowed hell, and bound the old devil; and afterwards ascended to heaven and prepared a way of return for those who shall merit it. When this was told to the noble Kaiser Constantine, then became he very joyful in mood, and sent his mother Helena with a great army to the city of Rome to the bishop, and bade them earnestly beseech him that he would come and baptize him. Then immediately the bishop thanked God for this, and baptized the King in the name of the Father, the Son, and the Holy Ghost, and firmly strengthened him in the true faith. And he then brake in pieces and destroyed all the idols, and consecrated churches there, and appointed all ecclesiastical orders according to the ordinances (of the Church). After that the great Kaiser Constantine was confirmed in the true faith, then began he to learn the divine lore and to read the mæran behatenan sige. ⁊ mearcode him on heafde halig rode tacen. ⁊ on his guðfanan gode to wurðmynte; Ða sone on mergen het se kasere constantinus gewyrcan ane gyldene rode on þære ilcan gelicnesse. þe he on heofenum swa mærlice scinende geseah. ⁊ heo beforan him beran het ongean* þa hæþenan. Sona swa hio on ꝥ halige rode taken beseagon. þa wurdon hio sona afyrhte. ⁊ to fleame gehwyrfde. ⁊ constantinus se mære kasere þa sige hæfde. ⁊ his fyrd þa hæþenan ofsloh! ⁊ hi eac sume on þære ea wurdon adrænete; on þisum dæge se ælmihtiga god sealde mycelne sige þam mæran kininge constantine. þurh ꝥ mycele mægen þære mære *Christes* rode. Æfter þam þe se mære kasere eft häm gewænde to his ageure byrig into rome. þa het he him to gelangian ealle þa ealdormæn. ⁊ þa boceras þæs iudeiscan folces. ⁊ acsode hiom hwæs tacen ꝥ bion mihte þe he on þære heofenan swa mærlice scinende geseah. Hio þa cwædon hit is ꝥ mycele ⁊ ꝥ mære heofenlice tacen. þe þæs lifigendan godes sunu on þrowode. Ða ꝥ geacsodon þe þær cristene wæron. þa coman hio hrædlice to ðam mæran kasere constantine. ⁊ swiþe bliþum mode him bodedon þa halgan þrynesse. ⁊ be þam halgan tocyme. þæs acænnedan godes sunu. on hwylce wisan he *akænned wære þurh mænniscne lichaman of þære halgan fæmnan *sancta* marian. ⁊ tealdon him þa þrowunga þe ure hælend on þære rode ðrowode. for mankynnes hælo. ⁊ alesednesse. ⁊ hu ure drihten on byrgenne wæs bebyriged. ⁊ on þam ðriddan dæge undeaþlice of deaðe aras. ⁊ helle gehergode. ⁊ þone ealdan diofol geband. ⁊ scoþþen to heofenum astah. ⁊ þider weg gerymde þam þe ꝥ geearnian willað. Ða þis þam mæran kasere constantine geteald wæs. þa wearð he swiðe bliðe on mode. ⁊ asende þa his moder elénan mid myclum werode to rome byrig to ðam[1] biscope. ⁊ hine giornlice biddan het. ꝥ he rædlice him tocome ⁊ hine gefullade; þa sona se biscop þæs gode þancode. ⁊ hine gefullode on fæder naman. ⁊ sunu ⁊ on þæs halgan gastes. ⁊ hine fæstlice trymede. to þam rihtan geleafan. ⁊ he þa ealle hiora diofol-geld tobræc. ⁊ towearp. ⁊ him þær cirican gehalgode ⁊ ealle cirielice hades gesette be ændebyrdnesse. Ða sioððen se mæra kasere constantinus *wæs getrymed mid rihtan geleafan. He þa liornian ongan þa godcundan lare. ⁊ þa halgan cristes bec

* [leaf 11.]

Constantine gains a victory through the Cross.

He consults the Jews about the Cross.

* [leaf 11, back.]

[1] MS. ðá.

Constantine is baptized.

* [leaf 12.]

holy books of Christ. When he had learned in the holy books in which place our Lord was anhanged on the cross, then sent he his mother the holy woman Helena with a large army to the great city Jerusalem, that she might enquire there concerning the holy cross; and he bade her that she should build churches in that same place where she, through God's assistance, might find the holy cross. The blessed queen Helena then put her trust firmly in God Almighty and departed. When she entered into the great city of Jerusalem, then bade she to be assembled before her all the Jewish folk. When they came before her then spake she unto them, thus saying: "I know, having learnt in your prophetical books, that you were from the first chosen by Christ himself; and ye know how our Lord wrought divine miracles—many blind he caused to see, and to the deaf he gave hearing, and drove out devils from demoniacs, and cleansed the lepers, and raised the dead to life, and healed many and divers diseases; and your elders through the devil's lore doomed the Redeemer, the Almighty Lord, deliverer of the earth, to death, and hanged him on the cross; and he on the third day arose from the dead. And your hearts are yet hardened so that ye may not understand nor acknowledge the true Creator of the earth, the Saviour and Redeemer; but the curse still abideth over you, which your elders themselves asked for in the passion of our Lord, when they said, 'His blood and the vengeance of his blood be upon us and upon our children.' But choose ye now the wisest men of your kin so that they may rightly answer that which I shall ask them." And they then in great fear went out, and earnestly considered what the question should be. And then they chose a thousand of the best of the learned Jewish men and brought them before the holy queen. Then spake the holy queen Helena: "Take heed now to my words. Behold! have ye not learned in your prophetical books concerning the advent of the begotten Son of God, and how our Saviour wes hanged on the cross as his own will was. So ye yourselves have learnt all these things and know them, and yet will not now understand what I wish to enquire of you." They answered and said, "Tell us, lady, wherefore thou spakest so sternly to us?" And she answered and said, "Go out and choose you of these the men who are best learned rædan; þa he geliornod hæfde on þam halgan bocum. on hwylcere stowe ure drihten on rode ahangen wæs! þa sende he his moder þa halgan fæmnan elénan mid mycelum werode to þare wuldorfullan byrig hierusalem. to þam ꝥ hio þær ofaxian scolde þa halgan rode. ⁊ he hire behead ꝥ hio scolde on þære ilcan stowe cirican getimbrian þær hio þurh godes fultum þa halgan rode gefindan mihte; Seo eadige cwen eléna þa fæstlice hire hiht gesette on gode ælmihtigum. ⁊ tóferde; Þa hio incode on þa wuldorfullan byrig ierusalem. þa het hi hiore togesamnian eall ꝥ iudeisce folc; þa þa hi coman beforan hire. ða spræc hio hiom to. ⁊ þus cwæð; Ic wat ⁊ geliornod hæbbe on eower witegungbocum ꝥ ge wæron fram frymðe gecorene fram criste selfum. ⁊ ge witan hu ure drihten godcunde wuldre geworhte. fela blinda he onlihte. ⁊ deafum *hearenunge forgeaf. ⁊ deofla heof mannum adræfde. ⁊ reofli[e]e he geclænsode. ⁊ deade he to life arærde. ⁊ mænige mistlice untrumnessa he gehælde. ⁊ eowre eldran þone ælmihtigan drihten middaneardes alesend þurh diofles lare to deaðe gedemdon. ⁊ on rode ahengon; ⁊ he on þam ðriddan dæge of deaðe aras! ⁊ get eowre heortan aheardode siondon ꝥ ge ne magon ongeton ne oncnawan þæne soþfæstan scyppend middaneardes hælend; [⁊ alesend; ac] seo awyrgednes[1] ofer cow wunað. þe eower yldran abædon sylfe on þæra þrowunga ures drihtnes. þa hio cwædon sio his blod ⁊ his blodes wrác. ofer ús. ⁊ ofer ure bearn; Ac geceosað eow nu þa wisestan mæn of eowre mægðe to þam ꝥ hio me rihtlice ⁊wyrdan magon þæs ic hiom axian wille; ⁊ hio þa mid mycelum ege uteodon. ⁊ giornlice þohtan hwæt seo acsung beon scolde. ⁊ hio þa gecuron þusend þara betst gelæredra iudeisera manna. ⁊ þa toforan þare halgan cwene gelæddon. Ða spræc seo halige cwen eléna. underniimað nu mine word. la hu ne lior*nodon ge on eowrum witegung-bocum be þam tocýme þæs áncennedan godes sunu. ꝥ ure hælend ahangen wæs on róde swa his agen willa wæs. swa ge selfe ealle þa þinc witan ⁊ cunnan. ⁊ nu get ge ongytan nellað þæs ic eow acsian wille; Hi andswarodon hire. ⁊ cwædon; sege us hlæfdige. for hwi þu us þus stiþlice word tosprece; Hi ⁊swarode ⁊ cwæð. gað ut ⁊ geceosað eow of þisum þa weras þe betst gelærede

Helena goes to Jerusalem to seek the Cross.

She consults the Jews.

* [leaf 12, back.]

[1] In the MS. *se* is wrongly added to *awyrgednes*.

The Jews are in great fear.

A thousand of the most learned Jews come before Helena.

* [leaf 13.]

that they may show me this day all the things which I shall ask of them." Then they with great dread went out from the queen, and discussed among themselves and anxiously considered what the question might be. Then spake there one called Judas, "I know indeed what the question will be: it is about the holy cross on which our elders hanged the Nazarene Saviour. If this queen will ask about this, then consider whether ye will declare it unto her, for we know assuredly that afterwards all the ordinances of our elders shall be destroyed." He said then again, "Zaccheus, my old-father (grandfather), said to my father, and my father to me, thus saying, 'My dearest child, when there shall be an enquiry concerning the holy cross, on which our elders hanged the Saviour Christ, then take heed that thou reveal it ere thou be quelled to death, for never any longer shall the Jewish folk have sovereignty, but the kingdom shall belong to those who believe in the Almighty God, because that he is truly the Son of the living God.' Then answered I my father and said, 'My father, if our elders knew that he was the Son of the living God, wherefore did they hang him on the rood?' Then said my father to me, 'Juda, my dearest son, I was never of their mind, nor aided them in their counsels, but I ever spake most strongly against their speech (counsel), because I always believed on the holy and marvellous name of the Son of the living God, whom our elders hanged for envy, and for wrath doomed him to death, and hanged him on the cross; and he was laid in the tomb, and on the third day, of a truth, arose from the dead; and after his miraculous resurrection he appeared to his beloved apostles; and thy brother Stephen firmly believed in him, and therefore the Pharisees and Sadducees then doomed him to death and with stones beat him (to death). Then said he, "My Lord, impute thou not these sins unto them, which they work upon me."' Then said my father again unto me, 'I advise thee, my dear son, that thou continually and firmly believe on Christ, the Son of the living God. Then shalt thou have life with him ever in eternity.' These things my father Simon said to me, as I have now said them unto you. Take thought now whether ye will declare it unto her if she will ask you about it." They answered and said, "We never before heard these words nor these things which thou now sayest unto us. If this queen shall ask about these

bion. ꝥ hio me on þisum dæge ealle þa þinc gecyþan magan þe ic heom acsian wille. Hio þa mid mycelum ege uteodon fram þara cwena. ⁊ heom betwionan gefiit hæfdon. ⁊ geornlice þohtan hwæt seo axung beon mihte; þa spræc þær án iudas wæs gehaten. Ic wat soþlice hwæt þeos axung bion wile. ymbe þas halgan rode þe ure yldran þone nazareniscan hælend on ahengon. Gif þeos cwen þises axian wille. þonne behealdan ge hwæþer ge hit hire gecyþan willen. for þan we witan soþlice ꝥ sioððen ealle ure yldrena gesetnesse toworþene bioþ; he cwæð þa eft. Zachéus min ealde fæder sæde minum fæder. ⁊ min fæder *sæde me ⁊ cwæð to me. min bearn ꝥ liofesta þoñ seo axung gewurþe ymbe þa halgan rode. þe ure yldran hælend crist on ahengon. þoñ warna þu þe ꝥ þu hio kyðe. ær þam þu to deaðe gecwylmed wurþe. forþam næfre ma iudeisc folc læne ne rixað. Ac þoñ biþ þæra manna rice þe gelefað on þone ælmihtigan god. for þam þe he is soþlice þæs lifigendan godes sunu; þa ⁊swarode ic minum fæder ⁊ cwæð. fæder min gif ure yldran wysten ꝥ he wæs crist þæs lifigendan godes sunu for hwi ahengon hi hine on rode; þa cwæð min fæder to me. Iuda min bearn ꝥ leofesta næs ic næfre on heore geþeahte. ne heom æt þære spræce ne gefultumede. Ac ic æfre swiþor ongean hio spræc. forþon þe ic ongeat simble his þone halgan ⁊ wundorlican naman þæs lifigendan godes sunu. þæne ure yldran for andan ahengon. ⁊ for graman to deaðe gedemdon. ⁊ hine on rode ahengon. ⁊ he wæs on byrgene gelegd. ⁊ on þam þriddan dæge soþlice of deaðe arás. *⁊ æfter his wuldorfullan æriste he hine ætewede his gecorenum liorninecnihtum. ⁊ þin broþer steffanus fæstlice on hine gelefde. ⁊ þa forþam þa fariseiscan ⁊ sundorhalgan hine to deaðe fordemdon. ⁊ hine mid stanen oftorfedon. þa cwæð he min drihten ne wit þu heom þas synna þe hi on me wyrcað. þa cwæð min fæder eft to me ic lære þe min liofa bearn ꝥ þu anrædlice ⁊ fæstlice gelyfe on crist þæs lifigendan godes sunu. þoñ hæfst þu lif mid him á on ecenesse. Þas þinc me sæde min fæder symon. swa ic eow nu gesæd hæbbe. þæncað ge nu hwæþer[1] ge hit hire cyþan willað gif hio eow þises axian wille. Hi andswarodon ⁊ cwædon. Ne geherde we næfre ær þas word ne þas þinc þe þu nu segst. Gif þeos

Judas says what he knows of the Cross.

* [leaf 13, back.]

His grandfather Zaccheus had given him information.

* [leaf 14.]

Stephen the martyr the brother of Judas.

[1] MS. þwæþer.

things then take heed to thyself that thou never disclose it unto her. We know it not nor are able (to know)." When they were thus speaking among themselves, then called them thither the queen's soldiers and commanded that they should quickly come before the great queen. When they stood before her, then said she unto them, "Of a truth I say that I will burn you all with fire except ye reveal to me truly the holy cross of Christ." Then became they immediately much terrified, and presented to her then the one who was called Judas, and said to her, "Lady, this (man) is true, and he is the most skilful and learned of us, and he is able to show thee all the things which thou askest of us." The queen let them all go, and took Judas alone and said to him, "Now is thy life or death in thine own power; choose now whichsoever thou wilt." Judas then answered and said, "If any man be hard pressed with hunger, and one lay before him stones and loaves, will he ever be so foolish as to eat the stones and to leave the bread?" Then answered him the great queen Helena, "If thou wilt live in heaven or on earth, then show me where the holy cross of Christ is preserved." Judas answered her and said, "I know not nor can, because it was done more than a hundred years ago, and I am young, and do not remember it." The great queen Helena answered him, "I have read in the holy books of Christ that the place is called Calvary—in which our Lord's cross is preserved. But make known to me where the place is, or I will command thee to be put to death by hunger." Then Judas again answered her and said, "I know not the place (nor can I), for I was not born then." Then commanded the queen Helena that they should take him and put him in a deep pit without meat or drink, and then dwelt he there seven days and seven nights; and then on the seventh day Judas called up from the pit and thus said, "I entreat and conjure you to take me out of this pit, and I will show you the holy cross of Christ." When he was out of the pit then went he to the place in which our Lord was hanged. When he came thither then he stretched out his arms and prayed to Christ, and thus said, "My Lord and Saviour Christ, thou who createdst heaven and earth and sea and all creatures which are therein, I entreat thee for thy great mercy that thou reveal to us thy holy cross, upon which thou sufferedst cwen þises axian wille þonne warna þu þe ꝥ þu hit hire næfre ne cyðe. We hit nyten ne ne cunnen. Ða hio þus hiom betweonan spræcen. þa cliopodan þare cwene cæmpan þider. ⁊ hio hetan ꝥ hio rædlice coman toforan þare mære cwenan. þa hio beforan *hire stodan. þa cwæð hio hiom to. Soðlice ic secge ꝥ ic eow ealle on fyre hate forbærnan. buton ge me soþlice gecyþan þa halgan cristes rode. Hi wæron þa sona swiþe afyrhte geworden. ⁊ scaldon hire þa ænne þe iudas wæs gehaten. ⁊ hire to cwædon. Hlæfdige þes is soþfæst ⁊ he is gleawest úre gelæred ⁊ he mæg þe ealle þa þinc gecyþan þe þu us acsost. Seo cwen forlet þa hi ealle ⁊ nam iudan ænne. ⁊ him tocwæð. Nu is on þinum agenum gewealde ge þin lif ge þin deað. geceos nu swa hwæþer swa þu wille; he ⁊swarode iudas þa hire. ⁊ cwæð. Gif hwylc man si hearde ofhingred. ⁊ man him lecge toforan stanas ⁊ hlafas. hwa is æfre swa dysig. ꝥ wille etan þa stanas ⁊ lætan þa hlafas. Him þa tocwæð seo mæra cwén eléna gif þu wille libban on heofenum oððe on corþan. þoñ cyþ þu me. hwær sio halige rode cristes gehealden sy; Iudas hire ⁊swarode ⁊ cwæð. Ic nat hit. ne ne can. for þan hit wæs gedon mare þonne for hundtiontigum gærum. ⁊ ic com iung ⁊ ꝥ ne geman. him andwyrde seo mæra cwen. eléna. Ic hæbbe geræd on þam halgum cristes bocum ꝥ seo stow hatte *caluarie locum þe ure hælendes rod on gehealden is. Ac gecyþ me hwær sio stow sy. oððe ic mid hungre hate þe acwellan; Hire ⁊swarode þa iudas eft. ⁊ cwæð. Ne ic þa stowe ne can ne ic þa gyt geboren næs; þa bebead seo cwen eléna ꝥ hine man náme. ⁊ sette on ænne diopne scað buton éte ⁊ buton wǽte. ⁊ þa wunode he þær seofan dagas ⁊ seofan niht. ⁊ þa on þam seofoðan dæge [ða] cliopode iudas up of ðam scaðe. ⁊ þus cwæð. Ic eow bidde ⁊ halsige ꝥ ge me of þisum scaþe úpatéon. ⁊ ic eow getæce þa halgan cristes rode; Ða he of ðam scaðe wæs. þa fór he to þare stowe þe ure hælend on ahangen wæs. þa he ðider com. þa aþenede he his handa. ⁊ to criste gebæd. ⁊ ðus cwæð. Min drihten hælend crist þu þe gescope heofenas ⁊ corþan ⁊ sæ ⁊ ealle gesceafta þe on þam siondon. Nu bidde ic þe drihten for þinre mycelan mildheortnesse. ꝥ þu ætywic us þine þa halgan rode. þe þu on þrowodest.

The Jews know nothing of the Cross.

* [leaf 14, back.]

Helena threatens to burn them to death unless they reveal the Cross.

Judas is detained.

He refuses to disclose the Cross.

* [leaf 15.]

He is cast into a pit.

He promises to say what he knows. He goes to Calvary.

(death) and redeemed mankind, cause to ascend from that place the sweetest smell of all precious perfumes, that I may firmly believe on thee, thou that art King of all kings, thou that livest and reignest ever in eternity." When Judas had finished this divine prayer, then immediately all the place quaked, and there arose from that place the sweetest smell of all the most precious perfumes. Then forthwith Judas marvelled greatly and thus said, "I say of a truth that the Son of the living God is the Saviour and Redeemer of all mankind that will believe in him. I now entreat and conjure thee, my Lord Jesus Christ, that thou blot out my sin, that I may be in the number (of the elect) with my brother Stephen, of whom many good deeds are written (in the book) among the miracles of the apostles." When he had said these words then he took a spade and delved the earth. When he had delved twenty feet in the earth then found he three roods; and forthwith then he was very joyful. He took the three roods and bore them to the great city of Jerusalem before the great queen Helena. She then said to Judas, "Tell me on which of these roods our Lord was anhanged. I know that two of them are those of the two malefactors who were hanging on each side of him." Then Judas knew not what to say unto her, but took the three roods and set them in the midst of the great city of Jerusalem, and there awaited the glory (manifestation) of the Lord. Then it came to pass this day at noon that they brought in a young man that was dead. Then was Judas very glad of this, and said to the great queen Helena, "Lady, now may ye perceive the might of our Lord Jesus Christ." Thereupon Judas bade them set down the corpse, and he then took one of the roods and laid it upon the dead body, and then prayed very earnestly to God Almighty for his name and for his great mercy (and he also bad all the people to pray) that God Almighty would show, through his great might, which cross it was that he himself was hanged upon for the salvation of mankind. The body lay still as dead as it was before. He then took the second rood, but it was all the same. So he took the third, and then forthwith the man arose alive and whole, and blessed the name of the Lord. And all those who were there blessed, praised, and magnified the name of the Lord. Then was the malicious devil of hell stirred up with anger and with

⁊ mancyn alesdest. ⁊ do ꝥ þær astige upp of þære stowe se swetesta stæne ealra diorwurþra wyrt-gemanga. ꝥ ic þonne fæstlice on þe gelefe. ꝥ þu eart *ealra kyninga kyning. þu ðe liofost. ⁊ rixast á on ecnesse. þa iudas þis godeunde gebed gefylled hæfde. þa sona biofode eal seo stow ⁊ þær astah úp of ðære stowe se sẃetesta stǽne. ealra diorwurþesta wyrtgemanga. þa sona iudas ðæs myclum wundrode. ⁊ þus cwæð. Ic soþlice secge ꝥ se ancænneda godes sunu is hælend. ⁊ nergend. ealles mancynnes. þe on hine gelyfan wyllað. Ic þe nu bidde ⁊ halsige min drihten hælend crist. ꝥ þu adilegie mine synna ꝥ ic mote bion on þæm gerimtæle mid minum broþer steffane þe fiola goddra dǽda siond be him awritene. gemang þara apostola wundor-gewurcum; þa iudas þas word gecweden hæfde. þa genam he ane spada. ⁊ dealf þa eorþan. þa he hæfde gedolfen twentig fota on þære eorðan. þa fand he þrio roda. þa wæs he sona swiþe bliþe. Genam þa ða þrio rodan. ⁊ bær hio to þære wuldorfullan byrig. ierusalem. toforan þare mære cwene elenan. Hio cwæð ða to iudan *sege me on hwyle þiosse roda ure hælend ahangen wære. Ic wat ꝥ þa twa siondon þara twegra scaðena þe on twam healfeon his hangiende wæron. þa nyste iudas hire ꝥ to secgenne. Ac genam þa ða þrio roda ⁊ gesette heo onmiddan þære wuldorfullan byrig ierusalem. ⁊ þær gebád drihtnes wuldres. Þa hit wæs æt none þæs dæges. þa bær man ænne geongne cniht forðferedne. Ða wæs iudas þæs swiþe bliþe. ⁊ cwæð. to þære mæran cwene elenan. Hlæfdige nu ge magon oncnawan þa mihte ures drihtnes hælendes cristes; hwæt iudas het þa settan ꝥ lic ⁊ genam þa þa ane rode ⁊ legde uppe þam deadan bæd þa swiþo giorne god ælmihtigne for his naman ⁊ for his mæran mildheortnesse. ⁊ eall ꝥ folc ealswa biddan het. ꝥ god ælmihti scolde geswuteligan þurh his mæran mihte hwyle sio ród wære. þe he self on ahangen wæs for mancynnes hælo. Se lichama læg swa fórð dead swa he ǽr wæs. He genam þa oþre. þa wæs hit eal ꝥ ilce. Þa genam he *þa þriddan. þa arás se cniht sona libbende ⁊ gesund ⁊ drihtnes naman bletsode. ⁊ ealle þa þe þær wæron bletsodon ⁊ heredon ⁊ mærsodon drihtnes naman. Þa wæs se niþfulla diofol on helle mid corre ⁊ mid

Judas offers up a prayer.

* [leaf 15, back.]

They dig up the ground and find three crosses.

* [leaf 16.]

They bring them to Jerusalem.

The true cross is discovered by means of a dead body.

* [leaf 16, back.]

hot-heartedness, and he therewith loudly roared and thus said, "Lo! what man is this that hath now betrayed me? O thou Nazarene Jesus! through thy passion thou hast regained to thyself all the souls that I formerly by myself had betrayed. O thou Judas! what is this that thou hast now done to me? Erewhile I, through one Judas, the betrayer of Christ, was honoured, and I drew much people to hell, but through this Judas I am degraded." Then Judas became filled with the Holy Ghost and thus spake, "May the Saviour who liveth and reigneth sink thee into the deep abyss of hell!" Forthwith was the devil no longer anywhere to be seen or heard. When the blessed queen Helena heard this, she marvelled much at the great faith which Judas had in God, and she commanded that the cross should be worked up with gold and with silver and with precious stones (gems), and that churches should be built in that same place in which the holy rood was found, as her son Constantine had previously ordered. And Judas was then baptized by the city bishop (metropolitan), and the bishop changed Judas' name and after he was baptized called him Quiriacus. And he afterwards flourished so greatly that, after the death of the bishop, he was elected and consecrated a bishop. Then began Helena to enquire very earnestly concerning the nails which had been driven through the hands and feet of our Saviour. She commanded them to bring to her the holy bishop Quiriacus, who was formerly called Judas, and said to him, "I bid and conjure thee that thou make a search for the nails with which our Saviour was fastened to the cross." And forthwith the holy bishop, with his mass-priests and with his deacons and with the believing folk, departed thither to the place called Calvary, and bore with him the holy rood. When they came to the place, then he raised his eyes up to heaven and secretly beat on his breast and thus said, "My Lord Jesus Christ, I pray and beseech thee for thy great and exalted mercy that thou show me the nails with which thy holy body was fastened to the cross." When he had spoken these words, all the people said "Amen." And there came up a great light from the place in which the holy rood was discovered, and there appeared the nails shining and glistening in the earth like the purest gold. All those who were there spake and thus said, "Now may we know and understand of

hatheortnesse astyred. ⁊ he þa swiþe hlude rýmde ⁊ þus cw*æ*ð. Hwæt is la nu ꝥ me beswicen hæfð. Eala þu nazarenisce hælend þurh þine þrowunga þe þu getuge to þe ealle þa sawla þe ic ær þurh me beswican hæfde. Eala þu iudas hwæt is þis ꝥ þu me nu gedon hæfst. Ær ic þurh þone iudas cristes belæwend wæs gewurþod ⁊ ic mycel folces to helle geteah Nu ic þurh þisne iudan ca*m* fram aworpen. Iudas wearð þa gefylled mid þa*m* halgan gaste ⁊ þus cw*æ*ð. Se hælend þe liofað ⁊ rixað þe besænce on þone diopan helle grund. Sona þa næs se diofol þær nahwær gesewen ne gehered. Đa hio þis geherde seo eadige cwen elena. þa wundrode hio swiþe þæs mycelan geleafan þe iudas. to gode hæfde. ⁊ hio þa halgan cristes rode bewyrcan het mid golde ⁊ mid seolfre. ⁊ mid diorwurþu*m* gimmu*m*. ⁊ cirican het geti*m*brian *on þære ilcan stowe þe seo rod on afunden wæs. Swa hire sunu constantinus ær beboden hæfde; ⁊ iudas þa fulluht underfeng æt þa*m* burh-biscope. ⁊ se biscop iudas naman awænde. ⁊ hine het quiriacu*m* sioððen he gefullad wæs. ⁊ he þa scoþþen mærlice geþeah. ꝥ æfter þæs biscopes forðsiðe. he wearð to biscope gecoren. ⁊ gehalgod. Đa ongan *sancta* elena swiðe giornlice axian þa næglas þe ures hælendes handa ⁊ his fet þurh adrifene wæron. Hio het hiore togefeccan þone halgan biscop cwiriacu*m*. þe ær wæs iudas gehaten. ⁊ hi*m* to cw*æ*ð. Ic þe bidde ⁊ halsige ꝥ þu ofaxie þa næglas þe ure hælend on þære róde mid gefæstned wæs. ⁊ he sona se halga biscop mid his mæsseprestu*m* ⁊ mid his diaconu*m*. ⁊ mid þa*m* geleaffullu*m* folce þider for. to þære stowe caluarie locu*m*. ⁊ mid hi*m* beran het þa halgan rode; þa hio to þære stowe coman þa ahof he his eagan up to heofenu*m*. ⁊ digellice on his briost beot. ⁊ þus cw*æ*ð. Min drihten hælend crist. Ic þe bidde ⁊ halsige for þinre mycelan ⁊ mæ*ran mildheortnesse. ꝥ þu me gecyþe þa nægelas þe þin halige lichama on þæra rode mid afæstned wæs; þa he þas word gecweden hæfde. þa cw*æ*ð eal ꝥ folc amen. ⁊ þær có*m* mycel leoht up of þære stowe þe seo halige rode on afunden wæs. ⁊ þær ætywedon þa næglas. ⁊ on þare eorþan scinan ⁊ blican swa ꝥ seloste gold; ealle þa þe þær wæron. spræcon ⁊ þus cwædon. Nu we magon

Satan's complaint.

The Cross is richly ornamented.

* [leaf 17.]

Judas is baptized.

Helena inquires for the nails of the Cross.

* [leaf 17, back.]

Judas discovers the nails.

a truth that the (only) begotten Son of God is the Saviour and Redeemer of all mankind that believe in him. And then the holy bishop St. Cyriacus, with great joy and gladness, took the nails and brought them to the worshipful queen Helena; and forthwith she bowed her knees and inclined her head to the earth, and inwardly she prayed to the nails, and earnestly began to consider to what purpose she might best employ the nails. Then came there a voice from heaven and said, "Take the nails, Helena, and command them to be forged on thy son the Emperor Constantine's bridle, then shall he obtain victory and peace in every battle." And then she did as was bidden her through the Holy Ghost, and she then gave many gifts to the bishop Quiriacus. And the holy bishop had so many gifts from God that he through his divine prayers healed many divers diseases. And the blessed queen Helena again returned to the city of Rome, and made known all these things to the great Kaiser Constantine, and she bade all her folk that they should ever keep this day, on which Christ's holy rood was found, in great honour. The Jews had taken Christ's holy rood, through the devil's lore, and had hidden it under the earth one hundred and thirty-three years, but the merciful Lord would not permit that the cross on which he himself had willingly suffered and redeemed all mankind should be any longer concealed, but that it should be gloriously manifested, as we have before told you, on this day, for his praise and honour, and for our heal and preservation from all the devil's temptations. It is meet that we ever honour this day with church-going and with alms-deeds and with holy prayers, so that we may so sanctify ourselves through the holy rood of Christ that we may escape all assaults of devils in this life and their fellowship in the future life. And may our Lord, who suffered on the holy rood, so help us that we may observe what our Lord's will is, and what is needful for ourselves; and ever let there be thanks to him because he suffered for us, and to him ever be praise and honour for all his goodness which he hath shown to mankind, for ever and ever to all eternity. Amen.

onenawan ⁊ ongeton soþlice. ꝥ se acænneda godes sunu. is hælend. ⁊ lysend ealles maneynnes. þe on hine gelefað; ⁊ he þa se biscop *sanctus* cwiriacus mid myeelre blisse ⁊ mid gefean. gena*m* þa næglas ⁊ hio brohte to þare arwurþan cwene elenan. ⁊ heo sona heore eneowe gebygde. ⁊ hire heafod ahelde to þære corþan. ⁊ inweardlice hio gebæd to þam næglan. ⁊ giornlice þencan ongan. hu hio ymbe þa næglas betst gedon mihte. Da co*m* stæfn of heofenu*m*. ⁊ cwæð. Nim þas næglas eléna. ⁊ heo besmiþian hát on þines sunu bridle constantinus þæs caseres. Þænne gefærð he sige. ⁊ sibbe on æghwylcu*m* *gefeohte. ⁊ heo þa swa dyde swa hire beboden wæs. þurh þone halgan gast. ⁊ hio þa gifede myeele þine þa*m* biscope ewiriace ⁊ se halga biscop swa myeele gife hæfde æt gode. ꝥ he þurh his godeunda gebeda mænige mistlice untrumnessa gehælde; ⁊ heo þa seo eadige cwen eléna eft ongean fór to rome byrig. ⁊ ealle þas þinc þa*m* mǽran kasere constantine geeydde. ⁊ heo budon þa eallu*m* þa*m* folce. ꝥ heo symble þysne dæg mid myeelre arwurþnesse healdan seoldon. þe seo halige cristes rode on afunden wæs; þa indéas naman þa halgan cristes rode þurh diofles lare. ⁊ hio behyddon under corðan. an hund geara ⁊ þri ⁊ þrittig geara; þa nolde se mildheorta drihten geþafigen þe on hire self willes þrowode. ⁊ on þa*m* rode taene eall maneyn alysde. ꝥ heo behyd alæne wære. ac heo wuldorfullice geswutelode eal swa we ær beforan cow rǽddon. on þisu*m* halgan dæge! him selfu*m* to lofe ⁊ to wurðmynte. ⁊ us to hæle. *⁊ [g]escyldnesse wiþ ealle diofles costnunga us gedafenað ꝥ we þisne dæg. simble wurþian mid ciric-socnu*m*. ⁊ mid ælmesdædu*m*. ⁊ mid halgu*m* gebedu*m*. ꝥ we þurh þa halgan cristes rode us gebletsian moton. ꝥ we ealle diofla on þisu*m* life. ⁊ on þa*m* towcardan hynþa. ⁊ midwununga forbugan magon. ⁊ motan; we drihten þe on þære halgan rode þrowode us gefultumige ꝥ we hit swa to healdan moton swa ures drihtnes willa si. ⁊ us s[e]lfu*m* þearflic si. si him simble þane þæs þe he for us þrowode ⁊ si him simble lof ⁊ wuldor ealre[1] his godnessa. þe he maneynne geeyd hæfð. a on ealre wuruld a wuruld a on ecnesse. AMEN.

St. Quiriac took the nails to Helena.

A heavenly voice bade her to forge them on her son's bridle.

[leaf 18.]

Helena returned to Rome, and related all these marvels to her son.

All folk were bidden to honour the day on which the Cross was found.

* [leaf 18, back.]

Let us bless ourselves through the Cross from all wiles of the devil.

[1] MS. *ealrē*.

To God be honour and glory for ever and ever.

II.

Þe HOLY RODE*.

[Ashm. MS. Bodleian Lib. 43.]

[fol. 63 *b.*] [1 treo. 2 deþe. 3 þurf. 4 þulke. 5 þat we. 6 furst ibouȝt.]

Þe holi rode þe swete tre[1] ! riȝt is to habbe i*n* mu*n*de
  Þ*at* haþ fr*am* st*r*onge deþ[2] ibroȝt to lyue ! al mankunde
Þoru[3] a[4] tre[1] we[5] were uerst uorlore[6] ! *and* u*er*st ibroȝt
  to g*r*ou*n*de

[7 And siþþe þurf a treo to lyue.]

And þoru a tre seþþe to lyue[7] ibroȝt· ihered be þulke
  sto*u*nde
Al [h]it com of one more ! þ*at* ous to deþe broȝte[8]

[8 brouȝte 9 aȝe. 10 bouȝte.]

And þ*at* ous broȝte[8] to lyue aȝen[9] ! þoruȝ[3] ih*esus* þ*at* ous
  boȝte[10]

[11 Of þe treo. 12 omitted. 13 þe.]

Of þe appeltre[11] þ*at* our uerste[12] fad*er* ! þen[13] luþ*er* appel
  nom

[14 ich wole. 15 ȝou nou. 16 þe. 17 man. 18 sinne. 19 his. 20 ȝurne. 21 þeȝ hit.]

In þe maner*e* þ*at* ichulle[14] ȝou[15] telle ! þe swete rode com
Þo adam our[16] uerste fad*er*[17] ! þe su*n*ne[18] hadde ido
And idriue was out of p*ar*ais ! *and* eue is[19] wif also
Aft*er* milse ȝerne[20] hi c*r*ide ! þei it[21] late were

[22 MS. *And*, H. Ane. 23 louerd.]

Ane[22] bi-heste [he] hadde of our lord[23] ! þo me hi*m* drof
  out þere

[24 omitted. 25 whan. 26 fulfuld.]

Þ*at*[24] wen[25] þe tyme wer*e* uolueld[26] ! our lord[23] hi*m* wolde
  biþenche

[27 mid. 28 smirie. 29 aquenche.]

And wiþ[27] oile of mylse smerie[28] hi*m* ! *and* his su*n*ne[18]
  quenche[29]

[fol. 64.]

Gret hope hadde to þis biheste ! adam euermo
In þe ualeie of ebron ! he lyuede i*n* tene *and* wo
Twei sone he hadde seþþe ! caym *and* abel
Þat on slouȝ þat oþ*er* uor en-vie ! as ȝe witeþ wel

* Collated with Harl. MS. 2277 (imperfect).

II.

HOU ÞE HOLY CROS WAS Y-FOUNDE*.

[Vernon MS. Bodleian Lib.]

ÞE holy Rode, þe swete treo· riht is to hauen in muynde, [fol. 28 b, col. 2.]
Þat haþ from strong deþ i-brouht· to lyue al Monkuynde,
Þorwh a treo we weore for-lore· and furst i-brouht to grounde,
Þorwh a treo seþþe to liue i-brouȝt· I-heried beo þulke stounde!
Al hit com of one More· þat vs to deþe brouȝte,
And þat vs· to lyue aȝein· þorwh Ihesus þat vs bouȝte;
Of þe treo· þat vre furste Fader· þe luþer Appel of nom·,
In þe Maner· þat ich ow telle wole· þe swete Rode com:
¶ Þo Adam vre furste Fader· þe sunne hedde i-do
And i-driue out of Paradis·, and his wyf also,
After Milce wel ȝeorne he criede·, þeiȝ hit late were;
A bi-heste he hedde of vr lord·, þo me him drof out þere,
Þat whon þe tyme weore folfuld· vr lord him wolde bi-þenche,
And mid Oyle of merci smere him· and his sunnes quenche:
Gret hope hedde Adam· to þis bi-heste euer-mo:
In þe valeye of Ebron· he liuede mid teone and wo:
Twey sones he hedde seþþe·, Caym· and Abel:
For Envye· þat on slouȝ þat oþur·, And þat ȝe witeþ wel:

Through a tree mankind were ruined, and through a tree were saved.

God promised Adam the Oil of Merci when he was driven out of Paradise.

Adam and Eve lived in great hope of this.
In Hebron they lived in sorrow and woe.
Two sons they had, Cain and Abel.

* The Title is taken from the Index.

Þo caym hadde his broþ*er* aslawe ⸝ iflemd he was þ*er*uore
Þo adam isei þ*a*t he hadde ⸝ is twei sones uorlore
He wep *and* made deol Inouȝ ⸝ lord he sede þi*n* ore
Ney wo*m*man ichabbe to muche ibe ⸝ Incle com ney hire na*m*more
Þre harmes ichabbe þoru hire iheued ⸝ my-sulf u*er*st uorlore
And myne sones boþe alas ⸝ *and* of al wo*m*man is more
Nolde adam come þo ney is wif ⸝ two hondred ȝer ne more
Vor wo þat he hadde uor hire ⸝ *and* eu*er*e he lyuede i*n* sore
Seþþe he hadde toknyṅge of our lord ⸝ þat he scholde to is wif wende
Ne dorste he noȝt be þ*er* aȝen ⸝ an sone he hadde atenende
Seth he let is name *ne*m*pne ⸝ *and* seþþe he hadde mo
Al is lif þe seli mo*n* ⸝ ladde i*n* tene *and* wo
Þo he was of nyne hondred ȝer ⸝ *and* two *and* þritti old
Þe strengþe hi*m* failede of is lymes ⸝ is bodi bicom al cold
He ne miȝte noȝt swynke aboute þe erþe ⸝ þe wed*us* up to d*ra*we
Of is lif he was anuyd ⸝ he wilnede be of dawe
He sat *and* carede of is lif ⸝ he clupede is sone seth
Sone he sede icham weri ileued ⸝ ic*h* wilny muc*h*e my deþ
Þo ic*h* was idryue of p*ar*ais ⸝ our lord bihet me þere
To smer*e* me wiþ þe oile of mylce ⸝ we*n* it tyme were
So longe ichabbe abide þ*er*-aft*er* ⸝ þat I ne may libbe na*m*more
To p*ar*ais þou most þ*er*-aft*er* go ⸝ *and* bidde hi*m* mylce *and* ore

* *n* not quite clear.

Þo Caym hedde his broþur i-slawe· i-flemed he was þer-fore :
Cain slew his brother, and was banished.

20 Þo Adam say3 þat he hedde· boþe his sones for-lore
He wep and made deol i-nouh· : "lord," he seide "þin ore !
Neih wommon ichaue to muche i-beo·, I nule come neih hire no more !
Adam says that he will come near his wife no more,

Þreo harmes ichabbe for hire i-had·, my self furst for-lore,
24 And nou my sones, welawey ! · of Al. wommon is more" :
nor did he for more than 200 years.

¶ Þo nolde Adam come neih his wyf· two hundred 3er and more,
For wo þat he hedde i-had·, and euere he lyuede in sore :
From vr lord toknynge he hedde seþþe· þat he scholde to his wyf wende :
Adam and Eve come together again.

28 Ne dorste he not beo þer a-3eyn· : A child he hedde atte ende,
Eve bears him another son, Seth.

Seth ! he let his nome nempne·, and seþþen heo hedden mo :
Al his lyf þis seli mon· liuede in teone and wo :
¶ Þo he was of Nyne hundred 3er·, and two and þritti old,
When Adam was 932 years old he was too feeble to work.

32 His strengþe faylede of his Limes·, his bodi bi-com al cold ;
Mihte he not aboute þe corþe swynke·, ne þe weodes vp to drawe ;
Of his lyf he was a-nuy3ed· he wilnede to ben of dawe :
He was tired of his life.

He sat· and Carede of his lyf·: he clepte his sone Seth :
[fol. 20, col. 1.]

36 "Leoue sone· icham weri of-liued·, ich wilne aftur my deþ :
He tells Seth that he must go to Paradise for the Oil of Mercy.

Þo ich was i-driuen out of *par*adys·, vr lord bi-het me þere
Wiþ Oyle of Milce smere me· whonne hit tyme were ;
So longe ichabbe þ*er*-aftur a-bide· þat ich may libbe no more :
40 To Paradys þow must þ*er*-after go· and er en hi*m* Milce and ore ;

Þe angel þou schalt þer Ifynde ∫ þat drof me out at þe ȝate
Say ich abide þulke biheste ∫ me þencþ it comeþ to late
And þat elde me haþ ouercome ∫ þat I ne may libbe longe
MS. *auonde.* Bede hi*m* þat ich deie mote ∫ *and* þe oile of mylce auonge[1]
Ine can na*n*ne wei quaþ is sone ∫ þude*r*ward ich wene
Leue sone quaþ adam ∫ þe wei is wel i-sene
Wen þou comst to þe ende of þis ualeie ∫ a grene wei þou schalt we*n*de
Þat riȝt euene estward geþ ∫ to pa*r*ais last þe on ende
Þer-bi wende þi mod*er* *and* ich ∫ þo ich pa*r*ais uor-let
Eue*r*ich stepe þat we on stepe ∫ uorbarnde und*er* our uet
Ne myȝte neue*r*eft þer gras growe ∫ *and* al þe oþer wei is grene
For þe foule su*n*ne þat we dude ∫ our stapes worþ isene
[fol. 64 *b.*] Þer-by þou myȝt wiþþoute defaute ∫ to pa*r*ays euene gon
Seth nom is fad*er* blessyng ∫ *and* wende hi*m* uorþ anon
Þe stapes he vond uorwelwed ∫ as is fad*er* hi*m* sede
Þo he to þe ȝate com ∫ he ne dorste go ner vor drede
An angel com sone to þe ȝate ∫ *and* esete wat he soȝte
He sede þat to hi*m* an ernde ∫ fram his fad*er* he broȝte
Þat he was old *and* weri ilyued ∫ *and* þat him longede sore
After þe swete oyl of mylce ∫ uor he ne myȝte libbe na*m*more
Ȝe quaþ þe angel is he so ∫ he ne schal þe*r*-of noȝt doute

An angel stands at the gate of Paradise.

Þe Aungel þou schalt þere fynde· þat drof me out atte ȝate:
Sey þat ich a-byde þat ilke bi-heste·, ac hit comeþ wel late,
And þat Elde me haþ ouercome· þat i ne may libbe not longe;
Bidde him þat ich dye mote· and þe Oyle of Milce a-fonge":

Seth says he knows not the way.

¶ "I· con no wey," quaþ his sone, "þiderward þauh ich wene":

Adam bids him go to the head of the valley, and to follow the green path.

"Leue sone," quaþ Adam þo·, "þe wei is wel i-sene,
Whon þou comest to þe hed of þis valeye·, a grene wey þou schalt fynde,
Þat geþ as euene as he may· to paradys þe on ende;

He will also see the path by which his parents left the Garden of Eden.

Þer biȝonde þi Modur and ich·, þo we Paradys forleete,
Euerich stude· þat we on stepten· for brende al wiþ vre fete;
Ne mihte neuer eft· gras þer-on grouwe·, and al þe oþur wey is grene,
For þe foule sunne þat we duden· vr fet-steppes beoþ euer sene;
Þerbi þou miht wiþ-oute defaute· to Paradys euene gon·":
Seth! nom his fadur blessynge·, and þe wey þiderward nom;
Þe steppes he fond ful wel i-wered· as his fader him sede:

Seth reaches Paradise.

Þo he to þe ȝate com· he dorste go no ner· for drede·:
¶ An Angel þer com sone to þe ȝate· and asked what he souhte:

He delivers his message.

He seide· a tiþinge to him· from his fader he brouhte,
Þat he was Old· and weri of-liued·, and þat he was alonged sore
After þe Oyle of Milce·, þat him was bi-hote·, for he miȝte libbe no more:
¶ "Ȝe," quaþ þe Angel, "is he so·? he ne schal þer-of nout doute:

Put In þin heued at þe ȝate ⁝ *and* stond þi-sulf wiþþoute
He pulte In is heued as he bed ⁝ *and* bi-huld al aboute
So murie ne þoȝte him neuer in no stude ⁝ þei he stode him-sulf wiþþoute
So gret delit he hadde *and* Ioie ⁝ of þe foules murie song
Of þe swete med al-so ⁝ *and* of þe floures þer among
Of ech maner frut þat he sei ⁝ þat smolde also swote
Þat of ech maner vuel as him þoȝte ⁝ amon miȝte habbe þer-of bote
Him þoȝte ȝif he moste þere ⁝ biholde In eny stounde
Euermo he myȝte In Ioie be ⁝ his lymes hol *and* sounde
Amydde þe place þat was so uair ⁝ he sei an vaire welle
Of wan alle þe wateres þat beþ anerþe comeþ ⁝ as þe þe bok deþ telle
Ouer þe welle stod a tre ⁝ wiþ bowes brode *and* lere[1]
Ac it ne bar noþer lef ne rynde ⁝ as it norolded were
A neddre it hadde biclupt aboute ⁝ al naked wiþþoȝte skynne
Þat was þe tre *and* þe addre ⁝ þat made adam uerst do sunne
Efsone he bihuld In ate ȝate ⁝ þe tre him þoȝte he sei
Vaire ileued *and* iwoxe ⁝ up to heuene an hei
A ȝong child he sei up þe tre ⁝ in smale cloþes iwounde
Þe more of[2] þe tre him þoȝte tilde ⁝ þoru-out helle grounde
His broþer soule abel ek ⁝ him þoȝte In helle he sei
Þe angel him drof þo fram þe ȝate ⁝ þat he nas nammore þer nei
Þe child he sede þat þou iseiȝ ⁝ a noueward þe tre
Godes sone it was þat wole anerþe ⁝ uor þine fader sunne be
And þe oile of milce wiþ him bringe ⁝ wen þe tyme Iuelle is
And smere þer-wiþ *and* bringe of pyne ⁝ þi fader *and* alle his

[1] ? sere.
[2] MS. *of to.*

Pult in þyn hed· here atte ȝate·, and stond þi-self wiþ-oute": *Seth is told to put his head inside the gate.*
He pult[e] in his hed·, as he bad·, and bi-heold al aboute;
So murie þouȝte him neuere in no stude·; þeiȝ his bodi weore wiþ-oute,

. . . . . .
. . . . . .
. . . . . .
. . . . . .

¶ Him þhouȝte· ȝif he moste þere· bi-holden eny stounde,
Euermore he mihte in ioye libbe·, in limes hol and sounde·:
¶ Amidde þe place· þat was so feir· he sauh a feir welle, *He saw there a well that supplies all the waters of the earth.*
Of whom alle þe watres on corþe comeþ·, as þe Bok vs deeþ telle;
Ouer þe welle stod a treo·, wiþ bowes brode and lere[1],
Ac hit ne bar. Lef· ne Rynde·, bote as hit for-Oldet were; *Also a tree leafless and bare, embraced by an adder.*
A· Neddre hit hedde bi-clupt a-boute·, al naket wiþ-outen skynne;
Þat was þe treo· and þe Neddre· þat furst made Adam do synne:
He bi-heold eft sone in atte ȝate·, þat treo eft sone he seih, *He looked in again and saw a tree reaching to Heaven—in the top he saw a baby in small clothes.*
Swiþe feir hed· and i-woxen· vp to heuene an heih;
A-nowarde he sayh· a ȝong smal child·, in smale cloþes i-wounde:
Þe Roote of þe treo him þhouȝte tilde· a-doun to helle grounde; *The root of the tree reached to Hell, where Abel his brother was.*
Abeles soule his broþur also· him þhouȝte in helle he seih;
Þo drof þe Angel· him from þe ȝate· þat he no more ne seih:
¶ "Þe child," quaþ þe Angel·, "þat þou seȝe· anouwarde on þe treo, *The child in the tree was God's son,*
Þat was Godus sone· þat wolde on corþe· for þi fader sunnes beo,
And þe Oyle of Milce bringe mid him· whon þe tyme i-fuld is *who should bring the Oil of Mercy to man.*
To smere þer-wiþ· and bringen of peyne· þi fader and alle his":

[1] ? sere.

Þe angel wende to þulke tre : an appel þ*er*-of he nom
And tok seth þ*er*-of þre curneles : þo he to hi*m* com
And bed hi*m* þulke cu*r*neles legge : vnd*er* is fad*er* tonge
And burie hi*m* we*n* he were ded : *and* loke wat þ*er*-of spronge
Seth wende aȝen as he com : uor þe wei was wel isene
[fol. 65.] Vor þe stepes were al uorbrend : *and* þe oþ*er* wei al grene
Þo he was ho*m* aȝen[1] icome : his fad*er* he fond ded
Þe cu*r*neles he dude vnd*er* is[2] tonge[3] : as þe angel[4] hi*m* hadde ised
And seþþe[5] he burede hi*m* as riȝt was : i*n* ualeie[6] of ebron
And of-swonke is owe[7] mete[8] : he nuste no betere iwon
Wiþþy*n*ne an[9] vewe ȝer þ*er*-aft*er* : þis cu*r*neles go*n*ne [ups]p*r*inge[10]
Þre [faire] ȝerden[11] þ*er* woxe of[12] : vaire þoru alle þinge[13]
Þo hi were iwoxe to[14] þe lengþe : of an elne[15] ic*h* wene
In þulke stat hi stode longe : *and* cue*r*more grene[16]
Vorte moyses þe p*r*ophete : aboute eode[17] i*n* þe londe
To lere þat folc of isr*ael* : [and] þo vond he þe ȝerdon stonde
Lo her he sede[18] gret toknynge[19] : of þe holi t*r*inyte
Fad*er* *and* sone *and* holi gost : of þis ȝerden þre
Vp he he*m* nom[20] wiþ gret honu*r* : *and* in auair[21] cloþ he*m* wond[22]
A swote smul þ*er* com out of[23] : þat smulde[24] i*n*-to al þat lond[25]
Te *con*fermy [þe] bet[26] is lawe : he ber[27] he*m* uorþ in[28] is hond
Ech sikemo*n*[29] [þat] þ*er*to hopede : is hele ano*n*[30] he vond.
To teche þat folc þe riȝte[31] lawe : þe ȝerden aboute he ber

1 aȝe.
2 his.
3 tunge.
4 þangel.
5 siþþe.
6 þe val.
7 omitted.
8 so in H., but read *mede*.
9 a.
10 vpspr*i*nge.
11 þreo faire ȝurden.
12 omitted.
13 fairest of alle þinge.
14 omitted.
15 MS. *helve*.
16 andallegate faire and grene.
17 ȝeode.
18 seide.
19 tokning.
20 Vp hi nome.
21 fair.
22 hi wounde.
23 þer-of.
24 smilde.
25 londe.
26 þe bet.
27 her bar.
28 on.
29 sik man.
30 sone.
31 riȝt.

¶ Þo wende þe Angel· to þulke treo·, an Appel þer-of he nom ;
Þreo Curnels he tok him þer-of seþþe·, þo he to him com,
And bad him þulke Curnels· legge vndur his fader tonge
Whon he weore ded· and i-buried·, to loke what þer-of spronge :

The Angel takes an apple off the tree and gives NOTA. three kernels of it to Seth. He is to lay them under Adam's tongue when he is dead.

¶ Seth· wende a-ȝeyn as he com·, þe wey was wel y-sene,
For þe stappes weore· al for-brend·, and þe oþur wey al grene :
Þo he was hom a-ȝein i-come· his fader he fond ded ;
He dude þe Curnels vndur his tonge·, as þe Angel him bed,
And seþþe buriede him, as riht was·, in þe Vaal of Ebron,
And bi-swonk his owne mede·, þo he nuste non oþer whon :

When Adam died Seth did as he was bidden.

¶ Wiþ-Inne a fewe ȝer þeraftur· þis Curnels bi-gonne to springe ;
Þreo smale ȝerden þer woxen·, feire þorwh alle þinge ;
Þo heo weoren i-woxen to þe lengþe· of an Elne, ich wene,
In þulke stat heo stoden longe· and euere-more grene,

After a few years the pips began to grow.

Three small trees grew up. For a long time they remained only an eln long.

¶ Forte Moyses þe prophete· code her in þis londe
To leren þe folk of I[s]rael·, and he fond þe ȝerden stonde :
"Lo her," he seide, "gret toknynge· of þe holy Trinite,
Of Fader· and Sone· and Holigost· : of þeose ȝerden þre" :
Vp he hem nom· wiþ gret honour·, in feir cloþ he hem wond ;
A· swote smel· þer com a-non out of·, þat smelde in-to al þat lond :
To Confermen bet his lawe· he bar hem forþ in his hond ;
Vche seek mon· þat þer-to hopede· his hele a-non he fond :
To teche þat folk þe rihte lawe· þe ȝerden wiþ him he beer,

Moses found the trees and took them up.

He bore them forth in his hand and healed the sick with them.

And eke to hele sikemen*!* two *and* fourti ȝer
Seþþe he deie scholde[1] ! þe ȝerden he sette er
Vnder þe hul of tabor ! deide him sulf[2] þer
Þer stode þe ȝerden grene ! mo þen[3] a þousend ȝer
Vorte Se*int* dauid þe kyng com ! þ*at* was of gret power
So þ*at* he was þoru þe holi gost ! ihote vorte heie[4]
To þe hul of tabor ! i*n* þe lond of arabie
Þ*at* he þulke ȝerden þre[5] ! vette *and* wiþ hi*m* nome
Nye dawes[6] he was þud*er*ward ! ar[7] he þud*er* come
Wiþ g*r*et hon*ur* he nom he*m* up: þo he þe ȝerden vond[8]
Þe suotnesse þ*at* þ*er*-of com ! velde al þ*at* lond
Wiþ g*r*et melodie of is harpe ! Se*int* dauid þe ȝerden nom[9]
And[10] to ier*usa*lem he*m* [he] ladde ! *and* nyþe dai[11] hom he com
In a derne stude[12] he he*m* sette ! uor it was i*n* þe euenynge[13]
Vorte amorwe þ*at* he iseie[14] ! wud*er*[15] he myȝte he*m* b*r*inge
A morwe þo he com þ*er*to ! to one hi were alle icome
And Imored so uaste also[16] ! þ*at* hi ne miȝte awei be [i] nome[17]
Þ*at* alle þre bicome[18] to on ! wat[19] bitokeneþ þis
Bote þ*at*[20] fad*er* *and* sone *and* holi gost ! al o god it is
Se*int* dauid aboute þis holi ȝerde ! a strong wal let rere[21]
And nom gode ȝeme hou it woxe[22] ! f*r*am ȝere to ȝere
Þ*at* he myȝte at[t]e laste iwete[23] ! hou old þ*at*[24] tre were
Wiþ a cercle of seluer he bond ! ech ȝeres seute þere*
So þ*at* wiþþi*n*ne[25] þritti ȝer ! þis[26] tre wox[27] wel heie[28]
Ac it[29] ne wox[27] na*m*more[30] þ*er*-aft*er*[31] ! as hi wuste[32] bi þe [siluer][33] beie
Ac eu*er* i*n* on þ*er*-aft*er* ! swiþe vaire it stod[34]
Se*int* dauid it hon*ur*ed[35] wel ! uor he wuste [þ*at*] it was good[36]

[1] Siþþe þo scholde deye.
[2] silf.
[3] more þan.
[4] hie.
[5] þreo ȝeorden.
[6] Neoȝe dayes.
[7] er.
[8] nom.
[9] þe suotnesse . . . . ȝerden nom. These two lines are omitted in H.
[10] omitted.
[11] þe neoȝeþe dai.
[12] In a durne stede.
[13] þeueninge.
[14] iseȝ.
[15] whoder.
[16] omitted.
[17] beo ynome.
[18] þreo come.
[19] what.
[20] omitted.
[21] dude arere.
[22] hou long ! hi were. [fol. 65 *b*.]
[23] wite.
[24] þis.
[25] in.
[26] þe.
[27] wax.
[28] heȝe.
[29] heo.
[30] nomore.
[31] afterward.
[32] H. omits as hi wuste.
[33] from H.
[34] Ac euere afterward ! faire ynou hit stod.
[35] onurede.
[36] god.

* H. omits line 132.

And helede þer-wiþ seke Men·, two and Fourti ȝeer·:
¶ Seþþe þo he dyen scholde· þe ȝerden he sette er
Vndur þe Hul of Tabor·, and dyede him-self þer:
Þo stoden þe ȝerden grene· More þen A þousund ȝeer
Forte seint Dauid· þe kyng com· þat was of gret pouweer,
So þat he was·, þorwh þe holigost·, i-hote forte heiȝe
To þe Hul of Tabor·, in þe lond of Arabye;
Þat he þulke ȝerden fette· and heom wiþ him nome:
Nyne dayes· he was þiderward· er he þider come:
Wiþ gret honour he nom hem vp·, þo he þe ȝerden fond:
Þe swotnesse þat þer-of com· fulde al þat lond:
Wiþ gret Melodye of his Harpe· seint Dauid þe ȝerden nom,
And heom hom to Jerusalem· þe Niþe day hom he com;
In a priue stude he hem sette·, þo hit was in þe Euenynge
Forte a Morwe þat he seȝe· whodere he hem miȝte bringe;
A Morwe· þo he com hem to· to one ȝerde heo weren alle i-come,
And i-Mored also faste· þat heo ne mihte ben a-wey i-nome;
¶ Þo heo weoren alle· to on by-come· what bi-tokneþ þis
But Fader· and Sone· and Holigost· and al o god hit is?
¶ Seint Dauid· a-boute þis ȝerden· a strong wal he lette arere,
And nom good ȝeme· hou longe he woxe·, from ȝere· to ȝere;
Wiþ a Cercle· he bond hym a-boute·, ȝer after ȝere,
Þat he mihte atte laste i-wite· hou old þat treo were;
So þat wiþ-Inne þritti ȝer· þis treo wex wel heiȝe,
Ac hit wox no more afterward·, and þat he wuste· bi þe seluerne byȝe;
Ac euere in on afterward· Feir and Grene hit stod;
Seint Dauid· hit honourede wel·, for he wuste þat hit was good:

Before he died he planted the trees under Mount Tabor. There they stood until David found them.

[fol. 29, col. 2.]

David took them to Jerusalem.

The three trees became one, as a sign of the Holy Trinity.

David built a strong wall around the tree.

He put a silver ring around, to see how much the tree increased yearly.

Þo Seint dauid hadde ido ꞉ þe sunne of[1] lecherie
And manslauȝt þo[2] he let sle ꞉ vor[2] his owe wif vrie[3]
And our lord nom þer-of wreche gret ꞉ swiþe sori he bicom
His penaunce he dude vnder þis tre ꞉ þat he þer-uore nom
Þer he made eke þen[4] sauter ꞉ his sunne[5] vorte bete
Þe raþer[6] it him was uorȝeue ꞉ uor þat[7] [holi] tre so[8] swete
Þo bigon[9] he eke[10] uor is sunne ꞉ þe holi[11] temple to[12] rere[13]
Swiþe noble in ierusalem ac he deide[14] ꞉ in þe fourteþe[15] ȝere
Þe kyng salomon is sone ꞉ þat kyng was seþþe þere
After him þe temple bulde ꞉ þat he ȝare were
Two *and* þritti ȝer he was þer[16]-aboute ꞉ *and* is fader fourtene also
So þat it was six *and* fourti[17] ȝer ꞉ ar[18] þat worke[19] were ido
Þo þe[20] work was al-mest ido ꞉ hem[21] vailed a vair tre
Þat holi tre[22] was fairest þo ꞉ þat hi myȝte awer[23] ise
Salomon it[24] let velle *and* hewe[25] ꞉ as queinteliche as he miȝte
And let it mete *and* make[26] more bi a fot ꞉ þen is riȝte
And broȝte it [in]-to is riȝte stude[27] ꞉ *and* lacy[28] wolde it þer
Þo was it bi a[29] fot to schort ꞉ [as euene] as hi mete it er
Þe carpenters it let[e][30] adoun ꞉ in strong[31] wraþþe *and* grete
To noþing þat hi it broȝte to ꞉ hi ne miȝte it make[26] Imete
A brugge ouer an olde[32] dich ꞉ hi made[33] hit ate[34] laste
Þo hi ne miȝte in þe temple ꞉ to non oþer wore it caste

[1] off. [2] ffor. [3] wyff ffrie. [4] makede ek þane. [5] sinnes. [6] whatlikere. [7] ffor þe [8] omitted. [9] bigan. [10] ek. [11] olde. [12] omitted. [13] arere. [14] H. omits ac he deide. [15] fourteoþe. [16] H. omits þer. [17] þritti. [18] er. [19] work. [20] þat. [21] him. [22] þe holi treo. [23] owar. [24] hire. [25] hewe and falle. [26] makie. [27] stede. [28] legge. [29] o. [30] lete. [31] stronge. [32] old. [33] makede. [34] atte.

¶ Þo seint Dauid i-sunged hedde þe sunne of lecherie,
And Mon slauht þo· for Bersabe· he lette slen Vrie,
Vr lord nom þer-of wreche gret·, swiþe sori he bi-com;
Vndur þe treo· his penaunce he dude· þat he þer-fore nom;
Þer he made þe Sauter·, his sunnes forte bete,
And þe raþere hit him was for-ȝiue· for þe holy treo so swete:

David did penance for his adultery and murder under this tree. Here too he made the Psalter.

¶ Þo bi-gon he eke· for his sunne· þe holy Temple to arere,
Swiþe noble in Jerusalem·, ac he dyede in þe fourteneþe ȝere:

David died,

¶ His sone, þe kyng Salomon·, þat after him· kyng was þere,
After him· þe Temple bulde forþ· þat heo folliche redi were:
Þeraboute· he was þritti ȝer·, and his fader fourtene also;
So þat hit was· foure and fourti ȝer· er þat work weore i-do:

and Solomon his son reigned in his stead. Solomon builds the Temple.

Þo þat werk· was almest redi· hem faylede a feir treo·:
Þat holy treo was þe feireste þo·, þat me mihte owhere i-seo;

When the work was almost done they wanted a goodly tree.

¶ Þe kyng Salomon hit let hewen·, As qweynteliche as he mihte,
And let hit nymen and make more· bi a fote þen his rihte;
Þo hit was brouht to rihte stude· and i-laced scholde beo þer,
Þo was hit· bi a foote to schort·, as euene as heo meeten er;
Þe Carpunter hit leyde a-doun· in strong wraþþe and grete,
To no þing þat he hit euere dude· he ne mihte hit maken i-meetete:

They take up this holy tree, but the carpenters can do nothing with it.

¶ A brugge ouer an Old dich· heo maden þer-of atte laste,
For wraþþe þat heo ne mihten· to non oþur werk hit caste:

They make a bridge with it across an old ditch.

Þ*er* ouer eode[1] mony[2] amo*n* ! þe wule[3] it þ*er* lay
Nuste [noȝt] alle wat it was ! þ*at* defoulede it aday[4]
Þe quene of saba com þ*er*uorþ ! *and*[5] anon so heo it isei[6]
Honu*re*d[e][7] it [wel] vaire *and* sat akne[8] ! heo nolde come þ*er*ney[9]
Bi anoþ*er* wei heo wende uorþ ! to salomon heo com
As heo hi*m* hadde wide[10] isoȝt ! to lerny of is wisdom
Þoru g*race* þ*at* our lord[11] hire ȝef[12] ! to salomo*n* heo sede
Þat þ*at*[13] tre ne scholde noȝt ligge þer ! ȝif[14] he dude bi hire rede
Vor þ*er* scholde ȝut a mo*n* ! deie on[15] þulke tre
Þoru wam[16] al þe lawe of giwes ! destrued scholde be
Salomo*n* it let nyme sone ! *and* vnd*er* erþe[17] it caste
Wel depe[18] [fur] fram alle men[19] ! *and* burede[20] it swiþe[21] vaste
So longe so it þ*er*-aft*er* were[22] ! a uair walle[23] þ*er* sprong
And a uair [water] seþþe wiþ god[24] fisc ! boþe dep[25] *and* long
Mony[26] sikeme*n* þ*er*[27] come ! *and* hor vet wesche þere[28]
Oþ*er* hoden[29] oþ*er* baþede al ! pur hol anon [hi] were
Þat wat*er* hi honu*r*de muche[30] ! *and* wolde þ*er*-Inne wade
Ac hi nuste noþi*ng*[31] of þe tre ! þ*at* al þe v*er*tu made
Seþþe it was þ*er*-aft*er* longe ! þ*at* our lord anerþe[32] com
And þ*at* folc bispek[33] is deþ ! *and* hor red[34] þ*er*-of nom
Þis tre bigon to flete[35] anon ! as our lordes[36] wille was
Þe giwes come *and* fou*n*de þ*at* tre[37] fletynge þ*er*[38] bi cas
Hi nome it vp uor it was vil ! *and* ileie hadde þ*er* longe
And made[39] þ*er*-of þe holi rode ! our lord [þer] on to honge

[1] ȝeode. [2] meni. [3] while. [4] aledai. [5] omitted. [6] iseȝ. [7] Honurede. [8] akneo. [9] þerneȝ. [10] ȝurne. [11] louerd. [12] ȝaf. [13] þe. [14] if. [15] in. [16] wham. [17] vrþe. [fol. 66.] [18] deoþe. [19] MS. *mem*. [20] burie. [21] wel. [22] So þat longe þat þer afterward. [23] welle. [24] MS. *gret*, H. god. [25] fisch gret. [26] Meni. [27] þat þer. [28] hire fet wette þere. [29] Here honden. [30] moche. [31] noȝt. [32] an vrþe. [33] MS. *bispeke*, H. bispac. [34] and here red. [35] fleote. [36] louerdes. [37] fonde þe treo. [38] omitted. [39] makede.

Þer ouer eode mony a Mon·, þe while þat hit þer lay,
160 A nusten not alle· hou holy hit was·, þat *þer* ouer eoden al day:
¶ Þe Qween of Saba· com þer forþ·, ac anon þo heo hit seih,
Honourede hit feire· and sat a-kneo·, and nolde not come þer neih;
Bi a-noþur wey heo wende·, to kyng Salomon heo com,
164 For heo hym hedde wel wyde i-souht·, to leorne of hi*m* wisdom;
Þorwh grace, þat vr lord hire ȝaf·, to kyng Salomon heo sede
Þat treo ne scholde ligge þer·, ȝif he dude by hire rede,
For þer scholde a mon ȝit dye· on þat ilke treo,
168 Þorwh whom· Al þe lawe of Gywes· distruyȝed scholde beo:
¶ Salomon hit let nyme sone· and vndur corþe hit caste,
Wel deope and fer from alle men·, and buriede hit wel faste;
So longe so hit þer-afterward was· a wel feir welle sprong,
172 A feyr watur wiþ gret * sich·, boþe deop and long;
Mony seke· þat þer comen· and wusch heore feet þer-on,
Oþur heore honden·, oþur baþeden al·, heore hele hedden anon:
Þat watur heo honoureden muche· and wolden þer-Inne wade,
176 Ac heo nusten no þing of þe treo· þat al þe vertu Made:
Seþþe longe þer-afturward· þat vr lord on corþe com,
Anon· þo þat folk by-speek his deþ· and heore Red þ*er*of nom,
Þat treo bi-gon to fleoten a-non·, as vr lordes wille was:
180 Þe Gywes comen· and founden þat treo· fleotynde þer bi cas,
Heo nomen hit vp· and for hit was foul· and i-leye hedde *þer* longe,
And maden þer-of þe holy Roode·, vr lord þer-on to honge;

The Queen of Sheba came thereby, but would not cross it.

She persuaded Solomon to remove the tree.

Solomon buried it.

A well sprang up there.

* *? god fisch.*

Many sick people bathed therein and were healed.

When our Lord came on earth the tree began to float.

The Jews thereof made the HOLY ROOD.

And[1] þe tre was vil *and* old: *and* to vili our lord also[2]
And[3] ȝut hem þoȝte þat[4] tre to vair: þat he were þer-on ido
Þe croys[5] after our lordes[6] deþ: vnder erþe hi caste
Þer hi him to deþe dude: *and* burede it[3] þere[7] vaste
And[8] boþe croys eke þer-wiþ: þat þe þeues henge[9] on er
Þer hi leie ar[10] hi were ifounde: mo þen an[11] hondred ȝer
Þo[12] titus *and* vaspasian: ierusalem nome
And destruede[13] alle þe giwes: þat neuereft þer hi ne come
And al þat lond was ibroȝt: In þe emperours hond of rome
And wiþ is men al biset: to nyme þer-to[14] gome
Seþþe þer com an emperour: þat het adrian
Swiþe heþene *and* luþer[15] ek: *and* worrede[16] ech cristene-man
He wuste war þe rode lay: þat god was on ido
And þat cristenemen þe[17] stude honured[e]: wenne[18] hi [miȝte] come þer-to
He let a temple of maumet': in þulke stude arere
Þat me ne vond noþing to loute[19] to: bote maumet' þere
Wenne[20] cristenemen miȝte þuder stele: hi ne dorste[21] vor doute
And ek aȝen hor[22] herte[23] it was: to eny maumet' aloute
Hi bileuede so al[24] þulke stude: and muchedel uor fere
So þat wiþþinne an[25] vewe ȝer: no cristenmon [ne] com þere
So þat þulke stude was: vor-lete[26] mony aday[27]
Þat no cristenmon ne paynym[28]: nuste war þe rode lay.

[1] For.
[2] to vyle oure louerd also.
[3] omitted.
[4] þe.
[5] croice.
[6] louerdes.
[7] wel.
[8] omitted.
[9] honge.
[10] er.
[11] tuo.
[12] omitted.
[13] destreignede.
[14] þerof.
[15] liþer.
[16] werrede.
[17] þat.
[18] whan.
[19] aloute.
[20] whan.
[21] þerste.
[22] here.
[23] hurte.
[24] omitted.
[25] a.
[26] forȝute.
[27] meni odai.
[28] cristene man ne payn.

For þat treo· was for-oldet· and heo heolden vr lord luþer also;
184 ȝit hem þhouȝte· þat treo to feir· þat he weore þer-on i-do:
ÞAt Crois seþþe· aftur vr lordes deþ· depe vnd*ur* þe corþe heo hit caste,

After Christ's Crucifixion the Jews buried the Crosses.

Þer as heo hi*m* to deþe dude· and burieden hit swiþe faste;
And þe twey Croyses eke þ*er*-bi· þat þe þeoues hengen on þer:
188 Þ*er* heo lyȝen· er heo weore weoren i-founde·, mo þen two hundred ȝer,

There they lie 200 years.

¶ Forte þat Tytes· and Vaspaȝian· wiþ al heore folk come,
And al þe Gywes hedden distruyed· and heore pouwer by-nome·,
And al þat lond was i-brouht· in-to þe Emp*er*ours hond of Rome,
192 And mid his Men i-fuld· and bi-set· to nyme þer-of Goome:
¶ Ac seþþe þer com an Emperour·, þat hihte Adrian,

Adrian knew where the Rood was,

Swiþe heþene· and swiþe luþer·, and werrede vche cristene man;
He wuste wher þe Rode lay· þat God was oune i-do
196 And cristene men þe stude honoureden· whon heo mihten come þer-to,
He lette a temple of Maumetes· in þulke stude arere,

and built a heathen temple on the spot.

Þat me mihte not fynde· to loute to· bote Maumetes þere;
Whon Cristene Men· mihten þider stele·, heo durste nout for doute,

[fol. 29 *b*, col. 1.]

200 An eke a-ȝeyn herte hit was· to eny Maumete· a loute,
So þat heo bi-leueden þulke stude·, and also for fere
Þat wiþ-Inne a fewe ȝer þ*er*-after· no cristene mon com þere,

Christians forsook the place.

So þat þulke stude was· for let mony a day,
204 Þat no c*r*istene mon ne Painym· nuste where þe Rode lay:

At last all knowledge of the Cross became lost.

A noble emp*er*our þ*er* com seþþe / þ*at* het *con*-stantyn
In batail he was so muche / þ*at* þ*er* nas of no fyn
Seþþe com is fon *and* wo*n*ne / muchedel of is londe
He ȝarkede aday is ost / aȝen he*m* vorte[1] stonde
As he toward batail[2] wende / he bihuld up an hei
Hi*m* þoȝte þ*at* a uair croys[3] / up i*n* heuene he sei[4]
Lettres he sei[4] þ*er*-on iwrite / he bigon he*m*[5] to rede
Wiþ[6] þes[7] signe þou schalt / maist*er* be þulke[8] lett*r*es sede

. . . . . .

. . . . . .

Þe emp*er*our þis vnd*er*stod / þei he heþene were
A croys[9] he let make[10] sone / þ*at* is men byuore[11] hi*m* bere
In stude[12] of is[13] ban*er* / to batail[2] he wende a-non
And þoru[14] ve*r*tu of þe holi croys / he ou*er*com is fon
And þe maist*r*ie *and* al is lond won[15] / In a [lute] stounde þere
Muche aft*er*ward[16] he þoȝte[17] seþþe / wat þulke signe were
Þe wisost[e][18] men of [al] is lond / biuore hi*m* he let b*r*inge
And enquered[e][19] of þe croys / wat were þe toknynge
Hi sede þ*at* at ier*usa*lem / god was [i]do[20] on rode
And þat þe giwes hudde þat[21] crois / as hi vnd*er*-stode
Wen[22] ichabbe[23] þ*er* þoru[24] quaþ þe emp*er*our / myn fon[25] ibroȝt to gro*u*nde
Ne worþ[26] ic*h* neu*er* bliþe i*n*[27] herte / ar[28] þe holi crois be ifou*n*de

1. for to.
2. bataille. [fol. 66 *b*.]
3. croice.
4. seȝ.
5. he hem bigan.
6. þurf.
7. þis.
8. þuse.
9. Ane croice.
10. makie.
11. tofore.
12. stede.
13. n.
14. þurf.
15. wan.
16. after.
17. soȝte.
18. wiseste.
19. enquerede.
20. ido.
21. þulke.
22. whan.
23. ich haue.
24. H. omits þer þoru.
25. mi fon.
26. worde.
27. of.
28. er.

Seoþþe þer com an Emperour· þat het Constantyn;
In werre and batayle he was so muche·, þat þer nas no fyn;
Seþþe comen his fon and wonnen· muchedel of his londe;
208 He ȝarkede a day his Ost· a-ȝeyn heom forte stonde;
¶ As he touward þe Batayle wende· he bi-heold vp an heiȝ,
Him þhouȝte þat a feir Crois· In heuene þat he seiȝ;
Lettres he sayȝ þer-on i-write·, he hem bi-gon to Rede·:
212 "Wiþ þis signe þow schalt Mayster beo·," þulke lettres sede,
"And wite þe from þy fon·, by daye· and eke by nihte,
Whon þow þenkest þer-vppon·, spede þou schalt in fihte":
¶ Þe Emperour þis vndurstood·, þeih he Heþene were,
216 A· Crois he lette make sone· þat his Men by-foren him bere,
In-stude of his Baner·, In Batayle a-non,
And þorwh þe holy Crois· he ouercom alle his fon
And won þe Maystrie·, and al his lond· in a luytel stounde þere:
220 Muche he þouhte þer-afterward· what þulke signe were;
Þe wiseste Men of al his lond· bi-fore him he lette bringe,
And enquerede of þe Crois· what weore þe tokenynge:
Heo seiden him· þat in Ierusalem· God was don on þe Roode,
224 And þe Gywes þat Crois hudden þere·, as heo hit vndurstode:
"Whon ichabbe," quaþ þe Emperour, "þer þorwh· my fon i-brouht to grounde,
Ne worþ ich neuere glad of herte·, er þe holy Cr[o]is beo i-founde":
Þo þe Emperour· of þe holy Roode· so feir Miracle i-seiȝ,
228 He let him Baptiȝen of seint Siluestre·, þe Pope þat þo was neih:

Then came Constantine who won many battles.

His enemies made war upon him.

As he went to battle he saw a fair Cross in the sky, upon which was written 'By this sign thou shalt be conqueror.'

He caused a cross to be made and borne before him in battle, and so conquered his enemies.

He made enquiry concerning the Cross.

He was told that the Jews had hidden it.

Constantine was baptized by Pope Silvester.

. . . . . .
. . . . . .
. . . . . .
. . . . . .

Nota. Eleyne þ*at* is mod*er* was ! to ier*usa*lem he sende
To seche aft*er* þe holi crois ! *and* heo gladliche vorþ wende
Þo heo com þud*er* heo let crie ! as heo hadde hir*e* red Inome
Þ*at* alle þe giwes of þe cite ! biuore hir*e* scholde come
Þo þe giwes i-so*m*ned wer*e* ! hi [hadde] schor[t]liche g*r*et[1] fer*e*
Gret *con*seil hi nome þ*er*-of ! wat þe encheson wer*e*
Þo sede on þ*at* het Iudas ! ic*h* wene þ*at* ic*h* wot.
Wat þis somounce amounty[2] schal ! ȝif ic*h* [hit] telli[3] mot
Ic*h* wene þe quene enqueri wole ! as heo haþ iþoȝt
Aft*er* þe rode þ*at* ihesu c*r*ist ! was on to deþe ibroȝt
Þ*at* non of ȝou be so wod ! þ*er*-of iknowe be[4] !
Icholle[5] ȝou telle (ȝou) i*n* *con*seil ! wat my fad*er* tolde me
Þo my fad*er* Symeon ! i*n* is deþ vuel lay
In co*n*seil he was to me iknowe ! þo he þen[6] deþ isai
Iudas he sede leue sone ! ȝif it bitideþ so
Þ*at* me enqueri of þe rode ! þ*at* god was on ido
Loke þ*at* þou be iknowe þ*er*-of ! raþ*er* þe*n* me þe quelle
Þ*at* sachee my fad*er* tolde me ! i*n* co*n*seil ichulle þe[7] telle
He sede me a lute biuore is deþ ! þ*at* he was ate[8] dede
To burie i*n* caluarie hul ! þe rode þoru comun rede
Leue[9] fad*er* ic*h*[10] sede þo ! wat ciled[11] ȝou alas
Wi wolde ȝe hi*m* to deþe do ! wen he god was
He sede þoru me nas[12] it noȝt ! ac vor he wiþ sede

[1] hi hadde schortliche grete.
[2] amounten.
[3] telle.
[1] þat non of ȝou ne beo iknowe ! ne so wod ne beo.
[5] Ich wole.
[6] þane.
[7] ich þe.
[8] atte.
[9] Leoue.
[10] he.
[11] cileþ.
[12] nis.

ÞE holy Rode· I-founde was·, as ich ow wolle now telle:
Constantin þe Emperour· heþene folk gon faste quelle,
For heo vr lord Ihesu crist· to strong deþ brouhte;
232 Alle þe heþene Men þat neih him were· sone he brouhte to nouhte:
Eleyne þat his Modur was· to Ierusalem heo sende
To sechen aftur þe holy Rode·, And heo gladliche forþ wende;
Þo heo com þidere· heo lette crie·, as heo red hedde i-nome,
236 Þat alle Gywes of þe Citéé· to-fore hire scholde come:
Þo þe Gywes i-somened were· heo hedden ful gret fere;
Gret counseil þei nomen þer-of· what þe enchesun were;
¶ Þo seide on· þat hette Iudas·, "Ich wene þat ich wot
240 What þis Somouns amounti schal·, ȝif ich telle mot:
Ich wene· þat þe Qweene enquere wole·, as heo haþ i-þouht,
Aftur þe Roode þat Ihesu crist· to deþe was onne i-brouht;
Þat non of ow· ne beo so wod· þat þer-of i-knowe be,
244 In Counseil ich ow telle wole þat my fader tolde me:
¶ Þo my Fader Symeon· in his deþ vuel lay,
In Counseil he was to me i-knowe· þo he on him þe deþ i-say;
"Iudas," he seide, "leoue sone·, ȝif hit bi-tydeþ so
248 Þat me enquereþ after þe Rode· þat Ihesus was on i-do,
Loke þat þou beo a-knowe þer-of· er þat me þe quelle;
Þat Zachéé my Fader tolde me· in Counseil ich wol þe telle:
He seide me a luytel bi-fore his deþ· þat he was atte dede
252 To burien hire· vppe Caluarie Hul·, as heo nomen alle to rede":
¶ "Leoue Fader," i seide, "þo· what eylede ow Allas
Whi wolde ȝe hym to deþe do·, whonne þat he good was":
¶ He seide· "bi me nas hit nout· ac for þat he wiþ-sede

Constantine's mother, Helena, goes to Jerusalem to seek the Cross.

She summons the Jews before her.

Judas tells the elders concerning the Cross.

Simeon, his father, had disclosed to him where the Cross was hidden.

Though Jesus was innocent the Jews put him to death.

[1] Mi. [2] oure lawe ⁝ dude him þe dede.
Myne[1] felawes of hor lawe ⁝ hi hi*m* broȝte to deþe[2] 256
Seþþe hi dude hi*m* i*n*[to] sepulcre ⁝ ac he aros to lyue

[fol. 67.] [3] þe. [4] wonden. [5] þe.
Fr*a*m deþe þen[3] þridde dai ⁝ myd is wounden[4] viue
Þen[5] fourteþe dai þ*er* aft*er*ward ⁝ to heuene he wende an hei
In þe lond of gallile ⁝ as al þ*at* folc isei 260

[6] Twelf monþ. [7] þerafter. [8] monȝ.
Twel[f] monþe[6] it was þ*er* aft*er*ward[7] ⁝ *and* half ȝer[8] *and* more
Þ*at* steuene þ*at* was my broþ*er* ⁝ preched[e] of godes lore[9]

[9] prechede his lore. [10] Oure. [11] stenden.
Our[10] giwes hi*m* ladde wiþþoute [þe] toun ⁝ *and* henede[11] hi*m* wiþ stones

[12] brusden.
And to st*r*onge [deþe] hi*m* bro ȝte Inouȝ ⁝ *and* debrusede[12] al is bones 264

[13] after þe Midewynter ⁝ to deþe.
Þe morwe aft*er* mydwynt*er* dai ⁝ to deþe[13] hi hi*m* broȝte
And nou he is i*n* [þe] Ioie of heuene ⁝ þ*at* he þo aboȝte
Þo Iudas hadde þis tale itold ⁝ þe giwes sede as hi stode

[14] so.
Telle ne hurde we neu*er* er ⁝ þ*us*[14] muche of þe rode 268
Þo þe tyme was icome ⁝ biuore þe quene hi come

[15] Cheoseþ. [16] ȝeo. [17] holie.
Cheseþ[15] anon quaþ þe quene ⁝ on of þis twei dome
Lif *and* deþ ȝou is biuore ⁝ cheseþ weþ*er* ȝe[16] wolleþ
Bote ȝe me fynde þe suete[17] rode ⁝ bre*n*ne echone [ȝe] scholleþ 272

[18] tofore. [19] eȝe. [20] grede.
Gret fur heo let make ⁝ biuore[18] hor al*r*e eie[19]
Þe giwes bigonne to *cr*ie[20] loude ⁝ þo hi þ*a*t fur iseie
Ȝif eny mon wot þ*er*-of hi sede ⁝ þa*n*ne wot Iudas
Vor sachee is fad*er* fad*er* ⁝ of gret power was 276
Þulke tyme þ*at* ihe*su*s was ⁝ on þe rode ido

[21] and alle þoþere go.
Þe quene let nyme þo Iudas ⁝ *and* alle þe oþ*er*[21] lette go

[22] bad. [23] no.
And bed[22] hi*m* be iknowe anon ⁝ he nolde uor none[23] þi*n*ge

Mine felawes of vre lawe· þerfore heo him brouhte to dede;
Seoþþe heo him in þe Sepulcre dude·, ac he a-ros to lyue

but he rose again to life the third day.

Fro deþe· þe þridde day· mid his woundes fyue;
Þenne þe fourtiþe day þer-afterward· to heuene he wende an heih,

On the fortieth day he ascended to heaven.

In þe lond of Galilēē· þat al þat folk i-seih:
Twelf Moneþ hit was· þer-afterward·, and half a ȝer· and more,
Þat Steuene· þat my broþer was· preche gon of his lore;

Stephen, the brother of Judas, was stoned for preaching Christ's lore.

Oure Gywes· him hedde wiþ-oute þe toun· and stenede him wiþ stones,
Þerwiþ to deþe heo him brouhte· and to brusede his bones:
Þe Morwe after Mid-wynter-day· to deþe heo him brouhte,
And nou he is in þe Ioye of heuene· and he hire a-bouhte":
¶ Þo Iudas hedde his tale i-told· þe Gywes seiden, as heo stode,

Helena again sends for the Jews;

"We ne herde telle neuer er· þus muche of þe Roode":
Þo þat þe tyme was· bi-fore þe Qweene heo come,
"Cheoseþ seide þe Qweene þo· of þeose tweye dome;
Lyf· and Deþ· is ow bi-fore·, cheseþ wheþer ȝe wollen,
But ȝe· þe Holy Roode me bringe· Brenne vchone ȝe schullen":

she threatens them with death if they will not show her where the Cross is hidden.

Gret Fuir heo lette make· bi-fore heore alre eiȝen;
Þe Gywes bi-gonne to crie loude· þo heo þe fuir i-seiȝen,
And seiden· "ȝif þer-of eny wot· þenne wot Iudas,
For Zachee· his Fader· fader· of gret pouwer was,

They say that Judas knows all about it.

Þulke tyme þat Ihesus was· on þe Roode i-do":
Þe Qweene· þo lette nyme Iudas· and þe oþere heo lette go,

The Queen retains Judas and sends the rest away.

And bad him ben A-knowe·, and þo he nolde for no-þinge

[fol. 29 b, col. 2.]

Þe quene him lette wel uaste bynde ! and in strong prison bringe[1]
Þer wiþþoute mete and drinke ! seue dawes he lay
Vor hongur he bigon to crie ! wel loude þen seueþe[2] dai
And sede bringeþ me of þis wo ! and ichulle ȝou lede
Þer ich wene þe rode be[3] ! as my fader me sede
Þo he out of prison com ! myd muche folc he wende
To þe place as[4] þe rode was ! as is fader him kende
Þo he to þe place com ! he sat adoun akne
Lord he sede ȝif it is soþ[5] ! þat þou[6] god and man be
And þat þou [of marie] were ibore ! send ous here þin[7] grace
And toknynge þat we fynde mote ! þe rode In þisse[8] place
Anon so Iudas hadde þis bone ! to our lord ibede[9]
Þe hul bigon to quake ! and out of one stede
Þer sprong[10] out a smoke and wende an hei ! and muche place fulde
Suettere smul ne myȝte be ! þen þe smoke smulde
Þo Iudas þis isei ! loude he gan crie
Ihesus is one[11] al-miȝti god ! ibore of maide marie
Wod is þat bileueþ oþer ! as ichabbe mony a-day[12]
Take ichulle to cristendom ! and uor-sake þe[13] giwes lay
He let him cristeny hasteliche ! and þo he icristned was
And let him nempne[14] quiriac ! þat er het Iudas
Þo nome hi spade and schole[15] ! and ner þe place wende
Depe[16] hi gonne to delue ! þer as þe smoke out[17] kende[18]
So þat hi founden roden þre ! þo hi hadde idolue longe
Our lordes rode and þe[19] oþer two ! þat þe þeues were on an-honge
Biside our lord him to scende ! þo nuste hi of þe þre[20]

[1] let in strenge bringe ! and wel faste bynde.
[2] þe soueþe.
[3] beo.
[4] þer.
[5] Louerd he seide if hit beo soþ.
[6] þu.
[7] þi.
[8] þis.
[9] Anon so Iudas hadde ! to oure louerd his bone ibede.
[10] smot.
[11] omitted.
[fol. 67 b.]
[12] meni o day.
[13] omitted.
[14] nemny.
[15] schoule.
[16] Deope.
[17] vp.
[18] wende.
[19] omitted.
[20] Biside oure louerdes croice hi gonnen hi fynde ! þo nusten hi of þe þreo.

280 Þe Qweene him lette þo faste bynde· and in-to strong prison bringe,
Wiþ-oute mete· and drinke· þer seue dayes he lay;
For strong hunger loude he criede· þene seueþe day,
And seide· "bringeþ me of þis wo· and ich ow wole telle and lede
284 Þer-as ich wene· þat þe Roode beo·, as my fader me sede":
Þo he out of *pri*sun com· mid muche folk he wende
To þe place þer þe Roode was·, as his fader him kende;
Þo he to þe place com· A-doun he sat on kneo,
288 Lord he seide·, "ȝif hit is soþ· þat þow· God and Mon beo,
And þat· þow of Marie weore i-boren· send vs nou þi grace
Sum toknynge· þat we fynde mowe· þe Roode in þis place":
¶ Anon· þo Iudas þis bone hedde· to vr lord i-bede,
292 Þe Hul bi-gon to qwake· and out of one stede‸
A· smoke sprong out· and wende an heiȝ·, and muche place fulde,
Swettore þing nas neu*er* non· þen þe smoke smulde‸
Þo Iudas þis i-sayh· loude he bi-gon to crye,
296 "Ihe*su*s is one Almihti God·, i-bore of Mayde Marie;
Wood is· þat eni oþur by-leeueþ· as i-chabbe mony a day,
Taken i-chulle to Cristendom· ich forsake Gywene lay":
He let him cristene hastiliche· and þo he i-cristened was,
300 He let hi*m* nempnen Quiriak· þat er· he hette Iudas":
¶ Þo nomen heo spade and[1] schouele· and ner þe place wende,
Deope heo gonne to delue· þer as þe smoke out wende;
So þat heo founden Roodes þreo· þo heo hedden i-doluen longe,
304 Þe Roode þat God was on i-do· and þat þe twey þeues were on an ho*n*ge
Bi-syden vr lord· hi*m* to schende·, ac he nuste whuch of þe þreo

Judas is thrust into prison, and kept without food.

On the seventh day he offers to tell all he knows about the Cross.

He is taken to Calvary, and offers up a prayer.

The Cross is discovered.

Judas becomes a Christian, and is called Quiriac.

[1] MS. *sand.*

Three Crosses are discovered.

Þat[1] holi croys þat hi soȝte ! wuch[2] it myȝte be
And[3] naþeles hi nome alle þre ! *and* toward toune bere
To cleyne þe gode quene ! wiþ wel glade[4] chere
Bi þe wei ate[5] heie non[6] ! me gan aȝen hem[7] bringe
A ded [ȝung] man vp an bere[8] ! toward buriynge
Quiriac nom þe one[9] rode ! *and* ef[t]sone þe oþer
And leide vp[10] þis dedeman ! ac he ne aros vor noþer
Hi leide þe þridde him upon ! *and* he aros wel blyue
And bigan to þonky godes sone ! þat broȝte him fram deþ[11] to lyue
Þo com þe deuel ȝollynge[12] norþ ! [*and*] loude he gan[13] grede
Alas nou is my myȝte ido ! euermo[14] he sede
Ihesus *ihesus* wat þenestou ! al[15] folc to þe lede
Þou hast her in-warde iȝeue man ! þing[16] þat ich mest ofdrede[17]
Þoru wan[18] ich was verst ouercome ! *and* nou icham al [ibrouȝt] to grounde
Alas þulke sori wule[19] ! þat it[20] was euer ifounde
Vor Inabbe power non so gret ! anerþe among manne
Ȝif hi makeþ þe fourme of þe croys ! þat Ine mot anon þanne
Þer-uore ichot[21] þat ech man ! wole nou þat soþe ise
Þat þe croys me haþ[22] ouercome ! *and* al bileue me
Alas alas þis[23] tyme ! nou ich worþ [al] vor-sake
Iudas Iudas wat was þe ! wi wostou þus on[24] take
Þoru þat[25] Iudas was ihote ! *ihesus* to deþe ich broȝte
And þoru Iudas icham[26] ouercome ! *and* ibroȝt to noȝte
Me ne tid[27] neuereft[28] strencþe[29] non ! bote eny mon wole[30] wiþ[31] wille
Seruy[32] me to paie is flese ! is soule vorte spille*

Nota.

[1] þe.
[2] which.
[3] Ac.
[4] gode.
[5] atte.
[6] none.
[7] him.
[8] in a here.
[9] nom þat o Rode.
[10] vpe.
[11] deþe.
[12] ȝullinge.
[13] loude gan to.
[14] for euere.
[15] alle.
[16] þu hast her a man iȝeue ! þing.
[17] drede.
[18] wham.
[19] while.
[20] he.
[21] ich wot.
[22] makeþ.
[23] þisne.
[24] ou so.
[25] þurf on þat.
[26] ich was.
[27] tit.
[28] neuere.
[29] strenȝe.
[30] omitted.
[31] bi.
[32] Suy.

* originally *spulle* but altered to *spille*.

Þe holy Crois þat heo souhten· whuch of þe þreo hit mihte beo;
Ac noþeles heo nomen alle þreo· and toward toune hem bere

As they were going toward Jerusalem,

To Eleyne þe goode Qweene· wiþ wel glade chere;
Bi þat hit was heiȝ non· me gon aȝeyn hem bringe
A ded Monnes bodi· vppon A bere· to-ward buryinge;

they meet men bearing a corpse.

Quiriak nom þis o Rode· and eft-sone þe oþer,
And leyde vppe þis dede Mon·, ac he ne a-ros for nouþer;

They apply the Crosses to the body.

He leyde þe þridde him vppon· and he a-ros wel blyue,
And bi-gon to þonke Godes sone· þat him brouhte to lyue:

The Holy Rood causes the corpse to revive.

¶ Þo com þe deuel ȝellynde forþ· loude he gon crie and grede,
"Allas nou is my power a-go·," her-after more he sede;

The Devil came yelling and complaining that his power had been taken from him.

"Ihesus Ihesus· what þenkestou·, Alle folk to þe lede,
Þou hast here in Monnes warde· þing þat ich mest drede,
Þorw whom· ich furst was ouercome· and nou I· am al to grounde;
Allas þulke sori while· þat heo was euere i-founde,
For ich nabbe nou· power so gret· on eorþe a-mong Menne;
ȝif me fourneþ enes þe Crois· anon ich mot go þeonne,
Þer-fore ich wot þat eueri mon· wol nou þe soþe i-se,
Þat þe Crois me haþ ouercome· and al my power bi-nome me;
Allas þat ich þis tyme i-sayh· nou ich worþ al forsake!
Iudas Iudas· what was þe· whi woldestou þus on take,
Þorwh on Iudas þat was i-hote· Ihesue to deþe was i-brouht,
And þorw a Iudas ich am ouercome· and i-brouht to nouht;

A Judas had brought Jesus to death, and by a Judas Satan was brought to nought.

Strengþe ne worþ me neuer non· bote eny mon wole mid wille
Seruen me to payen his flesch· his soule forte spille;

Wen[1] my strengþe is me bynome⸵ vondi ich mot [mid] gynne
And myd treson ȝif ich may⸵ eny man to me wynne[2]
I ne may her no leng bileue⸵ vor þat[3] me þencheþ longe
Vor þat[4] croys þat is me so[5] ney⸵ In pyne icham wel[6] stronge
Go henne[7] anon quaþ Iudas⸵ ne com her neuereft more[8]
I-founde it is þei it late be⸵ þat ouercome haþ al[9] þi lore
He þat her þis dede man⸵ fram deþe broȝte to lyue
Pulte þe [her] wiþ is power⸵ In-to helle grounde blyue
Muche was þat[10] Ioie of þe crois⸵ þat [men] made[11] þo þere
Wiþ gret song *and* procession⸵ þe quene hi it[12] bere
Iudas nom þo cristendom⸵ *and* þo he ibaptised was
He let him nempne[13] quiriac⸵ þat er[14] het Iudas
Þe quene of seluer *and* [of] gold⸵ an[15] riche scryne wroȝte
And[16] of ȝymmes presiouse[17]⸵ *and* þe rode þer-on broȝte
Vp[18] þe hul of caluary⸵ þer hi þe rode founde
A noble chirche heo let rere⸵ ihered be þulke[19] stounde
Þo desired[e][20] þe quene muche⸵ after þe nailes þre
War-wiþ our lord was⸵ Inailed to þe tre
Quiriac þat het er Iudas⸵ wende[21] to þe place
As þe crois ifounde was⸵ *and* bad our lordes grace
Þat he ȝif is wille were⸵ þe þre nailes him sende
Þe nailes wiþ gret liȝtinge⸵ out of þe erþe wende
Quiriac þonkede oure lord crist⸵ wiþ gret Ioie he is[22] nom
And tok hem cleyne þe gode quene⸵ þo he to hire com.

. . . . . .

. . . . . .

. . . . . .

. . . . . .

1 Whan.
2 eni soule awynne.
3 þis.
4 þe.
5 omitted.
6 ful.
7 hunne.
8 com þu her nomore.
[fol. 68.]
9 ouercomeþ al.
10 þe.
11 makede.
12 his.
13 nemni.
14 erst.
15 a.
16 omitted.
17 preciouses.
18 Vpe.
19 þe.
20 desirede.
21 ȝeode.
22 hem.

Whon my strengþe is neih by-nome· fonde ich mot wiþ ginne
And mid tresun ȝif ich may· eny Men to me winne;
I· may here no lengore bi-leue· for þis me þinkeþ longe,
For þe Crois þat is me bi-fore· in peyne ich am wel stronge":
¶ Iudas seide·, "go henne a-non· ne cum þou here no more,
I-founden is þeih hit late beo· þat ouercomen haþ al þi lore;
He þat her is· þe dede mon· fro deþ i-brouht to lyue
Pult te wiþ þi pouwer al· in-to helle wel blyue":
Muche was þe Ioye of þe Crois· þat me þo made þere,
Wiþ gret song· and processioun· þe Qweene heo hire bere;
¶ Iudas nom cristendom· and þo he i-cristened was
He let him nempne Quiriac· þat er heihte Iudas:
¶ Þe Qweene of Seluer and of Gold· A gret Schrine heo wrouhte,
And of ȝymmes preciouse· and þe Roode þer-Inne brouȝte,
Vppe þe hul of Caluarie· þer heo þe Roode founde;
A Feir Churche heo lette a-rere· i-heried beo þulke stounde!
¶ Þo þe Qweene· desirede muchel· aftur þe nayles þreo,
Wherwith vr lord was· I-nayled to þe treo;
Quyriac· þat er hihte Iudas· wende to þe place,
Þer as þe Crois i-founde was·, and bad vr lord of grace
Þat God, ȝif his wille were·, þe þreo Nayles him sende;
Þe Nayles· wiþ lihtynge gret· vp of þe corþe wende;
Quiriac þonkede Ihesu crist· wiþ gret Ioye he hem nom,
And tok hem Eleyne þe goode Qweene· þo he to hire com;
¶ Þus was þe holy Roode i-founde· þe þridde day of May
Þat we clepeþ in holichirche· þe Holy Roode day;
Quiriac· þat þe holi Roode fond· Bisschop seþþe he was,
In heuene he is nou seint Quiriac· þat furst hette Iudas;

Judas bids Satan begone, for his power is at an end.

"May Christ thrust thee quickly into Hell," he said.

The Queen made a great shrine of silver and gold and placed the Rood therein.

A fair church she then reared.

Then she sent for Judas, and bade him make search for the nails.

Judas finds them.

Thus was the Rood found on the third day of May.

.   .   .   .   .   .

.   .   .   .   .   .

.   .   .   .   .   .

.   .   .   .   .   .

Þe Holi rode was[1] ifou*n*de ! as ȝe witeþ[2] i*n* may
And[3] an-hansed was[4] i*n* septembre ! þe holi rode day
Mony[5] aȝer was[6] bitwene ! riȝt is þ*at* we[7] telle
Of eiþ*er* feste aft*er* oþ*er*[8] ! nouþ*er* bileue I nelle
A kyng þ*er* was i*n* perce þo[3] ! cosdroc was is name
Cristeme*n* þ*at*[9] he fond ! he broȝte alle[3] to schame
Wiþ his power he won[10] also ! alle þe londes[11] þ*er* aboute
Þo he com to ier*usa*lem ! of þe sepulcre he was i*n* doute
Þ*at* our lord[12] was on[13] ileid ! anon so he þis isei[14]
Vor al is power þ*at* was so luþ*er*[15] ! he ne dorste[16] come þ*er* nei[17]
Ac[3] a p*ar*tie of þe suete croys ! þat *Sainte* Eleine þed*er*[18] broȝte
He tok wiþ hi*m*[3] *and* wende aȝen ! na*m*more þud*er*[19] he ne þoȝte
Of þulke tre he was wel[3] p*ro*ut ! þei he[3] hi*m*-sulf luþ*er*[15] were
A swiþe hei tour of gold *and* selu*er* ! he let hi*m* sone rere[20]
Ȝy*m*mes *and* stones p*re*sious[21] ! þ*er*-aboute he let do
Þe fourme of so*n*ne *and* mone ! *and* of[3] ste*rr*es[22] also
Seyne as it he*m*-sulf were ! *and* turne[23] aboute vaste
As þondri*ng*[24] he made[25] eke ofte ! þ*at* muche folc[26] agaste
Þoru[27] smale holes myd queyntise ! þ*at* wat*er* ofte[28] þere
He made[25] valle adoun to g*rou*nde ! riȝt as it reyn were
As veruorþ as couþe eny man ! make[29] myd queyntise

[1] þat was. [2] wite. [3] omitted. [4] heo. [5] Meni. [6] was hit. [7] me. [8] Of hire festen as hi falleþ. [9] Of cristene men al þat. [10] wan. [11] al þat lond. [12] louerd. [13] þeron. [14] hit iseȝ. [15] liþer. [16] þerste. [17] þer neȝ. [18] þider. [19] aȝe ! nomore þider. [20] silf arere. [21] preciouses. [22] þe sterren. [23] turnde. [24] a þundre. [25] makede. [26] meni men. [27] þurf. [28] þat folc iseȝ ofte. [29] makie. [fol. 68 b.]

[Fol. 30, col. 1.]

By-seche we þe holy Roode· þat brouhte þe deuel to grounde,
And seint Quiriac· and seint Eleyne·, þorwh whom heo was i-founde,
Þat heo bi-sechen God for vs·, þat on þe Roode schedde his blood,
Þat we mote to þe ioye of heuene come· þat is so swete and god. Amen·

Beseech the Holy Rood, St. Quiriac and St. Helena, to intercede for us with God, so that we may come to Heaven's joy.

ÞE holi Roode was i-founde· as ȝe witeþ in May,
Honoured he was seþþe· in Septembre· þe holi Rode day;
Mony a ȝer þer was by-twene·, riȝt is þat we telle,
Hou þis feste was by-gonne· for-soþe lyȝen i nulle:

The Holy Rood was found in May, honoured it was in September.

A kyng þer was on eorþe þo·, Cosdre was his nome,
Cristene Men þat he mihte fynde· he brouȝt hem alle to schome;
Wiþ his luþer power he won also· al þe londes þer-aboute,
Þo he com to Ierusalem· of þe sepulcre he hedde doute,

There was a king named Cosdre, a persecutor of Christians.

He conquered many lands.

Þat vr lord was Inne i-leyd· a-non so he þis i-seih,
For al his power þat was so luþer· ȝit ne dorst he come þer neih,
Ac a partye of þe swete Crois· þat seint Eleyne þider brouhte
He tok wiþ him· and wende a-ȝein· no more þidere he ne þouhte;
Of þulke treo· he was wel proud·, þeih he him-self heþene were,

He came to Jerusalem, and took possession of a part of the sweet Cross, of which he was very proud.

A· swiþe heiȝ tour of Gold and Seluer· he let him sone a-rere,
Of ȝimmes· and of stones precious· þer-aboute he lette do;
Fourme of Sonne· and of Mone· and of Sterres also
Schinen·, as hit hem-self were·, and tornen a-boute faste,
And þundringe he made ek· þat þe folk ofte a-gaste,
Mid smale holes þorwh queyntyse· þat watur ofte þere
He made hit ofte to grounde falle· as þeiȝ hit Reyn were,
As ferforþ as couþe eny mon· make mid queyntyse.

He reared a high tower,

and imitated the heavens, with sun, moon, and stars, &c., and also thunder and rain.

Þe fourme as it an heuene were ! he made[1] on[2] alle wise
Wende aboute myd[3] queyntise ! *and* as reyn ofte reyne[4]
Ac me such wel selde luþ*er* prute[5] ! come to gode[6] fine
Anouewar is[7] tour amydde al þis ! is[8] sege he let rere
In is riȝt half he made an sege ! is on sone he sette þere[9]
To sitte hi*m*-sulf as[10] a god ! i*n* heuene as þei it were
As it were in stude of godes sone ! þ*at* no*n* defaute nere[11]
In is lifthalf he made[12] anoþ*er* ! a uair cok he let vette[13]
In[14] stude of þe holi gost ! i*n* is lifthalf bi hi*m*[15] sette
And[16] sat hi*m*-sulf al amyde ! þe fad*er* as þei it were
And sone *and* holi gost biside ! gret[17] prute was þere
Nou was þis a wond*er*[18] hyne ! *and* a wond*er* god also
And[19] cu*er* me þencþ he was abast[20] ! *and* also[21] hi*m* com to
Eraclius þe emp*er*our þ*at* c*r*istene was of[22] rome
Of þis mysuaryngc prute ! hurde[23] telle ilome
Wiþ is ost he wende i*n*-to is lond ! and worrede[24] on hi*m* uaste
In is heuene he[25] sat as a god ! þ*at* noþi*n*g hi*m* ne agaste
So þ*at* is eldest[26] sone ! he het wende[27] ate laste
Aȝen þe emp*er*our wiþ[28] is ost ! *and* of[29] þe lond hi*m* caste
Vor hi*m* ne dedeyned[30] noȝt vor hi*m*[31] ! of is heuene ene[32] aliȝte
Na*m*more[33] þen it were a god ! wiþ erþliche me*n*[34] to fiȝte
His oþ*er*[35] sone wiþ[36] is ost : aȝen þe emp*er*our wende[37]
Þo hi toward þe[35] batail come ! hor ciþ*er* to oþ*er* sende
Þat hi bitwene he*m*-sulue two ! þe[38] batail scholde do
And al hor ost[39] stonde *and* biholde ! *and* none[40] come þ*er*to
And weþ*er* of hem aboue[41] were ! habbe scholde þe myȝte
Of oþeres me*n* *and* al is lond ! aft*er*[42] is wille diȝte[43]
Þo þis vorward ymad was[44] ! harde[45] hi smyte to grounde

1 makede. 2 in. 3 bi. 4 gan ryne. 5 me seoþ selþe prute. 6 MS. *godes*. 7 þe. 8 a. 9 H. omits this line. 10 on. 11 H. omits this line. 12 sette. 13 to him me fette. 14 As in þe. 15 lifthalf me. 16 He. 17 moche. 18 maister. 19 Ac. 20 hit was a bastard. 21 þat. 22 at. 23 he hurde. 24 werrede. 25 omitted. 26 vlþeste. 27 omitted. 28 and. 29 out of. 30 deignede. 31 H. omits vor him. 32 omitted. 33 No more. 34 mid an vrþlich man. 35 omitted. 36 mid. 37 forþ wende. 38 þat. 39 þost al. 40 þat noman ne. 41 wheder aboue oþer. 42 and after. 43 hit diȝte. 44 was ymaked. 45 to-gadre.

Þe fourme as hit heuene were· he made on alle wyse;

. . . . . .

A-nouwarde his Tour· amidde al þis· his sege he lette a-rere,
In his Riht half he made a sege· his o sone he sette þere,
To sitten onne him-self· as a God· in heuene· as þeih hit were:
In-stude as þeih hit were godes sone· þat no de-faute nere;
In his Luft half· he made a-noþur· and feir he lette fette
In-stude of þe holi-gost·, bi his Luft half· he him sette,
And sat him-self a-midde· þe Fader as þeih hit were;
And sone· and Holi-gost· bi-side· gret pruyde was þere:

He set himself up as God the Father. His son personated God the Son, and a third person represented the Holy Ghost.

. . . . . .

Eraclius þe Emperour· þat cristene was of Rome,
Of þis mis farinde pruyde· he herde tellen ofte and i-lome;
In-to his lond· he wende wiþ his Ost· and werrede wiþ him wel faste;
In his heuene he sat as a God·, as þeih him no-þing ne a-gaste,

'Eraclius,' Emperor of Rome, heard of this, and made war upon Cosdre.

. . . . . .

Him ne deynede not ones for him· of his heuene a-lihte,
No more þen hit weore a God· wiþ erþliche mon to fihte;
His sone· a-ȝein þe Emperour· mid his Ost he sende,
Þo he to þe Batayle come· er eiþer to oþer wende,
Þat heo bi-twene hem-selue two· þe Batayle scholde do,
And al heore Ost· stonde and bi-holden· and no mon come þer-to,
And wheþer of hem so a-boue were· habbe scholde þe mihte
Of þe oþeres Men· and his lond· after his wille dihte;
Þo þe forward was ymad· to-gedere heo smite to grounde,

But the heathen Emperor would not alight from his heaven.

His army was conquered by Eraclius,

And foȝte as it was hor riȝte ? *and* made[1] harde wou*n*de
Ate[2] laste þe emp*er*our ? þen oþ*er* ou*er*com
And as vorward was al is folc ? i*n* is bau*n*done nom
And let he*m* c*r*istny echou[3] ? *and* siwy aft*er* his[4] wille
And þis luþ*er* kyng sat eu*er* atom ? i*n* is heuene wel[5] stille
As a[5] god *and* nuste noȝt ? þ*at* he was byneþe ibroȝt
And so vuele his me*n* hi*m* louede ? þ*at* hi ne warnde[6] hi*m* noȝt
Þis emp*er*our hi*m* wende vorþ ? i*n*-to[7] þis heuene an hei
He[8] vond hi*m* sitte as a god ? his sone hi*m* sat wel ney[9]
Heil be þou he sede þou[10] false god ? i*n* þi*n* false heuene ifou*n*de
Nym þi*n* sone *and* þi*n* holi gost ? vor ȝe beþ ney[11] aswou*n*de
Bi hi*m* þ*at* þou þe makest[12] aft*er* ? þ*at* þolede uor ous[13] wou*n*de
Bote þou wole on hi*m* bileue ? þou schalt [her] i*n* astou*n*de
Of myn hond[14] þolie deþ ? *and* þi prute be ibrouȝte to gro*u*nde
Vor al þi*n* heuene Iuele bileue ? ne[15] uor mark ne pou*n*de
Nai sertes quaþ þis oþ*er* ? þou ne schalt me [noȝt] so lere
Þ*at* ichulle abuye[16] to eny ma*n* ? bote he herre[17] þe*n* ic*h* were
Þe emp*er*our drou out is swerd ? *and* smot of is heued riȝt þere
His ȝonge sone þ*at* sat hi*m* bi ? þ*at* was i*n* is teþe[18] ȝere
He let hi*m*[19] cristny *and* make[20] kyng ? of al is fad*er* lond
His me*n* he ȝef al þat selu*er* clanliche ? þ*at* he þ*er* uond
Myd þe gold *and* myd þe selu*er* ? þ*at* he vond also þere
Þe chirche*n* þ*at* þe oþ*er* hadde destrued ? þ*er*-wiþ he let rere
And made alond[21] þ*er*[19] wel bileued ? *and* libbe i*n*[22] godes lawe
Alle þ*at* nolde t*ur*ne to god[23] ? he[24] broȝte sone of dawe

[fol. 69.]

[1] makede.
[2] and atte.
[3] euerechon.
[4] suy him to.
[5] omitted.
[6] tolde.
[7] to.
[8] and.
[9] and his sone him neȝ.
[10] H. omits he sede þou.
[11] beoþ neȝ.
[12] makedest.
[13] þolede harde.
[14] myne honden.
[15] omitted.
[16] ich wole abowe.
[17] bote. heȝere.
[18] teoþe.
[19] omitted.
[20] makie.
[21] makede þat lond.
[22] bileoued ? al in.
[23] on god bileoue.
[24] hi.

And fouȝten as heore riȝte was· and maden harde wounde,
Ac atte laste· þe Emp*er*our· þe oþur ouer-com
And al his folk·, as forward was·, in his baundun nom,
¶ He lette cristen eu*er*ichone· and suwen hi*m* to his wille;
Þis luþer kyng sat euere a-tom· In his heuene wel stille,
As A God· and nuste not· þat he was bi-neþe i-brouht,
And so vuel he was bi-loued of his men· þ*at* heo nolden hi*m* telle nouht;

and his kingdom fell into his hands. He compells the people to become Christians.

¶ Þis Emp*er*our hi*m* wende forþ· in-to his heuene an heih,
He fond hi*m* sitte þ*er*e as a god· his sone hi*m* sat wel neih;
"Heil," he seide·, "sire false god· in þis false heuene i-founde,
Mid þy sone· and mid þin hori-gost·* ȝe beþ neih a-swounde;
Bi hi*m* þat þou makest þe aftur· þat for vs þolede wounde,
But þou wolle on hi*m* bi-leeue· þou schalt here in a stounde
Of myn hond þole deþ· and þi pruyde ben i-brouht to grounde;
For al þin heuene y nul bi-leue· ne for Mark· ne for pounde":

Eraclius finds Cosdre on his throne in his false heaven.

* *sic*: hori gost—a dirty ghost? (intended as a pun.)

He bids him come down and believe on Jesus Christ.

¶ "Nay Certes," qu[o]d þis oþ*er*·, "þou ne schalt me not so lere,
Þat ich to eny mon schule a-bouwe· bote he herre þen ich were":
¶ Þe Emp*er*our drouȝ out his swerd· and smot of his hed riht þere:
His ȝongeste sone· þat bi hi*m* sat· þat was in his tenþe ȝere,
He let hi*m* cristene and make kyng· of al his fader lond;
His Men he ȝaf al þat seluer· þat he þere fond,
¶ Mid þe Gold and riche þinges· þat he fond þere;
Þe chirches þat þe schrewe destruyde· he lette þ*er*-wiþ vp a-rere,
And made al þat lond in god bi-leeue· þere in Godes lawe;
Alle þat nolde t*ur*ne to God· he brouȝt hem sone of dawe:

Cosdre refuses to obey, and loses his head. His son, ten years of age, is baptized. Eraclius rebuilds the ruined churches.

Þe holi crois[1] þat he vond þere ꝰ þat god was on ido
Adoun he nom wiþ gret honur ꝰ *and* ladde wiþ him also
To þe boruȝ[2] of ierusalem ꝰ *and* þo he com þer biside
Vp þe hul of olyuet ꝰ an stounde he gan abide
Al þat folc aboute him com ꝰ wiþ gret honur myd alle
And þonkede god of þat[3] cas ꝰ þat hem dude[4] þer biualle
Þat þe swete holi crois ꝰ aȝen[5] moste come
Þat þe luþer kyng cosdroe ꝰ hem hadde er bynome
Þe emperour wende adoun þe hul[6] wiþ vair procession
Þen[7] wei þat our lord wende ꝰ toward is[8] passion
Þo he com to þe boruȝ[9] : *and* wolde In ate ȝate
A uair miracle our lord[10] sende ꝰ þat he ne moste com In[11] þer-ate
Vor þe stones þat were þer[12] aboue : adoun anon aliȝte
And bi þe wal stode euene uorþ[13] ꝰ þat nomon In ne miȝte
Sori was þis emperour ꝰ *and* al is[14] folc also
And dradde þat hi vnworþe[15] were ꝰ such holi þing to do
Þer was wop *and* cri[16] Inouȝ ꝰ on god þat he hem sende
Som grace ȝif is wille were ꝰ þat hi saucliche In wende
Þo[17] stod an angel ouer[18] þe ȝate ꝰ a crois he huld an honde
Sire emperour he sede þulke tyme ꝰ þat our lord[19] was her alonde
Þo he com In at þis ȝate ꝰ to be to deþe ido
Vp an[20] seli asse he rod ꝰ *and*[21] in feble cloþes also
He ne com[22] wiþ no gret noblcie ꝰ so[21] as þou dost nou
Wiþ riche cloþes ne oþer prute ꝰ þei he were as hei as þou
Mid þis word he wende aȝen þis emperour[23] anon
And liȝte adoun *and* alle is cloþes ꝰ caste of euerichon
Anon to is scerte *and*[24] is breche ꝰ sore wepynde wiþ[25] alle
Þe stones arise vp aȝen[26] ꝰ þat were adoun Inalle
And lie[27] euerich in is riȝte stude ꝰ as hi hadde er ido
And þe ȝat up as it was er ꝰ þe wei clene also

1 Rode.
2 burgh.
3 omitted.
4 him was.
5 aȝe.
6 wende þo anon.
7 þane.
8 þe.
9 burȝ.
Nota.
10 louerd.
11 er he cam.
12 þer were.
13 bi þoþer wal stod þerforþ.
14 and þis.
15 vnworþi.
16 duol.
17 þer.
18 aboue.
19 louerd.
20 vpon a.
21 omitted.
22 com in.
23 aȝe ꝰ þemperour.
[fol. 69 b.]
24 scherte and to.
25 mid.
26 aȝe.
27 eye.

Þe holy Crois þat he fond þ*er*e· þat vr lord was onne i-do,
A-doun he nom wiþ gret honour· and ladde wiþ hi*m* also
To þe Borwh of Ier*usalem*·, and þo he com þer bi-syde
Vppe þe Hul of Olyuete· a stounde he gon a-byde;
Al þe folk a-boute hi*m* com· mid gret honour wiþ-alle
And þonkeden God· of þat cas· þat hem was bi-falle,
Þat þe swete holi Crois· a-ȝein moste come,
Þat þe luþur kyng Cosdre· hem hedde er bi-nome;

He took the Holy Rood and brought it to Jerusalem, and placed it upon the Mount of Olives.

¶ A-doun of þe hul wende þe Emp*er*our· mid feir p*ro*cession
Þulke wey þat vr lord wende· to-ward his passion;
Þo he com to þe borwh· and wolde in atte ȝate
A feir Miracle vr lord sende· þat he ne mihte in þ*er*-ate;
For þe stones þat a-boute were· a-doun a-non a-lihte
And stooden euene a-boute bi þe oþur wal· þat no mon in ne mihte;
Sori was þe Emp*er*our· and al his folk also
And dredden þat heo not worþi weoren· a such holy þing to do;
Þ*er* was wepynge and cri i-nouh on god· þat he hem sende
Su*m* grace·, ȝif his wille were·, þat heo to þe Borwh wende;

Then with a great procession he carried the Cross to Jerusalem. But the stones of the City's walls stood round about, and prevented Eraclius from entering the gates of Jerusalem.

¶ Þo stod þ*er*-bi an Aungel· a Crois hee heold an honde:
"Sir Emp*er*our," he seide·, "þulke tyme· þat vr lord was here a-londe,
Þo he com in atte ȝate· to deþe to ben i-do,
Vppon a sely Asse he Rod· in feble cloþus also,
He com wiþ no gret nobleye· so as þou dest now,
Wiþ riche cloþus· ne wiþ oþer pruyde·, þeih he were as heih as þou":

An angel appeared, and rebuked the Emperor's pride.

¶ Mid þis word he wende a-ȝeyn· þe Emp*er*our a-non
A-lihte a-doun· and his cloþus· of caste euerichon,
Anon to his schurte· and his Brech· sore weopinde wiþ-alle;
Þis stones risen vp aȝeyn· þat weren er doun i-falle,
And lay· vche in his rihte stude· as heo hedden er i-do,
And þat ȝat opene as hit was er· and þe wey clene also;

Eraclius took off his rich clothes, even to his shirt. Then the obstacle was removed, and the gates became open.

Þe *emperour* þe swete rode nom[1]: *and* al auote[2] In bar
Þ*at* folc siwede hi*m* wiþ g*r*et p*r*ece[3]: g*r*et Ioie *and* blisse[4] was þar
Anon þ*er* com so suote smul[5]: as it f*r*am heuene were
Þ*at* al þ*at* co*n*treie[6] fulde: *and* alle þ*at* stode[7] þ*er*e
Þe emp*er*our ber þ*at*[8] croys: i*n*-to þe te*m*ple an hei
He gan synge þis nywe[9] song: byuore[10] alle þ*at* were þ*er* ney
Þou croys bri3tore to þis wordle[11]: þe*n* alle þe sterren be[12]
Þou art to honouri to þis me*n*: *and* awel to louye tre[13].
Holier þe*n* alle[14] þi*n*g: þou one worþi were
Þ*at* þou þe frut[15] of al[16] þe wordl: al one vp þe[17] bere
Þou suete tre þ*at* bere on þe: þe suete nayles þre[18]
And þe suete berþene[19] of godes sone: þ*at* was ido on þe[20]
Saue nou al þis co*m*panye: þ*at* igadered her[21] is
And here to-gadere to-dai[22] ibro3t: i*n* þi*n* heryngе iwis
Þis song song þe e*m*p*er*our: þ*at* wel[23] is 3ut vnd*er*stonde
Vor 3ut me it syngeþ i*n* holi chirche: we*n*[24] me bereþ þe crois an ho*n*de
Þ*at*[25] folc honoured ek þe crois: as me[26] my3te come þ*er*to
Wiþ offri*n*g *and* eke[23] wiþ song: *and* wiþ oþ*er* melodie also
Þis was þe holi rode day: þ*at* i*n* septembre is
Þ*er*uore me halweþ 3ut þe*n*[27] dai: i*n* holi chirche iwis:

[1] nom þe swete Rude.
[2] afote.
[3] prute.
[4] H. omits and blisse.
[5] swet smyl.
[6] þe contray aboute.
[7] al þe stede.
[8] bar þe.
NOTA canticum.
[9] þisne nue.
[10] tofore.
[11] MS. wor[l]dle.
[12] beo.
[13] to luye treo.
[14] þan eni.
[15] tresour.
[16] omitted.
[17] þu.
[18] also.
[19] burdoun.
[20] on þe was ido.
[21] her igadered.
[22] to dai to gadere.
[23] omitted.
[24] whan.
[25] and þat.
[26] hi.
[27] halþ þane.

Þe Emperour nom þis swete Rode· and al a fote him beer;
Þat folk suwede him wiþ gret pres· gret Ioye and blisse was þer,
Anon þer com so swete a smul· as þei hit from heuene were,

A sweet smell came from heaven.

Þat al hit smulde wiþ gret Ioye· þat in þe cuntre weren þere;
¶ Þe Emperour bar þis swete crois· in-to þe temple an heih,
He gon singe þis newe song· bi-foren alle þat weore þer neih:

The Emperor bore the Cross into the Temple. A new song he sang before all the people,

"ÞE Crois brigtore to þis world· þen Alle þe sterres beo,
Þou art to honoure of alle men· and muche to loue of alle treo;

in honour of the Holy Rood.

Holiore þou art þen al þat is· for þou one worþiore were,
Þat þou þe tresor of al þis world· al one vppe þe bere;
Þow swete treo· þat bere on þe· þe swete Nayles also,
Þe swete burþene· of Godus sone· þat on þe was i-do,
Saue nou al þis cumpanye· þat i-gederet her is,
And here to-day to-gedere i-brouht· in þin heryinge i-wis":
¶ Þis song soong þe Emperour· þat wel is vnderstonde,
For ȝit me hit singeþ in holichirche· whom me bereþ þat crois an honde;

It is still sung in Holy Church.

Al þat folk honurede ek· þat Crois· so feire so heo mihten do,
Wiþ offringes· and wiþ song· and wiþ oþure melodyes also;
¶ Þis was þe holi Rode day· þat in Septembre is
Þerfore me honoureþ in holichirche· þulke day ȝit i-wis:

This was the feast of the Holy Rood, which is observed in September.

[fol. 71.]

SEyn quiriac þat biscop was ! prechede godes lawe
Iulian þe luþer emperour ! broȝte him of lif dawe[1]
Vor þe suete rode þat he fond ! and uor[2] men þat[3] þerto drouȝ
To bileue men[3] on ihesu crist ! uor he it huld al wouȝ
Seint quiriac was þo biuore þe emperour ibroȝt
He het him bileue on hor maumet'[4] ! and þo[3] he nolde noȝt
His riȝt hond he smot[5] of verst ! ich do he sede þis
Vor[6] hast ofte iwrite þer-wiþ ! aȝen our lawe iwis
Þou gidi[7] hound quaþ Seint quiriac ! wel hastou do bi me[8]
Of a good þoȝt[9] þou were wel vnderstonde ! wel auȝte ich blesse þe
Vor bynome is me[10] þulke lyme ! þat me haþ ofte to sunne idrawe
Vor ichabbe[11] ofte iwrite[3] þer-wiþ ! aȝen ihesu cristes lawe
Þe wule[12] ich was a luþer[13] giw ! and on him ne bileuede noȝt
Þo þis emperour isei[14] ! þat he nolde[15] turne is þoȝt
He made him drynke led iweld ! and In is mouþ halde[16] it þere
Euer sat þis gode mon ! as him noþing nere
Vp a gredire hi[17] leide him seþþe ! ouer[18] a gret fur and strong
To rosti as me deþ verst[19] flesc ! grece was þer among
Vor[20] þat fur was al of grece[21] ! and col[22] and salt was ek þerto
And of is flesc þat was vorbarnd[23] ! þe wounden hi selte[24] also
Þo[25] he[26] ne miȝte þer-wiþ turne is þoȝt ! ne to deþe him bringe
He[26] þoȝte ȝif he[27] miȝte him turne ! wiþ eny oþer gynne[25] þinge
Quiriac he sede biþench þe bet ! and do after my lore
And ȝif þou nelt honure our godes[28] ! bote þou wolle do more

[1] him siþþe of dawe. [2] for he. [3] omitted. [4] here Maumetȝ. [5] let smyte. [6] For þu. [7] wode. [8] ido me. [9] aue gode dede. [10] bynyme me. [11] ich haue. [12] while. [13] liþer. [14] þo þemperour. þis iseȝ. [15] nolde noȝt. [16] hulde. [17] gredil he. [18] vpe. [19] fersch. [20] For þo. [21] al afure. [22] gresse. [23] forbrend. [24] hi silte þe wounde. [25] omitted. [26] Hi. [27] if hi. [28] nelt god honure.

Seint Quiriac þe Bisschop· prechede Godus lawe:
488 Iulian þe luþur Emperour· brouht him seþþe of dawe,
For þe holi Roode· þat he fond·, and for he men þer-to drouh
To bi-leeue on Ihesu crist· for al he heold hit wouh;

St. Quiriac preached God's law.

Þo þe Emperour hedde seint Quiriac· bi-fore him i-brouht
492 He bad him leeuen in heor Maumetes·, and þo he nolde nouht,
His riht hond he let furst of smyte· And al i-do he seide þis :—
"For þou hast wel ofte· þer-wiþ i-write· aȝein vr lawe i wis":

He was put to death by the Emperor Julian, because he would not worship idols. His right hand was first smitten off.

¶ "Þou gidi hound·" seide þis gode Mon·, "wel hastou i-do by me,
496 Of my good þou weore wel vnderstonde· wel ouȝt i blesse þe,
For þou hast bi-nome me þulke lime· þat haþ me ofte to sunne i-drawe,
For ich habbe þer-wiþ ofte i-write· a-ȝeyn Ihesu cristes lawe,
Þe while þat ich was Gyew· and on him bi-leeuede nouht:"

He rejoiced at this, because with that hand he had written against Jesus Christ.

500 Þo þe Emperour saiȝ þat he nolde· nout tornen his þouht
He ȝaf him drinken welled led· and in his mouþ helde þere,
Euere sat þis gode mon· as þeih him noþing nere;

Julian caused him to drink boiling lead, but it injured him not.

Vp A Gledeire he leide him seþþe· ouer a gret fuir and strong,

Then they laid him on a gridiron.

504 To Rosten as me deþ versch flesch· grees was þer Among,
For þat fuir was· al of Col· and greee· and þat salt was eke þer-to,
And of flesch þat was eke for brend· þe woundes he salte also,

They roasted him, and salted his wounds.

Þo heo ne mihte torne þer-wiþ his þouht· ne to deþ him bringe,
508 Heo bi-þouhten hem· ȝif heo mihte· wiþ eny oþer þinge;
¶ "Quiriac" he seide· "þenk on þi-self· and do aftur my lore,
Ȝif þou nult not· vr godes honoure· bote þow wolle more,

But they could not alter his determination to remain a Christian.

Þei[1] *þat* þou nart cristene no ȝt[2] ! and ichulle[3] de-boner be
And Murilif[4] þou schalt lede ! *and þat* þou schalt ise
Þe gode mo*n* nolde do aft*er* hi*m* þo[5] ! a caudron he let fulle
Wiþ seþing oile vol Inouȝ ! *and* let hi*m* þ*er*-Inne pulle[6]
Þ*er*-Inne he seþ þe*n*[7] godemo*n* ! vorte he weri was
Þe godemo*n* herede our lord c*r*ist[8] ! and noþe[9] worse he[10] nas
So þat þe e*m*p*er*our isei ! þat he ne miȝte hi*m* ou*er*-come
Wiþ a swerd he smot hi*m* þoru þe herte[11] ! þo[12] he was out Inome
And is soule to heuene wende ! aft*er* þis torme*n*tynge [fol. 71 *b*.]
God uor þe loue of Sei*n*t quiriac ! to þulke Joie ous bringe.

[1] Sai.
[2] cristine nert noȝt.
[3] ich wole.
[4] þe murie lyf þat.
[5] nolde after him do.
[6] þeron pulte.
[7] þe.
[8] Eure crist herede þe gode man.
[9] neuere þe.
[10] him.
[11] þurf þe side.
[12] and þo.

Sey þat þou nart· cristene nout· and ich wolle de-boner beo,
And murie lyf þou schalt lede þer-afterward·, and þat þou schalt i-seo":
Þo þe gode mon nolde don after him·, a Caudrun he lette fulle
Wiþ Oyle· and let hit seþen faste· and let him þer-Inne pulle;
Þer-Inne he seþ þe gode Mon· forte þat he weri was:
Þe gode Mon heriede vr lord euere and neuer þe worse him nas;
Þo þe Emperour i-sauȝ· þat he ne mihte him so ouer-come,
With a swerd he smot him þorwh þe herte· þo he was of þe Baþe inome;
His soule wente to þe Ioye of heuene· aftur his tormentynge,
Crist for þe loue of Seint Quiriac· to þulke Ioye vs bringe A. M. E. N.!

[They then put him in a cauldron of boiling oil,]

[but he was none the worse.]

[Then they smote him through the heart, and his soul went to heaven.]

III.

THE STORY OF THE HOLY ROOD*.

* [Harleian MS. 4196. fol. 76*b*. col. 1.]

De morte primi parentis Ade
et *de incepcione crucis* Christi.

When Adam was 930 years old and on his death bed,

When adam oure form fader dere
Was of elde nyghen hundreth ȝere,
And þarto [thritt]y*, þan he kend
Þat his life drogh nere þe end;

* nearly effaced,

he bad Eve call all his sons before him to receive his dying blessing.

Þan said he vntill eue, "þou sall
All my suns bifor me call,
Þat I may blis þam or I dy."
And als he bad scho did in hy;

[fol. 76 *b*, col. 2.]

Scho cald [þam] vnto him þat tide,
Þai come and stode all him biside,
Als he in his sekenes lay,

His sons ask their father what ails him.

And vnto him þus gan þai say:—
"Fader, what harm es þe on hand,
Þat þou es in þi bed ligand,
And wharto hastou cald vs heder?"

He replies that he is ill-bestead and has his fill of pain and sorrow.

Þan said he to þam al to-geder:—
"Suns," he said, "I far ful ill,
Of pine and sorow I find my fill."

They ask him to tell them what pain and sorrow are like.

And þai answerd and said ogaine:—
"Fader tell vs what es payne,
And how it es sorow to haue,
Say vs þe suth, so god þe saue;
For whils we in þis werld haue bene,
Of sekenes haue we seldom sene."

Seth tells his father that his sickness arises from a longing for the fruits of Paradise,

Þan said seth, "for suth I trow,
Fader, þat þou ȝernes now
Of *para*dis fruit forto ett mare,
Of þe whilk þou has etin are;

And þarfor ligges þou sorowand swa,
Bot say to me and I sall ga
Sone vnto paradis ȝate,
And I sall grete þare in þe gate;
I sall mak site and sorows sere,
And so I hope god sall me here,
And send sum angell me to gete
Sum of þat fruit þat þou wald ett."

and declares his readiness to go there, if he can find the way, and procure, by means of sorrowful supplication, some of the fruit.

Adam vnto seth þan telles:—
"I ȝerne no fruit, ne no thing els,
Bot I haue dole with-owten dout,
And euil in al my lims obout."

Adam says he wants no fruit.

Þan said seth and þai all bidene,
"We wate neuer what euil es to mene;
Tell vs what thing þe greue þus,
Wharto suld þou laine fra vs?"

Seth desires to know what it is Adam wants.

Als he lay þan þus said he:—
"Al my suns herkins to me!
When god had made me with his will
Ȝowre moder þan he made me till;

Adam tells his sons of their parents' disobedience.

In p*ar*adis sone he vs sett,
And gaf vs leue al fruit to ett;
He outtoke no thing bot a tre
Þat he forbed bath hir and me;
In middes of p*ar*adis it stode,
And was knawing of ill *and* gude;

How they ate of the forbidden tree in the middle of the garden.

Þe est he put in my powsté
And þe north at my will to be,

The East and North were under Adam's control,
[fol. 77.]

And till ȝowre moder he toke þat tide
Bath þe west and þe sowth syde;
And twa angels he toke vs till,
Vs forto were fra alkins ill;

while Eve held sway over the West and South sides of the garden.

Till on a tyme, sons, suth to say,
Oure angels went fra vs oway,
Bifor god þaire wirschip to ma;
Þan [com] þe fende þat es oure fa,

On a day Adam and Eve's good angels went away to do honour to God.

The devil, taking advantage of their absence, caused our first parents to eat of the forbidden fruit,

And in ȝowre moder fand he stede,
And did hir do efter his rede;
Sone scho ette, als he hir red,
Of þe fruit god vs bath for-bed;
Scho bed it me and I ette sum,
And þus bigan oure care to cu*m*;
Þe gerrard þus gan hir bigile,
And me also, allas þat while!

whereforeGod was displeased,

Þan of oure werk was god il paid,
And als sone vnto me he said:—

and threatened Adam and Eve with divers penalties.

'Adam, for þou has left my lare
And broken þe bode þat I bad are,
And mare wroght efter þi wife,
Þan efter me þat lent þe life,

Upon Adam's body sixty and ten wounds were to come, from head to foot.

Vnto þi bodi sal I send
Sexty wowndes *and* ten to lend,
Right fra þi heuid vnto þi hele,
Eghen and eres and ilka dele;
And all þi lims on ilka side
Witht sorows sall be ocupide.'"
He said, "suns, god has sent þis thing
Vntill vs and all oure of-spring;

But as the remedy for this God promised them the *oil of mercy.*

Bot oure lord god almighty
Said we suld haue oile of mercy,
In þe werldes end, if we wald craue,
Of all þis site vs forto saue;"
All on þis wise when he had talde,

Adam's sorrow is so great that he bewails the lack of medicine.

He feled sorows ful many-falde;
He cried and said him self vnto,
"Allas! caytif what sall I do;
Þat slike sorows er to me send,
And has no medsin me to mend!"

Eve thereupon weeps and prays God for forgiveness,

When eue herd þat he said swa,
Scho wepid and had ful mekell wa,
And vnto god fast gan scho call,
"Lord forgif me þir angers all!

I wroght þe werk, þat wate I wele,
Wharfore we haue þis dole ilkdele."
Scho praied adam on þis manere,
"Lord lat me haue þi sorow sere,
For sertes I did all þe syn
Wharfore þou es þir angers in."
Þan adam answerd hir vntill,
"It may noght be wroght at oure will,
Oure lord of heuyn þat has it send
Thurgh his might he may it mend."

and desires to bear Adam's punishment.
[fol.77, col.2.]

Adam þan vnto seth gan say:
"Sun of a thing I sal þe pray,
Forto wend als I sall þe wys
Vnto þe ȝates of paradis,
And at þe ȝates, when þou cu*m*es right,
Þou sal mak sorow in goddes sight;
Fall to erth and powder þe,
And pray god haue mercy on me,
For þan þ*ar* auenture send sall he
Sum of his angels to þat tre,
Of whi[l]k springes þe oile of life,
Þat medeyn es to man and wife,
Þar forto send me sum dele,
Þan hope I þat my care sal kele."

Adam beseeches Seth to go to the gates of Paradise,

and to pray to God to send him some of the *oil of mercy*, a medicine for "man and wife."

Þan answerd seth and said in hy,
"To do þi will I am redy,
Bot þe bus teche to me þe way,
And what I sall to þe angell say."
Adam said, "sun tell him till
How þat I haue angers ill,
And tell him also of þis thing
How þat my life es nere ending;
And pray him me to certify
Of þe oile of mercy weterly,
Þe whilk god hight me of his grace,
When he me put out of þat place;

Seth says he is quite ready, if his father will teach him the way and what to say to the Angel.
Adam directs him to tell the Angel that he is near his death,

and wishes to have the *oil of mercy* which was long ago promised him.

If he now þat sand to me will send,
Of all my sorow it sall me mend:"

The way, Adam says, is easy. A green path reaches even unto the gates of Paradise.

"And sun," he said, "I sall þe say
Wharby þou sall ken þe way:
Þou sall sone find a grene gate
Euyn vnto paradis ȝate;

Turning eastward many footsteps will be seen,

Wend estward *and* for no thing let,
Vntill þou in þat way be set;
Þan many fotesteps saltou se,
Bath of þi moder and of me;

which were made by Adam and Eve when they were driven out of Eden.

For by þat ilk way went we twa,
Þi moder and I with-outen ma,
When we war put out of þat blis
To won in midelerth for oure mis;
And þe sin of vs twa allane,
Was so grete and god with-gane,

[fol. 77 b.]

For wherever their feet touched, there the grass withered and dried up.

Þat in what stedes oure fete gan fall,
Þare groued neuer gres, ne neuer sall,
Bot euermore be ded and dri,
And falow, and fade, for oure foly;
Þus saltou find, with-outen mis,
Right to þe ȝates of paradis."

Seth departs for Paradise.

Seth es went, with sorows sad,
Furth right, als his fader bad,

He finds the withered steps.

And hastily he fand þe way,
Als adam vntill him gan say,
With welkit steppes, many ane,
Als his fader bifore had gane;
And euen he held þat ilk gate

which bring him to Eden. He falls down on his face, casts dust on his head,

Vntill he come to paradis ȝate:
On his face þan fell he downe
And kest pouder opon his croune
Ful mekill murni[n]g gan he make,
And sorowed for his fader sake;

and cries to God for the *oil of mercy*

And vnto god fast gan he cri
Of adam forto haue mercy,

And oile of mercy him to send,
So þat he might in liking lend:
So als he made his praiers fast,
God sent saint michael at þe last;
He bad þat seth he suld vp rise
And said vnto him on þis wise:—

that should restore his father to health. While Seth is fast praying, St. Michael appears and bids him to rise.

"Seth," he said, "what sekes þou here?
I am michaell goddes messangere,
My lord of heuyn has ordand me
Ouer all his men keper to be;
And sertanly to þe I say,

"I am," he says, "God's 'messenger,' and 'keeper' of all God's men.

Þat þe thar nowþer grete ne pray
Efter þe oile of mercy here,
For þou gettes it on no manere,
Vntill a tyme if þou tak tent
When fiue thousand ȝere er went,
Twa hundret and twenty þar-till,
And also aght als es goddes will;

It is useless to weep or pray here for the *oil of mercy*, for you will never get it until 5228 years have elapsed.

Þan sal god send doun his sun
Crist in-to þe werld at won;
For mannes sins þan sal he dy,
And so fra bale he sall þam by;
Grauen he sall be in a stede

Then shall God send Christ to die for man's sin.

And rise þe thrid day right fra þe ded,
And lif ogayne, in lim and lith;
And adam þan sall rise him with;
Adam and all his of-spring,
Þat god vntill his blis will bring;

On the third day he shall rise from the grave, and Adam shall rise with him,

With crist þan sall þai right vp ryght
And wende to won in lastand light;
Þan sal þi fader right vp rise
And wend to welth in paradis;

[fol. 77*b*, col. 2.]

and ascend to heaven.

And þat same crist als I tell þe
In þe flum sal baptist be;
To saue man saules he sall be send
And all fals trowth he sall defende;

Christ shall be baptized in the Jordan.

He shall give the oil of mercy to the repentant sinners.

Þe oyle of mercy sal he gif
Till all þat in his law will lif;
And till all þat will sese of sin

He shall give them endless bliss.

Sal he gif blis þat neuer sal blin;
Þan sall þi fader cum fra paine
And dwell in paradis ogayne;
Þarfore if þou þi fader se

Tell thy father his days draw to an end.

Say him als I haue said to þe,
'His daies er dreuen vnto þe end,
Langer in þis life may he noght lend.'

But first do what I am about to tell you.

Bot first now, or þou wend oway,
Sall þou do als I þe say;

Go to the gate of Paradise, put in thy head, letting thy body stand without; if thou seest any marvels come again and tell them to me."

Wende vnto paradis ȝate
And put in bot þi heuid þarate,
And lat þi body stand þaroute,
And luke what þou sese þe obout;
And if þou any selkuth se
Cum ogayne and tell to me."

Seth did as he was bidden.

Seth went and did on þis manere,
And saw ful many selkuthes sere;

He heard there noise and noble smell.

He herd þare noyse and nobill smell,
Swetter þan any tong might tell;

He saw gay herbs and trees, and heard plenty of birds' songs.

Gay herbes and trese þare gan he se,
And fowles sang ful grete plenté;

In the midst of Paradise he saw a well out of which flowed four streams, that watered all the world.

In middes of paradis saw he right
A well þat was schinand ful bright,
Of þe whilk foure flodes ran out,
And went ouer al þe werld obout;
He saw of þa foure flodes clere
Come al þe water in þis werld here;

Above the well he perceived there stood a fair tree, having many branches, but barkless and leafless.

Obouen þe well persayued he
Whare þare stode a ful faire tre,
With branches þaron maniane,
Bot bark ne lefe ne had it nane;
Þan had seth meruail in his mode
Whi þat tre so naked stode;

He believed that the tree stood thus bare on account of his parents' sin.

And wele he hopid, his hert with-in,
Þat it was for his fader sin,
Als þe steppes war þat he had sene;
Þat neuer bare none herbes grene,
And all for þe sin of þam twa,
Þarfor he trowed þe tre was swa;
Al þis thoght when he had left,

[fol. 78.]

Looking about a second time,

In ogaine þan luked he eft,
And hastily þan gan he se
A meruaile of þe mekill tre;

the tree appeared to reach to heaven, and was covered with bark and leaves.

Him thoght þat it stode vp ful euyn
And rechid on heght right to þe heuyn,
And bark inogh þar-on was sene
With leues þat was gay and grene;

In the top of the tree he saw a little child wrapped in swaddling clothes.

And in þe crop of þat tre on hight
A litill childe he saw full right,
Lapped all in clathes clene,
Als it right þan born had bene,
So till his sight it semed ȝing,
He had grete meruaile of þis thing;

He looked down on the ground, and the roots of the tree seemed to reach to the uttermost ends of hell, and he seemed to see the soul of his brother Abel.

Vnto þe erth þan luked he
And saw þe rotes of þat same tre,
Weterly him thoght þai fell
In-to þe vtterest end of hell,
And þare him thoght he had a sight
Of his broþer saul ful right,
Abell þat was sakles slaine.

Then went he to the Angel again, and told him all that he had seen, and asked the meaning of it all.

Þan to þe angell he went ogayne
And tald vnto him albidene,
Als he þare had herd *and* sene;
He pried þe angell tell him mare
Of þe childe þat he saw þare;

The Angel tells Seth that the child is the Son of God,

Þe angell answerd him in hy,
And said what it suld signify;
"Þe childe þat þou saw in þe tre,
Þe sun of god for suth es he,

His schewing here noght els it ment

who shall be sent from heaven to earth, and also restore his father to bliss. That he is the oil of mercy promised to Adam,

Bot þat he sall till þe erth be sent;
He sall fordo þi fader syn,
And vnto welth ogayne him win;
He es þe oile of mercy right,
Þe whilk was to þi fader hight,
When he fra paradis gan wende,
Thurght formast fanding of þe fende;

and he shall bring Adam and all his offspring from bale to endless bliss.

Fra bale to blis þis barn sal bring
Þi fader and all his of-spring[1],
Þat ordaind er in þe werldes ende,
Fra wa till endles welth to wende."

Then the Angel takes three kernels of the tree that caused our bale and gives them to Seth and speaks as follows: "Within three days after thy return Adam shall die and be buried. When he is laid in earth put these three kernels into his mouth, for of them shall three 'wands' spring; the first shall be a cedar tree, the second a cypress, and the third a pine tree. These wands betoken the Trinity. The cedar is the Father, the cypress the Son, and the pine the Holy Ghost." Seth departs with the kernels and reaches home.

Þe angell þan toke kirnels thre
Þat war tane of þat same tre,
Of þe whilk oure bale bigan,
And vnto seth þus said he þan:—
"With-in thre daies when þou cumes hame [fol. 78, col. 2.]
Sall þi fader dy Adam,
And in a graue he sall be graid,
And, when he es in erth so laid,
Þir kirnels þat I gif þe to
Þan in his mowth þou sall þam do,
For of þam sall thre wandes spring,
And ilkone sall be of sere thing:
Þe first of cyder suthly es,
Þe secund sal be of cypres,
And þe thrid of pine sal be;
And þai bitaken þe trenité,
In þe cyder þe fader alweldand,
And in cypres þe sun we vnderstand,
In þe pyne þe hali gaste bi skill."
Þus tald þe angell seth vntill,
And when he was þus kyndely kend,
Hastily hamward gan he wend,
And hame also with him he had
Þe kirnels als þe angell bad.

[1] MS. *of of spring.*

De obitu primi parentis ade.

When seth had wroght all on þis wise
And cumen hame fra paradise,
Vntill his fader fast gan he fare,
Als he lay in sekenes sare,
And tald vnto him albidene
How he had done whare he had bene,
And how þe angell gan him hete
Þat he suld haue his bale to bete,
Oile of mercy fra god send
To saue him in þe werldes end.
When adam herd him sogat say,
Þa wordes ful gretely gan him pay,
And in his life þan anes he logh,
For he hopid forto win fra wogh,
And forto be saued sertainely;
Þarfore to god þus gan he cry,
"Lord me list no langer lif,
Mi gaste in-to þi hend I gif
Forto wis it at þi will,
In whilk stede so it sall go till."
Þus he died with-in þe thrid day
Als þe angell vnto seth gan say;
Þan had he lifed in þis werld here
Nien hundreth and threty ȝere;
For mans kinde was þan so strang,
Þat þai moght wele lif so lang.
When he was ded þus als I tell,
Both wife and barnes opon him fell
And lay opon þe cors criand,
Heuid to heuid and hand to hand,
Þai trowed to turn life him vntill,
For þai kowth þan none oþer skill;
And als þai murned with dreri mode,
Michaell come and by þam stode,
And oþer angels gudely graid,

He tells his father of his journey,

and how that the *oil of mercy* should be sent to save him at the world's end.

These words pleased Adam, and for once in his life he laughed.

He thanked God for his grace

and gave up the ghost. When Adam died he was 930 years old.

Man's nature was then vigorous, and he might live to such an age.

[fol. 78 *b.*]

When Adam died, his wife and bairns fell upon him and lay crying upon the corpse, head to head and hand to hand, for they thought to restore him to life. But Michael appeared to them and thus spake to Seth, "Weep no more, for it is God's will.

And vnto seth al þus he said:
"Wepes namore, bot bese still,
For þus it es my lordes will,
Þat I sal teche here ȝow vnto
How ȝe with þis cors sall do;

Take up the corpse and I will shew you what to do with it." They took up the body, and followed the Angels, all singing "full solemnly" to the Vale of Hebron, where they graved Adam.

Takes him vp and wendes with me,
For in erth sall he bereed be."
Þai toke þe cors vp þam omang,
And þe angels bifore gan gang
Singand all ful solempnely,
And makand nobill melody;
To þe vale of ebron þai him broght
And groue him þare, als þam gude thoght.

Adam's bairns were greatly astonished at all this, but the Angel tells them that the dead must be buried in earth or stone, for all that are born shall die.

Þan al his barnes awonderd ware
Of þe sight þat þai saw þare;
Þe angel said þan to þam in hy,
"Of þis thing haues no ferly,
For als we now do him vnto
So sal ȝe with ȝowre ded men do;
Gers beri þam in erth or stane,
For all sall di þat life[1] has tane."

Seth then thinks of the kernels and puts them under his father's tongue.

Seth þan opon þa kirnels thoght,
Þat he fra paradis had broght;
In his fader mowth he þam did
Als þe angell gan him bid;

Of those three kernels sprang three trees from which great marvels arose.

Of þa kirnels thurgh goddes grace
Wex thre wandes in litill space,
And of þa wandes grete ferlis fell,
Als men may here me efter tell;
Ful mekill sele was to þam sent,
Als men may here wha takes entent;

De *tribus uirgis in ore ade crescentibus*

In Adam's mouth these wands stood until Noah's time, after the flood, 1072 years.

In adams mouth þir wandes stode,
Till tyme of noie efter þe flode,
Þat was to wit with-outen were,
A thowsand sexty and twelue ȝere;

[1] MS. *lifi*.

And furth ȝit groued þai in adam
Fra noie till tyme of abraham,
Fra abraham ȝit stode þai þen
Vntill þe cumyng of moysen;
And nowþer flitted fer no nere,
And ilkone groued by þam self sere;

They went on growing until the time of Moses, and removed not from their place.

[fol. 78 b. col. 2.]

Ane elne of lenkith þa wandes ware
And all þis time wex þai nomare,
Bot in astate ay war þai sene,
And euer grouand in like grene;
Lang efter þat tyme þus bifell
Þat þe childer of israel
Went with moyses thurght þe se,
Fra pharao and his menȝé,
Þat mekill wa had to þam wroght,
And in grete bondage had þam broght;

Each increased an ell in length and no more. In this state they continued until the exodus of the Israelites from Egypt.

Þai past þe se bath hale and sound,
And pharao and his men war dround;
And when þaire fase war þus for-done
To þe vale of ebron come þai sone,
And als þai in þat dale gan dwell
Forther-mar þan þus bifell;
Opon ane euyn als moyses ȝode
He saw whare þir thre wandes stode,
Þat are in adams mowth was sett,
And with grete honore he þam grett;
"For suth," he said, "þir wandes mene
Þe trinité þam thre bitwene,
Þat on þis wise er samin sett,
For in þe rote all war þai mett."

The Israelites crossed the Red Sea in safety, but their foes were drowned. Then the folk came to the Vale of Hebron, wherein they did dwell. One evening as Moses was walking along he saw the place where the three wands were. He greeted them with great honour, knowing that they were the sign of the Trinity.

Þa wandes þan thoght he forto take
Wirschip to þam forto make;
And fra þe erth when he drogh þam out
So nobil smell was þam obout,
And so gude sauore gan þai fele,
Þat his men wend wonder wele

He drew them out of the earth, and so noble a smell arose that all the folk weened that they had at last reached the Land of Promise, for which they thanked God with might and main.

Þat þai had bene cumen right,
To þe land of hest þat þam was hight;
Al his folk þai war ful fayne
And loued god with might *and* mayne:

Moses took the three wands and wrapped them in a clean cloth.

Moyses toke þa wandes schene;
And lapped þam in clathes clene,
And als a relik obout þam bare,
With wirschip, als þai worthy ware:

They were thus kept together for forty-four years, and all that were worm-smitten or torn by wild beasts were cured by touching the wands.

Ay whils þai dwelled so in fere,
And þat was foure *and* fourty ȝere,
And all þat war with wormes smeten,
Or els with wilde bestes beten,
And þai might neght þa wandes nere
Þai suld als fast be hale and fere,
So þat defaut suld þai find nane,
Thurgh towcheing of þe wandes allane:

[fol. 79.]

It came to pass that the Israelites lacked water, and displayed a want of trust in God.

So it bifell þe folk had care
For þat þam wanted water þare,
And in þaire hertes þai bigan
To be mis-trowand ilka man,
To god þai groched al bidene;

Moses tells them to have faith, and water shall be given them.

And moyses said to þam in tene,
"Mistrowand men herkins to me,
If ȝe in trowth will stedefast be,
We sall gett water grete wane
Here out of þis hard stane."

God had commanded Moses to smite the flint twice.

For god had bidden him on þis wise
Þat he suld strike on þe flint twise,
And largely þan suld it gif
Water þat þai with might lif;

which when he had done, abundance of water came forth.

Þan with his wand þe stane strake he
And water went out grete plenté,
Þat men and bestes had þaire fill
Of wat*er* at þaire awin will;

But Moses took all the merit of this miracle,

And for moyses toke all þe mede
And loued noght god for his gude dede,

Ne gert þe folk na louing make
To him þat sent it for þaire sake,
Þarfore oure lord god all-mighty,
Said vnto moyses opinly,
Þat he suld noght þa childer bring
Vnto þe land of his heteing,
Þat was þe land of promisiowne,
Þat he had made vnto þam boune.

therefore God sa'd that he should not bring the children of Israel unto the Land of Promise.

Þan moyses wist and wele he kend
Þat his life drogh nere þe ende;
To þe hill of thabor þan went he
And þare he sett þir wandes thre,
By-side a water vnder þat hill,
For he hopid it was goddes will
Þat gude werk suld with þam be done;
Þan efter þis he died sune.

When Moses knew that his end was near, then went he to the Mount Tabor and there he planted these three wands beside a stream under the hill,

and soon after this he died.

Quomodo dauid tulit uirgas in ierusalem.

Still þan stode þa wandes þare
A thowsand ȝere *and* wex nomare,
Bot in astate ay gan þai stand
Till d*auid* was king of iews land;
And þat was a lang tyme bitwene,
And euer þai groued ilyke grene;

After this the wands remained in the same state for 1000 years until David became king of the Jews.

Þan dauid was thurgh þe haly gaste
Warned þat he suld wende in haste,
In-to þe land of araby
Till þe hill of thabor hastily,
Þe thre wandes þare forto fett,
Þat moyses þe p*ro*fett had sett;
To ierusalem þat þai war broght
For thurgh þam suld be wonders wroght,
And diuers dedis done bidene,
And efterward so was it sene;
Þus when dauid warned was
Till araby sone gan he pas,
To þe hill of thabor fast he ȝode,

Through the Holy Ghost David went into the land of Arabia, to the hill of Tabor, where he found the three wands.

[fol. 79, col. 2.]

Whare þir ilk thre wandes stode;
Vnto þe stede he went full euyn,
Als he was warned with god of heuyn;
And when he of þe wandes had sight
He honord þam with all his might,

He took them out of the ground and there arose a sweet smell and noble melody.

And toke þam vp out of grounde;
And swilk a smell þare was þat stounde,
And noise and nobill melodi
Of diuers maners of minstralsy,
Þat dauid and his menȝé wend
Þe haly gaste had þare descend,
So mekill mirth gan with þam mete
Of nobill noyse and sauore swete;

David laid the wands together in a case of bright silver.

Þan dauid laid þa wandes in fere
In a kase al of siluer clere;
He sang ful fast so was he faine

As he went along, sick men were healed through virtue of the wands.

And on þis wise he went ogayne;
And als þai went so by þe strete,
Seke men many gan þai mete,
All war þai helid in gude degré,
Thurgh vertu of þa wandes thre.

Glad and blithe David came unto his country, and on the ninth day he reached Jerusalem.

Dauid was ful glad and blith,
Vnto his cuntré come he swith;
Þe nyend day efter hame come he
To ierusalem þe riche ceté,
Bot night it was thurgh goddes will
When þai come þe ceté vntill,
On þe wandes had dauid thoght
With wirschip whare he sett þam moght,

He then planted the "wands" in a "dike," and set trusty men to watch them,

And in a dike he did þam right
Biside his castell all þat night,
And seker men he sett to wake,
So þat þai suld no harmes take;

and he intended on the morrow to find a better place for them.

On þe morn he thoght to seke a space
To plant þa wandes in honest place,
Forto be keped honestly,

And wirschipd als þai war worthy.
To rest he went es noght at laine,
And sone at morn he come ogaine;
He fand his wandes hale and sowunde
Ful fast grouand on þe grounde,
And þar-of grete wonder him thoght,
Bot remu þam þan wald he noght,
For in his hert he trowed right
Þat þai war sett thurgh godis might;
Þar-fore he lete þam stand þare still,
And bad þat none suld negh þam till;

When he came to look at them in the morning, he [fol. 79 b.] found them growing fast in the ground, but he did not attempt to remove them.

And forto dwell with-outen dout
He made a stif wall þam obout,
Stalwurthly of lime and stane,
So þat negh to þam suld nane.

For a safeguard he built a stiff wall of lime and stone around them.

Þe same lenkith ȝit war þai þare,
Als moyses in desert þam bare;
Bot þus when dauid sett þam has,
Þan wex þai so þat wonder was,
Þe body wex in a hale tre
And þe crop was branches thre;
And for it wex so dauid made
A serkell al of siluer brade,
And bad þat it suld sawded be
All obout þe haly thre,
Þat he might wit, with-outen were,
How mekill it wex ilka ȝere;

The wands were then of the same length as in Moses' time. But now in a short time they grew and became one great tree with three branches springing from the top. David made a silver circle (ring) to mark the growth of the trunk year by year.

For it wex grete thurgh goddes *grace*
And also lang in litill space;
In þat stede þan stode it þare
Threty ȝere and sumdele mare,
And wex ful fast, I vnder-stand,
For þe tyme was nere cumand;
Þan dauid wex dreri in mode,
For in his hert he vnderstode
Þat [he] a sinful man had bene

For thirty years the tree stood in this spot and increased yearly. David, knowing that he had been a sinful man, made his moan to God, and, sitting under this holy tree, to

And vnt[o] god he gan him mene;
Sitand vnder þat haly tre,
Grete sorow in his hert had he,
And in his sorowing said he þus,
Miserere mei deus et c'.

make amends for his sins, he composed the whole of the "psalter-book;" and in remission of his sins he began to make a kirk. For twenty-four years he went on building day and night. But God bids him to build no more, on account of his sinful life.

And so he made his mis to mende
Þe sawter buke right to þe ende;
And in remission of his syn
To mak a kirk he gan bigin,
And þare-obout he begged fast,
Till foure and thwenty ȝeres war past;
And bisid him both day and night
With werkmen þat war wise and wight;
And for he was a synfull man
Of god þus was he warned þan:—
"A hows to me saltou neuer make,
And þat es for þi sinnes sake."

[fol. 79 *b*, col. 2.]

David desires to know who is to build God's house.

Dauid answerd and said in hy,
"Lord, wha sall make þi hows bot I,
Wha sall vnto þi werk tak tent,
Sen vnto me no sele es sent."

He is told that his son Solomon shall complete the work.

"Salomon þi sun," said he,
"Sall mak a temple vnto me,
Þat euer-mare sal be in minde,
And in mencing omang man-kinde."
Þan dauid wist righ[t] wele inogh,
Þat his life fast till ende drogh,

David then calls all the elders of the city to him,

Of þat ceté gert he call
Þe eldest men *and* maisters all;
And hastily þai come him till
Forto wit what was his will;
Þan vnto þam al þus said he,

and bids them crown Solomon his son as king. Thus he gave his crown away

"Takes salomon my sun for me,
For, sirs, als sune I sal be ded,
And god has chosen him *in* my stede;
His corown so he gaf oway

And so he died þat ilk day;
Þan in a grafe þai gan him graue,
Whare kinges suld þaire beriing haue,
With sang and grete solempnité,
Als fell to swilk a lord at be.

and died that same day, and was buried with regal solemnity.

Quomodo salomon perfecit templum.

Salomon was corond king,
And led þe land at his liking;
Moste sutile werkmen has he soght
And on þe temple fast þai wroght,
And endid it of masonry
In þe space of ȝeres twa *and* thretty;
Forto tell all his fader tyme
And efter þe wirking of him;

Solomon was crowned king,

and in thirty-two years he completed the Temple.

And when it suld till end be brogh[t],
Þe wrightes þat þe timber wroght
A mekill balk þam bud haue ane,
In þat cuntré þai kouth find nane,
Þai soght in toun and in ceté,
And nowre-whare might þai find a tre,

When the Temple was almost finished, the carpenters wanted a large beam, and sought far and wide for a suitable one.

Þat wald acorde vnto þaire met,
Bot þat þat dauid king had sett;
It forto take þe king cumand
And bad it suld no langer stand;
Þan doun þai hewit þat haly tre
So þat þaire werk might endid be;
Þai caried it vnto þe kirk
And ordand werkmen it to wirk;
Þe maisters has þaire mesure tane,
Þe lenkith threty cubites and ane;

At last they found the tree planted by David. Solomon bad them hew it down. When this was done, they took the measure of it, and found it to be 31 cubits in length.

[fol. 80.]

Þai polist it and made it plaine,
Bot all þaire wirking was in vayne;
When it was made efter þaire merk,
Þai wand it vp vnto þe werk
And langer þan þai fand þe tre,
By a cubet þan it suld be;

After polishing it they found that it was one cubit too long.

Of þat fare þai war vnfaine,
And sune þai gat it doun ogayne

They took the beam and shortened it, and on measuring it again they found it to be shorter than the right size. Thrice they altered it, but they could not get the right measure.

Eft þai toke þaire mesures þan,
And kuttes it als wele als þai can;
"Do wind it vp" biliue þai bid,
Bot al was in waste þat þai did;
Þan was it schorter þan þe assise
Thrise wroght þai with it on þis wise;
Acorde to þat werk wald it noght,
Þar-of þam all grete wonder thoght;

Then they sent for Solomon,

Þai cald þe king for he suld se
How þai had wroght with þat tre,
For mekill tene was þam bitid,
Sen þai war al so crafty kid;
When salomon saw it was swa,

who ordered the tree to be placed in the Temple,

In-to þe temple he gert it ta,
And bad þat it suld honowrd be,
For sum might trowed he in þat tre;
Anoþer balk þan haue þai soght,
And al þe werk till end þai wroght.
Þe haly tre, on þis manere,

where it lay many a year between two pillars of the kirk. Solomon bad that once a year every man should visit the Temple and honour this holy tree.

Lay in þe temple many a ȝere,
Twa pilers of þe kirk bitwene,
Þe king gert kepe it þare ful clene,
And made þe custom in þat cuntré,
And bad þat ilka man suld be
In þat stede anes in ilka ȝere,
And ilkone on þaire best manere
Þat haly tre forto honowre
Þat seþin bare oure sauioure.

So it befell upon a year that all the country far and near went to honour this tree. Among this company was a woman that had no faith

So it bifell opon a ȝere
Al þe cuntré, fer and nere,
Vnto ierusalem þai went
To honore þat tre with gude entent;
A woman was þare þam omang
Þat in hir hert ay hopid wrang;

Scho soght þeder þe sight to se
And trowed no vertu in þe tre;
Hir thoght it was scorne in hir wit
Þat oþer men so honord it;
Maximilla was hir name,
Scho sat þaron hir self to schame,
And for scho trowed no might þarin;
Hir clathes biliue bigan to brin
Als herdes þat had bene right dry,

[fol. 80, col. 2.] Maximilla was her name; but, as she was sitting by herself her clothes took fire and burnt like tow.

Þan cried scho loud, thurgh prophecy,
And said, "my lord mighty ihesu
Haue mercy and on me þou rew."
When þe iews herd hir on ihesu call,
Grete tene in hert þan had þai all;
Þai said "scho sklanders oure goddes euyn
For a new god we here hir neuyn";
Þai bad þat bald men suld be boune
To haue hir tite out of þe toune,
And sune, with-outen oþer rede,
Þai staned hir vnto þe ded;

"Lord Jesu," she said, "have mercy and pity upon me." The Jews were angry that the woman had slandered their God by the mention of a new one, and bade bold men turn her out of the town, and stone her to death.

Scho was þe first þat suferd schame
For þe neueni[n]g of ihesu name.
It was þaire custum, als men knew,
Þat who so neuind þat name ihesu,
He suld be staned to ded als sone
And so was with þat woman done.

So she was the first Christian martyr, and all who mentioned the name of Jesus were commanded to be stoned.

De probatica piscina.

Ful many when þai saw þis sight
Honord þe tre with all þaire might,
And þarto made þai more loueing
Þan vntill any oþer thing;

Many who saw this sight honoured the tree with all their might.

Þarfore þe iews thoght grete despite,
And to þat tre þai went ful tyte;
Out of þe toun þai did it draw,
For men þar-in no might suld knaw,
For þai saw grete worde of it went,

The Jews took offence at this and drew the tree out of town,

And men þarto toke mekill entent
And many men honord it mare,
Þan goddes þat in þe iewri ware;
Þarfore þai ordand þam omang
Þat na more worde of it suld gang,
Bot for vertu þat was þar-in

but were afraid to break or burn it. So they cast it into a ditch.

Þai durst it nowþer breke ne brin;
In to a dike þai gan it kast,
So to be wasted at þe last,
Þarfore in þat dike þai it did;
Bot god wald noght þe might war hid,
Sen þat so grete word of it went,
Þarfore his sande þarto he sent;

But every day, between "underon" and "prime," God's angel came to this [fol. 80 b.] tree, and moved the water in the ditch,

Euer-ilka day a sertaine tyme,
Bitwix þe vnderon and þe prime,
His angels to þat haly tre
Ful oft-siþes men might þam se,
Þai moued þe water in þat tide
And wesche þe tre on ilka side;

and all that were sick and sore, if they might only get into the water when it moved, were cured of their sickness.

And all men þat war seke and sare
If þai in þat tyme might be þare,
When þe water was moued swa;
Wha so might first in-to it ga,
If he had neuer so mekill bale,
Hastily he suld be hale
Thurgh vertu of þat haly tre;
Þis was knawin in ilk cuntré,
For mani þat blind *and* croked ware
Hastily war þai helid þare;

Then the Jews took the tree out of the water,

So when þe iews p*er*sayued right,
Þat thurgh þe tre was schewid slike might,
Þai said it suld noght lang be swa;
Out of þe water þai gan it ta,

and turned it into a bridge over a "beck" (brook), so

And ordand it to be a brig,
Ouer a-noþer bek to lig,
For so þai trowed þat mens fete,

And bestes þat went by þe strete,
Suld cu*m* and ga all ouer þat tre
So þat it suld wasted be;
For grete despite in hert þam thoght
Þat wonders thurgh it war wroght.

> that it might be worn out by the feet of men and beast.

Þus lay þis tre þare, als I tell,
Vntill þe sage quene, dame sibell,
Come to ierusalem on a ȝere,
Wisdom of salomon to here;

> Thus this tree lay until Dame Sheba came to Jerusalem to hear of Solomon's wisdom.

And by þat side hir gate was graid
Whare þis haly tre was laid,
And sone when scho þar-of had sight
Scho honord it with all hir might,
Kneland doune on aiþer kne,
Swilk vertu trowed scho in þe tre;

> Passing over this bridge she honoured it with all her might,

Hir clathes gert scho þar-on lig,
And bare fete went scho ouer þe brig;
Thurgh p*ro*phecy þan þus scho said—
"Þis ilk tre þat here es laid
A verray signe wele may it seme
Of a domesman þat all sal deme,
Als lord and maister moste mighty,
Þus may þis signe wele signify."

> She laid her clothes thereon and barefooted went over the bridge. She said the tree was a true sign of a doomsman who should judge all men as lord and master.

Scho lended þare ay whils hir list,
Grete wit of salomon scho wist;
And seþin ogayne gan scho ga
To hir cuntré þat scho come fra,
And þat tre euer scho gan honowre
Þat seþin bare oure sauiowre;
Þis haly tre lay in þat stede,
Vntill þat crist suld suffe[r] dede,
When dome was gifen ordand was he
Forto be hanged opon a tre,
Þat als a cros þan suld be wroght;
On swilk a tre þan had þai thoght,
Sone a iew stode vp in hy,

> [fol. 80 b, col. 2.] This tree lay in that place until Christ should suffer death. He was condemned to be hanged on a tree fashioned like a cross.

The Jews think of the tree "laid over the lake,"

And þus he said thurgh prophecy:—
"Þe kinges tre, I rede, ȝe take,
Þe whilk ȝe laid ouer þe lake
To make a cros both large *and* lang
Þe kyng of iews þar-on to hang."
To þis þai all assented þan,
And rathly out of þe toune þai ran;
Þai toke þe tre þan þare it lay,
Þe thrid part þai hewed oway,
And of þe rembnand haue þai made

and from it they make a cross eight cubits long.

A large cros, bath lang and brade;
Viij cubites þai made it lang
With-outen þat in þe erth suld gang,
And aþer side of cubites thre
Þat abouen þe heuid suld be;

When it was finished they took it to Pilate, who was well pleased with their work.

When it [was] made þus at þaire will,
Þe cetè sone þai broght it till,
To pilate went þai ful gude spede,
He held him wele paid of þaire dede.

De fabrice clauorum.

The cross is made but the nails are wanting. The Jews run to a smith out of the town, and bid him make three nails.

E cros es made, als it sall be,
Bot þan þam nedes nayles thre;
Þe iews war ful redy boune
And ran for na[i]les in-to þe toune;
Vnto a smith þai come ful sone
And bad, "belamy, biliue haue done,
Make thre nayles stif and gude
At naile þe prophet on þe rode";
When þe smith herd þaire entent,
How þat ihesu suld be schent,

The smith, believing Christ to be a true prophet,

In hert he had ful mekyll wa
Obout þe nayles forto ga,
For of ihesu he vnder-stode
Þat [he] was prophet trew *and* gude;
Þarfore wele in his hert he thoght
Þat for him suld no nayles be wroght;

does not intend to make the nails.

He answerd þam with wordes fre
And said "ȝe gett none nailes for me,
God has sent on me his merke
So þat I may wirk no werk;"
In his bosum he hid his hand
And said he hurt it on a brand,
"Þar-on," he said, "I haue slike pine
Þat I hope my hand to tyne."
Þan answerd þe iews kene
And said vnto him all in tene:
"All for noght þou feynes þe,
All þi sare-nes will we se,
And bot we find þi tales trew
Ful sare it sall þi seluen rew."
Þus thai thret him in þaire saw,
And gert him þare his hand out draw,
Þan was þare schewed in þat place
Grete gudenes, thurgh goddes grace;
His hand semed als it war sare
And hurting had it neuer þe mare;
Þe iews saw þat it was so,
And namore said þai him vnto;
Furth come þan þe smithes whife,
A fell woman and full of strife,
By þe iews þare þai stode,
Scho spac hir husband litill gude;
"Sir," scho said, and loud gan cry,
"Sen when had þou slike malady;
Ȝistereuen, when þe day was gane,
Euill on þi handes had þou nane,
And sen sekenes es sent to þe
Þir men sall noght vnserued be,
Þai sall haue nayles or þai ga,
Als sone my self sall þam ma."
Scho blew þe belise ferly fast,
And made þe yren hate at þe last.

But he answers the Jews with bold words: "No nails you get from me, for I have burnt my hand on a [fol. 81.] brand,

and I expect I shall lose my hand."

The Jews did not believe the smith, but bade him show them his hand,

which they saw hurt as he had said (though in reality it was not).
So they made no more ado about the matter.
But out came the smith's wife, a cross-grained scolding woman.
By the Jews she stood, and said little good of her husband.
"Since thou art sick," she said, "these men shall not go away unserved."

So she set to work and made the nails herself,

the Jews all the while lending her a helping hand.

Þe iews helppid hir forto smite
So þat thre nayles war made ful tite;
Hir husband saw and stode ful still,
He durst noght say þat scho did ill;

They were very roughly made, but the Jews gladly took them,

Þai war full grete and rudely wroght,
Bot þarfore þai forsuke þam noght,
Bot sone, when þai þir nailes had,
Furth þai went with hert ful glad,
And hastily þai toke þe gate

and brought them to Pilate.

Vntill þai come to sir pilate.

IV.

FINDING OF THE CROSS.

[Harleian MS. 4196, leaf 149, back, col. 2.]

De Inuencione sancte crucis.

MEn aw to honure euer omang
Þe cros þat al our hele on hang;

The Cross ought always to be held in honour.

And how þat haly tre was fun,
Was þis feste ordand and bigun;
Þat tre vs aw forto do honoure
Þat bare oure lord and oure sauioure.

Constantine was true in word and deed.

Whils Constantyne þe nobil king
Lifd here in erth in grete liking,
Trew he was, in dede and saw,
And lely lifed he in his law;

In Rome he reigned as Emperor.

In Rome he regnid als Emperoure,
And gouerned it with grete honoure;
So in his tyme, trewly to tell,
All on þis maner it bifell:—

The Greeks and folk of Barbary gathered together to fight against Rome.

Þe grekis and þe folk of barbary
Geders ful grete cumpany,
Forto gif batail ogaynes rome,
And so by strenkit it to ouercum;

When Constantine heard of this he was sore afraid,

And when king Constantine herd tell
Off al þis fare, how it byfell,
In his hert he had grete drede,
For ful grete power gun þai lede;

but prepared to defend his land.

He ordand him grete cumpany
Of men of armes and archery
His land with fighting to defend,
And to hald it fro his enmis hend;

But as he lay upon a night, before the day that they should fight, it seemed to him that he looked toward heaven,

And als he lay opon a night,
Bifore þat day þat þai suld fight,
Him thoght he lukid to heuyn on high,

and saw the Cross on which Christ died, and a voice spake thus to him

And in þe aire him thoght he sigh
Þe same cros þat crist was on done,
And a voice sayd þus to him sone:

“Arrange thine arms in this same manner, then shalt thou overcome thy enemies. In this sign put fully thy trust, then shalt thou have no cause for fear, for by this thou shalt have [leaf 150.] victory.”

“Ordayne þine armes on þis kin wise,
Þan sal þou ouercum þine enmise;
And in þis figure fully þou trayst,
Þan thar þe no thing be abaist;
Mak þis in þine armes forþi,
Þan sall þou haue þe victori.”
In hoc vince.

On awaking he was very joyful. Up he rose with a light heart, and went to Helena the noble Queen, and told her of his dream. Full glad was she of the tidings, and she caused a cross to be made to be carried before the Emperor.

He wakkend þan and was ful glad,
For he so gude herting þan had;
Vp he rase with hert ful light
And to his moder he went ful right,
Þat was saynt Elyne þe noble quene,
And tolde vnto hir ilkdele bidene;
Of þis tithing scho was ful fayne
And gert ordan, with al hir mayne,
Þat he suld haue swilk armes dight,
Als he had sene by gastly sight;
His awin armes sone doun war laid
And þe cros in his scheld purtraid,
Byfore him in batayle to bere,

So he went forth to the war, and through the Cross overcame his enemies.

And so he went furth to þe were;
And thurgh þe vertu of þe croyce,
Als he was warned by gastly voyce,
Al his enmis he ouer-come
And broght þe victori to Rome.

St. Helena was very joyful that her son had returned safe, and with might and main honoured the Cross. But of the Cross they knew nothing, nor indeed of Jesus.

Saint Elyne þan was wunder fayne
Þat hir sun was cumen safe ogayne,
And þat ilk figure of þe rode
Honurde þai with mayn and mode;
Bot of þe cros no thing þai knew,
Ne no thing wist þai of Ihesu,
Ne no thing wist þai what it ment
Þat þai honurd with gude entent.

Þan king Constantine gert call
Of Iewry þe maisters all,
Forto enquere by þaire clergy
What thing þat signe suld signify:
Þai said, "sir, lely we ȝow hete,
Byfor þis tyme was a *pro*phete
Hight ih*es*u*e*, and [in] þis same Cetè
Was he hanged on swilk a tre;
Ful many men þarbi was mend,
And grete vertu þarof was kend,
Bot sone efter þe iews it hid,
For no might suld of it be kid,
And how it was hid sal ȝe here.
Sir, it bifell in þis manere—
When ih*es*u*e* vnto ded was done,
Þe iews þan tok þaire counsail sone,
Forto hide þat ilke haly tre,
So þat it suld noght honurd be;
Vnder þe grete hill of caluary
Þore groue þai it ful priuely,
With two crosses þat thenes on hang,
And also þe nayles þat war strang;
Al kest þai priuely in a pyt,
So þat no man suld of þam wit;
Þore haue þai liggen, on þis maner,
Sethin more þan two hundreth ȝere,
Sethin Tytus and vaspasian come
And destroyd mony iews of Rome;
For right als þai boght ih*es*u fre
For thritty penis of þaire monè,
So war þai sold to þaire enmy
Euer thritty iews for a peny;
On þis wise war þai al broght doun,
Vnder þe Emp*er*oure subieccione,
So þat no man wun þore sald
Of þe Emp*er*ure bot þai wald hald,

Then Constantine called together the masters of Jewry, and asked what the sign signified. They said that before this time there was a prophet, named Jesus, who was hanged on such a tree in this same city. Many were healed thereby, and recognised its great virtue. Soon after the Jews hid it, so that it should not be honoured.

They graved it under the hill of Calvary, along with the crosses of the two thieves.

[leaf 150, col. 2.]

Here they have lain more than 200 years. After this Titus and Vespasian came and destroyed many Jews, for just as they bought Jesus for thirty pence, so were they sold to their enemies every thirty Jews for a penny.

Far and wide are they sown. No Jew has a house of his own.

And sethin als wide als þai er saun
Has no iew hous of his awyn;
Swilk maystris war made þam omell,
And efter þat tyme þus bifell:—

When Sir Adrian was Emperor of Rome, the Christians were persecuted.

In Rome ane Emperoure was þan
Þat named was sir adrian,
Cristen law wald he none ken,
Bot euer distryed al cristenmen;

He well knew where the Cross was hid,

Þis Emperoure wele vnderstode
Whore his elders had hid þe rode,
And herby persayued he it right,

for Christian men came to honour the holy place, the Mount of Calvary,

For cristen men both day *and* night
Come to honure þat haly stede,
And bousomly þore made þaire bede;
Þai honurd þe mount of caluary,
In wirschip of þe cros namely.
And þis Emperoure of Rome
Wist cristen men so þeder come,

so he built a heathen temple upon the mount.

Þe cros he wold noght þethin take,
Bot þus he ordand for þaire sake
In þat same place to edify
A temple for þaire maumetry,
For cristen men suld þan forbere
In þat stede to mak prayere;

No Christians ever after came there to pray, so the Cross passed out of mind.

Þan cristen men þat place refused,
None of þam efter þeder vsed,
And so it wurthed at þe last
Þe cros al out of minde was past,
And þat was for no man herd say
Þarof ne in what stede it lay.

Long after this temple was destroyed and the place was overgrown with thorns and briars.

Lang efter þe temple of maumetry
Was all distroyd fro Caluary,
Þan groued þe stede with thornes *and* breris,
And of þe cros no thing men heris;
For two hundreth ȝeres war omell,
Bitwix þe tymes þat I of tell.

[leaf 150, back]

þan Constantine was Emperoure
And rewlid rome with grete honoure;
Vnto him was tolde in þat tyde,
140 How þat þe iews þe cros gun hide.
Vnto his moder he said in hi,
"Moder, sen we haue þe victori
And myne enmise þus er slone,
144 Thurgh vertu of þe cros allone,
And clerkis has told to ȝow and me
þat criste was ded on swilk a tre,
Ful fayn I wold þat tre war soght
148 And sone vnto more honure broght."
þan said his moder, saynt Elyne,
"Sun, for suth I sal noght fyne
þat haly tre or I haue fun."
152 And sone hir way scho has bigun,
Furth scho went with faire menȝé,
To ierusalem, þat riche ceté.
And when þe iews herd hereof tell
156 þat þe quene come þam omell,
Grete wunder had þai albidene,
What thing hir cu*m*ing suld bimene.
And al þe iews sone did scho call
160 To cum into þaire comun hall,
þe sertayn suth hir forto lere
Of thinges þat scho wold enquere;
Here-fore þe iews had mekil dout,
164 þai gedird togeder in grete rout,
And priuely þai ask þis thing,
What was þe caus of þe quenes cu*m*ing.
And sum, als þai had herd of hir,
168 Said scho come for þe cros to spir,
Waron crist vnto dede was broght,
And ilkone said þai knew it noght;
So was þore ane þat hiyght Iudas,
172 þat grete mayster omang þam was;

Unto Constantine it was told how the Jews had hidden the Cross.

Constantine tells his mother Helena that he would like to find the Cross upon which Christ had suffered.

Helena determines to discover it,

and goes to Jerusalem.

When the Jews heard of her coming they were in great fear and dread.

Helena calls them into their common hall, and says there are certain things which she wishes to know.
The Jews take counsel together as to what the questions might be.

Some said that she had come to enquire about the Cross of Christ, but they said they knew nothing of it.

Saint simyon sun for suth was he,
And Simyon was sun of ȝaché.
Þis Iudas said, "sumdele I mene

Judas tells the Jews what Simeon his father had told him on his death-bed.

Of thinges þat here bifore has bene;
Simyon, my fader, als ȝe sall here,
Told vnto me on þis manere :—
When he wist wele sune forto dy

"'If any one enquires after the Cross, do not disclose where it is to be found, unless it be [leaf 150, back, col. 2.] to save thy life.'

'Sun,' he said, 'herkin me in hy,
A counsail sall I tel to þe,
Þe whilk I will you hald priué;
If it bifall, sun, in þi liue
Þat any spir, oþir man or wiue,
Or efter þe cros will þe ass,
Þat ihesu crist on hanged was,
Or þai þarfore do þe to dede,
Tell þam vnto swilk a stede,
Þat now es waste *and* al vnkid,
For þore I wote wele was it hid;
And if þou may þi ded escheu,

He told me where the Cross was commonly reported to be hid."

Þan wald I þat no man it kneu.'
Þus tald he to me in what stede
Þai groue þe rode bi comun rede,
Bot if we any oþer wise mai do,
I rede we tel noman þarto."
Þan had þai meruail in þaire mode
For þai herd neuer are of þe rode;

Hereupon the Jews came before Helena,

Þan come þai furth, ilkone bidene,
In comun hall bifor þe quene.
Sone on þis wise scho said þam to—

who threatened to put them to death unless they made known to her where the Cross was hid.

"Dose swith and chese one of þir two,
Whethir ȝow es leuir to suffer dede,
Or els to tel me in þis stede
Whore cristes cros in erth es hid,
And bot ȝe do, als I ȝow bid,

To show them that she was in earnest she caused a fire to be made.

Ilkone ȝe sall be brint þis day."
And sone a fire scho did puruay,

And when þai saw þe fyr on brede,
In þaire hertis þan had þai drede:
Vnto þe quene al gun þai cry,
"Lady, of vs here haue mercy,
For we wote no thing how it was;
If any wote þan wote Iudas,
For he was ane old prophet sun,
Þe laws wele better mai he cun;
His elders war of þe alde state,
And of þaire werkes sumdel he wate."

This frightens the Jews, who declare they know nothing of the Cross, but that one Judas knows all about it.

Þan lete scho al þo oþer go,
And Iudas toke hir vnto;
And for he wald tell no resoun,
He was done in depe dungeoun,
And þore he lay in mirknes grete,
Seuyn dayes, with-outen drink or mete.
For hunger he cried on þe seuynd day,
"Saue me and I sall yow say
Whore ȝe sall fynd þe rude tre,
Als my fader tolde vnto me;
Vnto me es þis mater dym,
Bot sum knawing I haue by him."

Helena takes Judas and lets the others go. Because Judas was obstinate she cast him into a mirk dungeon, where he remained seven days without food. On the seventh day he declares his willingness to disclose where the Cross is hid.

Fro prisun þan was Iudas tone,
And furth went with þam ilkone
Vnto þe mount of Caluary;
Þam folowd ful grete cumpany.
And when þai come whore þai wald be,
Þan Iudas knelid doun on his kne,
He said, "lord, þat all has in waldë,
If tales be trew þat men has talde,
If þou be he þis werld bigan,
And verrayli es both god *and* man,
And of a maiden in erth was born,
Als sere prophetis haue said biforn,
Send us sum takening of þi grace,
To find þe rude tre in þis place,

[leaf 151, col. 1.]

Forth Judas goes to Calvary, followed by a great company. When he came where he wished to be, he knelt down and prayed God to send some token of the Cross.

Wharon þi self wald suffer dede,
If it be hid here in þis stede."

As soon as Judas had done praying the hill above began to quake, a great smoke arose, and gave forth a sweet smell.

Als Iudas þus gun his prayers make,
Þe hill obouen bigan to quake,
And þarof rase a ful grete reke,
Bot þat was ful wele smelland smeke;
Ful mekil mirth was þam omell,
Fo[r] neuer man feld swetter smell;

Then Judas cried aloud, "Of a truth, Lord Christ, thou art the Saviour of the world, who was born of the chaste maiden; unto Thy law I will betake me, and for ever forsake the Jew's law."

Þan Iudas fast bigan to cry,
And he said ful stedfastly,
In veritate, christe, *tu es redemptor mundi*,
"In suthfastnes, lord criste, I trow,
Þe sauioure of þis werld es þow,
Þat born was of þe mayden chaste,
And sall be euer of mightes maste;
Vnto þi law I wil me take,
And þe Ieus law euer I forsake."

Then they made Judas a Christian, and changed his name to Quiriac. He afterwards became a bishop.

Þan cristen man þai gan hi*m* mak
And turned his name to Quiriak,
Sethin was he Bisschop i*n* hali kirk,
And hali werkis oft gun he wirk.

They noted where the smell came from, and grubbed about the place until they found three crosses.

Þai biheld whore þe smel come out,
And fast grubed þai þore obout;
So depe þai grubbed *and* so fast,
Thre crosses fand þai at þe last;
Ane of crist both large and lang,
And oþer two þat theues on hang,
Bot þore was noman þat knew
Whilk was þe cros of ihesu.

Then Quiriac prayed God to send them the nails,

Þan Quiriak prayd, with hert and hend,
Þat god suld þam þe nailes send
Þat nayled crist þe rude vnto;
And sune when he had prayed so

[leaf 151, col. 2.]

Thre nayles aperd vnto þare sight,
In þe erth schineand ful bright;
Þai toke thre nayles *and* crosses thre

And bare þam to þe riche cetć ;
Ful mikel folk come þam ogayne
And of þare fare þai war ful fayne ;
And on a bere þore gun men bring
A ded bodi vnto þe beryiing.
Quiriak bad þam þat it bare
Set doune þe bere omang þam þare,
So forto p*ro*ue þare, or þai pas,
Whilk of þa crosses cristes was ;

and forthwith there appeared three nails shining in the earth. Joyfully they return to the city. They meet men bringing a corpse upon a bier. Quirinc bids them set the bier down.

Quiriak fast vnto god prayd
And ane cros to þe cors he layd.
And sethin ane oþer he laid þartill,
Bot ȝit euer lay þe bodi styll ;

Then he laid each cross upon the dead body.

Þe thrid cros þan he toke forþi
And layd it vnto þe ded body,
And als sune als it neghed nere
Þe cors rase up, both hale and fere ;

When the third cross touched the corpse it rose up whole and sound.

And al þe folk þat saw þat sight
Loued god, with al þaire might ;
And so þai past into þe toun,
With a fful fayre p*ro*cessioune ;
Al loued þai god, with ioyful mode,
And saynt elyn scho bare þe rode ;

Forthwith they passed into the town with great procession, and St. Helena bore the Cross.

Þan sone omang þam herd þai ȝell
A ful grete dyn of deuils of hell ;
Þai cried, "allas and wayloway,
For dole what sal we do þis day ;
Þe tre es funden whilk we suppose
Sall ger vs all oure pouwer lose,
For we haue power in no place,
Whore men on þam þat takin mase ;

But a great yell and din of devils was heard among them crying "Allas and welladay, what shall we do this day, since the Cross is found and deprives us of all power in this place ?

Now mun oure power fro us pas,
Wo wurth þe while it funden was !
For fro þat figure bihoues vs fle
So with man-kind ouercu*me*n er we ;
It puttes oway all oure powere,

Woe worth the time it was found !

But we care not for all the crosses men can make, provided we can make them commit deadly sin."

So þat we mai noght negh it nere,
Bot-if we may with any gyn
Mak þam to do dedly syn;
Þan with þam wil I wun and wake,
For all þe crosses þat þai can make,
Bot I may neuer no man spill
With syn, bot-if þam seluin will;
Asay I sall, with sere sutelté,
To ger men syn and serue me."

[leaf 151, back, col. 1.] "Thou wicked devil," said Quiriac, "wend thy way into the deepest hole of hell, evermore in dole to dwell."

Quiriak said þan to þe fende
"Þou wikked deuil þi way þou wende,
Vnto þe deppest hole of hell,
Euermore in dole to dwell;
For funden es now þe haly tre
Þat fellis þi pride *and* þi pousté."

Then the fiends vanished with a hideous cry.

Þe fendes þan with hidose cry
Vanist fro þam ful sudanly;
Þan went þai furth with meri mode
Vnto þaire temple þai bare þe rude.

Queen Helena made a silver case, adorned with gold and gems, and enclosed therein the Holy Cross.

Þan þe nobil quene Eline
Gert mak a case of syluer fyne,
With gold and precius stones plenté,
And closid þarin þat haly tre;
And on þe mount of caluary

She built a church on the Mount of Calvary, and put the Cross therein. Men came from all quarters to honour the Cross, and many marvels were wrought by it.

Gert scho mak a kirk in hy,
And þore scho set þe haly tre
Of all men honord forto be;
And sone when it was þeder broght,
Fro sere sides me*n* þeder soght,
And ful grete grace was þore schewd,
And grete releue to lerd and leude;
Thurgh cristen land so es it kend,
Þat fro þe fendes it mai us fend,
So þat þai may do us none ill,
Bot-if oure self assent þartill;
For in werld has he no powere,

Night ne day to negh us nere,
If we his werkis will forsake,
And cristes cros opon vs make.
356 God *gra*nte us grace so to honoure
Þe cros þat bare oure sanioure,
Þat we may to þat blis be broght,
Whilk crist with his blode to us boght.

The Cross may defend us from the devil, if we keep ourselves free from sin.

Let us ever honour the Cross, so that we may be brought to that bliss which Christ purchased with his blood.

V.

THE UPLIFTING OF THE HOLY ROOD.

For the confirming of our faith, and to the glory of our Lord, we honour with songs of praise two days in the year on account of the Holy Rood, (ever) since it was discovered.

The Jewish folk hid it (the cross) with evil intention. They would not that this treasure (the cross) should become a comfort to men. But the blessed Helena afterwards discovered it there, through the revelation of Christ, as He marvellously had manifested it; and she divided the rood as the Lord had instructed her, and left one portion in that same city in which Christ had suffered, as the writings inform us, enclosed in silver; and she went home afterwards with the other portion of the precious tree to her dear son, in order to strengthen his faith.

Now we celebrate the day on which it (the cross) was found in honor of our Saviour, who would suffer on it. It is after Easter in the year's course; and we observe in harvest time with holy ministrations a second festival—that on which it (the cross) was brought again to Jerusalem, as we shall hereafter relate. It happened, unfortunately, as very often it still does, that the heathen nations invaded the land, and an impious king called Cosdrue came with a great army to the Holy Rood where Helena had placed it, in the aforesaid Jerusalem. Impiously bold, he harrowed then the land, and took the Holy Rood home to his own country. He was so uplifted and so wicked a ruler, that he would be God; and wrought then of silver a high steeple in the form of stone-work, and with shining gems surrounded all the house, and in the

V.

[ÞÆRE HALGAN RODE UPAHEFEDNYS*.]

WE WURÐIAÐ MID LOF-SANGUM FOR URES GELEAfan trymminge twegen dagas on geare drihtne to wurðmynte for þære halgan rode siððan heo afunden wæs. [Cotton MS. Julius E vii, leaf 155, back.]

Þa iudeiscean hi behyddon mid hetelicum geðance. noldon þ se maðm wurde mannum to frofre. ac seo eadige helena. hi eft þær afunde þurh cristes onwrigennesse swa swa he mid wundrum geswutelode. ⁊ to-dælde þa rode swa swa drihten hire gewissode. ⁊ forlet þa ænne dæl on þære ylcan byrig. þe crist on þrowode. swa swa us cyþað gewritu. mid seolfre bewunden. ⁊ wende ham siððan mid þam oþrum dæle þæs deorwurþan treowes to hire leofan sunu his geleafan to getrymmenne.

The Jews hid the Cross, but Helena found it.

She took home one portion of the precious tree.

Nu freolsige we þone dæg þe heo on afunden wæs. þam hælende to wurðmynte þe wolde on hire þrowian. se bið ofer eastrum. on ymbryne þæs geares. ⁊ we healdað on hærfest mid halgum þenungum oþerne freols-dæg on þam þe heo geferod wæs eft to hierusalem swa swa we her æfter secgað. Hit gewearð for yfelnysse swa swa for oft git bið. þ þa hæðenan leoda þ land gehergoden. ⁊ sum arleas cyninceg cosdrue gehaten com mid miccl̄um here to þære halgan rode. þær helena hi gesette on þære foresædan hierusalem. gehergode þa þ land. ⁊ þa halgan rode genam ham to his earde. arleaslice dyrstig. He wæs swa up-ahafen. ⁊ swa arleas brega. þ he wolde beon god. ⁊ worhte þa of seolfre ænne heahne stypel. on stanweorces gelicnysse. ⁊

Two days are celebrated in honour of the Cross.

Cosdrue invaded Jerusalem, and took away the Holy Rood.

* The title in the MS. is 'XVIII. KL. OCTOBR*is*. EXALTATIO *Sancte* CRUCIS.'

upper-story he wrought his throne all of red gold; and wonderfully drew out water by means of pipes, for he would cause rains, as if he himself were God. But he was nevertheless very foolish, for the rain might not be of service to any one. He laboured then still more to manifest his power, and bade the earth to be delved secretly with craft, so that horses ran constantly about the house through the secret trenches, dinning with their feet, for he would work thunder. Nevertheless was he witless.

He sat then in the house as High God, and placed the Holy Rood beside his throne, as it were for a companion in his impiety. He then sat there from that time forth, and to his son he assigned all his kingdom. But Christ destroyed him. An emperor there was in those days, named Eraclius, a Christian, of mature age, and undaunted in war; and he adorned his belief with good works, and honoured God's servants with benevolent mind.

Then came Cosdrue's son against the emperor Eraclius, for he desired to win his kingdom in battle. Then it was settled between them both, that they two should boldly go to single combat on the bridge of the river, and he who should get the victory should wield the kingdom, without the loss of the men who had come with them. Then they all said that if any man would assist either of them, forthwith he should be seized and with crippled limbs should be cast into the river.

They then went both on the bridge together, and the believing (faithful) emperor killed the enemy of God, Cosdrue's son, and he afterwards wielded all his kingdom, and rode to Cosdrue. Then all the army joyfully submitted to Eraclius, and he received them and brought them to baptism. And no one would make known to Cosdrue the battle (which had lately taken place), because he was hateful to all his people.

Then Eraclius went up to the steep upper-floor, and quickly said to the impious Cosdrue these words: "Life I will grant thee if thou wilt forthwith believe now on the Saviour Christ, and wilt promise that thou wilt be baptized, and I will be thy friend, and I will let thee have this land in thy possession; if thou then dost otherwise thou shalt be put to death."

Then would not Cosdrue believe on Christ, and Eraclius forthwith drew out his sword and beheaded him, and commanded him to be buried. He took his younger son, a boy of ten years old, and baptized him, and

mid *scinendum gymmum besette eall þ hus. ⁊ on þære upflora eall mid readum golde his cynestol geworhte. ⁊ wundorlice mid þeotum wæter ut-ateah wolde renas wyrcan. swylce he sylf god wære. ac he wæs ful dysig forþan þe se rén ne mihte nanegum[1] fremian. He swanc þa git swiðor wolde geswutelian his mihte. ⁊ het delfan þa eorðan digellice mid cræfte. swa þ hors urnon embe þ hus gelome þurh þa digelan dica dynigende mid fotum wolde þunor wyrcan gewitleas swa ðeah.

* [leaf 156.]

Cosdrue tries to be like God,

1 [MS. *nanegum*.]

and imitates miracles.

He sæt þa on þam huse swa swa healic god. ⁊ gesette þa halgan rode to his heahsetle up swilce him to geferan on his fracodnysse. He sæt ða þær swa forð. ⁊ his suna betæhte ealne his cynedom. ac crist hine fordyde. Sum casere wæs on þam dagum cristen. ⁊ gelyfed. eraclius gehaten. unearh on gefeohtum. ⁊ he his geleafan geglengde mid godum weorcum. ⁊ godes þeowas wurþode mid wel-willendum mode.

Eraclius lived at this time. He was a true Christian.

Ða com þæs cosdruan sunu togeanes ðam casere. wolde mid gefeohte gewinnan his rice. Ða gewearð him bam. þ hi beald-lice twegen to anwige eodon on þære éá brycge. ⁊ seðe sige gewunne weolde þæs rices butan þæra manna lyre þe him mid comon. Hi þa ealle geewædon þ gif ænig man wolde heora oðrum fylstan. þ man hine sona gefenge. ⁊ foredum sceancu*m* into þære éá wurpe.

He came against Cosdrue's son,

Hi eodon þa begen on þære briege togædere. ⁊ se geleaffulla casere alede þone godes feond cosdrues sunu. ⁊ he siððan geweold ealles his rices. ⁊ rád hi*m* *to cosdrue. þa beah eall se here bliðe-lice to eraclio. ⁊ he hi underfeng. ⁊ to fulluhte gebigde. ⁊ nan man nolde cyþan cosdrue þ gewinn. forðan þe he wæs andsæte eallum his leodum.

and defeated him.

* [leaf 156, back.]

Eraclius þa astah to þære sticolan upflora. ⁊ cwæð to þam arleasan ardlice þas word. Lifes ic þe geann. gif þu anrædlice gelyfst nu on hælend crist. ⁊ cwyðst þ þu wille to fulluhte gebugan. ⁊ ic þin freond beo. ⁊ ic þæ læte habban þis land to gewealde. gif þu þonne elles dest. þu scealt deaþe sweltan.

Þa nolde se cosdrue on crist gelyfan. ⁊ eraclyus sona his swurd ateah. ⁊ hine beheafdode. ⁊ het bebyrigan. ⁊ nam his gingran sunu siððan to fulluhte tyn wintra cnapa. ⁊ him cynedom forgeaf

Eraclius slew the unbelieving Cosdrue.

gave up to him the kingdom, and then delivered to his (own) army the high steeple, with all the silver; but he himself took the gold and gems into God's church. Then he carried the rood, with a procession of the people, again to Jerusalem, eagerly and joyfully.

Riding quickly, they came at last to the aforesaid city; and the emperor sat on a royal horse, as was most pleasing to him. But when he would enter (the city) then was the gate closed, so that the stones fell suddenly together, and so it was wrought into a wall.

Then were they terrified on account of that wonderful token, and forthwith looked sorrowfully to heaven, and saw our Lord's precious cross shining there; and God's angel bore it above the gate and thus said:

"When that the heavenly king, Christ Himself, entered in through this same gate to His own passion, He was not clothed with purple, nor adorned with royal crown, nor rode He through this stone gate on a steed, but on the back of an ass He meekly rode as an example to men, that they should shun pride." And after these words the angel went up. Lo! then the emperor quickly alighted, thanking God for the lesson; and he took off his purple and his girdle of pall. Then he went with naked feet and took the rood, praising God with shedding of tears.

Then befell a divine miracle to the stone-work. When the emperor came with meekness to them, then the stones parted and the gate opened tself. There was also another marvel, so that a winsome (delightful) odor steamed on the holy cross, when it was on its way home, through the land and filled the air; and the people rejoiced on account of this, being filled with the odor.

No perfume could give out so delightful a smell. And then the emperor exclaimed with joy: "O thou marvellous rood on which Christ would suffer and quench our sins with His precious blood! O thou rood shining more than the bright stars of middle earth! Greatly art thou to be loved, O holy and winsome tree; thou wert worthy to bear the prize of all middle earth! Be mindful of this assembly which is here gathered together for the honour of God!"

Then the emperor exalted the Holy Rood in that same place in which it stood at first, before the impious king, Cosdrue, took it therefrom. On that day the true Saviour marvellously manifested His power through the illustrious cross, so that a dead man arose on that day, and four bedridden

betæhte ᵭa his here þone heagan stypel. mid eallum þam seolfre. ⁊ he sylf genam ꝥ gold. ⁊ þa gymmas. into godes cyrcan. Ferode ᵭa þa rode mid þæs folces meniu ongean to hierusalem georne mid blisse.

Eraclius carries the Cross back to Jerusalem.

Hi comon þa ætnextan eaflice ridende to þære foresædan byrig. ⁊ sæt se casere on kynelicum horse swa him geewemast wæs. ac þa þa he inn wolde. þa wearþ ꝥ geat belocen. swa ꝥ þa stanas feollon færlice togædere. ⁊ wearþ geworht to anum wealle swa.

Hi wurdon þa afyrhte. for þam færlican taene. ⁊ beheoldon sarige sona to heofonum. ⁊ gesawon drihtnes rode deorwurᵭlice þær scinan. ⁊ godes engel hi bær bufan þam geate ⁊ cwæᵭ.

A wonderful token appears to him.

Þa þa se heofonlica cyning crist sylf inferde þurh þis ylce get to his agenre þrowunge. næs he mid purpuran gescryd. ne mid cynehelme geglenged. *ne he on steda ne rád. þurh þis stænene geat. ac on assan hricge he rád eadmodlice mannum to bysne. ꝥ hi modignysse onscunion. ⁊ æfter ᵭysum wordum gewende se engel up. Hwæt ᵭa se casere eaflice lihte þancigende gode þære wissunge. ⁊ dyde of his purpuran. ⁊ his pellenan gyrlan. eode þa mid nacodum fotum. ⁊ genam þa rode mid agotenum tearum god wurþigende.

* leaf 157.]

Wearᵭ þa godes wundor on þam weorc-stanum þa ᵭa se casere com mid eadmodnysse to. þa tocodon ᵭa stanas. ⁊ geopenode ꝥ get. Wæs eac oþer wundor swa ꝥ wynsum bræᵭ. stemde on þære halgan rode þa þa heo hamwerd wæs. geond ꝥ land. ⁊ þa lyfte afylde. ⁊ ꝥ folc þæs fægnode. afylde mid þam bræᵭe.

Eraclius enters the city with befitting humility.

A winsome odor steams from the Cross.

Ne mihte nan wyrt-bræᵭ swa wynsumlice steman. ⁊ se casere þa clypode mid blysse. Eala þu wundorlice ród. on þære ᵭe crist wolde þrowian. ⁊ ure wita adwescan mid his deorwurþan blode. Eala þu seinende ród swiþor þonne tungla mære on middan-earde micelum to lufigenne. halig treow. ⁊ wynsum. þe wurþe wære to berenne ealles middan-eardes wurþ. gemunde þisne heap. þe her gegaderod is gode to wurᵭmynte.

The Emperor's address to the Cross.

Þa ahof se casere þa halgan rode up on þære ylcan stowe. þe heo on stod æt fruman. ær þan þe se arleasa cyning eosdrue hi gename. On ᵭam dæge geswutelode se soᵭfæsta hælend wundorlice mihte. þurh his þa mæran rode. swa ꝥ an dead man aras

The exaltation of the Rood.

ones were there wonderfully healed, and ten lepers from their lingering disease, and many maniacs regained their senses. And many sick ones were healed of various diseases at the Holy Rood for the honour of Christ. And the emperor afterwards performed many good deeds there, and endowed God's churches with lands and sustenance, and restored God's praise. He went then to his royal seat to Constantinople, with great faith meditating upon God's greatness. Now is the day called in Christian books *Exaltatio Sanctæ Crucis*, that is in English speech, Uplifting of the Holy Rood, because that it was exalted with great honour on the foresaid day to the honour of the Lord.

It is nevertheless to be noticed that it (the cross) is widely distributed, by means of frequent sections, to every land. But the spiritual token (signification) is with God ever incorruptible, though the tree be cut in pieces. The heavenly sign of the Holy Rood is our banner against the fierce devil, when we bless ourselves boldly through God with the sign of the cross and with right belief.

Though a man waver wonderfully with his hand, nevertheless it is not a blessing except he make the sign of the holy cross, and forthwith the fierce fiend will be terrified on account of the victorious token. With three fingers must a man make the sign and bless himself for the Holy Trinity, which is a glory-ruling God. Sometimes priests say that Christ's betrayer (traitor), the impious Judas, shall not hereafter be condemned in the great day (of doom) to the deep hell, and they say that he may excuse himself to Christ, as if he of necessity committed that treachery against Him. But against that we say that Christ's word is not false. He said concerning Judas, that it were better for him that he were not born, than that he should be His betrayer. Neither the Jews nor that secret traitor were compelled by God to that horrible intention, but when that Christ, who seeth all things, saw their evil will, He then turned it to good, so that their wickedness became to us for salvation. Each man who does evil with evil intention is guilty before God, though he may benefit some, and each man who does good with good will, hath his reward of God, though he may do harm to some by it, because the righteous judge giveth to each the reward according as he himself might determine (will) and his will might dictate to him. Now are the Jews and the shameless

on þam dæge sona. ⁊ feower bedrydan þær wurdon wundorlice gehælede. ⁊ tyn lic-þroweras. fram heora langsumum broce. ⁊ fela *wode menn heora gewit underfengon. ⁊ manega untrume fram myslicum coþum þær wurdon gehælede. æt þære halgan rode. criste to wurðmynte. ⁊ se casere siððan fela goda gedyde þær. ⁊ godes cyrcan gegodode. mid landum. ⁊ bigleofum. ⁊ godes lof geedniwode. Ferde ða to his cynestole to constantinopolim mid micelum geleafan godes mærða smeagende. Nu is se dæg geewæden on cristenum bocum. *Exaltatio Sancte crucis.* ꝥ is on englisere spræce upahefednyss þære halgan rode. forþan þe heo wæs ahafen mid healicum wurðmynte on þam foresædan dæge. drihtne to lofe.

* leaf 157, back.

Eraclius returns to Constantinople after celebrating the "Uplifting of the Holy Rood."

Is swa þeah to witenne ꝥ heo is wide todæled. mid gelomlicum ofcyrfum to lande gehwilcum. ac seo gastlice getacnung is mid gode æfre á unbrosnigendlic. þeah þe se beam beo to-corfen. ꝥ heofonlice tacn þære halgan rode is ure gúðfana wiþ þone gramlican deofol. þonne we us bletsiað gebylde þurh god mid þære rode tacne. ⁊ mid rihtum geleafan.

The Holy Rood is our banner against the devil.

Þeah þe man wafige wundorlice mid handa ne bið hit þeah bletsung buta he wyrce tacn þære halgan rode. ⁊ se reða feond biþ sona afyrht for ðam sige-fæstan tacne. Mid þrym fingrum man sceall senian. ⁊ bletsian. for þære halgan þrynnysse. þe is þrim-wealdend god. Hwilon cweþað preostas. þæt cristes læwa iudas se arleasa eft ne wurðe fordemed on þam micelan dæge. to þam deopan helle. ⁊ cweþað ꝥ he mage wið crist hine betellan. swilce he neadunge gefremode ꝥ facn wið hine. Ac we cweðað þær togeanes. ꝥ cristes word ne bið leas. he cwæð be þan iudan. ꝥ him wære betere ꝥ *he geboren nære þonne he his læwe wære. Næron þa iudeiscan ne se dyrna læwe þurh god geneadode. to ðam gramlican geþeahte. ac þa þa crist geseah. se þe gesihð ealle þing heora yfelan willan. þa awende þe hit to gode. swa ꝥ heora yfelnyss us becom to hæle. Ælc man þe yfel deþ mid yfelum willan. is scyldig wið god. þeah þe hit sumum fremige. ⁊ ælc man þe god deð mid godum willan hæfð his mede æt gode. þeah þe hit hearmige sumum. for þan þe se rihtwisa dema deð ælcum þa mede. be þam þe he sylf wolde. ⁊ his willa him dihte.

How the sign of the Cross should be made.

* [leaf 158.]

Judas and the Jews will be punished for their treatment of Christ.

traitor (Judas), who plotted against Him, guilty of Christ's death (though that it became to us for everlasting redemption), and none of them shall ever come to Christ's kingdom unless they repent them of their sin and turn to Christ. The Saviour is so merciful, that He would have mercy upon His own murderers if they would turn and pray for His mercy, as many of them did, as for instance the centurion who wickedly pierced Him (Christ) in His holy side, and afterwards turned to Him. The centurion was named Longinus. He saw then how suddenly the sun became dark from midday until noon, and all middle earth trembled, and rocks burst asunder; then he turned to Christ, smiting his breast, saying loudly, *Vere Filius Dei est hic*—Truly this (man) is the Son of God. He then renounced his employment, and proceeded to the apostles, and was by them instructed in the faith, and with baptism was washed from his former deeds.

Then he distributed all his goods in alms, and lived in purity as Christ's own servant (thain) in great abstinence, and preached to the heathen the true faith and forgiveness of sins, and put down idolatry, and performed miracles in God's name, until a cruel judge put him to death with great torments.

But he wrought many marvels before the judge, amid the torments, and blinded the judge through the power of God, that men might know how merciful the Saviour is who had magnified him so. Then was he beheaded for the sake of the Saviour, whom he had before cruelly wounded on the cross, and he (now) dwells eternally in glory with Him. The heathen judge who put him to death was named Octavius. But he came afterwards to the place where he was slain, and sought his body, praying for forgiveness, with weeping and lamentation. Then forthwith he saw with sound eyes, being enlightened by the same who had before made him blind. Then the judge sumptuously buried the body of Longinus, and believed on Christ, ever glorifying God until he departed this life. Glory and praise be to the benevolent God, who reigneth ever eternally. Amen.

Nu synd þa iudeiscan. ⁊ se sceamlease læwa cristes deaðes scyldige. þe syrwdon be him. þeah þe hit us become to ecere alysednysse. ⁊ heora nan ne becymð to cristes rice næfre. butan þam þe hit gebettan. ⁊ gebugan to criste. Swa milde is se hælend ꝥ he miltsian wolde his agenum slagum gif hi gecyrran woldon. ⁊ biddan his miltsunge. swa swa heora mænig dyde. swa swa se hundredes ealdor. þe hine hetelice stang on his halgan sidan. ⁊ siððan him beah to. se hundredes ealdor hatte longinus. He geseah ða sona hu seo sunne aþystrode. fram mid-dæge oð non. ⁊ eall middan-eard bifode. ⁊ stanas toburston. þa beah he to criste sleande his breost. ⁊ secgende hlude. *Vere. filius dei est hic.* Soþlice þæs is godes sunu. He forlet ða his folgoð. ⁊ ferde to þam apostolum. ⁊ wearð gelæred to geleafan þurh hi. ⁊ mid fulluhte aþwagen fram his fyrlenum dædum.

None of them shall come to Christ's kingdom unless they repent.

Longinus pierced Christ's side.

He dælde þa his ealita ealle on ælmyssan. ⁊ on clænnysse leofode. swa swa cristes *ðegen. on mycelre forhæfednysse. ⁊ þam hæþenum bodade þone soþan geleafan. ⁊ synne forgifennysse. ⁊ towearp deofolgild. ⁊ wundra gefremode on godes naman. oð ꝥ sum gramlic dema hine gemartyrode mid micelum witum.

He afterwards believed in [* leaf 109, back.] Christ, and died a martyr.

Ac he worhte fela wundra ætforan þam deman. betwux þam tintregum. ⁊ ablende þone deman þurh godes mihte. ꝥ menn mihton tocnawon hu mildheort se hælend is. þe hine mersode swa. He wearð þa beheafdod for ðæs hælendes naman. þone þe he ær gewundode wælhreowlice on rode. ⁊ wunað on ecnysse on wuldre mid him. Octauius hatte se hæþena dema þe hine acwealde. ac he com siððan þær he ofslagen wæs. ⁊ gesohte his lic biddende forgifennysse mid wope ⁊ heofunge. Þa geseah he sona gesundfullum eagum. þurh þone ylcan onliht þe hine ǽr ablende. ⁊ se dema þa deorwurðlice bebyrigde longines lichaman. ⁊ gelyfde on crist æfre wuldrigende god. oð ꝥ he gewát of life. Sy wuldor ⁊ lof þam wel-willendan gode. seðe æfre rixað on ecnysse. AMEN.

He was beheaded by Octavius.

Octavius was afterwards converted.

VI.

HOW ÞE HALI CROS WAS FUNDIN. BE SEINT ELAINE*.

* [Fairfax MS. 14, Bod. Lib. fol. 88 *b*, art. 63.]

We all ought to honour the Cross.

The Jews hid the Cross from the Christians.

For 200 years it lay hidden.

Of þe rode now for to rede
 ihesus criste he be mi spede,
þat þare-on suffred sorouful pine
to lause vs fra our wiþer-wine;
we agh to buxumli hit bere,
for hit of bote is our bauere,
baþ on bodi *and* in hert,
againe alle our care hit is our quert.
quen ihesus þer-of was vn-done,
þe iewes hid hit efter sone
fra cristen men hit to blinde;
laþ ware ham þai sulde hit finde,
þai wiste þe cristen walde hit kepe
for-þi in erþ þai grofe hit depe
vnder erþ, *and* oþer twa
quare-on þe theuis hang on squa;
þe riȝt rode þai went to dille
out of þe cristen mennis skille,
þat if wiþ chaunce men on ham hit
quilk þai sulde haue þai sulde noȝt witt:
¶ bot crist, þat nane is to him like,
walde noȝt late his dere relike,
squa noteful þing, squa lang be hid,
þat he ne walde þat hit ware kid.
quen hit had bene ij. hundre ȝere
vnder erþ, þat druri dere,
to bote of baþ our saule *and* life,
he did hit be fundin þorou a wife:

a duȝti wife, þat hiȝt Eline,
was moder of king costantine,
ho fande hit, qua-sum wil wite h*it* now,
herkin *and* I sal tel hit ȝou.

Helena found it.

Als in stori. I. red *and* fande,
quen costantine was liuande
of rome þen was he emp*er*our,
againe heþin folk stiþe in stoure;
be-tid a tide þat heþin lede
come him batail for to bede;
sa mikil folk þai wiþ ham led
þat costantine was sare a-dred.
þai come tille him þat ilk niȝt
atte þai sulde on þe morne fiȝt.
¶ A man þat seleouþ faire was graide
come to þe kinge *and* þus he saide :—
" costantine loke vp *and* se
til heiue*n*-warde *and* conforte þe."
he lokid vp *and* in þat siȝt,
he sagħ [þar] cristis crosse ful briȝt;
a titel sagħ he þar-on lye,
"here-in þou salle haue victorie."
þen did þe king*e* make [of] a neyuen[1]
suche a cros as he sagħ in heyuen[2];
and vp in trauþ he ras stedefast
and braþeli on his faas he brast,
and did þat cros be-for him lede
and felled dou*n* þat cursid lede;
þai felle, þai fled þa wiþ*er*-wine,
þe victorie has king*e* costantine
þorou þe croice *and* c*r*istis miȝt,
and þorou þaire stedfast trauþ in [d]riȝt.

Constantine is about to fight a battle with heathen folk.

[fol. 89.]

In the night he sees a divine manifestation of the Cross.

By this token he gains the victory over his enemies.

Þen sende þe king constantine
sandis til his moder eline
for to do seche, wiþ-outen hone,
þe cros þat c*r*iste on was done,

He sends his mother to look for the Cross.

[1] read *an euen*.

[2] read *heuen*.

to finde þat hali tree sum quare
and make a kirke be raisid þare.
Beneiras and Ansiers were her messengers.
benciras *and* ansiers,
þ*er* twa men was messagers,
þai ware sende to þe quene *fra* rome;
bot herkenis how þai gaue dome.
¶ þis lauedi had þen hir wiþ
The story of the good goldsmith, who owed a Jew a sum of money, and who was to forfeit its weight in flesh if he did not pay the debt when due.
a c*r*isten man, was gode goldsmiþ,
quat þing þat ho him of walde mouþ[e]
atte hir deuise make he couþe,
bot pouer he was of litil aȝt.
and to a iew mikil he aȝt
a sou*m*me of money for to amount,
and askid him ful harde a-count;
þe couenaund was made ful harde
and saide he made him suche forwarde,
if he his money muȝt noȝt gett,
þat he sulde ȝilde him for his dett
þat ilk weȝt at þer was lesse
he sulde ȝilde of his awen flesse.
The debt was not paid, and the Jew demands the penalty.
þe dai Is past, þe dette vn-quit,
þe bodi be-houis be leue for hit.
¶ þe c*r*isten dred ful sare þe pine,
bot þe iew walde neuer fine.
baþ to þe quenis court þai come,
þe iew þrali bad gif him dome.
sharp grundin knife in hande he bare,
þe c*r*isten[1] stode nakid be-for him þare;
þai walde for money had him boȝt,
bot g*ra*nte of þe iew gatte þai noȝt;
of raunsou*n* na mare þen a risshe
walde he take bot of his flesshe.
Beneiras and Ansiers try the case.
¶ Saide benciras *and* ansiers:—
"þou sal haue broþ*er* al þi fers,
þe quene has biddin vs to deme
And al þat resou*n* is to queme,

[1] MS. has *iew* altered to *cristen*.

say vs how þou wil him diȝt
and we salle giue þe dome ful riȝt."
¶ "how," saide þe iew, "bot be my lay,
þat werst þat euer I. can or may,
his eien first putt out I. sal
and his hende smite of wiþ-al;
tonge *and* neise wil I. noȝt saue,
til atte I al my couenande haue."

The Jew says that he shall first put out his debtor's eyes, then cut off his hands, next his tongue and nose.

¶ þe messagers him gaf ansquare
"þen semis hit noȝt þou wil hi*m* spare,
take þou þe flesse we deme þe,
squa atte þe blode mai sauid be;
a drope of blode if atte þou tine
we gif ȝou dome, þe wrange is þine;
al if his flesshe was salde *and* boȝt
his blode to selle neu*er* he þoȝt;
þe fallis þe flesshe, we ar wele knawen,
kepe him þe blode þat is his awen."

The judges tell him to take the flesh, but no drop of blood.

¶ þen saide þat iew, "be saint driȝtine
me þink þe wers p*ar*t is mine;
to take þe flesshe if I. assay
þen þe blode wil ryn a-way;
for-done ȝe haue me wiþ ȝour dome,
and þat make ȝe romains of rome;
maugrefe þ*er*-fore mote ȝe haue,
alle þat suche a dome me gaue."

The Jew says that he is getting the worst of the bargain, for the blood must run away if he cuts the flesh.

"A curse on you for your decision against me."

¶ beneiras þen saide, "p*ar*fay
alle has þis court herde þe missay,
me *and* my felaw sir ansiere;
þou has missaide riȝt foule here,
we wil missay þe na wiȝt,
bot ellis of þe we wil haue riȝt;
þe lauedi, for ho did vs leue,
ho bad vs riȝtli dome to giue,
and þe soþ we haue þe saide,
þ*er*-fore þou dos vs now vpbraide."

The judges answer that they are determined to do what is right.

¶ þe lauedi bad, wiþ-outen lite,
iugement on him þai sulde giue tite,
[fol. 89 b.] for sieure was ho þan of site,
þat þe cristen man was quite.
þe iew was dampned, so at þe quene
sulde al his catel haue be dene,
In hir merci his tonge to take,
þat in hir presence suche wordis spake.
þe iew him þuȝt selcouþ tene
atte þis dome at was sa kene,
and saide on hiȝt, atte al muȝt here,
"me ware leuer ȝou to lere
quare lijs ȝour lordis rode tree,
þen þus smartli dampned be."
¶ "god wate frende," þen saide eline,
"þou sal be quite of alle þi pine
if þou wil do as I. þe bid,
to shew vs quere þat cros is hid."
"lauedi," he saide, "be my lay,
þe soþ ȝet can I. noȝt say;
bot sette me a certaine day
þat wiþ my maistris speke I may,
I salle þe bringe tiþande of hit,
þe quilk bleþeli þou walde witt"
¶ "Gladli," ho saide, "here I þe hiȝt
of a day respite *and* a niȝt;"
¶ saide elaine, "certis bot þou hit finde
of baþ þine eien þou sal be blinde."
¶ þe iew him sped tawarde his tide,
ouer his day durst he noȝt bide;
na selcouþ if he dred him sare,
he wiste þe quene walde him noȝt spare;
til hir he went better spede,
and saide, "lauedi I. knaw my dede,
priuely be-houis vs fare,
and folowes me wiþ-outen mare."

They condemn the Jew, and declare his goods to be forfeited to the queen.

The Jew then offers to show them where the Cross is, if they release him from this penalty.

He asks time to make the necessary inquiries.

Helena tells him that he shall lose his eyes if he does not find the place of the Cross.

On the day appointed he came before the queen, and bids her follow him without delay.

þar-fore he went him sone in hy
vn-to þe mount of caluary;
and oþ*er* folk went wiþ þe quene,
þidder þai went al bedene.
¶ sone quen þai þaire praier makid,
þe erþ vnder ham hit shakid.
þen saide þe iew þat al þis herde,
"c*r*iste þou art sauiour of þis werde!"
his claþis he kest, al bot his serke,
to make him nemil vn-to his werke;
siþen he toke a spade in hande,
lange he dalue, bot noȝt he fande;
¶ quen he riȝt depe had dellui[n] sare,
mare þen xx. fote or mare,
þai fande iij. crossis; an was þ*at* ilk*e*,
bot wiste þai noȝt quilk was quilk,
þe quilk muȝt be þe lordis tre,
and quilk muȝt þe theuis be:
wiþ mikil ioy *and* mikil gle,
to þe tou*n* þai bare þa þre;
þ*er* ware þai done in c*er*taine place,
for to a-bide our lordis grace.
Aboute midward of þe day *and* mare
a dede man cors forþ þai bare;
saint elaine made hir praier þare,
so did al þe folk was þare,
þat c*r*ist sulde ham takening shaw
his awen dere tree to knaw.
on aiþ*er* tree þe cors on rane,
bot alwais lay hit stil as stane;
¶ þe þrid þai touchid wiþ his hide,
and vp he rase wiþ-outen bide,
and spac wiþ a bliþ voyce,
and þus gatis he hailsed þe croice:—
"god loke þe cros p*r*ecious þinge,
on þe hang*e* þat heiest king*e*;

He brought the queen and other folk to Calvary.

The Jew, with spade in hand, set to work, and after digging twenty feet or more, he found three crosses.

They carried the crosses to the town with great joy.

About mid-day they tested the crosses by a dead body.

As soon as the corpse touched the Cross of Christ, it rose to life, and addressed the Cross.

menskid wiþ his flesshe was þou,
of alle trees maste of vertu ;
he has þe halghed at mast con ken,
and þe salle mensk al *cr*isten men."

The Cross is carried to the Temple.

¶ þis miracle sene wiþ mani man,
þai bare hit to þe temple þan ;
þe Iewes to þe baptim ran,
þ*er* was *cr*istened mani a man.
quen þat cros was broȝt in
men muȝt se þing*e* is ȝet to myn,

The tree, of which the Cross was taken, was still in the Temple, and gave out a sweet smell,

for þat tree þ*at* hit of was shorne,
as talde is in þis boke be-forne,
and al-wais in þat temple lay,
and ȝet was funden þ*er* þat day ;
hit ȝalde of hit sa squete a smel,
how gode hit was can I. noȝt tel ;
þe smelle ou*er* al þe temple spred,
and þ*er*-wiþ amendid ilka sted ;

by which its connection with the Cross was manifested.

and bi þat smelling*e* muȝt man se
hit was shorne of þat ilk tree.
¶ a iew þ*at* mikil had herde *and* sene,
he talde þe soþ vn-to þe quene,
and saide, his eldris talde him be dene,
quatkin a tree hit sulde haue bene ;
quen ho had herde al his resou*n*,
þen can ho make hir orisou*n*,

[*fol. 90.*]

þat god wit*er*ing sulde sende hir sone,
whar ho sulde þat cros done.

God bids the queen divide the Rood into four parts. One part was to be left in the Temple, another part was to go to Rome, the third to Alexandria, and the fourth to Rome.

¶ our lorde hir sende an angel wise,
and bad hir dele hit in foure p*ar*tise ;
þe tane sulde in þe temple lende,
to rome men sulde þe toþ*er* sende,
til alisaundre to bere þe þrid,
þe firþ to bere hir Seluin mid,
to costentine wit*h* hir to wende,
and alsqua did. þat lauedi hende.

¶ In foure pecis þai hit smate,
of þe quiche got hit wate;
þai did riȝt *with* ij. as god ment,
til rome *and* alisaundre ham sent;
þe þrid þai left in þat cité,
as in stede of auctorité;
þe firþ led hir wiþ cline
vn-to hir sone king costantine;
to mete hir ȝode mani baroun,
wiþ grete *and* faire processioun;
wiþ-in þe kirke of saint sophie
þer haue þai sette hit richelie;
was neuer ȝet na tree in lande
sa riche ne sa faire shewande;
Men was wonte to come to se
at ilke paskis þat hali tree.
daies iiij. ham sette for stage
þe emperour wiþ his baronage,
¶ a-pon þe day of mandee;
þe riche quene wiþ hir meyne,
a-pon þe friday efterwarde[1],
of pardoun for to serue hir part;
þe clergi on þe seterday,
þat kepers ware of cristen lay;
wiþ-outen case þer daies þre
þis cros was þen, *and* man mote se;
¶ *and* hit was talde of mani man,
at a licour þer-of ranne,
þat wiþ betinge was bote of bale,
and sekenes diuers to make ham hale;
a vessel, þat hit ware noȝt tint,
stode vnder þat licour for to hint,
for to dele vn-to þe vnfere,
to sende ouer al þe cuntree sere.
ÞE grace of god is grete *and* gode,
þat giuis vs ensaumple of þe rode;

The queen divided the Rood as she was bidden.

She took a portion of it to Rome, and placed it in the "*Kirke of St. Sophie.*"

The ceremony connected with the finding of the Cross occupied four days.

[1] MS. *ofter-warde.*

A liquor ran from the Cross, and healed many sick folk.

Some of the liquor was caught in a vessel, and sent into divers countries.

ma miȝt*es* has our lorde wroȝt
þen ani man mai þink in þoȝt:

Many men only believe what they have seen.

bot man of trauþ is squa vnsely,
þai traw noȝt bot þai se wiþ ey;
and þat vnneþis wil þai traw,
wiþ-outen signe of grete v*er*tu.
me þink, if ȝe þe soþ haue soȝt,

But since the world has been made, miracles of the Cross have appeared, right and left, in diverse places.

þat syn þe werlde was first wroȝt,
miraclis of þe crossis miȝt
has oft standen in stede *and* riȝt,
ouer *and* vnder, riȝt *and* left,
in þis compas god has al weft;
¶ bot-if man of him-selue be blinde,
vm-þink him wele he sal hit finde,

The Cross is mentioned in the Old Law.

þe liknes of þis tree sa trew
was in þe alde laghe, be-for þe new,
and in þe new laghe alsqua sere,
þat sum ar gode of for to here.

This tree (of the Cross) was planted in Paradise.

¶ I þink þis is þat tree of blis
þat riȝtwisnes to bundin is.
had adam fundin hit atte hande,
þar-wiþ he muȝt had life lastande;
þat plauntid hit is in p*ar*adis
and dos þe dede vp for to rise.

Adam took shelter under it when he had sinned.

¶ *and* adam, quen he wroȝt had woghe,
vnder þis tree he him droghe,
þat did him god to resou*n*
and did him hope of p*ar*dou*n*.

The cry of Abel's blood came from it, when slain by his brother.

þe blode of abel hit crid als,
quen him had slaine his broþ*er* fals;
wiþ-in þat cry was grete þing hid,
þat in þis cros now is kid.
and dede, for soþ, had bene noe,
had noȝt him saued þat tree.

The four corners of Noah's ark were made of the wood of this tree.

of foure corners þe arche was made,
als has þe cros of lange *and* brade;

þe dore of þe arche a-pon þe side,
and þ*er* was ih*esus* wounded wide;
qua wil vm-þink*e* him in his mode
mai finde mani takenis of þe rode.
¶ Our lorde gaf moises a wande
to wirk*e* maist*ri* wiþ in hande;
sum time was hit wor*me*, su*m* time ȝerde,
as men I.-nogh*e* has saide *and* herde
þat wele be takenid. þat cipres,
þ*er*-of was warnis[t][1] moises,
baþ in worde *and* in dede.
quen isr*ae*l of egipt ȝede,
of þat blessed lambis blode,
a cros was made in signe of rode;
þa at cros had on ham drawen,
our lorde ham sauid as for his awen;
and al þa oþ*er* ware bot tint
and taȝt vn-to þe angels dint.
¶ quen þe nedderes þat ware fel
stanged þe folk of israel,
quen þai welk in wildernes,
vnder þe warde of sir moyses,
a nedder was sette a-pon a tree,
þat quen þe stanged muȝt se
þe nedder on þe tree þ*er* hange,
þai ware alle warisht of þaire stange.
¶ quen þai sagh*e*, as þai did oft,
moises lift his hende on loft,
þe quilist he helde his hende on croice,
ay herde his awen folk þe voice.
¶ quen strife was a-boute presthede,
in þe dais a-mange þe iewes lede,
to xij. men taȝt þai wandes xij.,
ilkan merkid his him-selue,
and saide quilk wande beris blome
sulde haue þe presthede wiþ dome;

Moses's wand came from this tree.

At the Exodus we read that the Israelites were saved by the sign of the Cross. [fol. 90 *b*.]

Moses raised up a cross in the wilderness, by which those who were stung by adders were healed.

In the dispute about the priesthood twelve wands were chosen, each one bearing a mark.

[1] MS. *warnis*.

The priesthood belonged to him that had a cross upon his 'wand.'

þ*er* florisht an, as ȝe haue herde,
þe cros a-pon þat ilk ȝerde.
¶ Heliseus on oþer-wise
did a dedeman for to rise;
þe staf þat he a-pon him did
þe crosse hit bare to tak in hede.

David, when he went to fight with Goliath, bore a token of the Cross.

¶ quen dauid faȝt againe þat etin
has he noȝt his staf for-ȝetin;
vn-to þe bataile he hit bare,
muȝt na king*e* squorde do mare.

The sign of *Tav* betokens the Cross.

þe signe of tav. in alde lawes
be-takenis cros in our dawes,
þe men at þar wiþ blessed ware
hit helped ham fra mis-fare;
tav *and* cros baþ ar as an,
bot. tav has ȝerde a-bouen nan.
of croice in þe alde testament
was mani bisening, qua to cowde tent,

The Cross is the banner of Holy Kirk.

¶ croice is, qua-sum[1] wil or nay,
baner of hali kirk to-day;
man has noȝt herde þat folc be lorne
þat hali crosse has wiþ ham borne.

It enables man to conquer his enemies.

bot has be-tid, baþ now *and* are,
þe lesse folk ouer-come þe mare,
þ*er* croice was stad atte ani fiȝt,
if þe dude be tane wiþ riȝt.

Of the Cross the first man and woman was made.

Of cros to telle for-gete I noght,
of cros þe formast man was wroȝt,
of cros þe first of alle wifis;

By the Cross we were redeemed.

of cros god boȝt our saule liuis,
þ*er*-on he gaf him-self raunsou*n*,
and of him-self made gunfanou*n*.
þe cros of medicine beris bote,
baþ in frute *and* als in rote;
in cros hit was for vs þe flour
þat we haue þorou sa grete honou*r*.

[1] MS. *quasim.*

a riche liknis ay beris hit,
hit is þe heued of hali writte,
foundement. of our clergie,
rewle hit is of haly vie.

The Cross is the head of Holy Writ, the foundation of our clergy, and the rule of Holy Life.

makid hit is of foure and þre,
now is hit talde bot for a tree;
nokis foure *and* trees þrin,
syn þe þrid was done þer-in.
In trees þrin *and* faure parates
I. vnderstande þe vij. artis;
of iiij. *and* iij., qua tellis eyuen,
he sal hit noumbre make of vij.
þou do to gedder x. *and* ij.
þe laghis twin sal þou finde squa;
In x. sal þou finde þe halde,
in tale of twa þe new is talde.

It is made up of four (nails) and three (woods), by which we may understand the seven arts. Multiply four by three, and it gives us the sum of the Old and the New Law (ten commandments of the Old Testament, two of the New).

man has on croice his schaping knawen,
and he him-selfe on vij is drawen,
baþ in bodi *and* saule, I. say;
þe bodi of elementȝ twies tway,
þe saule hit has of strengthis þrin,
þat takin of cros þai bere wiþ in.

Man is composed of seven elements, the body of four and the soul of three.

¶ quen god þat ordeins alkin state,
of alle in his for-þoȝt he wate,
ferlely puruaied he an;
a cros of tree *and* noȝt of stane,
bot þat was for to make mende
of þe tree þat was defende:

There is a good reason why the Cross was made of wood and not of stone.

his cros he has wroȝt with craft,
hit beris schap til alkin shaft.
wele did moises þat hit fande,
and dauid als þat fot þe wande,
and salamon þat fel hit did;
and ho þat hit fande, quare hit was hid,
elaine at squa gerne hit soȝt,
and til our note now has hit broȝt,

The world is full of the name and the smell of the

ho delt hit wisely as ho wilde,
þat al þis werlde hit is fulfilde
of þe name *and* of þe smelle,
for-þi is gode þ*er*-of to telle.

[fol. 91 *b.*]

Cross.

St. Helen found the nails,

Eline ne walde noȝt for lete
þe naylis, in hende *and* fete
þat driuen ware; ful ȝorne ho soȝt
til ho ham fand, fund ho noȝt,

and worked them up into the bridle of Constantine,

a werk of ham ho wroȝt ful fine
In bridel of king costantine;
was na cristal als briȝt,
ne sa shene to mani siȝt;
quidder-sum[1] he ferde þat sire,
þe bridel briȝtnes bare of fire;

and many were converted by it.

mani þat sagh þat bridel briȝt
t*ur*ned to þe g*ra*ce of goddis miȝt.

Constantine bore them about for three years.

costantine ham bare iij. ȝere,
quen he droghe til his endinge nere,
out to þe bridil he ham laȝt,
and to be side þe crois ham taȝt,
þat mani v*er*tu siþen wroȝt,
þorou miȝt of c*r*ist þat vs boȝt;
at costantine noble *and* in fraunce
god has made mani mustraunce.

The nails are now at St. Denis.

¶ At saint denis is his crou*n*,
wiþ þa nailis redy boun;
mani man come seke *and* sare
at þaire hele had fundin þare.

This story is now finished. Whoso can tell this tale better, let him do so. I tell it as I found it. There are many divers stories of the Rood

¶ now þe crois is broȝt til ende,
þe crois miȝt mote vs defende;
qua-sum[1] þis tale can bet*er* tende,
for c*r*istis loue he hit amende;
þis tale, queþ*er* hit be il or gode,
I fande hit writen of þe rode.
mani tellis diuersli,
for þai mai finde diue*r*se story,

[1] MS. *sim.*

[1] MS. *sim.*

¶ þat fande þe crois he hiȝt Iudas;
made bisshop of þe toun he was,
and his name was turnid þus,
þat he was calde quiriacus:
¶ quen fundin was þis hali crois,
þe warlaghe saide on-loft *with* vois:—
"a ha Iudas! quat has þou done,
þou has me greued, I warne þee sone
at þou did þat cros kiþe,
þou salle rew hit mani siþe;
þorou hit ware mani saulis myne,
þat I am ferde now to tyne;
noȝt for-þi I. wil noȝt nyte,
ful wele I sal þi dedis quite;
a-noþer kinge gaine þe sal rise
þat sal make þe to grise,
and do þe suffer sa mykil shame,
at þou sal nite ihesu name;
and þis was saide be tirand an.
þat quiriac was of siþen slan:
¶ þat findis cry quen Iudas herde,
neuer þe mare was he ferde,
bot waried he þat quiþer-wine,
and saide, "crist þat is lorde myne,
he deme þe in-to helle depe,
euer in wellande wa to wepe."
Þat hali crois, I of haue red,
quar-on ihesus for vs was spred,
hit is our shilde *and* our spere,
againis þe feinde for to were;
ilk day in were we weinde
bot þat ihesu vs grace sende,
þorou þe crois a-gaine þe fende
to be our socour at our ende.

Some say Judas found the Cross,

and that Satan was enraged thereat.

The devil threatened Judas with his vengeance.

[1] MS. *didis*.

Judas bade the fiend depart into hell deep, "*ever in boiling woe to weep.*"

The Cross is our shield and spear against the devil. It will be our succour at our ending day.

VII.

EXPOSITION OF THE HOLY ROOD*.

* [Harl. 4196, leaf 177, col. 2.]

In festo exaltacionis sancte crucis.

There was a king of Persia named "Chodroas," who had a son and heir and many servants.

A king sum tyme in cuntré was,
Þat had to name king chodroas,
A sun he had þat was his ayre,
And oþer menzé many and faire.
Of þe cuntré of pers was he king,
And all þe land at his dedeing.

Every city and town were under his hand. He set up a throne, and commanded his subjects to [leaf 177 *b*, col. 1.] call him the King of kings, God, and Lord of lords.

He gert ilk cetté and ilk toune
Vnto his biding be so boune,
Þat in a trone up he him sett,
And cumand þam with-owten lett
Þat king of kinges þai suld him call,
And allso god grettest of all,
And lord of lordes both loud and still,
And none on melde[1] mete him untill.

He was not satisfied with this only, but went to Jerusalem, and threatened the Christians, and destroyed their churches.

Zit was noght þis in þat sesowne
Inogh till his confusione;
Bot to ierusalem he went,
And said all suld be schamely schent
Þat trowed on crist or on his lay.
Þar-to he dose all þat he may,
In ierusalem þaire kirkes he stroyde,
And cristen men ful gretly noyed.

He took his journey towards the Holy Sepulchre with the intention of destroying it, but turned back for fear.

He toke his wai þan to þe graue
Whare crist was layd þat vs sall saue,
It to destroy with all his mayn;
Bot for ferdnes he turned ogayne,
And durst do no thing at þe kyrk,

[1] Read *molde*.

Bot wikkedly þus gan he wirk.
Saint Eline þe nobill quene,
Þat lang bifore his tyme had bene,
Fand þe cros[1] þat men cald þe rode,
Þat ihesue died on for oure gude,
And to ierusalem scho it broght,
And graithed it þare als hir gude thoght,
In siluer and go[l]d al bidene,
For þat it suld be kepid clene,
And þat same kirk gert scho make
Coriosly for þat cros sake,
For men suld hald þat haly tre
In honore als it aw to be.
Bot þis ilk king chosdroass[2],
When he wist whare þis ilk cros was,
He gert his men with grete maystry
Haue it forth with him in hy
Out of ierusalem cetté,
And broght it whare him liked to be.
When he was þus cumen hame ogayn,
Of his iorné he was ful fayne,
And hastili þan[3] gert he dight
A faire toure all off siluer bright;
He made it nobilly for þe nanes,
Within all ful of precius stanes.
A trone of gold þarin he sett,
With precius stanes all ouer plett,
And þarein gert he gayly dyght,
Like son and mone and sternes bright;
Also zit gert he mak þarin
Propirtese by preué gyn,
Þat it was like untill a heuyn;
And rayn þarfro cumand ful euyn
And preué whistils war omang
Made euyn like to angels sang.
Þare in þat toure als him gude thoght,

The Cross that the noble queen Helena had found, she brought to Jerusalem, and adorned it with silver and gold. For the preservation of the same she made a church, where men might go and honour the holy tree.

This impious king, when he knew where the Cross was, took possession of it, and carried it away with him to his own country.

He raised a fair tower of silver adorned with precious stones. Therein he set a throne of gold, ornamented with precious stones. By representations of the heavenly bodies, he made the tower look [col. 2.] like heaven, and caused rain to descend therefrom. He even imitated the song of angels by means of secret whistles.

[1] MS. *cors.*

[2] MS. *chosoroass.*

[3] MS. *þant.*

In this tower he raised a seat for himself, and set the Holy Cross beside him. There he sat like a god, and bade all his subjects call him such. He assigned the kingdom to his son.

A sege untill him self he wroght,
And þare he gert with mekill pride
Set þe haly cros him biside.
Þar als a god he sat in stall,
And so he bad men suld him call.
His kingdom and all his riallté,
Vntill his sun haly gaf he;

For many a day he practised his cursed "maumetry," leading the folk in the devil's law. Thus with the devil we will let him dwell, and of his son we will now talk. Eraclius lived at this time, a noble and Christian king.

And on þis wise þat curst caytiue
In maumetry wald lede his liue.
And so he did full many a day
Ledeand þe folk in fendes lay.
Þus with þe deuil we lat him dwell,
And of his son I sall now tell.
A nobill king of cristendum,
Þat namen was heraclium,
Was gouernowre of grete [empire]
Soucrainly als lord and syre;

He had a wife and children, and led his life in Christ's law. The son of "Chosdroas" was envious of the Christian king's renown,

Childer he had and worthly wife,
In cristes law he led his life.
Þan þis son of chosdroas
In his hert euill angerd was
Þat þis cristen king had name
More þan he or his sire at hame.
Þarfore he ordand him in hy,

and made preparations to fight against him, and to destroy him, if possible.

And gaderd a grete cumpani
Of sarzins by his assent;
And with ful grete ost es he went,
With þis cristen king to fight,
And to destroy him if he might.

Eraclius, hearing of this, gathered together a large Christian company to defend his kingdom.

Bot sone eraclius herd tell,
Of þis falshed how it bi-fell.
He ordand him full hastily
Of cristen men grete cumpany.

The two armies met at a certain place near a river.

Bot als it was oure lordes will,
When aither come oþer vntill,
In place whare þai swld batayl take,

On þis wisse gan þai couenant make.
A water was þam twa by-twene,
And a brig all ouer it clene.
Þe sarzyn was mekill of brede and lenth,
And traisted mikill i*n* his awin strenkth.
Þarfore þis forward gan he ma
To do þe batail bitwix þam twa.
And þat þe cristend man suld mete hi*m*
In middes þe brig was ouer þe brim,
And wheþer so might maistri win
On his side suld þe bataill blin;
And he suld haue i*n* his pousté
All þat þai bath had, land and fe.
To þis couenant assented þai bath,
And þarto band þai þam with ath,
Þat if þaire men on owþir side
Come forto help þam in þat tide,
Þai suld be cut for þaire iornay,
Þaire armes and þaire legges oway,
And so be kasten in þe flode,
And saue þam suld none erthly gude.
When bath þe sides war sworn þar-till,
Þis couenand lely to fulfill,
Þe twa lordes[1] on þe brig[2] met,
And aiþer hard on oþer set.
Ful fast þare faght þai tow in fere,
And none oþer durst negh þam nere.
Þan cristen men, with hertes fre,
Prayed to ihesu crist, þat he
Suld send þaire prince þe victory,
Als he for þam on rode wald day,
And all þai praied þan with a voice :—
"Thurgh vertu of þi haly croyce,
Whar-thurgh þou wan þe victori
Of þe fende, oure fals enmy,
Þou grante þis day oure prince to wyn

The son of "Chosdroas" proposed to Eraclius to decide the contest by a battle between the two on the bridge of the river. The Sarasin was great in breadth and length, and

[leaf 178, col. 1.]

trusted much in his own strength. He who came off conqueror was to have the other's possessions.

To this plan both consented, and bound themselves with an oath to cripple and throw into the stream any one who should come to their assistance.

The two lords met on the bridge of the river, and set hard on each other.

The Christians with one voice prayed that their lord might have the victory over the false Sarasin.

[1] MS. *lorde lordes.*
[2] MS. *bring.*

Þe maistri ouere zon fals sarzyn."
On þis manere all prayed þai fast;
And ihesuc herd þam at þe last,
And ordand to his trew serwand
Of þe sarzin to hawe ouer[1] hand,
And to destroy him in þat place.
Bliseed be he þat gaf slike grace.
Sone when þe sarzins saw þis sight,
How þaire maister to ded was dight,
Swilk drede in hert had þai ilkane,
Þat þai oblist þam noght allane,
To hald þe couenand made byforne,
Bot new athes all haue þai sworn,
With eraclius forto stand,
In ill and gude, with hert and hand,
And wilfully all hale hete þai,
Forto leue on cristes lay,
And forto bycum cristen men,
And crist for þaire god euer to ken.
Sone when eraclius saw þat sight,
He resayued þam with hert ful light,
And cownsaild þam with wordes fre,
Þat þai suld all baptist be,
And trow in crist with gude entent,
And to his saw all þai assent.
So war þai baptist all þat day,
And lifed euer in cristes lay.
Veraclius[2] when þis was done,
In-to pers puruaid him ful sone,
And with him all þat cumpany
Þat bifore lifed in maumetry.
And als he went thurgh-out þat land,
All þe folk þat he þare fand
Ouþer war þai baptist sone
Or els þai war vnto ded done.
Þus conquert he all þat cuntré,

Christ heard them and gave His faithful servant the victory.

[1] MS. *ever*.

When the heathens saw that their master was killed, they were so terrified that they swore new oaths to stand with Eraclius in evil and good, and with heart and hand. Willingly they promised to become followers of Christ.

[col. 2.]

Eraclius received them with joyful heart, and had them all baptized that very day.

[2] So in MS.

Then Eraclius set out for Persia, and on his way he induced the people to become Christians. Those that refused were put to death.

Till he come tyll þat same ceté,
Whare Cosdroas so sitand es
Als a god in grete reches.
Into þe toure he went full sone
And fand him sitand in his trone,
Dubbed obut with pricius stanes,
And dight ful nobilly for þe nanes.

He came to the city of "Cosdroas," where he found the emperor sitting like a god on his throne.

Biside him stode þat haly tre
Þat þai had soght so forto se;
And soucrainly for þat tre sake,
Wirschip to him gan þai make.
Þan cosdroas was full affraid,
And þus Eraclius to him said :—
"If þo will haue þi life in land,
Als I say sall þou vnder-stand,
For þou has done þis tre honore,
Þat bare ihesu oure sauyore;
All if þou did it noght for him
Vnto þe grante I life and lym.
At þe reuerence of þis haly tre,
If þo will trow in ihesu fre,
And forsake all þi mawmetry,

Beside him was the Holy Cross. When Eraclius's men saw that sight, they did honour to "Cosdroas" for the sake of the Cross. Eraclius thus spake to the heathen king: "Forasmuch as thou hast done honour to the Cross of Christ, I will spare thy life if thou wilt forsake all thy 'mawmetry,'

Þat þou and þi folk yn affy,
And turn þe unto ihesu crist,
And in his name will be baptist,
Þi life in land þan haue þou sall
And all þi kingdom still withall.

and turn to Jesus Christ and be baptized.

And if þou will noght do þis rede
With my swerd þou sal be dede."
Þis sarzin wald noght turn his mode,
To leue his fals goddes for no gude.
Þarfore Eraclius ful sone
Strake of his heuyd with-outen hone,
And bad þat he sul[d] haue beriing,
By-caus þat he had bene a king.
Þan þai toke þat haly tre.

If thou wilt not follow my advice, with my sword shalt thou be slain." The heathen king refused to become a [leaf 178 *b*, col. 1.] Christian, therefore Eraclius struck off his head without more ado.

With hymns and noble songs they took the Cross, and carried it away with them.

With ful grete solempnité,
And bare it[1] furth so þam omang,
With himpnes and with nobil sang.
And all þe folk þan war ful glad,
Þat þai þis haly tre þus had.
Hamward þai toke þe way in hy,
With mekill mirth and melody;

As they drew near Mount Olivet, which is on the way to Jerusalem, they came close to the gate of the city where Jesus entered when he came thither to suffer pain.

And als þai come in þe strete,
Doun ouer þe mownt of olyuete,
Als it fell i*n* þare iornay,
To ierusalem þe redy way,
Graithly furth þai held þe gate,
Vnto þai come till þat ilk zate,
Whare ih*esu*c crist went in ful playn,
When he come þeder at suffer payn;

Much folk of the town had assembled to see the procession of the Cross.

And mekill folk of þat same toune,
Þat war cumen with p*ro*cessiowne,
For wirschip of þe haly tre,
And su*m* þat reall sight to se,

Eraclius rode with much pride along with his nobles.

Eraclius him self gan ride
Bifor þe prese with mekill pride,
And oþer lordes þat with him ware,
Þe haly cros oma[n]g þam bare.
And þus, with grete solempnité,
Entred þai to þat ceté.

But when they attempted to enter the city, the gates closed like a wall of stone, and they saw no signs of any mode of entrance.

Bot when þai neghed þe zates nere,
Þis meruaill fell on þis manere.
Þe zates, þat bifore war wide,
Closed samyn sone in þat tyde,
Þat kenyng of zate was þare nane,
Bot all closed alls a wall of stane,
So þat þai might no takni*ng* se,
On whilk syde þai suld haue entré.

Sore afraid were they when they saw this miracle.

Sone when þai saw þis wonder dede,
In þaire hertes þai had grete drede.
Eraclius[2] and oþer ma,

[1] MS. *if*.

[2] MS. *Erachius*.

When þai saw þat it was swa,
Þai praied ihesue oure sawiowre
In þat case þam to socoure,
Thurgh uertu of þat haly tre,
Þat þai might win to þat ceté.
Þus praied þai all with drery steuyn,
Heueand up þaire heuides till heuyn;
And als þai loked so up on hight,
Þai saw ane angell schineand bright,
Euyn opon þe wall standand,
And þe signe of þe cros in his hand;
He stode obouen whare þe zate suld be,
And þir wordes on þis wise sayd he.
He said, "when crist of heuyn king,
Þat lord es of all erthly thing,
Þis same wai to þis ceté went,
Þare forto suffer[1] grefe turment,
In at þis zate he toke þe way,
Bot he come all on oþer array.
Grete hors for him none ordand was,
Bot sitand on a simple ass;
He was noght cled in kinges clething,
Bot pouerly went he in all thing;
He went noght with grete minstralsy,
Bot in his prayers ful preuely:
Ensaumple suthly forto gif
To þam þat in his law wald lif,
In him to trow with trew entent,
And mekely to wende als he went."
When þis was said, he went up euyn,
With grete light, till oure lord in heuyn.
Þe Emperoure þan Eraclius
Ful hertly thanked dere ihesue;
And all þe folk þat with him ware
War ful faine of þis ferly fare.
Sone of his stede doun es he light,

Eraclius and his company then prayed to God for help to enter the city.

[col. 2.]

As they looked up to heaven, they saw an angel shining bright standing on the wall with the sign of the Cross in his hand, and thus he spake to them: 'When Christ, heaven's king, entered this city by this gate, he had no great horse, but rode on a simple ass; He was not clad in king's clothing, but went in poorly—not with great minstrelsy, but with secret prayer."

Having thus spoken, the angel ascended to heaven. The emperor thanked God for the instruction he had received.

He then got off his horse,

[1] MS. *susfer*.

cast off all his gay clothing, his crown and ornaments,

And kest of all his clething bright,
His corown and his kinges array
And his dubbing he did oway,

and barefooted bore the Cross on its way.

And barefot went he on his fete,
Bereand þe cros[1] by þe strete.
And on þis maner did þai all.

[1] MS. *cors*.

Then the gates opened wide, and they entered with solemn song.

And when þe king come nere þe wall,
It opind and wex zates wide,
Als it had bene bifor þat tyde.
Þai entred þan with solempne sang,
Ful mekill mirth was þam oma[n]g;
And þe cros bare þai þam bitwene,
Till þe stede whare it bifore had bene,

The Cross was restored to its former place.

And up þai set it really,
And honord it als was worthi.

That day many miracles were wrought by virtue of the Cross. Blind men got their sight, crooked men were made [leaf 179, col. 1.] straight, the dumb and deaf were healed, and devils were chased out of many.

Þat day þare, thurgh þe cors allane,
War miracles wroght ful maniane,
Of sere blind men þat had þaire sight,
And crokid men war made ful right;
Of parlesy war helid grete wane,
And dum and defe ful maniane;
And leprous men had hele in haste,
And out of many war deuils chaste.
Þus war þai held ful grete plenté,
Thurgh vertu of [þat] haly tre,

Unto Christ be honour for ever and ever!

Þat bare ihesu oure sawiowre,
Vnto him be euer honowre.

VIII.

DISPUTE BETWEEN MARY AND THE CROSS*.

* [Vernon MS. fol. 315 b, col. 3.]

Disputacio inter Mariam et Crucem, secundum Apocrafum.

I.

Oure ladi freo·,
on Rode treo·,
made hire mon:
Heo seide on þe·
þe fruit of me·
is wo bigon:
Mi fruit I· seo·
in blodi bleo·
Among his fon,
Serwe I· seo·,
þe veines fleo·
from blodi bon:
Cros·! þou dost no trouþe!
On a pillori· my fruit to pinne,
He haþ no spot· of Adam sinne;
Flesch· and veines· nou fleo a-twinne,
Wherfore I· rede of routhe·:

Our gracious lady made the following complaints against the Rood-tree:—

On thee my fruit is woe-begone.

My offspring is fastened to a tree, spotless as he is.

Alas! flesh and veins are come in twain, and therefore am I sorrowful.

II.

Cros· þi bondes schul ben blamed,
Mi fayre fruit· þou hast bi-gyled;
Þe fruites Mooder· was neuere a-famed,
Mi wombe is feir·, founden vn-fuyled:
Chyld· whi artou not a-schamed

I, the mother of my child, was never defamed; my body is fair and spotless.

On a pillori· to ben I·-piled ?
Grete Iewes· þus weore gramed,
And dyede· for heore werkes wyled ;
In mournyng· I· may melte !
Mi fruit· þat is so holi halwed,
In a feeld· is fouled· and falwed ;
Wiþ grete Iewes· he is galwed,
And dyeþ· for Monnes gelte :

Great Jews sinned, and thou didst die for their wild works.
I melt in mourning, for my offspring is defiled.

By great Jews is he crucified, and dies for man's guilt.

III.

On account of the great Jews, gallows was upreared.

A deadly drink, O Cross, thou gavest to the Lord of life.
His veins did burst through the torture.

Defiled is my son, that never trespassed, with thieves that ever loved riot.
Why shall my son be nailed ?

FOr grete Iewes· galwes were greiþed,
Þat euer to Robbyng· Ronne ryf ;
Whi schal my sone· on þe beo leid,
Þat neuer nuyȝed· mon nor wyf ?
A drinke of deþ· soþliche seid,
Cros þou ȝeuest· þe lord of lyf :
His veynes to bursten· wiþ þi breid,
Mi fruit stont nou· in a strong stryf ;
Blod from hed· is hayled,
Fouled· is my fayre fruit,
Þat neuer dude· tripet ne truit
Wiþ þeues þat loueden· ryot and ruit ;
Whi schal my sone· be nayled ?

IV.

Thou, O Cross, art made to bear fools full of sin.
My son should be excused, and never ought his blood to run on thee.
With thieves must be hang far in fen.

Men may know me as a sorrowful mother.

Þorwȝ Iugement· þou art en-Ioynet
To bere fooles·, ful of sinne :
Mi sone from þe· schulde beon ensoynet,
And neuere his blod· vppon þe rinne ;
But nou is truþe· wiþ tresun teynet,
Wiþ þeoues to honge·, fer in fenne ;
Wiþ feole nayles· his limes ben feynet,
A careful Moder· men mai me kenne,
In Bales· I· am bounde !

Þat fruit was· of a Mayden born,
On a þeoues tre· is al to torn;
A Broche· þorw-out his brest bo[r]n
His holi herte· haþ wounde:

The Virgin's child is torn [fol. 310.] asunder on a thief's tree.

V.

Tre þou art loked· bi þe lawe
Þeoues· traitours· on þe to d[e]ye,
But now is trouþe· wiþ tresun drawe,
And vertu· falleþ in vices weye;
But loue· and treuþe·, in soþfast sawe,
On a treo· traytours· hem teye,
Vertu is· wiþ vices slawe:
Of alle vertues· my sone is keye,
Vertu· swettore þen spices!
In fot· and· hond· bereþ blodi prikke,
His hed is ful of þornes· þikke,
Þe goode hongeþ· a-mong þe wikke,
Vertu dyeþ wiþ vices·:

Truth is distorted by treason, and virtue is fallen in the way of vice (i.e. is treated like vice). Traitors tie love, faith, and soothfastness on the tree.

In foot and hand he bears bloody wounds. His head is full of thick thorns; the good man hangs along with the wicked.

VI.

Tre vnkynde! þou schalt be kud,
Mi sone step-Moder· I· þe calle:
Mi fruit was born· wiþ beestes on bed,
And be my flesch· my flour gan falle,
Wiþ my brestes· my brid I· fed;
Cros· þou ȝeuest him· Eysel· and Galle!
Mi white Rose· Red is spred,
Þat fostred was in· a fodderes stalle;
Feet· and fayre hondes!
Þat nou ben croised· I· custe hem ofte,
I· lulled hem· I· leid hem softe:
Cros þou holdest hem· hiȝe on lofte
Bounden· in bledyng bondes·!

Unkind tree, my son's stepmother I call thee. My child was born along with beasts. With my breasts I fed him. My white rose is become red, even he that was fostered in a "fodder's stall." Feet and fair hands that now are crossed, oft have I kissed and lulled them, and laid them softly down.

VII.

I lulled aloft my love, and with cradle band I bound him. On the Cross he hangs; on thy stair naked and exposed to the wild wind.

Mi loue· i-lolled vp in þe eyr,
Wiþ cradel bond· I· gan him bynde,
Cros he stikeþ nou· on þi steir,
Naked a-ȝeyn· þe wylde wynde:
Foules fourmen heor nestes· in þe eyr,
Wolues in den· reste þei fynde,
Bot Godes sone·, in heuene heir,
His hed nou leoneþ· on þornes tynde,

I may well be sorrowful. God's head hath no rest, but leans on his shoulder-bone, and thorns pierce his flesh.

Of Mournyng· I· may myune!
Godes hed· haþ reste non,
But leoneþ· on his scholder bon;
Þe þornes· þorwh his flesch gon,
His wo· I· wyte hit sinne:

VIII.

So high thou holdest my son that his feet I cannot kiss. I thrust out my lips, I outstretched my neck to kiss his feet. The Jews drove me from the Cross, and on me made their mouths amiss, their games and their jokes. O Cross, thou bearest my bird, beaten blue, along with fraudulent thieves.

Cros to slen· hit is þi sleiht,
Mi fayre fruit· þou berest fro blis;
Cros þou holdest him so heih on heiȝþ,
Mi fruites feet· I· mai not kis;
Mi mouþ I· pulte·, my sweore I· streiȝt
To cusse his feet·, soþ þing hit is:
Þe Iewes· from þe cros me keiȝt,
On me· þei made heore mouwes amis,
Heore games· and heore gaudes!
Þe Iewes wrouȝten· me ful wo:
Cros· I· fynde· þou art my fo,
Þou berest my brid·, beten blo,
A-mong þeose fooles fraudes·:

IX.

[Cross responds.]

Cristes cros· ȝaf onswere:—
Ladi to þe· I· owe honour,

Þi brihte palmes· nou I· bere ;
Mi schyning scheweþ· þorw þi flour,
Þi feire fruit· on me ginneþ tere ;
Þi fruit me florischeþ· in blod colour
To winne þe world· þat lay in lure ;
Þat Blosme Blomed· vp in þi bour,
Ac not for þe· al-one !
But for to winne· all þis world,
Þat swelte· vndur þe deueles swerd :
Þorw feet and hond· God let him gerd,
To A-mende monnes mone· :

Lady, thy fair fruit begins to ripen in me. It flourishes on me with bloody hue. In order to win the lost world that blossom bloomed in thy bower, but not for thee alone, but to win all this world, that died under the devil's sword.

X.

Adam dude· ful huge harmes,
Whon he bot A bite· vndur a bouh,
Wherfore þi sone· haþ sprad his Armes,
On a treo tyed· wiþ teone I-nouh ;
His flesch· is smite wiþ deþes þarmes,
And swelteþ heer-in· a swemly swouh ;
His Breste is bored· wiþ deþes swarmes,
And wiþ his deþ· fro deþ he drouh
Alle· his leoue freondes !
As Ozie spac· in *pro*phecie
And seide—"þi sone seinte Marie,
His deþ· slouȝ deþ· on Caluarie,
Ȝaf lyf· wiþ-outen endes· " :

Adam did huge harms when he bit a bite under a bough; wherefore thy son hath spread out his arms tied grievously to a tree. His flesh is smitten with death's dint, and he dies herein in a swooning faint. As Isaiah spake: "His death slew death, and gave [fol. 316, col. 2.] eternal life on Calvary."

XI.

Þe stipre· þat is vnder þe vyne set
May not bringe· forþ þe grape ;
Þeih þe fruit· on me beo knet,
His scharpe schour· haue I· not schape :
Til grapes· to þe presse beo set
Þer renneþ· no red wyn· in rape ;

The support of the vine produces not grapes. I have not sent the sharp shower to ripen the fruit hanging on me. No red wine

Neuere presse· pressed bet,
I· presse wyn· for kniht and knape:
Vp-on a Blodi brinke
I· presse a grape·, *with* strok and stryf,
Þe Rede wyn· renneþ ryf:
In Samaritane· God ȝaf a wyf
Þat leof licour to drynke:

comes until the grapes be set in the press. I press wine for "knight and knave." Upon a bloody brink I press a grape with stroke and strife. In Samaria God gave a woman that precious liquor to drink.

XII.

LAdi· loue doþ þe to alegge
Þi fruit is prikked· wiþ speres ord:
On Cros·, wiþ-outen knyues egge,
I· kerue fruit· of godes hord;
Al is al red·, Rib· and Rugge,
His bodi bledeþ· a-ȝeyn þe bord;
I· was piler· and bar a brugge,
God is weie·, witnesse of word;
God seiþ he is· soþfast weye!
Mony folk slod· to helle slider,
To heuene· mihte no mon þider,
Til god dyed· and tauȝte whider
Men drawen· whon þei dye·:

On Cross without edge of knife I cut fruit off God's treasure.

I was pillar, and bare a bridge. God is the way, the true way.

None went to heaven until God died, and taught them how thither men should go when they die.,

XIII.

Moyses haþ fourmed·, in his figour,
A· whit lomb·, and non oþer beste
Schulde be sacred vr saueour,
And be mete of mihtes meste;
I· was þat cheef chargeour,
I· bar flesch· for folkes feste;
Ihesu crist· vre saueour
He fedeþ· boþe lest and meste,
Rosted· a-ȝeyn þe sonne!
On me lay· þe lomb of loue,

In the Mosaic law a white lamb is the type of a saviour—the greatest of all meats.

I was that chief bearer (of sins). I bare flesh for the feast of folks. Christ, roasted in the sun, feeds both most and least. On me lay the Lamb of Love.

I· was plater· his bodi a-boue,
Til feet· and hondes· al-to cloue,
Wiþ blood· I· was bi-ronne:

I was the platter which bare his body, until feet and hands were rent asunder.

XIV.

Ȝit Moyses· in Rule haþ rad,
We schulde ete vr lomb· *in* sour ve*r*geous;
Sour ve*r*geous mai make· vr soules glad,
To serwe sore· for sunnes ours;
Sour ve*r*geous schal make· þe deuel a-drad,
For he fleecheþ· fro godes spous;
Beo a staf· stondeþ sad,
Whon ȝe fongen flesch· in godes hous,
Þat staf· is Cristes Crouche!
Stondeþ stifli· bi þat stake,
Whon *þat* ȝe fongen· flesch in Cake,
Þen schal no feond· maystri make,
Ȝoure soules for to touche:

Moses has bidden us eat our lamb with sour verjuice. Sour verjuice may gladden our souls, and cause the devil to tremble.

When ye eat Christ's flesh in God's house, stand stilly by the staff of Christ's Cross.

XV.

For *par*doun scheweþ· be a shrine,
Wiþ nayl· and brede· on bord is smite,
Rede lettres· write be lyne,
Bluwe· Blake· a-mong men pite:
Vr lord I· likne· to þis signe,
His bodi· vppon a bord· was bite,
In Briht blod· his bodi gan schyne;
Hou wo him was· may no mon wite,
Red vp-on þe Roode!
Vr *par*doun brede·, from top too to,
Writen hit was· wiþ wonder wo,
Wiþ Rede wou*n*des· and strokes blo,
Vre Book· was bounden in bloode·:

Pardon on a tablet, written with red letters, mixed with blue and black, is betokened by Christ.

His body upon a board was bent; the blood illuminated his body, that shone red upon the Rood.
Our pardon was written on his body from top to toe.

Our book was bound in blood.

XVI.

Adam drowned his ghost in bitter gall; instead of this gall God gave us mead; with sweet mercy the bitterness is quenched. His body was the book, the Cross was the board, when Christ was clenched thereon. Were a man ever so blessed a saint no prayer could get pardon for him, until book on board was spread, dinted and driven with sharp nails, till feet and hands were riven.

Adam· stod vp in stede,
In Bitter galle· his gost he dreint;
A-ȝeyn þat galle· God ȝaf vs mede,
Wiþ swete Merci· Bitter is queynt;
His Bodi was Book· þe Cros was brede,
Whon crist for vs· þ*er*-on was cleynt:
No mon gat *par*doun· wiþ no bede,
Weor he neuere· so sely a seynt,
Til book on bord· was sprad!,
Wiþ sharpe nayles· dunted and driue,
Til feet· and hondes· al-to riue;
His herte blod· vre book haþ ȝiue,
To make· vr gostes glad:

XVII.

[fol. 316, col. 3.]

I was the first press to squeeze out the wine. I bare a bridge to teach the way where seemly angels sit and sing. The Cross was a tablet of pardon. In book it is billed (written). When blood was written on Christ's body then was pardon obtained for sinners.

Cristes Cros· ȝit spac þis speche
Furst was I· presse· wyn to wringe,
I· bere a Brugge·, wei to teche,
Þer semely Aungeles· sitte and synge:
Lord of loue· and lyues leche
For þe was set· sely sacrynge,
To winne þe world· þat was in wreche;
Þe Cros was brede·, *par*doun to bringe,
Pardoun· In book is billed!
What is *par*doun· vppon to minne?
Hit is forȝiuenes· of dedly sinne;
Whon blod was writen· on cristes kinne,
Pardoun was· fulfilled:

XVIII.

[Respondit Maria:]

O Cross, wonder not though I be wroth.

Oure ladi seide· Cros of þi werk
Wonder þe not·, þeiȝ I· be wroþe,

Þus seide Poule·, Cristes clerk ; —
Þe feolle Iewes·, wiþ false oþe,
Iewes· ston hard, in sinnes merk,
Beoten a lomb· wiþ-outen loþe,
Softur þen watur· vndur serk,
Meode· or· Milk· medled boþe!
Þe Iewes· weoren harde stones!
Softur þen wat*ur*· or eny licour,
Or dewȝ þat liþ· on þe lilie flour
Was cristes bodi· in blod colour,
Þe Iewes wolden· ha broken his bones· :

The fell Jews, stone-hearted in dark sins, have beaten a lamb, softer than water under skirt; softer than milk or mead mixed together. Like hard stones were the Jews. Softer than dew on the lilly-flower was Christ's body in bloody colours.

XIX.

And mony A prophete· gan make mon,
And seide· "lord send us þi lomb
Out of þe wildernesses ston,
To fende vs· from þe lyon cromp :"
Of mylde mount of Syon
Be-com mon·, In A Maydens womb,
Made a bodi·, wiþ blessed bon,
In a Maidens blod· þi bodi flomb :
At Barreres· weore debate!
Þorwȝ stones· In þe wildernes
Men miȝte better· ha crepet I·-wis,
Þen bored· in-to heuene blis,
Til blod· brac vp þe ȝate· :

Many a prophet moaned, and said, "Lord, send us thy Lamb out of the stone of the wilderness, to defend us from the lion's paw."

Men might more easily creep through the stones of the wilderness than bore their way into heaven's bliss. But blood brake open the gate.

XX.

Sin monnes sone· was so nedi,
To beo lad· wiþ lomb mylde,
Whi weore gylours· so gredi
For to defoule· my faire childe?
Cros whi weore þou· so redi
To rende my fruit·, feor in fylde?

Why were beguilers so greedy to defile my fair child? O Cross, why wast thou so ready to rend my offspring?

[Cross replies:] Lady, to make the devil afraid, God shaped me as a shield against shame. I am a chosen, choice relick that no devil dare abide.

Ladi to make· þe deuel dredi,
God schop me a scheld·, schame to schilde,
Til lomb of loue· dyede!
And on me ȝeld þe gost· wiþ vois;
I· was chose· a Relik chois,
Þe signe of Ihesu cristes crois,
Þer dar no deuel· a-byde:

XXI.

Many folk I defend from their foe. [crux respondit:] Heaven's gates were closed close until the Lamb of Love died. Mankind was tied in hell until Christ died and rose. At noon the Lamb of Love said "It is finished." Mankind are unbound, and heaven's doors are opened.

Moni folk I· fende· from heore fos:
Cristes Cros· þis sawes seide:—
Heuene ȝates· weore closed clos
Til þe lomb· of loue dyede,
Þis is write· in tixt· and glos:
Aftur Cristes deþ· prophetes preide:
Til þe lomb of loue· dyed and ros
In helle pyne· monkynde was teyde:
At houre of his none!
Þe lomb of loue· seyde his þouȝt—
Nou is folfuld· þat wel is wrouȝt,
A Mon is out of bondes brouȝt
And heuene dores· vndone:

XXII.

The Cross said:

Wiþ þe Fader· þat al schal folfille,
His sone to heuene is an help,

I was a pillar and stood full still. The devil's sword was rendered useless.

I· was piler· and stod ful stille:
After oþur ȝiftes· now gostes ȝelp,
Þe fend· þat al þis world wolde kille,
His swerd he pulte vp· in his kelp;
To helle he horlede· from þat hille,
Beerynge· as a Beore whelp:

Christ's Cross hath cracked the devil's crown.

A beore is bounden· and beted!
Cristes Cros· haþ craked his croun,

Þe lomb haþ leid· þe Lyoun a-doun;
Þe lomb is lord· in eueri toun,
So Cristes blod· haþ pleted:

The lamb hath subdued the lion. The lamb is lord in every town.

XXIII.

In holy writ· þis tale is herde,
Þat goode ȝiftes· god vs ȝaf;
God seiþ him-self· he is schepherde,
And vche an heerde· bi-houeþ a staf;
Þe Cros· I· calle· þe heerdes ȝerde,
Þer-wiþ þe deuel· a dunt he ȝaf,
And wiþ þe ȝerde· þe wolf he werde,
Wiþ duntes· drof him al to draf:
Þe Cros· þis tale tolde!
Þat he was staf· in þe heerdes hond,
Whon schep breken· out of heore bond,
Þe wolf he wered· out of lond
Þat deuoured· cristes folde:

Christ is a shepherd, and [fol. 316 *b*, col. 1.] every shepherd needs a staff. The Cross is the shepherd's crook. Therewith he gave the devil a dint, and frightened the wolf, and drove him with the dints all to draff.

XXIV.

Ȝit seide· þe Meke Marie—
Roode· þou reendest my Rose al red:
Þreo Iewes coomen· from Caluari
Þat day· þat Ihesu þoled ded,
Alle þei seiden· þei weore sori,
For-dolled· in a drouknyng dred;
Þei tolden hem alle· wherfore· and whi
Heore hertes were colde·, as lumpyng led;
Þe furste· heore tale tolde!
Whon crist was knit· *with* corde on a stok
His bodi bledde· a-ȝein þat blok,
Þorw feet and hondes· nayles gan knok.
Þen gan myn herte· to colde·:

[respondit Maria.] O Cross, thou rendest my red rose. Three Jews came from Calvary the day Christ died, and said they were sorry and sore afraid. The first said: "On the Cross Christ's blood ran down the block. Through feet and hands nails were knocked. Then my heart began to grow cold."

XXV.

The second said: "It was not that that caused me to be sorrowful, so much as the setting up of the Cross after he was nailed thereon. Then the nails rent his hands and feet. The hard hat of thorns pierced his head. His joints were disjointed, I perceived. Then wept I water, and tears did flow; to care I was inclined."

Þe Secounde seide nay· not þat·
Þat dude serwe· in-to myn herte schete;
But whon þe Roode ros· *and* doun was squat,
Þe nayles· renten him hondes and feete,
Þorw-out his helm· þe harde hat
Þe þornes· in-to his flesch gan crepe,
His Ioyntes· vn-Ioynet· I· tok good gat;
Þo weop I· water· and teres leete,
To care I· was enclyned !
In cloddres of blod· his her was clunge,
Þe flesch was from· þe bones swonge,
Druiȝe drinkeles· was his tonge,
His lippes to clouen· and chyned· :

XXVI.

The third said: "Those pains you have told were the least he endured. Methought this pain was the greatest. All his flesh was flayed, and a sword went through Mary's breast. Out of the Cross the knife came then. She fell down in swoon thereat, but the Jews by tens and by twelves danced before her and mocked her grief."

Þe þridde seide· þis þouhte me lest
Of þeose peynes· and oþer mo,
Þis peyne þouhte me· peyne mest;
Al his flesch· he let of flo,
His Mylde Moder· stod him nest,
Loked vpward· And hire was wo,
A swerd swapped hire· þorw þe brest:
Out of þe cros· þe knyf com þo,
Þis siht sauh I· my-selue !
Þe swerd of loue· þorw hire gan launce,
Heo swapte on swownyng· þorw *þat* chaunce;
To scornen hire· þei gan daunce,
Iewes· bi ten· and twelue· :

XXVII.

Mary said: Since the three Jews

Sin Iewes made· so muchel mon,
To seon my brid·, bou*n*den in brere,

In sad serwyng· moste I· gon·
To seon blodi· my chyldes chere:
Fadres· *and* Modres· þat walken in won
Schul loue heore children· beo skiles clere;
Þeose two loues· weore in me al-on,
For fader and moder· I· was here,
Þeose two loues· in me weore dalt !
I· was fader· of his flesch,
His Moder hedde· an herte nesch,
Mi serwe flowed· as water fresch,
Weopyng· and wo· I· walt :

bewailed the sufferings of my son, it behoved me to give way to sorrow when I saw my son's face all bloody. Fathers and mothers both love their children. These two loves were centered in me. I was father and mother here.

XXVIII.

IN me weore tacched· sorwes two,
In þe fader· mihte non a-byde,
For he was euere· in reste and Ro,
Ioyned· in his Ioyes wyde,
I· serwed sore· for to sei so :
I· say whon þat my derlyng dide,
Wiþ duntes· he was to deþe i-do,
Vp-on a tre· his bodi was soyled ;
Whon trouþe is told· and darted !
Of alle Ioyes· God is welle,
Þer mihte no serwe· in him dwelle,
I· serwed sore· as Clerkes telle,
Mi pyne· was not departed· :

A father's and a mother's sorrow were felt by me. The father in rest and peace could feel no sorrow.

I sorrowed sore to see my darling done to death by dints, and his body defiled on a tree.

God is well of all joys, no sorrow could abide in Him.

XXIX.

ÞE hattore loue· þe caldore care,
Whon frendes fynde· heore fruit defoyled ;
Þe dispitous Iewes· nolde not spare,
Til trie fruit· weore tore and toyled ;
Neuer Mayden· Mournede mare,
I· sauh my child· ben surded and soyled,

The hotter the love, the colder the grief. The cruel Jews would not cease until the fruit was torn and spoilt.

[fol. 316 *b*, col. 2.]

I saw my son defiled, and my heart was torn by the sword of sorrow. For I saw my son bemoiled with blood, as Simeon had foretold.

Myn herte to-clef· wiþ swerd of care ;
I· sauȝ my brid· *with* blod bem-oyled [1],
As Symeon· seide beo-forn ! ,
Þe swerd of serwe·, scharp I·-grou*n*de,
Schulde ȝiue· myn herte a wou*n*de ;
In more wo· þen I· was bounde
Neuer*e* buirde· haþ born· :

[1] MS. *ben oyled.*

XXX.

At the crucifixion the dead did wake, the day turned to dun night, the mirk moon made mourning, the light leapt out of the sun, the temple walls did shiver and shake. The veils in the temple spun in two. O Cross, why wouldst thou not crack when righteous blood ran down thee, and when kin lost kin? Thou didst stand stiff as a mast when life departed.

ÞE dede· worþily· gan wake,
Þe dai t*ur*ned· to nihtes donne,
Þe Merke Mone· gan Mournyng make,
Þe lyht out leop· of þe sonne,
Þe temple walles· gan chiu*er*e· *and* schake,
Veiles i*n* þe te*m*ple· a-two þei sponne :
Cros· whi noldestou not crake,
Whon rihtful blod· on þe was ronne,
And kuyndes· losten heore kende ! :
Whon my fruit· on þe was fast,
Cros· whi weore þou not a-gast ?
Þow stod stif· as eny mast,
Whon lyf· left vp his ende· :

XXXI.

St. Denis said that the whole world went then to wreck. He saw the planets lose their brightness.

WHon þat Prince· of Paradys
Bledde· boþe brest· and bak :
An heþene clerk· was seint Denys,
He seide· þis world· wente al to wrak,
He sauȝ þe planetes passen· out of her*e* p*r*is,
Þe brihte sonne· gan waxen blak ;
Þe Clerk· þ*at* was so wonderly wys
Wonder wordes· þer he spak,

St. Denis said the day of doom draws to an end.

Denys· þis grete Clerk seide !
Þe day of doom· draweþ to an ende,

Al vr kuyndes· haþ lost vr kende ;
Til God þat dyed· for vch a kuynde
For Monnes kuynde deyde· :

All things did act against their nature while Christ was dying for all mankind.

XXXII.

Foules fellen· out of heore fliht,
Beestes gan Belwe· in eueri binne :
Cros· whon Crist· on þe was cliht,
Whi noldestou not· of mournyng minne ?
Þe Cros seide· ladi briht,
I· bar ones þi fruit· for monnes sinne,
More to amende· monnes riht
Þen for eny weolþe· þat I· gan winne ;
Wiþ blod· God bouȝte his broþer !
Whon Adam· Godes biddyng brak ;
He bot a bite· þat made vs blak,
Til fruit weore tied· on treo wiþ tak·,
O· fruit· for anoþer· :

Fowls fell out of their flight, beasts did bellow in their bins. O Cross, when Christ was fastened on thee, why didst thou not give way to grief? The Cross thus replies: "I did bear thy fruit for man's sins, more to amend man's right than to gain any wealth. Adam's biting a bit of apple made us all black, until a fruit was tied with tack on tree.

XXXIII.

Sin Cristes Cros· þat kepeþ ȝifte
Graunted· of þe fadres graunt,
I· was loked· I· schulde vp-lifte
Godes sone· and maydenes faunt,
No Mon hedde· scheld of schrifte ;
Þe deuel stod lyk· A lyon raumpaunt,
Mony folk· In-to helle he clihte,
Til þe crosses dunt· ȝaf him a daunt ;
Mi dedes are bounden· and booked !
Alle þe werkes· þat I· haue wrouht
Weore founden· in þe Faderes· fore-þouht,
Þerfore ladi· lakkeþ me nouht,
I· dude· as me was looked :

I was ordained to uplift God's Son, else there would be no shield against the devil.

The devil stood like a *lion rampant*, and many folk he carried off to hell, until the Cross's dint gave him a check.

XXXIV.

Through blood and water Christendom was wrought.

Þorw Blod· *and* Wat*ur*· cristendam was wrouht,
Holy writ· witnesseþ hit wel,
And in wille· of soþfast þouht,

And a man may be baptized in Christ's blood by virtue of true belief.

A Mon mai· be cristened skil;
Þat blod· þat us alle bouht
Digne cristenyng· gan vs del;
At cristenyng· crist for-ȝat vs nouht,
His blessede blod· whon we gan fel:
Maiden· Moder· and Wyue!

Christened we were in red blood when Christ bled on the Cross of Cypress and Olive.

Þi fruit haþ ȝiuen vs baptem,
Cristened we weore· In Red rem,
Whon his bodi bledde· on þe Beem,
Of Cipresse. and Olyue· :

XXXV.

Jesus said to Nicodemus that we must be born again, first in the flesh, next in the font.

AS Ihe*s*u seide· to Nichodem*us*
"But a Barn· be twyȝes born,
Whon dom*us*-day· schal blowen his bem*us*,
He may elles liggen· loddere for-lorn,
Furst of a wombe·, þer reuþe rem*us*,
Siþþe in a font·, þ*er* synne awey is schorn":
I· was cros· to monnes quem*us*,

[fol. 316 *b*, col. 3.]

I· bar þe fruit· þow bar bi-forn,
For þi beryng· Al-one!

Had I not borne Christ, mankind would have been left in a forlorn lodge, there to grunt and groan.

But ȝif I· hedde· I·-boren hi*m* eft,
From riche reste· mon hedde beo-reft
In a loren logge· I·-left·,
Ay· to grunte· and grone· :

XXXVI.

Thou art heaven's queen, thy

Þou art I·-Crouned· heuene quene,
Þorw þe burþe· þat þou beere,

Þi garlond is al· of graces grene,
Helle Emperesse· in heuene Empere:
464 I· am a Relyk· þat shineþ shene,
Men wolde wite· wher þat I· were,
At þe parlement· wol I· bene,
On domes-day· prestly a-pere;
468 Whon Ihesu schal seye· riht þere!
"Trewely· vppon þe Roode tre
Mon· I dyede for þe;
Mon what hastou· don for me·
472 To beon· my frendly feere·?"

garland is of green graces, and thou art even empress of hell. I am a relick that shines clear, and at the parliament to be held on Doomsday men shall see me appear. Then shall Jesus say: Man, I died for thee on the Cross; what hast thou done for me to be worthy of my friendly fellowship?

XXXVII.

At þe *parlement*· shul puiten vp pleynyng,
Hou Maydenes fruit· on me gan sterue,
Spere· *and* spounge· and sharp nayling,
476 Þorw þe harde hat· þe heued shal kerue,
Shul preie· to þat rihtful kyng:
Vche mon schal haue· as þei a serue,
Rihtful schul ryse· to riche restyng,
480 Truyt· and tripet· to helle shal sterue:
Mayden Meoke and Mylde:
God haþ taken in þe· his fleschly trene
I· bar þi fruit· leoþi and lene;
484 Hit is riht þe Roode· helpe to a-rene
Wreeches· þat wraþþe þi chylde·:

At that parliament complaint shall uprise.

Each shall have as they deserve that day. The righteous shall ascend to a rich resting-place. The wicked shall die in hell. I bore thy fruit, and it is right that I should help to arraign the wicked that injured thy child."

XXXVIII.

ÞE queen a-cordet· wiþ þe cros
And a-ȝeyn him spak· no more speche;
488 Þe queen ȝaf· þe Cros a cos,
Þe ladi of loue· loue gan seche,
Þeiȝ hire fruit· on him were· diȝt to dros,
Whon rendyng ropus· gan him reche:

The queen agreed with the Cross, and gave it a kiss.

She even be an to love the Cross.

Christ's Cross has kept us from loss, So does Mary's prayers and God our leech. The queen bore fruit first, and the Cross afterwards, to [d]eliver us from hell.

Cristes cros· haþ kept vs from los,
Maries preyers· And God vr leche,
Þe qween· and þe Cros· a corde:
Þe qween bar furst· þe cros afturward,
To feeche folk· from helleward,
On holy stayers· to steyen vpward
And regne· wiþ God vr lorde·:

XXXIX.

The Clerk that made this allegory of Mary's woe for our instruction was a witness of Christ's passion. But the Cross is a cold creature, deaf and dumb, though it has been here, metaphorically, endowed with life. None ever heard Christ's Cross speak, nor did our Lady lay any blame upon it.

ÞE Clerk· þat fourmed· þis figour
Of Maries wo· to wite som,
He saih him-self· þat harde stour,
Whon godes Armus· weore rent aroum;
Þe Cros is a cold· Creatour,
And euere ȝit haþ ben· def· and dom,
Þeiȝ þis tale beo florisshed· *with* faire flour,
I· preue hit· on Apocrafum;
For witnesse· was neuer foundet!
Þat neuere cristes cros spak,
Oure ladi leide· on him no lak,
Bot to pulte· þe deuel a-bak,
We speke· hou crist was woundet·:

XL.

In fleshly weed God did him hide. Of gentle maid was he born to bleed.

IN Flesshly wede
God gan him hede,
Of Mylde May
Was bore to blede,
As Cristes Crede
Soþly wol say;

[O]n a stock-like steed He rode, we read, in red array.

On a stokky stede
He Rod· we Rede,
In Red Array;

From devil's dread may

From deueles drede

Þat Duyk vs lede,
At domes-day :
Whon peple· schal parte· and pace ?
To heuene halle· or to helle woode,
Cristes cros· and cristes blode
And Marie preiers·, þat ben ful goode,
Grant vs þe lyf· of grace· Amen.

that duke lead us upon Doomsday.

When people shall part to heaven or to hell, may Christ's Cross and Mary's prayers obtain for us the life of grace.

Explicit disputacio inter Mariam
et Crucem. Secundum Apocrafum.

IX.

[* Douce MS. 126, fol. 90 b.]

[WITH AN *O* AND AN *I**.]

I.

God came into this world, and died for the love of man.

Godys sone þat was so fre,
  In-to þis world he cam,
And let hym naylyn vp-on a tre,
  Al for þe loue of man;
His fayre blod þat was so fre,
  Out of his body it ran,
A dwelful syȝte it was to se;
  His body heng blak *and* wan,
  Wiþ an O *and* an I.

His body hung black and wan on the Cross.

II.

The crown of thorns pierced his head.

To a pillar he was bound.

In his bitter passion he ever thought of man.

His coroune was mad of þorn
  And prikkede in-to his panne,
Boþe by hynde *and* a forn;
  To a piler y-bowndyn
Ihesu was swiþe sore,
  And suffrede many a wownde
Þat scharp *and* betere wore.
  He hadde vs euere in mynde,
In al his harde þrowe,
  And we ben so vnkynde,
We nelyn hym nat yknowe,
  Wiþ an O *and* an I.

III.

But-ȝif we loue hym trew*e*,
Hour*e* peynys ben in helle,
ȝarkyd euer*e* newe;
Who so wele loue trewe
Byhold ihesu on þe croys,
How he heng pale of hewe,
And cryde wiþ mylde voys.
Me þristiþ he gan to kalle,
Þe iewis herdyn þys,
Eysel meynt wiþ galle
Þey bedyn hym y-wys.
With an O *and* an I.

Love Christ, and look to the Cross,

and see how he cried for drink.

The Jews gave him vinegar and gall.

IV.

His þrist was to seyȝe
For loue of manys soule,
Hym longede for to deyȝe;
Who so be proud in herte
Þynk on god al-myȝt
And on his wow*n*dys smerte,
How rewly he was a-dyȝt;
Godys sone in trone,
Þat heyȝest is of myȝt,
Tok batayle a-lone
For oure loue to fyȝt,
With an O *and* an I.

Jesus longed to die.

For love of us he did battle alone.

V.

Þe batayle was so stronge,
At many a betyr wownde.
Þe ryche blod out spronge:
Trewe turtyl corounyd on hylle,
Þat heyȝest art of kynde,
Þy loue chaungyþ my wille.

In this battle the blood flowed out.

I will forsake the devil, and [fol. 91.] serve the gracious lady St. Mary.

Whan þou comyst in my mynde;
  Þe fend I forsake anon,
For on lady so hende;
  To seruyn þe lady þan wil I gon,
For ȝhe is of my kende,
  With an O And an I.

VI.

I am one of those whom thy sorrow has redeemed.

Ich am on of þo
  Þat þy sone bouȝte dere,
He schal me nat for-go.

A M E N.

X.

[WITH AN *O* FOR AN *I* *.]

[* Douce MS. 128, fol. 258.]

To thee who suffered for holy Church, I pray for joy.

As þou for holy churche ri3t
Bare þe blody face,
To þe y praye, boþe day *and* ny3t,
Of ioye sende me a space.
Wiþ an O. for *and* an I. a space for to a-byde,
Thu bere myn arnde to þat lord. þat bare þe blody syde.

Jesus, to thee I make my moan.

¶ Ihesu kyng in trone,
Lord in magesté
To þe y make my mone
Wiþ herte good and fre.

I have no friends, and I am very sorrowful.

Frendes haue y none
That wolde me knowe ne se,
My wonynge ys allone,
Lord wel wo ys me!
Wiþ an O. *and* an I. My wonynge is wel wykke,
Frendes haue y fewe, My fomen walkeþ þykke.

I have few friends, but many foes.

[* From Caxton's Golden Legend, third edition[1], 1493, fol. Cxxxi. col. 1.]

THE INVENTION OF THE HOLY CROSS*.

Of thynuencion of the holy crosse *and* first of this word Inuencion /

The holy Cross was found by Seth and others.

[* fol. Cxxxi. col. 2.]

THe Inuencion of the holy crosse is sayd by cause that this daye the holy crosse was founden· for tofore it was founden of seth in paradyse * terrestre / Lyke as it shall be sayde here-after : and also it was founden of salamon in the monte of lybane and of the quene of saba / in the temple of salamon And of the Iewes in the water of pyscyne· And on this daye it was founden of Helayne in the mounte of caluarye /

Time of the finding of the Cross.

The Gospel of Nichodemus tells how Seth went to Paradise for the oil of mercy.

[* fol. Cxxxi *b*, col. 1.]

THe holy Crosse was founden two hondred yere after the resurrexcion of our lord· It is redde in the gospell of nychodemus / that whan Adam wexed seek : Seth his sone wente to the yate of paradyse terrestre for to gete the oyle of mercy for to enoynte wyth alle his faders body : Thenne appyered to hym saint mychell thaungell and said to hym / traueyle not the in vayne / for this oyle. for thou mayst not haue it tyll fiue thousand and fyue hondred yere ben passed / how be it that fro Adam vnto the passyon of our lord were but fyue M *and* *xxxiij yere / In another place it is redde that the aungell broughte hym a braunche. *and* commaunded hym to plante it in the mounte of lybanye. Yet fynde we in another place : that he gaaf to hym of the tree that adam

[1] The first edition (1483) is in the British Museum, but was overlooked till this piece and the next were in type.

ete of And sayd to hym that whan þat bare fruyte he shold be guarysshed and all hool / Whan seth came agayn, he founde his fader deed and planted this tree vpon his graue / And it endured there vnto the tyme of salamon *and* by cause he sawe that it was fayre he dyde doo hewe it doun and sette it in his hows named saltus / *and* whan the quene of saba came to vysyte Salamon / She worshypped this tree by cause she sayde the sauyour of all the world shold be hanged theron / by whom the royame of the Iewes shall be defaced and seace: Salamon for this cause made it to be taken vp and doluen depe in the grounde, Now it happed after that they of Iherusalem: dyde doo make a grete pyte for a pyscyne: where as the mynysters of the temple shold wesshe theyr bestes þat they sholde sacrefyse / and there founde this tree / *and* this pyscyne hadde suche vertue that the aungels descended *and* meuyd the water / And the fyrst seek man that descendyd in to the water after the meuynge / was made hool of what someuer sekenesse he was seek of· And whan the tyme approched of the passyon of our lord / thys tree aroos out of the water and floted. aboue the water / And of this pyece off tymbre made the Iewes the crosse of oure lord / Thenne after this hystorye: the crosse by whiche we ben saued. came of the tree by whiche we were dampned / *and* þe water of that pyscyne had not this vertue onely of the aungel: but of the tree / Wyth this tree wherof þe crosse was made there was a tree that wente ouerthwarte· on whyche the armes of our lord were * nayled / And another pyece aboue whiche was the table / wherin the tytle was wryten: *and* another pyece wherin þe sokette or morteys was maade that the body of the crosse stood in: Soo that there were foure manere of trees That is of palme of cypres / of cedre and of olyue / Soo eche of thyse foure pyeces was of one of these trees: This blyssyd crosse was put in the erthe and hid by the space of an C yere and more· But the moder of themperour whiche was named helayne founde it in this manere For constantyn came wyth a grete multytude of barbaryns nyghe vnto the ryuer of the

The holy Cross in time of Solomon

It bestowed miraculous powers upon the pool of Bethsaida.

[* fol. Cxxxi. *b*, col. 2.]

The Cross consisted of four kinds of trees.

The Cross was hidden for more than one hundred years.

dunoc / whiche wold haue goon ouyr for to haue destroyed al the countré And whan constantyn hadde assembled hys hoost / He wente and sette them ageynst that other partye / but assone as he began to passe the ryuer: he was moche aferd / by cause he shold on the morn haue batayle / And in the nyght as he slepte in his bedde: an angel awoke hym· and shewed to hym the sygne of the crosse in heuen and sayd to hym: Beholde on hye on heuen / Thenne sawe he the crosse made of ryght clere lyght / and was wryten there vpon wyth lettres of gold / In this sygne thou shalt ouercome the batayle / Thenne was he alle comforted of this visyon / And on the morne / he put in his banere the crosse: and made it to be born tofore hym and his hoost. and after smo[te] in the hoost of his enemyes: and slewe *and* chaced grete plenté / After this he dyde doo calle the bysshoppes of the ydollis / *and* demaunded them to what god the sygne of the crosse appertcyned: *and* whan the[y] coude not answere somme crysten men þ*at* were there tolde to hym the mysterye of the crosse· and enformed him in the faith of the trynyté. Thenne anone he byleued parfytele in god / *and* dyde do baptyse hym *and after it happed that constantyn his sone remembryd the vyctorye of his fader: Sente to helayne his moder for to fynde the holy crosse Thenne helayn wen[t]e in to Iherusalem / and dyde doo assemble alle the wyse men of the countré: *and* wha*n* they were assembled / they wolde fayne knowe wherfore they were called: Thenne one Iudas sayd to them: I wote wel þ*at* she wyl knowe of vs where the crosse of Ihesu cryst was leyed: but beware you al / that none of you telle hyr / For I wote well thenne shal our lawe be destroyed For zacheus myn olde fader sayd to symon my fader / And my fader sayde to me at his deth: be wel ware: that for noo tourment that ye maye suffre / telle not where the crosse of Ihesu cryst was leyde For after that it shall be founden· the Iewes shall reygne nomore. but the crysten men that worshyppe the crosse shal thenne reygne. And verayly this Ihesus was the sone of god: Thenne demaunded I my fader: whe[r]fore had they hanged

Constantine's vision of the Cross.

By help of the token of the Cross he defeats his enemies.

[* fol. Cxxxii. col. 1.]

Helena goes in search of the Cross.

Judas tells the Jews some particulars relating to the Cross.

hym on the crosse sythen it was knowen that he was the sone of god. Thenne he sayd to me fayre sone I neuer accorded therto: But gaynsayd it alwaye / but the pharysees dyde it by cause he repreuyd theyr vyses / but he aroos on þe thirde daye and his discyples seeyng he ascended in to heuen / Thenne by cause that stephen thy broder bylyued in hym the Iewes stoned hym to deth / Thenne whan Iudas had sayde thyse wordes to hys felawes / they answerd we neuer herde of suche thynges· Neuerthelesse kepe the wel yf the quene demaunde the therof· þat thou saye nothyng to hyr / whan þe quene had called them / and demaunded theym the place where our lord Ihesu cryst had be crucefyed / they wold neuer telle ne ensygne hyr: Thenne commaunded she to brenne them alle / but thenne they doubted *and* * were aferde / *and* delyuerd Iudas to her [*and*] sayd / Lady this man is the sone of a prophete and of a Iust man *and* knoweth ryght wel the lawe / and can telle to you all thynge wat ye shall demaunde hym / Thenne the quene lete all the other go *and* reteyned Iudas wythout moo / Thenne she shewed to hym his lyf and dethe and bad hym chese whiche he wold· Shewe to me sayd she the place named golgata: where our lord was crucefyed by cause, and to the ende that we maye fynde the crosse / Thenne sayd Iudas it is two C yeres passed and more / and I was not thenne yet born / Thenne sayd to him the lady / by hym that was crucefyed. I shal make the perysshe for hungre. yf thou telle not to me the trouthe / Thenne made she hym to be caste in to a drye pytte / *and* there tourmented hym by hungre / and euyll reste. whan he had ben seuen dayes in that pytte / Thenne sayd he yf I myght be drawen out: he shold saye the trouthe / Thenne he was drawen out / and whan he came to the place / anon the erthe moeuyd and a fumme of grete swetenesse was felte in suche wyse that Iudas smote his hondes to-gyder for ioye· and said in trouthe Ihesu cryst thou art the sauyour of the world / It was so that Adryan the Emperour had do make in the same place where the crosse laye a temple of a goddesse by cause that all they that came in that place

The Jews would not tell Helena where the Cross was to be found.

[* fol. CXXXii. col. 2.]

Helena threatens Judas.

Judas at last consents to find the Cross.

shold adore that goddesse But the quene dyde do destroye þe temple / Thenne Iudas made hym redy and began to dygge / And whan he came to xx paas depe / he founde thre crosses and brought them to the quene / And by cause he knewe not whiche was the crosse of our lord he leyed them in the mydle of þe cyté: *and* abode the demonstraunce of god: *and* aboute the houre of none / there was the corps of a yonge man brought to be bu*ryed / Iudas reteyned þe byere *and* layed vpon it one of the crosses / and after the second. *and* whan he layed on it the thyrde / anone the body that was deed came agayn to lyf / Thenne cryed the deuyll in the eyre. Iudas what hast thou don: thou hast doon the contrarye that thother Iudas dyd / For by hym I haue wonne many sowles / *and* by the I shall lose many by hym I reyned on the people / and by the I haue loste my royame / Neuerthelesse I shall yelde to the this bountee For I shal sende one that shal punysshe the / and that was accomplysshed by Iulyan the appostata: whiche tourmentyd hym afterward[1] wha*n* he was bysshop of Iherusalem: and whan Iudas herde hym he cursed the deuyll and said to him Ihesu cryst dampne the in fyre perdurable / After this Iudas was baptysed *and* was named quyryache / And after was made bysshop of Iherusalem / wha*n* helayn had the crosse of Ihesu crist / and that she had not the nayles / Thenne she sente to þe bysshop quyryache that he sholde go to the place and seeke the nayles / Thenne he dyde dygge in therthe so long that he founde them shynyng as golde. thenne bare he them to the quene / and anone as she sawe them she worshypped them wyth grete reuerence· Thenne gaf saint helayn a parte of the crosse to her sone: And that other parte she lefte in Iherusalem closyd in gold: syluer· and precyous stones / And hyr sone bare the nayles to the emperour: And the Emperour dyde doo sette them in hys brydel [and] in his helme whan he wente to batayle: This rehereeth Eusebe whiche was bisshop of Cezar / how be it that other saye otherwyse: Now it happed that Iulyan the appostata dyde doo slee quyryache þat was bysshop of Iherusalem: by cause he had founden the crosse / For he

[* fol. Cxxxii. *b*, col. 1.]

The true Cross is found.

The devil rails at Judas.

[1] Orig. *afterwrad*.

Judas becomes a Christian and a bishop.

The finding of the nails.

Eusebius relates some of these matters.

hated * it soo moche / that where someuer he founde the crosse he dyd it to be destroyed for whan he wente in batayle ayenst them of perse he sente and commaunded quyriache to make sacrefyse to thydollis // And whan he wold not doo it he dyde do smyte of his ryghte honde / *and* sayd wyth this honde hast thou wryten many lettres / by whiche thou repellyd moche folke fro doyng sacrefyse to our goddes: Quyryache said thou wood hounde thou hast don to me grete proffyte. For thou hast cut of the honde wyth whiche I haue many tymes wreten to the synagoges that they sholde not byleue in Ihesu cryst: And now sythe I am crysten / thou hast taken fro me that whyche noyed me: Thenne dyde Iulyan do melte leed and cast it in his mouth *and* after dide do bringe a bedde of yron / *and* made quyryache to be layed *and* stratched theron / and after layed vnder brennyng cooles. and threwe therin grees and salte; For to tourmente hym the more / *and* whan quiriache moeuyd not· Iulyan themperour sayd to hym other þou shalt sacrefye our goddes / or thou shalt say at the leest thou art not crysten / and whan he sawe he wold do neuer neyther he dyde doo make a depe pytte ful of serpentes and venemous beestes and caste hym therin / *and* whan he entred· anone the serpentes were all deed / Thenne Iulian put hym in a cawdron full of boylynge oyle: and whan he shold entre in to it he blyssyd it and sayde / Fayr lord tourne this bayne to baptym of martyrdom / Thenne was Iulyan moche angry: *and* commaunded that he shold be ryuen thorugh his herte wyth a swerd and in thys manere he fynysshed his lyf,

The vertu of the crosse is declared to vs by many myracles For it happed on a tyme that one enchauntour hadde dysceiued a notarye: and broughte hym * in to a place: where he had assembled a grete conpanye of deuylles and promysed to him that he wold make him to haue moche rychesses And whan he came there he sawe one persone blacke sittyng on a gret chayer: and all aboute hym all full of horryble peple *and* blacke whiche had speres *and* swerdes: Thenne demaunded this grete deuyll of the enchauntour who was that clerke then

* f. l. Caxton, c. l. 2.

Julian the Apostate.

He is stretched upon burning coals.

He is tormented, cast into a pit full of serpents.

At last he is put to death.

Many miracles of the Cross.

* f. l. Caxton, col. 1.

chauntour sayd to him / Syre he is oures / thenne said the deuyll to him: yf thou wylt worshyp me and be my seruaunte / and renye Ihesu cryst: thou shalt sitte on my right side The clerke anone blessid hym wyth the signe of the crosse· and sayd that he was the seruaunt of Ihesu cryst his sauyour And anone as he had made the crosse / þe grete multytude of deuylles vanyshed awaye /

A company of devils were once put to flight by the sign of the Cross.

¶ It happed that this notari after this on a tyme entred wyth his lorde in to the chirche of saint sophye / and kneled downe on his knees tofore thimage of the crucifyxe: the whiche crucifyxe as it semed loked moche openly *and* sharply vpon him· Thenne his lorde made him to goo aparte on a nother side: and alway the crucifyxe torned his eyen towarde hym. Thenne he made him goo on the lefte syde / *and* yet the crucifyxe loked on hym Thenne was the lorde moche amerueylled / and charged hym *and* commaunded him that he sholde telle him wherof he had soo deserued that the crucifixe soo behelde and loked on him / Thenne sayd the notarye that he cowde not remembre hym of noo good thynge that he had done / sauf that on a tyme he wolde not renye ne forsake the crucifyxe tofore the deuyll / Thenne lete vs so blysse vs wyth the sygne of the blessid crosse that we may therby be kepte fro the power of our goostly *and* dedely enmye the deuyll / And by the merites of the gloryous passion that our sauyoure * Ihesu cryst suffred on the crosse after this lyf we maye come to euerlastyng lyf in heuen / A M E N.

How the Cross turned its eyes upon "a notary."

The sign of the Cross will enable us to keep out of the power of the devil.

[* fol. Cxxxiii, col. 2.]

XII.

THE EXALTATION OF THE CROSS*.

[* Caxton's Golden Legend, third ed. 1493, fol. CClxvii. *b*, col. 1.]

Here foloweth thexaltac*i*on of the holy Crosse /

THe exaltacion of the holy Crosse is sayd· by cause that on this day þe holy crosse *and* fayth were gretly enhaunced / and it is to be vnderstonde that tofore the passion of our lorde Ihe*s*u crist. þe tree of the crosse was[1] a tre of fylthe / for þe crosses were made of vile trees : *and* of trees without fruyt : for all that was planted on the mou*n*t of caluarie bare no frute It was a fowl place / for it was the place of þe torme*n*t of theuis : It was derk for it was in a derke place *and* wythout bewté / It was the tree of deth / for men weren * put there to deth. It was also the tree of ste*n*che / for it was planted amo*n*ge the caroynes / *and* after the passio*n* the crosse was moche enhau*n*ced / for the vylté was transported in to precyosité : Of the whiche the blessyd saynt andrew saith / O precious holy crosse god saue the : His bareynes was torned in to fruyte / as it is sayd in the cantycles / I shall ascende vp in to the palme tree : His ignobylité or vnworthines was torned in to sublymité *and* heyth The crosse þ*a*t was torment of theuis / is now born in the front of the*m*perours / hys derknes is torned in to lyght *and* clernesse wherof crisostom sayth the crosse *and* þe wou*n*des shall be more shinyng than the raies of the sonne at the iugement : his deth is co*n*uerted in to perdurabilyté of lyf / wherof it is sayd in the preface : that frowhens þ*a*t the deth grew / frothens the lyf resourded / and

The Cross a filthy tree.

[1] Orig. *wan*.

[* fol. CClxvii. *b*, col. 2.]

After the passion it was no longer a vile tree.

The Cross is brighter than the sun's rays.

the stenche is torned in to swetnesse canticorum j / This exaltacion of the holy crosse is solempnysed *and* halowed solempnly of the chirche: for the fayth is in it moche enhaunced: for the yere of our lorde vj C *and* xv our lorde suffryd his peple to be moche tormented by the cruelté of the paynems. And cosdroe kyng of perceens subdued to his empyre all the reames of the worlde / and he cam in to iherusalem and was aferde and adredde of the sepulcre of our lorde: And retourned: But he bare with him the parte of the holy crosse / that saynte Helene hadde lefte there:

How "Cosdroe" took away from Jerusalem a piece of the Cross.

Of the Impiety of "Cosdroe."

And thenne he wolde be worshypped of al the peple as a god. And dyde doo make a tour of golde and syluer / wherein precyous stones shone· And made there in the ymages of the sonne. and of the mone: and of the sterres And made that by subtyll conduytes water to be hydde. And to come downe in maner of Rayne.

And atte the laste stage. he made horses to drawe charyottes rounde *aboute lyke as they had meuyd the tour and made it to seme as it had thondred / and delyuerde his reame to his sone / and thus this cursid man abode in the temple *and* dyde doo set the crosse of our lorde by him *and* commaunded that he sholde be callyd god of all the people / And as it is rede in libro de mit[r]ali officio / The sayd cosdroe resident in his trone as a fader / set the tree of the crosse on his right side in stede of þe sone / *and* a cocke on his lyfte side in stede of the holy goost / and commaunded that he sholde be called fader / And thenne heracle the emperour assembled a grete oost / and came for to fyghte wyth the sone of cosdroe by the ryuer of danubye / And thenne it pleysed to eyther prynce: that eche of theym sholde fyghte one agaynst that other vpon the brydge / *and* he that sholde be vaynquysh *and* ouercome: his aduersarye sholde be prynce of thempyre wythout hurtyng eyther of bothe oostes / *and* soo it was ordeinyd *and* sworn· And who someuer sholde helpe his prynce. sholde haue forthwyth his legges *and* armes cut of: *and* to be plonged. *and* cast in to the ryuer: And thenne heracle commaunded him all to god / *and* to the

[* fol. CClxviii. col. 1.]

Of the contest between "Cosdroe" and "Heracle."

holy crosse / wyth all the deuocyon that he myghte: and thenne they foughte longe / and at the last our lorde gaaf the victorye to heracle: *and* subdued him to his empyre. The oost that was contrary and al the peple of cosdroe obeyed theym to the crysten fayth / and receyued the holy baptesme And cosdroe knew not thende of þe bataylle / For he was adoured *and* worshyped of all the peple as a god / soo that no man durst not saye nay to him And thenne heracle came to him / and fonde him sittyng in his siege of golde / And sayd to hym / For as moche as after the manere thou hast honoured the tree of the crosse / Yf thou wylt receyue baptim / and the fayth of Ihesu cryste / I shall gete it to the *and yet shall thou holde thyne trone[1] and reame wyth lytyll hostages / And I shal lete the haue thy lyfe / and yf thou wylte not· I shall slee the wyth my swerde / and shall smyte of thyne hede And whan he wolde not acorde therto: he dyde anone doo smyte of his hede / And commaunded that he sholde be beried: by cause he had be a kynge: And he founde wyth him one his sone of the age of ten yeres / whom he dyde doo baptyse. and lyfte him fro the fonte. And left to hym the reame of his fader. and thenne dyde doo breke that toure[2] / And gaaf the siluer to theym of hys oost / And gaaf the golde and precyous stones for to repaire the chirches that the tyraunt had destroyed / And took the holy crosse and broughte it agayne to Iherusalem And as he descended fro the mount of oliuete / and wolde haue entred by the gate: by whiche our sauyour went to his passion on horsbacke aourned as a kynge· sodenly the stones of the yates de[s]cended: and Ioyned theym togyder in the yate lyke a walle / and all the peple were abasshed / And thenne the angell of oure lorde appered vpon the gate holdyng the signe of[3] the crosse in his honde / And sayd: whan the kyng of heuen went to his passion by this gate / he was not arayed lyke a kyng / ne on horsback But came humbly vpon an asse / In shewyng the example of humylyté whyche he lefte to theym that honour hym / And whan this was said he departed and vanysshyd away / Thenne the emperour toke of his hosen, and

"Heracle" conquers "Cosdroe's" son.

*fo. fol. CClxviii. col. 2.

[1] Orig. *crone*

"Cosdroe" is slain.

[2] Orig. *toure*

"Heracle" carries away the piece of the Cross to Jerusalem.

[3] Orig. repeats *the signe of*

Barefoot and nearly naked he enters Jerusalem.

shone himself in wepynge. And despoylled hym of alle hys clothes in to his sherte /

[1] Orig. *toook*.

And took[1] the crosse of our lorde: and bare it moche humbly vnto the gate /

[2] Orig. *and And*. [* fol. CClxviii, *b*, col. 1.]

And anone the hardenesse of the stones felte the celestyall commaundement / and[2] * remeuyd anone. and opened *and* gaue entree vnto theym that entred Thenne the swete odour that was felte that daye whan the holy crosse was taken fro the toure of Cosdroe / and was brought aye*n* to Iherusalem fro soo ferre cou*n*tree / and soo grete space of londe retorned in to iherusalem in that moment / and replenysshyd it wyth all swetnes: Then*ne* the riht deuoute kyng began to say the praysynges of the crosse in this wyse O crux splen*d*idior / & c: O crosse more shinyng than all the steeres / honoured of the worlde rihte holy / and moost amyable to all theym whiche oonly were worthy to bere[3] the raunson of the worlde: Swete tree / Swete nayles / Swete yron: swete spere beryng the swete burdens / Saue thou this presente company. that is this day assemblyd in thy lawde *and* praysinges: And thus was the precious tree of the crosse reestablyshid in his place and thau*n*cyent myracles renewid For a dede man was reised to lyf / And iiij men taken wyth the palsei were cured *and* helid. Ten lepers were made clene: and xv blynde men receyuid theyr sight ayen / Deuylles were put out of men / and moche peple *and* many were delyuerde of dyuerse siknesses *and* maladyes. Thenne themperour dyde doo repayre the chirches. and gaaf to them grete yeftes: and after retorned home to his empyre: And it is sayd in the cronycles that this was done other while: For thei sawe that whan Cosdroe had taken many reames. he took Iherusalem / And zacharye the patriake. and bare awaye the tree of the crosse. And as heracle wolde make peas wyth him: the kyng cosdroe sware a grete othe: that he wolde neuer make peas wyth crysten me*n* *and* romayns yf they renyed not him that was crucifyed / and adoured the sone / And thenne heracle: whiche was armed: wyth faith bro*ughte his oost ayenst him: and destroyed *and* wasted the perciens wyth many

[3] Orig *here*.

Miracles were wrought by virtue of the Cross.

Other accounts are given of Heraclius and his opponent.

[* fol. CClxviii, *b*, col. 2.]

batailes that he made to theym / and made costdroe to flee vnto the cyté of thelyfonte / And at the last cosdroe had the flyxe in his bely / and wolde therfore crowne hys sone kyng / whiche was named mendasa And whan syroys his eldest sone herde herof / he made alyaunce wyth heracle / *and* pursued his fader wyth his noble peple *and* set him in bondes : and susteynid hym wyth brede of trybulacion *and* wyth water of anguysh And at the last he made to shote arowes at him bi cause he wolde not byleue in god / *and* soo deyed : And after this thyng he sent to heracle the patryarke. the tree of the crosse : *and* all the prysoneres / And heracle bare in to Iherusalem the precyous tree of the crosse And thus it is rede in many cronycles also. Syble sayth thus of the tree of the crosse / that the blessyd tree of the crosse was thre tymes wyth the paynems· as it is sayd in thystorye tripertyte : O thryes blessid tree / on whiche god was stratched / This perauenture is sayd for the lyf of nature / of grace : and of glory : whiche came of the crosse / At constantynople a Iewe entryd in to the chirche of saynt sophie / and considered that he was there alone / and saw an ymage of Ihesu cryst / And took his swerde *and* smote thymage in the throte / *and* anone the blood guysshid oute *and* sprange in the face *and* on the hede of the Iewe / And he thenne was aferde *and* took thimage / and cast it in to a pytte / And anone fledde away : And it happed that a crysten man met him and saw him all blody And sayd to him / fro whens comest thou thou hast slayne some man / and he sayd I haue not : The crysten man sayd verely thou hast com*m*ysed some omycide / For thou art all besprongе wyth the blood / *and* the Iew sayd. verely the god of the cryste*n* * men is grete and the fayth of hym is ferme and approued in all thynges / I haue smyten noo man but I haue smyten thymage of Ihesu Cryst· and anone yssued blood of his throte / And thenne the Iewe brought the crysten man to þ^e pytte / And there drewe out that hooly ymage· And yet is sene on this daye the wounde in the throte of thymage / And anon the Iewe bycame a good crysten man and was baptysed. In syrye in the Cyté of baruth

Some say that "Cosdroe" was shot to death with arrows.

The story of the Jew who smote an image of Jesus Christ.

[* fol. CClxix. col. 1.]

How the Jew became a Christian.

ther was a crysten man whiche had hyred an hous: for a yere / *and* he hadde sette thymage of the crucyfyxe by his bedde / to whiche he made dayely his prayers / and sayd his deuocion / *and* at the yeres ende he remeued and tooke an other hous. and forgate and lefte thymage behynde hym / And it happed that a Iewe hyred that same hous / And on a daye he hadde another Iewe one of his neyghbours to dyner: and as they were at mete / It happed hym that was boden in lokyng on the walle to espye this ymage / whiche was fyxed to the walle *and* began to grynne at it for despyte / And agaynst hym / that badde[1] hym / and also thretened and menaced hym: by cause he durst it kepe in his hous thymage of Ihesu of nazareth: and that other Iewe sware as moche as he myght. that he neuer hadde sene it / ne knewe not that it was there / And thenne the Iewe fayned as he hadde ben peased / and after went straite to the prynce of the Iewes / and accused that Iewe of that whiche he hadde sene in his hous: Thenne the Iewes assembleden and came to the hous of hym: And sawe thymage of Ihesu cryst / and they toke that Iewe and bete hym / And dyd to hym many Iniuryes / And caste hym out half dede of theyr synagoge / *and* anone they defowled thymage wyth theyr feet / and renewed in it all the tour*mentes of the passyon of our lord / and whan they perced his syde wyth the spere / blood and water yssued habun-dauntly in soo moche that they fylled a vessell / whiche they set ther vnder. And thenne the Iewes were abasshed and bare this blood in to theyr synagoge / and all the seke men and malades that ware enointed ther wyth / were anone guarysshed *and* made hooll: And thenne the Iewes told and recounted alle this thinge: by ordre to the Bysshop of the countree: and alle they wyth one wylle receyued baptyme in the fayth of Ihesu cryst / and the Bysshop put this blood in ampulles of crystalle and of glas for to be kepte / And thenne he called the crysten man that had lefte it in his hous / and enquyred of him who hadde made soo fayre an ymage / *and* he sayd that nychomedus hadde made it / And whan he deyde / he lefte it to gamalyell: and Gamaliel to zachee and zachee to Iaques / and Iaques to symon / And

How a Jew grinned at the Cross which he saw in a friend's house.

The Jew is beaten for keeping a cross in his house.

The cross was shamefully used.

[* fol. CClxix. col. 2.]

Blood came forth from the crucifix.

The Jews believed and were baptized.

[1] Orig. *hadde*.

had ben thus In Iherusalem vnto the destruction of the Cyté. And fro thens hit was born in to the Royame of agryppe of Crysten men / And fro thens it was brought agayn in to the countree. and it was lefte to me by my parentes by ryghtfull herytage / and this was done in the yere of our lord seuen hondred and l.

Migrations of the image.

And thenne all the Iewes halowed theyr synagogues in to the chyrches and therof cometh the custome that Chyrches ben halowed: For to-fore that tyme the aultres were but halowed only / and for this myracle the chyrche hath ordeyned / that the fyfte kalendas of decembre / Or as[1] it is redde in an other place: the fyfte ydus of Nouembre shold be the memorye of the passyon of our lord / wherfore at rome the chyrche is halowed in thonore of our sauyour / where as is kepte an ampulle wyth the same blood: *and* there a *solempne feste is kepte and done / *and* there is proued þe ryght grete vertu of the crosse vnto the paynems and to the mysbyleued men in all thynges / And saint gregory recordeth in the thyrde booke of his dyalogues: that whan andrewe bisshop of the Cyté of fundane suffred an hooly nonne to dwelle[2] wyth hym / the fende thenemy began Temprynte in his herte the beaulté of her / in suche wyse / that he thoughte in his bedde wycked *and* cursyd thynges / And on a daye a Iewe came to rome and whan he sawe that the daye fayled and myght fynde no lodgynge. he wente that nyght / and abode in the Temple of appollin / *and* by cause he doubted of the sacrylege of the place / how bee it that he hadde no fayth in the Crosse· yet he markyth *and* garnysshed hym wyth the sygne of þe crosse: thenne at mydnight whan he awoke / he sawe a companye of euyll spyrytes: whiche wente to-fore one Lyke as he hadde somme auctoryté of puyssaunce aboue thother by subiection / and thenne he sawe hym sytte in the middes a-monge the other: and began to enquyre the causes and dedes of eueryche of thyse euylle spyrytes: whiche obeyed hym / and he wold knowe what euylle eueryche hadde do / But gregory passyth the maner of this vysyon / By cause of shortnes· But we fynde semblable

Of the consecration of churches.

[1] Misprinted *at* in orig.

[* fol. CClxix, *b*, col. 1.]

[2] *dwedlle* in orig.

How bishop Andrew was tempted by the devil to give way to the lusts of the flesh.

A Jew in the temple of Apollo sees a company of evil spirits.

in þe lyf of faders / That as a man entryd in a Temple of thydollis / he sawe the deuill syttyng / and all his meyny aboute hym And one of thyse wycke spyrytes came and odoured hym / and he demaunded of hym / Fro whens comest thou and he sayde / I haue ben in suche a prouynce / *and* haue moeued grete warres: and made many trybulacyons and haue shedde moche blood· and am come[1] to telle it to the: and Sathan sayd to hym· in what tyme hast thou done this. and he sayd in thyrty da*yes and sathan sayd: why hast thou bee so longe there aboutes / and sayd to them that stode by hym: goo ye and bete hym / and all to-lasshe hym. Thenne came the seconde and worshypped hym / and sayd Syre I haue ben in the see / And haue moeued grete wyndes and tourmentys and drowned many shyppes / and slain many men / And sathan sayde how longe hast thou ben aboute this / and he saide xxij dayes. *and* sathan sayde hast thou done nomore in this tyme / *and* commaunded þat he shold be beten / *and* the thyrd came *and* said I haue ben in a Cyté and haue meuyd strynes and debate in a weddyng / And haue shed moche blood / *and* haue slayne þe husbond: *and* am come to telle the / and sathan axed / in what tyme hast thou done this: *and* he sayd in x dayes / *and* he sayd hast thou done nomore in that tyme / And commaunded them that were aboute hym to bete hym also: Thenne came the fourth and sayd / I haue ben in the wyldernes xl yere: *and* haue laboured aboute a monke *and* vnnethe at the last I haue throwen *and* made hym to synne of the flessh / *and* whan sathan herde that / he aroos fro his sete / *and* kyssed hym. and toke his crowne of his hede / *and* set it on his hede / and made hym to sytte wyth hym. *and* sayd thou hast done a grete thynge / and hast laboured more than all thother / *and* this maye be the maner of the vysyon: that saint gregory leueth: whan eche had sayd / one sterte vp in the mydle of them all / *and* sayd he had meuyd Andrewe agaynst the name[2] / And had meuyd the fourth parte of his flessh agaynst her in temptacion· *and* therto that yesterday he thought so moche in his minde on her that in the houre of euyn songe he gaf to her

Each devil renders an account of his actions to the chief devil.

[1] *came* in orig.

[* fol. CClxix, *b*, col. 2.]

One says he has caused tempests and shipwrecks.

Another is crowned for causing a monk to commit a sin of the flesh.

One of the fiends tells how he has tempted St. Andrew.

[2] So in first edition, but read *nonne*.

in Iapyng a buffet / *and* sayde pleynly þat she myght here it that he wolde synne wyth her: thenn[e] the mayster commaunded hym that he shold performe þat he had * begonne: *and* for to make hym to synne he shold haue a synguler victory[1] *and* rewarde amonge all the other / *and* thenne commaunded he: that they shold goo loke who that was that laye in the temple. And they wente *and* loked / *and* anone they were ware that he was marked wyth the sygne of the crosse: And they beyng aferd escried *and* sayd / veryly this is an empty vessell. alas he is marked / and wyth this voys all the companye of the wycked spyrytes vanysshed awaye / *and* thenne the Iewe all amoeuyd came to the bysshop: *and* tolde to hym all by ordre what was happed: And whan the bisshop herd this / he wepte strongly. *and* made to voyde all the wymmen out of his hous / and thenne he baptysed the Iewe. Saint gregory rehereeth in his dyalogues that a nonne entred in to a gardyne / and sawe a letuse / and coueyted that: and forgate to make the sygne of the crosse / and bote it glotonessly / and anone fylle doune and was rauysshe of a deuyl / and there cam to her saynt Equycyen / *and* the deuyll began to crye *and* to saye / what haue I doo I satte vpon the letuse / *and* she came and bote me and anon the deuyll yssued oute by the commaundement of the holy man of god: It is redde in thystorye scolastyke / that the paynems had pe[y]nted on a walle the armes of Serapis / and theodosyen dyde do put them out. *and* made to be peynted in the same place the sygne of the crosse / *and* whan the paynems and prestes of thydollis sawe that. anone they dyde them to be baptysed sayenge that it was gyuen theym to vnderstonde of theyr olders that tho armes shold endure, tyll that suche a sygne were made there. in whiche were lyf: And they haue a lettre. of whyche they vse that they calle holy / and had a forme that they sayd it exposed and sygnefyed lyf perdurable /

His master bids him to complete his work.

[* fol. CClxx, col 1.]

[1] Orig. *virtory*.

The devils find the Jew marked with the sign of the Cross, by which they are terrified and put to flight.

How a nun ate a lettuce without making the sign of the Cross, and was ravished by a devil.

XIII.

[* Royal MS. 17 A 27, fol. 72 b.]

THE SYMBOLS OF THE PASSION*.

O vernacule[1], i honoure him *and* the,
Þat þe made þorow his preuité;
[fol. 73.] Þo cloth he set to his face,
Þe prent laft[2] þere[3] þorow his grace,
His moth, his nose, his ine to,
His berd, his here[4] dide al so.
Schilde me for al þat in[5] my liue
I[6] haue singud[7] with wittus fiue,
Namlich with mout of sclaundering,
Fals othus[8] *and* bakbiting,

The Vernicle received the print of Jesus' face.

I have sinned, but, Lord, forgive me through sight of the figure I see before me.

The readings here given are from Additional MS. 11,748.

[1] veronicle. [2] by-left. [3] *omitted.* [4] here. [5] me fro dissece in al. [6] that y. [7] sinwed. [8] othis swore.

XIII.

THE SYMBOLS OF THE PASSION*.

[* Additional MS. 22,029.]

The *ver*nacul—I honowre hym [and the]
þ*a*t the made throwe hys pryuy[té];
The cloth*e* he set ovyr hys face,
4 The prynte he lefte ther, of hys grace,
Hys mowth*e*, hys nose, hys eyn too,
Hys berd, hys here he ded also.
Schyld me, lorde, for þat i*n* myn lyffe
8 That I haue synnyd *with* myn wyttys fyve,
Namelych*e* *with* mowth*e* of stlawndrynge,
Of fals othys and bakbytynge,

And made boste with toung al so
Of si*nn*us þat i haue do;
Lord of heuen, for-ȝeue it me
Þorow syht[1] of þe[2] figur þat i here se.

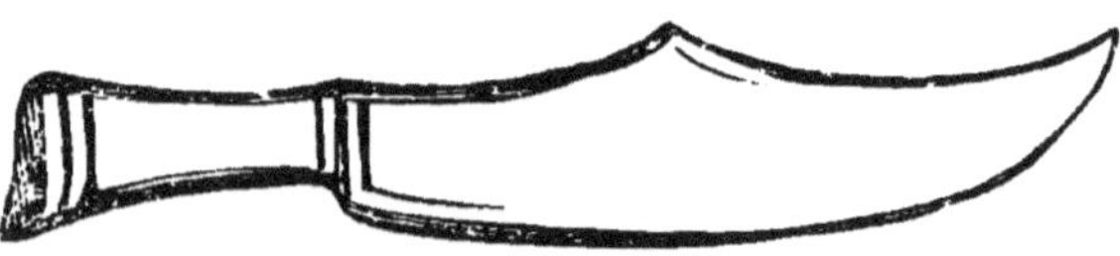

*Cultellus circu*m*sicionis.*

The knife of circumcision destroyed Adam's sin.

Þis[3] knif be-tokeneþ[4] circu*m*sicion,
He distroyet[5] sinne al *and* sum
Of oure formefadur adam,
Were-þorow þow[6] tok kynde of man;
From temptacioun of lecherie
Be[7] my socoure whan i schal diee.

[fol. 73 *b*.] May it succour me from the sin of lechery.

Pellicanus.

The pelican that feeds her young with her blood denotes Christ, who fed us with his blood, and is our father and our food.

Þe pelicane his blod did[8] blede
Þer-with his briddus for to fede,
Þit[9] be-tokenet on[10] þe rode
Oure lord us fede[11] with his blode,
Wen he us bouht out of helle
In ioy *and* blis with hi*m* to dwelle,
And bene our fadur *and* our fode,
And we his childurne meke *and* gode.

[1] vertu. [2] *omitted.* [3] the. [4] tokeneth the. [5] distryed. [6] we. [7] he be. [8] doth. [9] hit. [10] a-pon. [11] fedde.

And makyng boste *with* tonge alsoo
Of many synnys that I haue doo:
Lorde of heuyn, for-ȝeue it me
Throwe v*er*tew of the fygure þ*at* I here se.

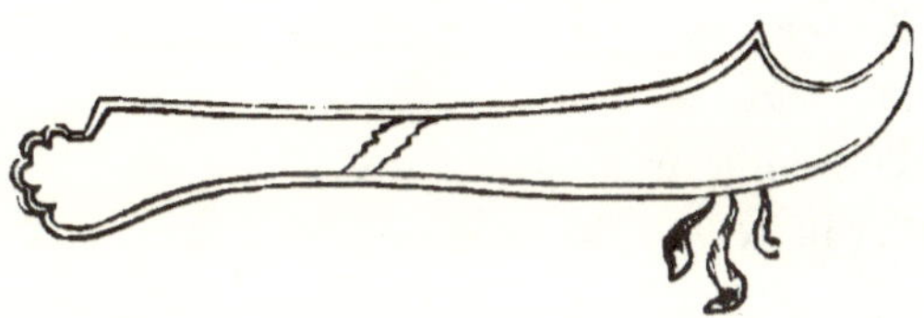

Thys knyffe betoknythe þe ci*r*cu*m*sysy[on],
That dystroyd owre synnys alle *and* su*m*
Of owre formfathyr adam,
Wher-thorowe we toke þe kynde of man.
From temptacyon of lecherye,
Lorde, kepe me tylle that I deye.

The pelycan hys blode dothe blede
Þer-*with* hys byrdys for to fede,
It betoknythe vppe-on the rode
Owre lorde fed vs *with* hys p*recius* blode,
Whan [h]e vs bowt owt of helle
In ioye and blys *with* hym to dwelle,
And be owre fathyr and owre fode,
And we hys chyldyr meke and good.

Triginta denarii.

May the thirty pieces of silver shield us from [fol. 74.] treason and covetousness.

Þe pens also þat iudas tolde,
Þat for[1] iesu crist was solde,
Vs schilde from tresun *and* couetyse,
Þer-in to die in no wise.

Lanterna.

May the lantern keep us from the night's sin.

Þe lantern þat me bar[2] in þe ly3t,
Wen crist was taken in þe ni3t,
Hit lyt[3] me from ni3tus[4] sine,
Þat i neuer be tak[5] þer-inne.

Gladii et fustes.

May the swords and spears keep me from fiends.

Suerdus *and* battus þat þey bere
Iesu crist þer-with[6] to fere—
From findus, lord, þow[7] kepe me
Of hem aferd þat i ne be.

[1] ther-fore. [2] men bare. [3] he kepe [4] dedely. [5] neuer deye. [6] with *omitted.* [7] thay.

The pens also that Iudas tolde,
  Wher-for i*esu* cryste was solde—
Lorde, schylde me from treson and couetyse,
Ther-i*n* that I deye in no wyse.

The lantern *þat* they bare in the lygth*e*,
  Whan cryste was takyn wit*h*-in þo nygth*e*—
Lord, kepe me from nygthys synne,
That I neuyr be take ther-In.

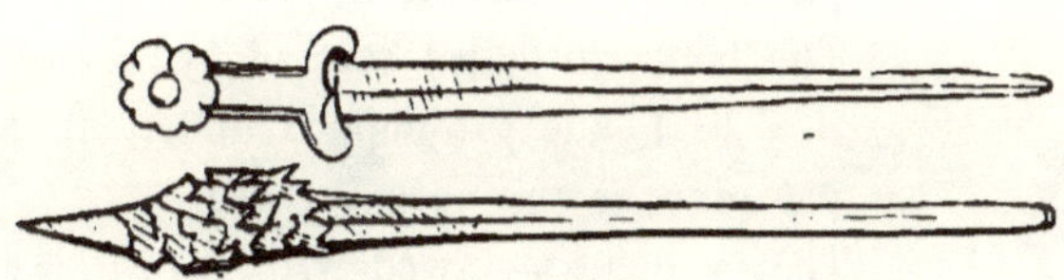

Swerdys and stauys that þei bere
  Ther i*esu* cryste to fere wit*h* there—
From fendys, lorde, kepe thow me,
Of them, lorde, a-ferd that I not be.

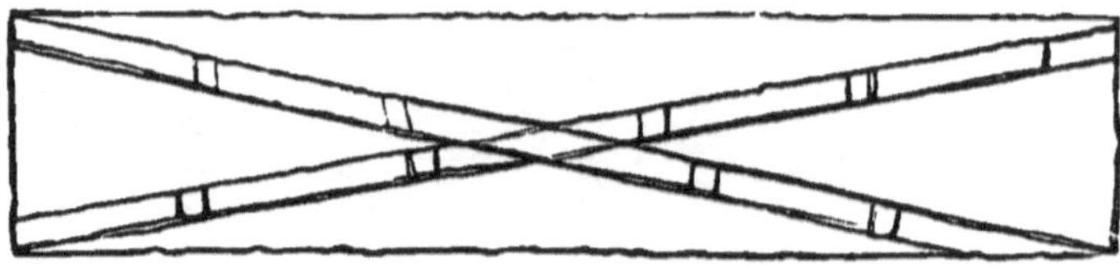

[fol. 74 b.]

The Jews brake Christ's head with a reed. If I wrong any man, may the sin be forgiven me on account of this stroke.

Arundines.

Crist had a stroke with a rede,
Þer-with þe iewes brak his hed[1];
With gud chere *and* milde moode
Alle he tholud[2] *and* stille[3] stode:
Wen i misdo or ani man me,
Hit be for-ȝyf for þat pité.

May the hand that smote thee under the ear be my succour against my sins of hearing.

[*Manus depillans* et *alapans*.
The hond, lord, þat tare of þyn here,
And þe honde þat flapped under þin here—
Þat pine be my socour there
That y haue y-sinwed *with* myn[4] here,
And of alle oþur synne al so
Þat wiþ myn eren haue y herkened to.][5]

[1] Wiþ a reed he hadde a strake,
Ther-with his heued þe iew to-brake.

[2] suffred. [3] stille he. [4] *with* myn *is in a later hand.* [5] From MS. 11,748.

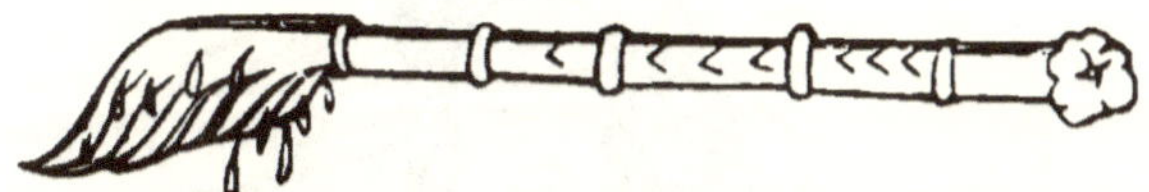

Uythe a zarde he had a stroke,
þer-*with* the iewys hys hede they broke;
With good chere and myld mode,
Alle he suffyrd and stylle he stode.
Whan I mys-do ar ony man do me,
It be for-zeve for that peté.

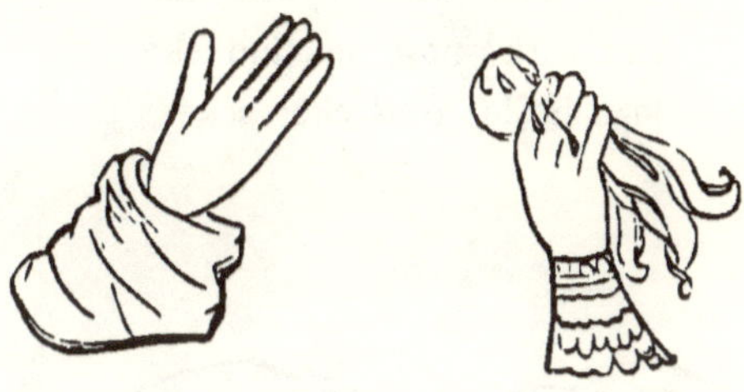

The handys, lorde, þat tare of thyn here,
And þe hande þat clappyd the vndyr þe ere—
For þat peyn, lorde, be myn socowre there
That I haue synnyd *with* pryde of here,
And all*e* othyr synnys also
That *with* erys I haue herkynd to.

The Jews put a cloth before the eyes of Jesus; may it keep me from the vengeance of ignorance, and of other sins that I have done.

Velamen ante oculos.

Þe cloth be-fore þin ine to,
To bobbe[1] þe þey knyt it so,
Hit kepe me from[2] ueniauns
Of childhod *and* of ignorauns,
And of other[3] sinnus also
Þat i haue with my ine do,
And with[4] nose smellud eke,
fol. 75.] Boþe ho[le] *and* eke[5] seke.

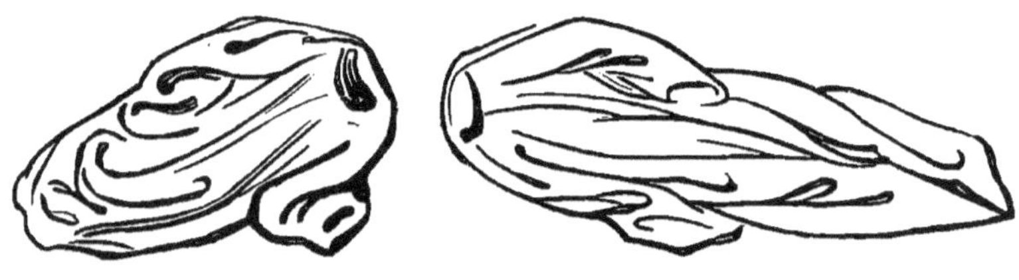

May the seamless white coat be my succour, since I have loved to indulge in soft clothing.

Tunica inconsutilis et uestis purpuria.

Þe whit cote þat hade sem none
And þe purpure þey layd both upon one[6],
Þey be my sokur *and* my helping,
Þat my bodi haþ[7] usud soft cloȝing.

[1] bobby. [2] fro eche. [3] alle. [4] wiþ my. [5] also. [6] laid loot up one.
[7] ther y haue.

The clothe be-forn thyn eyn too,
To bobbyn the they knyt it soo—
Lord, kepe me from vengawns
Of chyldhode and of ignorawns,
And eke synnys also
That I haue sene *with* myn eyn too,
And *with* myn nose smyllyd eke,
Bothe olde and seke.

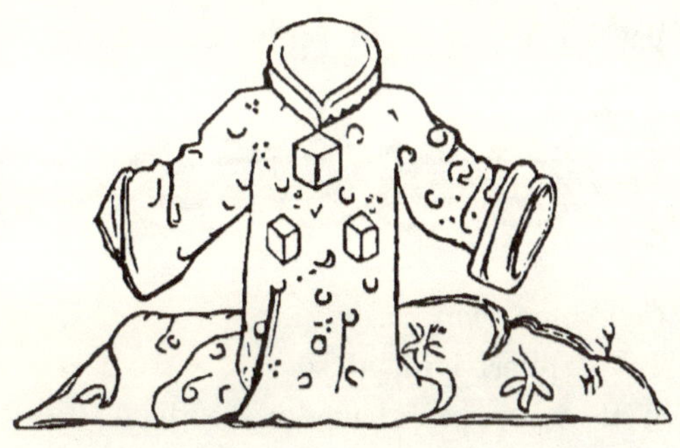

Thyn own cote that had seme non,
The purpylle þat they leyd lotte vppe-on—
Lorde, be myn socowre and myn helppyng
That myn bodye hathe vsyd mys clothyng.

Virge et flagelle.

May the rods with which he was scourged be my help against sloth.

With ȝerdes grete þow were to-dachud,
With scourges smert al to-lachud,
Þat peine me soker[1] of sinnus[2],
Of slouth *and* of idelnes.

Corona spinea.

[fol. 75 *b.*]

May the crown of thorns shield me from hell pit.

Þe coroune of þorn on þin hed þrast,
Þin her to-tar, þi skyn to-brast;
Schild[3] me from pein of helle pit,
Þat i haue deseruud þorow uan-wite[4].

Columpna cum corda.

May the bond that bound the Lord to the pillar release me from the bonds of unkind deeds.

To þe piler, lord, al so
With a rop þey[5] boundun þe to;
Þe senewes from þe bones brast,
So hard hit was draw *and* strened fast;
Þat bond me alese of bondes,
Of unkind dede *and* unkindnes[6].

[1] be my socour. [2] synne þis. [3] þat schild. [4] wane-wit [5] men
[6] Harde þay drowe *and* stryned faste;
Þe ȝenewys fro þe bonys to-barst.
Þat bond alese me and vnbynde,
Þat y haue *trespassed and* be vnkynde.
The words "and vnbynde" and the next line are in paler ink.

Uythe zardys grete þou ware alle to-daschyd,
W*ith* scorgys smerte alle to-laschyd;
Lord, socowre me of synnys thys,
Of stlowthe and eke of ydylnes.

The crown of thorn on þi hed preste,
Thyn here to-tere, thy skyn to-breste.
Lord, socowre me of synnys thys,
Of stlowthe and eke of Idylnes.

TO þe pyller, lorde, also,
W*ith* a rope men bownd þe too,
Hard drawe and streynyd faste;
The senews from þe bondys braste.
Lorde, lose me of bondys i*n* dystresse,
Thowe I ded onkend a-geyns kyndnesse.

*Uestigia saluatoris, quando exiuit per portam ierusalem, portando crucem, coronam spineam *coronatus, mille passus sic incedens, roseum cruorem distillando.*

[* fol. 76.]

Thou didst bear thy Cross and didst go out of Jerusalem.

Þow bere þe cros *and* toke þe gate
Out at ierusalemus ȝate;
Þin foot-steppus suet *and* gode
Wer sene þorow schedi[n]g of þi blod.

Thou didst meet with the women of Bethlehem and of Jerusalem, who wept for thy sufferings. Thou didst tell them to weep for themselves and their children.

Þer mettust þow with wy*m*me*n* of bedle*m*,
And al so with wy*m*men of ier*usal*em,
And alle[1] þey wepten for þi turment;
To hem þow seydust ap*er*tment,
"Ne wepe ȝe not for my wo,
But for ȝoure[2] self *and* ȝoure childurne also;
For hem ȝe moun ful sore wepe,
And salt teres for hem lete,
For þey schul haue turment hard
An hundert wintur her afterwart."

May those steps of thine give us pardon when we devoutly go on pilgrimage.

Þo steppus of[3] sine ȝif us p*ar*doun,
Wen we gon with[4] deuocioun
On[5] pilgremage on hors or fote;
Of alle oure sinnus[6] þey ben our bote.

[1] *omitted.* [2] ȝow. [3] Al þay stappis of oure. [4] we gooth wiþ good. [5] A. [6] sorwe

Thowe bare the cros ouyr the lake,
Owt of iheru*sa*lem at the gate;
Thy fote-steppys swete and good
Wer sene throwe schedyng of þi pr*ec*yus blode.
Þou mettyst wit*h* wome*n* of bethleem,
And also women of iherusalem;
Alle they wepyd for þi torment;
To them þou seyddyst a-p*er*te-ment,
"Wepe ȝe not for myn woo,
But for ȝowre childyr also;
For them ȝe maye sore wepe,
And salte terys for them lete;
For they schal haue torment hard
An hu*n*dyrd wyntyr here-aftyrwa[r]d."
Tho steppys for vs of g*ra*ce ȝeue p*ar*don,
Whan we goo, wyth*e* deuocyon,
On pylgrymage on hors ar on fote.
Of myn synnys, lorde, be myn bote.

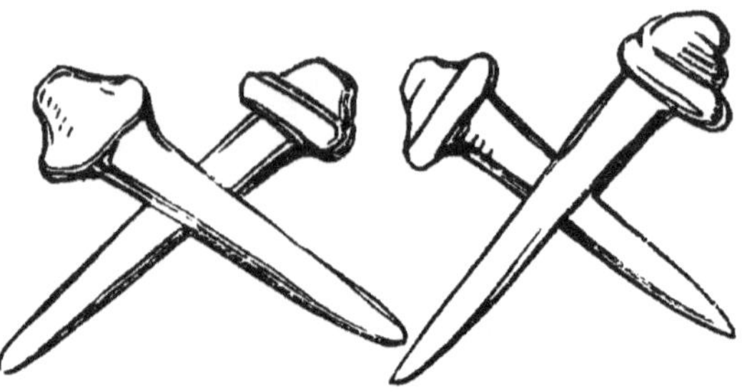

Claui.

[fol. 76 *b.*]

May the nails help me out of those sins that I have done with feet or hands.

Þe nayles þorow fet *and* handus to—
Þey helpe me out of sinne *and* wo
Þat i haue in my liue do,
With handus handult, with fet i-go.

Malleus.

May the hammer be my succour if I have smitten any with staff or knife.

Þe hamur bothe sterne *and* gret
Þat drof þe nayles þorow hond *and*[1] fete
Þey[2] be my socur[3] in my lyf,
Ȝif i[4] man smot with staf or knyf.

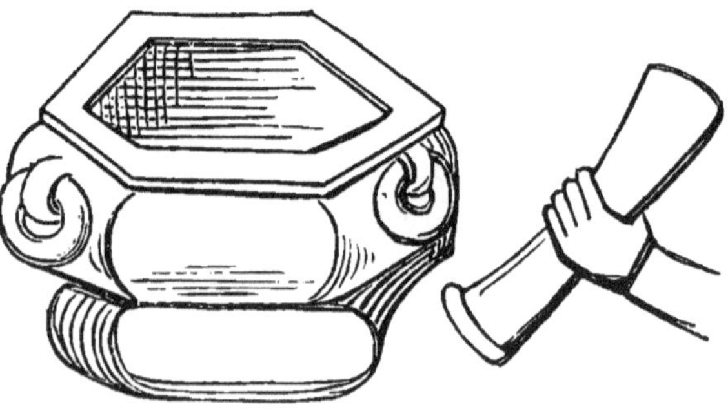

Vas cum felle.

[fol. 77.]

May the vessel of vinegar and gall keep me

Þe uescel with eysel *and* with galle
Kep me from þe[5] sinnus alle,

[1] nayles in cristis. [2] hit. [3] socour þat. [4] y eny. [5] *omitted.*

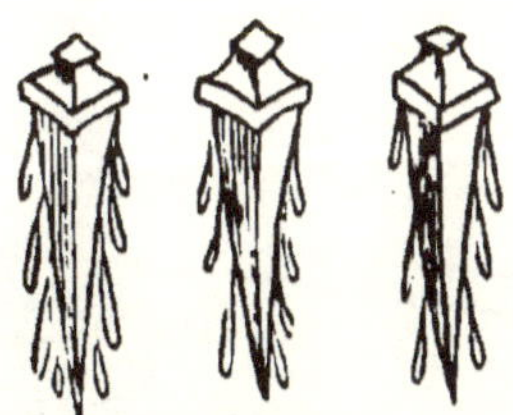

The naylys throwe fete and handys also,
  Lorde, kepe me owt of synne and woo,
That I haue *in* myn lyffe doo,
With handys handyld or on fote goo.

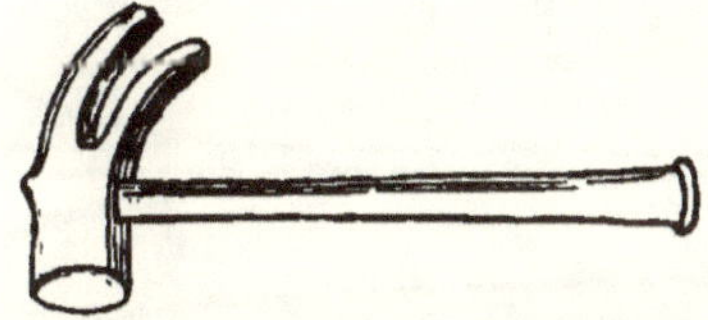

The hamyr bothe stern and grete,
  þ*at* droffe þ[e] naylys throw hand and fote,
Lord, be myn socowr *in* alle myn lyffe,
Iffe ony man stryke me *with* staffe or knyffe[1].

The vessel of aysylle and of galle,
  Lord, kepe me from þ[e] synnys alle,

[1] Lines 101–104 follow line 124 in the MS.

from sins hurtful to the soul.

Þat to þe soul is fowl uenim,
Þat i be not pusond þer-ine[1].

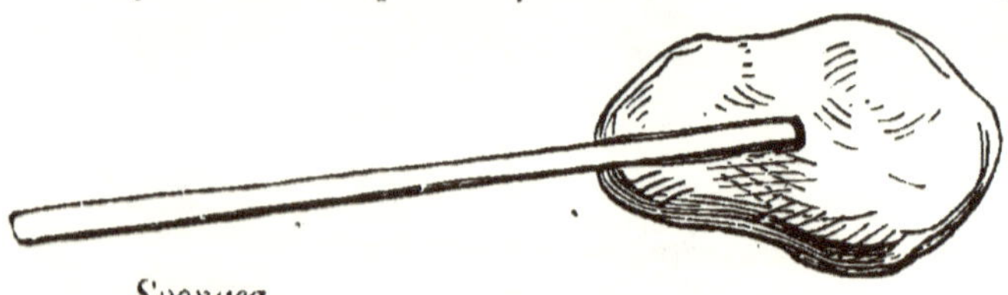

Spongea.

May the sponge save me when I die from the vengeance due to my sins of gluttony.

Þo þow thurstudust sor with-alle,
Þey ȝeufe þe eysel medult with galle;
Þat i haue dronken i*n* glotonie,
Hit saue me wen i schal diee,
Þat, lord, now i pray to þe
For þat greuauns þow suferdst for me[2].

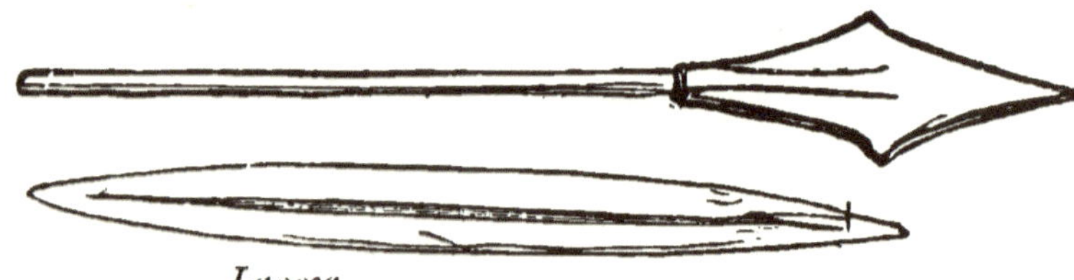

Lancea.

[fol. 77 b.]

May the spear that pierced thy side quench the sins of pride and disobedience.

Lord, þe scharp spere i-grounde
Þat in þin herd mad a wonde,
Hit kuench þe sine[3] þat i haue wrogt,
With al myn hert euel i-þowt,
And of my stout prid þer-to,
And myn unbuxumnes al-so.

Scala.

May the ladder preserve me

Þe laddur upset be enchesoun
Wen þow wer ded be take adoun[4],

[1] that men be nouȝt y-combred þer-yn. [2] ll. 113, 114 *omitted.* [3] synnes.
[4] to take þe doun; *originally,* by take a-doun.

That to sowle ben venym,
That I be not poysynd ther-in.

Whan þou thrystyd sore with-alle,
They gaffe the eysyll with byttyr galle;
Alle þat I haue dronke in glotenye
For-geue me, lorde, ar than I deye.

Lord, the spere so scharpe I-grownde,
Þat in thyn herte made a wownde,
It quenchyth the synne þat I haue wrowt,
With alle myn harte fulle ewle thowt,
And myn stowt pryd also,
And myn onbuxumnes ther-too.

The ledder, vppe-set be encheson
Whan þou war ded to be take a-down,

from dying in my sins.

Wen i ham ded in[1] ani sinne
Take me þat i ne die þer-ine.

Forceps.

May the tongs loose me from all my sins.

Þe tonges þat drow þe nayles out,
Of fet, of handes, al about,
And louset his[2] bodi from þe tre,
Of alle my sinnus þey lese[3] me.

[fol. 78.]

Iudeus spuens in facie christi.

Since Jesus suffered a Jew to spit in his face, may I be forgiven if I have insulted any man.

Þe iewe þat spit[4] in goddus face—
For he hit suffurd, he ȝyf us[5] grace;
Þat I haue reuilud or ani man me,
For þat despit for-ȝyf it be.

[1] on. [2] loosed þi. [3] loose. [4] spathe. [5] me.

Whan þ*at* I am In synne,
Lord, lete me not dey ther-in.

The pensynnys, þ*at* drewe þe naylys owt
Of fete and handys, alle a-bowt,
And losyd þi bodye from þe tre,
Of myn synnys, lord, lose þou me.

The iewys þ*at* spytte, lorde, i*n* thy face
Ʒe suffyrd alle, and gaffe them *grace*;
That I haue gylte or ony man me,
It be for-ȝeue for þ*at* peté.

Christ bore the Cross on his back. May the Cross give me grace to repent of my sins.

Christus *portans crucem in humero.*
Þe cros be-hind his bak-bon
Þat he þolud deth uppon—
ȝif me grace in my liue
Clene of sine me to schriue,
And þerto uerey[1] repentauns,
And here to fulfille my penauns.

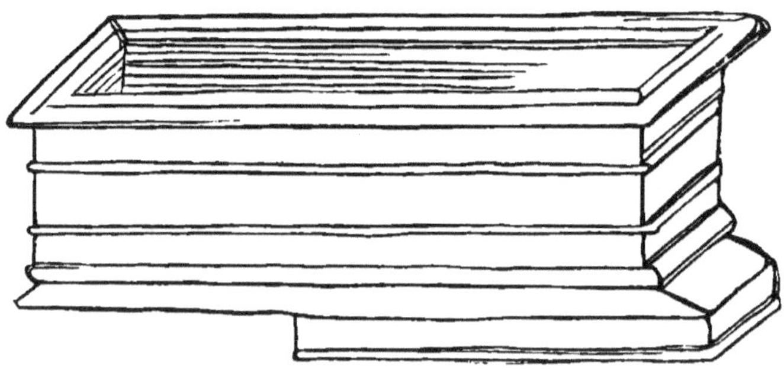

[fol. 78 *b*.]
May the sepulchre

Sepulcrum christi.
Þe sepulcur þat[2] þerinne was layde
His blessud bodi al be-bled[3]—

[1] al-so. [2] that he. [3] for-bleed.

The cros be-hynd þi bakke-bon,
  Þat þou suffyrd dethe vppe-on—
Lord, geue me grace, in my lyue,
Clene of synne me to schryue,
And þer-to very repentawns
With spas to performe myn penawns.

The sepulkyr wher-in þou war hyd,
  Þi blyssyd bodye alle for-bled—

send me, ere I die, true sorrow for my sins, so that I may be cleansed from them,

He me send, or þat[1] i deye,
Sorow of hert *and* ter of ye,
Cler *and*[2] clensud þat i be,
Or i to my graue tee;
So þat i mow[3] on domus day
To þe[4] dom cu*m* with-out dedli[5] fray
And wend to[6] blis in[7] cumpanie,
Þer[8] os[9] men schul[10] neuer dye,

so that I may dwell in everlasting joy.

But dwelle i*n* ioy wit oure lord riȝt[11],
Þer is euer day *and* neuer niȝt,
Þat last schal with-outen ende;
Now ies*u* crist [us][12] þidur send[13]. amen.

[1] *omitted.* [2] Clene. [3] mote. [4] thi. [5] *omitted.* [6] to þe. [7] wiþ. [8] MS. *þei.* [9] þat. [10] schal. [11] wiþ ouȝte driȝt, *read* oure Driȝt. [12] ous.
[13] MS. 11,748 adds two lines:—

Iesu, þat deidest one þe rode tree,
Graunte ous þis for charite. Amen.

Then follows at once:—

These armes of crist bothe god *and* man
Seint peter discriued ham.
What man þes armes ouer-ȝaith
And for hure synnes sory and schrine beeth
To seye hit a twelfe monthe eche day wiþ good chere
He haþ sixe thowsaund *and* seuen hundred and fiue and fifty ȝere
And half a ȝere *and* dayes thre
This is y-grauntyd for to be
And for the vernicle haue he may
Fourty dayes eu*er*yche day
And for the pytye with good chere
Grauntyd is sextene thowsaund ȝere
And sixe [an] thirty dayes þer-to
For to segge eu*er*y day A pater *noster* *and* v. Aue maria wiþ
o Crede.

Lord, grawnt me, ar þ*at* I deye,
Sorowe of herte wit*h* terys of eye,
Clene clensyd for thy mercye,
144 Er þ*at* I in myn graue lye,
So þ*at* I may at domys daye
To þ*at* dome cu*m* wit*h*-owt fraye,
And wend to blysse i*n* cu*m*pany,
148 Ther as men schalle neuyr dye,
But dwelle In blysse wit*h* þ*at* lord brygth*e*,
Wher euyr is day but neuyr nygth*e*,
And lest schal wit*h*-owt ende:
152 Ie*sus* cryste vs thedyr send!

*Gr*acia*rum* *acciones* *iesu* christo *stanti* *in* *sepulcro.*

[fol. 79.] I thank thee, Lord, for all thy sufferings.

I þank þe, lord, þat þow me wrout,
And with strong peynus þow me bout;
I þank þe, lord, with ruful entent
Of þi peynus *and* þi turment,
With carful hert *and* dreri mod,
For schedynd of þi swet blod.
What may i say þow hast don*e* for me?
Þi bodi was bonden to a tre,
With scourges knit þe knott*is*[1] grete
Þi blessud bodi was al for-bete,
On eu*er*i side turnnd *and* torne,
Also naked as þow were borne,
Þat hol sted was found none
Fro þe croun to þe ton.
Þi blessud bodi þer hit stod,
Al hit was be-helet in blod;
And when þow were so for-swong,
Among þe iues þey did þe hong,
With scharp naylus þorow hand *and* fet
Þey let þe hong til þow wer ded;
And aftur þi deth, to us sote,
Þey pittu*n* a spere to þin hert rote;

Thy body was scourged and beaten on every side, so that no whole place was to be found in thy whole body.

[fol. 79 *b*.]

They let thee hang until thou wert dead.
They thrust a spear into thy heart.

[1] MS. *knoctis*.

Þe wiked iwes with sturdi mode
Let þer-out strem þin hert blod.
Alas! lord, þi penus þow tholudust þo,
Oure sinnus hit mad so wellawo.
ȝese instrument*us* þat here p*er*tend[1] beþ
In memori of þi bittur deyt,
Þey hulpun hem to do þi passioun,
Þey help us to oure sauacioun;
For þey greuet þe ful sore,
Þin anguich wex so lenger þe more.
Lord, what may i for þat ȝylde þe?
Þow desirdust noȝt but loue of me.
Lord, þow ȝif me grace *and* myȝt
With al min hert to loue þe ryȝt;
In lyf *and* deth, in wele *and* wo,
Let neuur min hert turne þe fro,
And or hit so be for thing unwrest
For loue let, lord, min hert brest;
In a blessud tym þen was I bore,
When al my loue to þe is core.
But merci, lord, i þe prey,
Þow let me neuer in sine dye,
Werethorow i schuld dampned be;
Derworth lord, for þi pité
Þis graunt me, lord, i prey to þe,
For mari loue þi moder fre. amen.

May these symbols of thy passion help our salvation.

[fol. 80.]

Give me grace to love thee rightly.

Let me never die in my sins.

Grant me pity, dear Lord.

Þese armus of crist boþ god *and* man,
Sent petur þe pop discriuet hem.
Wat man þis armes ouer-se,
For his sinnus sori *and* schereuen be,
Þre ȝer of p*ar*don is þe su*m*me
Of sent petrus gr*a*nt, furst pope of rome;
And xxx popes aftur hi*m* þat were,
An C dayus ich yauf with gode chere;

[fol. 80 *b*.]

[1] Read *portraid*.

xxxviii bichoppus eke also,
Ich *gr*ant bi him self xl dayus þer-to.
Pope i*n*nocent mad a gret counsail
And al þis *con*fermed with-outen fayl.
And more p*ar*don ȝaf also.
iiii ȝere ii C dayus þer-to;
And ich bischop sayd to-for-hand
For syȝt of þe uernacul hath graunt
xl dayus to p*ar*don,
And þer-with-al her benisun.

May thy symbols preserve us from the "evil one."

And also who þat eu*er*i day
Þis armus of crist be-hold may,
Þat day he ne sal dee no wiked ded
Ne be cu*m*bert with þe kued;

May they preserve women labouring with child.

And also to wymen hit is meke *and* mild,
When þey trauelne of her chi[l]d.
Þe soum of weke*us* to se hit ich day
A. C. *and* xix *and* half get þow may,

[fol. 81.]

To sen it ich day in þe moneþ also
V. C. ȝer *and* xviii *and* xii wokes þer-to,
To sen it a twelf-moneth ich day enter
Haþ vi. M°. vii. C. v. *and* fifti ȝere
And half ȝere *and* dayes þre
Of p*ar*don, þus popus haþ graunted þe.

APPENDIX.

I.

DISPUTE BETWEEN MARY AND THE CROSS.

I*.

[Royal MS. 18 A 10, leaf 126 b.]

Listen to the controversy between Mary and the Cross.

O litel whyle lesteneþ to me
  Ententyfly, so haue ȝe blys,
Gode ensaumple here schul ȝe,
  Of noble Mater wrouȝt it is,
How Mary spak to þe rode tre,
  Whan her sone was in angwys;
Þe Cros answeryd þat lady fre,
  Ful myldely seiȝe clerkys wys,
¶ Þat þis tale haue made couþe;
  Þei haue expounced it by siȝt,
  A good ensaumple and a bryȝt;
  But Apocrifum þei holde it riȝt,
For tre spak neuere wiþ mouþe.

This story is apocryphal.

II.

Maria.

Our Lady made her moan to the Rood.

¶ Oure lady fre,
To þe rode tre,
  Sche made her mone.
And seyde, "on þee
Is fruyt of me
  Full wo-bygone:
With blody ble
My fruyt I gan see,

* The numbers are those of the corresponding stanzas in the text, pp. 131–149, the order being somewhat different.

Among hys fone:
Of Sorewe I see,
Hys veynes fle
Fro blody bone:

She accused the "tree" of a want of truth in punishing her child

¶ Tre, þou dost no treuþe,
On pilory my fruyt to pynne,
He haþ no spot of Adam synne,
Flessche and veynes fle atwynne,
Wherfore I rede of reuþe.

III.

"Cross, thy bonds are to be blamed for defiling my fair fruit,

¶ Cros, þi bondes schul be blamed,
My gode fruyt þou hast bigyled;
Þe fruytes modir was neu*er* famed,
My wombe is faire fou*n*de vnfyle[d]:
Child, why art þou noȝt aschamed
On pilory to be I-pyled,
As grete þeuys þat were gramed,
Þat deyeden þorouȝ her werkis wylde?
¶ Blode from hede is hayled,
Aꝉꝉ to-fowled is my faire fruyte,

that never did wrong.

Þat neu*er* dyd treget ne truyte
With þeuys þat loue ryot vnriȝte;
Why schal my sone be nayled?

IV.

¶ Þe grete þevys galowes were greyd,
Þ*a*t eu*er*e to robbe ronne*n* ryfe;
Why schal my sone þ*er*-on be leyde?

He never did harm to any.

He noyȝed neu*er* man ne wyfe.

A deadly drink thou givest thy Lord.

A drynk of deeþ soþely seyde,
Cros, þou ȝeuyst[1] þe lord of lyfe:
Hys veynes breke *with* þi breyde,
My fruyte stont i*n* stroke *and* stryfe:

[1] MS. ȝeu*yt*.

[leaf 127.]

¶ The faire fruyte of my flessche,
My leue childe *with*-oute lak,
For Adam goddis biddyng brak;
Þe blood ran on my briddes bak,
Droppynge as dewe on ryssche.

For Adam's sin the blood ran down my bird's back.

IV.

¶ The Iugement haue þei Ioyned
To bere fooles full of synne:
Ȝit scholde my sone fro þee be soyned,
And neuer hys blood on þe rynne;
But now is truþe *with* tresoun twyned,
With a þeef to henge fer in fenne;
With fele nayles hys feet be pyned,
A careful modir men may me kenne,
¶ In balys I am bounde:
Þe brid þat was of a mayde borne,
On þis tree is all for-torne;
A broche þorow hys breest was borne,
Hys hert now haþ a wounde.

Truth is now united to treason.

With a thief my son is hanged.

V.

¶ Tre, þou art loked by lawe
Þat a þeefe and a traytour on þe schal deye,
Now is truþe *with* tresoun drawe,
Vertu is falle by vicys weye;
Love and truþe and soþefast sawe,
On a tre traytours do teye,
Now is vertue *with* vyces slawe:
Of all vertues cryst is keye,
¶ Vertue is swetter þan spyces,
In foote and honde he bereþ blody prykke,
Þe heed is full of þornes pikke,
Þe goode hangeþ among þe wikke,
Vertue þus deieþ wiþ vyces.

O tree, thou art only made for traitors,

yet virtue is slain along with vice,

and the good hangeth among the wicked.

VI.

Thou, Cross, art my son's stepmother.

¶ Cros, vnkynde þou schalt be kyd,
My sonys stepmodir I þe calle:
My bridde was borne *with* beeste on bedde,
And by my Fleissche my fruyt gan fall[e],
And *with* my breestys my brid I fedde;
Cros, þou ȝyuest hym eysell *and* galle!
My white rose rede is spred,
Þat florysshed was in fodders stalle;

The limbs that I have caressed now hang aloft.

¶ Feet and faire handes
Þat now be croysed I kissed hem ofte,
I lulled hem *and* leyde hem softe:
And þou Cros haldes hym hiȝe alofte
Bounde in blody bandes!

VII.

[leaf 127 *b.*]

¶ My love I lulled vppe in hys leir,
With cradel-bande I gan hy*m* bynde,
Cros, he stikeþ vppon þi steir,
Naked in þe wylde wynde:

Naked he hangs in the wild wind.

Fowles formen her nest in þe eyr,
Foxes in den rest þei fynde,
But goddys sone and heuenys eir,
Hys hede holdeþ on þornes tynde,
¶ Of moornyng I may mynne:

He hath no rest, and the thorns pierce his brain.

My sonys hed haþ reste none,
But leneþ on þe schuldr*e* bone;
Þe þornes þorow þe panne is gone
Thys woo I wyte synne.

VIII.

So high, O Cross, thou holdest him, that I cannot kiss his feet.

¶ Cros, to sle hym is þi sleiþe,
My blody brid þou berest fro blysse;
Cros, þou holdest hym hiȝe on heiþe,
Hys fair*e* feet I may not kysse;

My mouþe I putte, my swere I streeche
Hys feet to kys;
Þe Iewes fro þe cros me keeche,
And on me make her mowe amys,
¶ Her game and her gawdes;
Þe Iewes wrouȝt on me wo:
Cros, I fynde þou art my fo,
My brid þou berist beten blo;
Among þes folys frawdys."

The Jews drive me from the Cross.

Cross, thou art my foe, thou hast beaten my bird blue."

IX.

¶ Cristys Cros þan ȝaf answere:—
"Lady, to þe I owe honour,
Þi bryȝt palme now I bere;
My schynyng scheweþ of þi flour,
Thy trye fruyt I to-tere;
Þi fruyt me florysschiþ in blood colour
Þe worlde to wynne as þou mayst here;
Þis blossom blomed i*n* þi bour,
¶ Not aƚƚ for þe alone,
But forto wynne aƚƚ þis werd;
Þat waltereþ vndir þe deueles swerd:
Þorowe foote and honde god lete hym gerd,
To amende mannys mone.

Sancta Crux.

Thy fruit flourishes in red blood;

it bloomed not alone for thee, but for all the world.

X.

¶ Adam dyd fuƚƚ grete harmes,
He bote a fruyt vnd*er* a bowe,
Þ*er*fore þi fruit spred hys armes,
On tre þat is tiȝed wi*th* tyndes towe;
Hys body is smyte ny þe þarmes,
He swelt wi*th* a swemely swow;
Hys breest is bored wi*th* deeþis armes,
And wi*th* hys deeþ fro deeþ vs drowe

Thy fruit is spread out on the tree for Adam's sin.

[leaf 128.]

¶ And att hys goode freendys,
As Isayas spak in *pro*phecye:
He seyde ‘þi sone, seynt Marye,
Hys deþe slowe deþe in Caluarye,
And leueþ *with*-oute endys’.

Thy son's death slew death on Calvary.

XII.

¶ Lady, love doþe þe alegge
Fruite prikkyd *with* sperys orde:
I Cros, *with*-oute knyues egge,
I kerue fruit best of horde;
Att is rede, Ribbe and rigge,
Þe bak bledeþ aȝens þe borde;
I am a pyler and ber*e* a brigge,
God is þe weye, witnesse one worde;
¶ God seiþ he is soþefast weye:
Many folk slode to hett slider,
To heuene noman cowde þider,
Til god deiȝed *and* tauȝt whider
Men drawe whan þei deye:

I cut the best of fruits.

Many folk went to hell ere Christ died for them.

XIII.

¶ And Moyses fourmed hys figo*ur*,
A whyte lambe, and noon oþ*er* beest
He sacred so our*e* sauyo*ur*,
To be mete of myȝtes meest,
And chosen cheef in hono*ur*,
I bar*e* fleissche to folkys feest;
I*es*u cryst our*e* creato*ur*,
Hys Flessche fedeþ leste and mest,
¶ Rosted aȝens þe sonne;
On me lay þe lambe of love,
I was plat*er*, hys body above,
Whan flessche *and* veynes att to-clove,
With blood I was bironne.

Christ is spoken of as a lamb in the Mosaic law.

I was a platter, and bore the lamb's flesh.

XIV.

¶ ȝit Moyses þis resoun rad,
'Ete ȝoure lambe *with* soure vergeous';
Sowre saws make þe sowle glad,
Sorowe for synnes oures;
Þat vergeous makeþ þe fende a-drad,
And fer fleþ fro goddis spous;
And bere a staaf and stonde sadde,
Whan flessche þe fediþ in goddis hows,
¶ Þis staf is crystis crouche;
Stonde þou styf by þis stake,
Whan ȝe fonge ȝowre fleissche in take,
Þan may þe deuyll no maystryes make,
ȝoure sowles to touche.

The paschal lamb was eaten with bitter herbs.

The eaters bore a staff.

The staff is Christ's Cross.

XV.

¶ Whan pardoun is schewed *with* a scryne,
With boke on bord *with* nayles smyte,
With rede lettres wryten blyne,
Blewe and blak among me pyte:
My lorde I likne to þat signe,
Þe body was bored *and* on borde bete,
In briȝt blode oure boke gan schyne;
How woo he was no wiȝt may wyte,
¶ Ne rede in hys rode;
ȝoure pardoun boke fro top to too,
Wryten it was full wonder woo,
Rede woundes and strokes bloo,
ȝoure boke was bounde in blode.

[leaf 128 *b*.]

Pardon is written in red letters.

Christ's bleeding body denoted our pardon.

Our book was bound in blood.

XXIII.

¶ In holy write þis tale I herde,
How riche ȝiftis god vs ȝaf;
God seiþ hym-self a good scheperde,
And euery herde byhoueþ a staf;

Every shepherd needs a staff.

The Cross is a shepherd's staff.

Þe cros I kalle þe heerdys ȝerde,
  Þerwith þe deuyl a dent he ȝaf,
With þat ȝerd þe wolfe he werid,
  With dyntes drofe hym alł to draf."
¶ Þe Cros þis tale tolde,
  How he was þe staf in herdis hande,
  Whan scheep borsten oute of bande[1],
  Þe wolfe he wered oute of lande
Þat deuouride crystis folde.

It drives the devil from Christ's fold.

[1] MS. *hande*.

XVIII.

[Mari]a. Mary replies.

¶ Oure ladye seyde, "Cros, of þi werk
  Wonder naȝt þei I be wroþe,
Þus seyde Poule, crystes clerk,
  To þe fikelł Iewes, with-oute oþe,
Iewes stone hard, with synnes merke,
  Þei bete a lambe with-oute loþe,
Softer þan water vnder serk,
  Milk or mede melled boþe:
¶ Þe Iewes were þe hard stonys.
  Softer þan water or mylk lycour,
  Or dew þat lithe on lily-flour
  Was cristes body in blode colour,
Þe Iewes brisseden hys bonys.

The Jews did beat an innocent lamb.

Stone-hearted Jews bruised the soft body of Jesus.

XX.

¶ Siþe mannys sone was so nedy,
  To be lad as a lamb so mylde,
Why were gylours so gredy
  To fowle so my faire chylde?
And Cros, why were þou so redy
  My fruite to foule fer in felde?"
Þe cros seyde, "to make þe deuyłł dredy,
  God schope me schelde schame to schelde,

Why were traitors so ready to defile my child?

"To make the devil afraid," said the Cross,

Sancta Crux.

"God shaped me as a shield.

[leaf 129.]

¶ Siþe lombe of love dyede,
And on me ȝelde hys goost *with* voys;
Men chose me a relyk choys,
Þe signe of Iesu Cryst*is* Croys,
Þer dar no deuyl abyede:

I am a choice relic; no devil can abide me.

XXI.

¶ Many folk, I defende fro her foos":
Cristes cros þis sawe he seyde:—
"Heuene gate was keiþed clos
Til lambe of love now he deyede,
It is write in tixt and glos:
For Cristis deeþ prophetes preyde:
Till lambe of love deyed and roos
In hell pyne many folk was teyde:
¶ In þe houre of hiȝest noone,
Þe lambe of love seide his þouȝt—
'All is fulfilled þat well was wrouȝt,
Man is oute of bondys brouȝt
And heuene dorys vndone':

The lamb of love opened the gate of heaven.

He brought man out of bonds, and undid heaven's doors.

XXXIII.

¶ And I was Cros and kepte þat ȝifte
Þat ȝeue was of fadres graunt,
I was loked I schulde vp-lifte
Goddis sone *and* Maydenes faunt[1],
Noman had schelde of scrifte;
Þe deuyll stode as lyou*n* rau*m*paunt,
Many folk he keighte to hell clifte,
Till þe dyntes of þe cros gan hy*m* adau*n*te:
¶ My dede is founde and boked,
All þe werke þat I haue wrouȝte
It was in þe fadres forþouȝte,
Louely lady, lak me nouȝte,
I dyd as I was loked.

I, Cross, was ordained to uplift God's Son.

The dints of the Cross daunted the devil.

[1] MS. *faint*.

XXXIV.

¶ In wat*er* and blood cristenyng was wrouȝt,
Holy writ witnessiþ it weƚƚ,
And in þe weƚƚ of worþi þouȝt,
Man is cristened to soule hele;
Þe blood þat aƚƚ þe world haþ bouȝt,
A digne *cr*istenyng he gan me dele;
Cryst in *cr*istenynge forȝat me nouȝt,
Hy[s] fressche blood whan I gan fele:
¶ Mayde modir and wyue!
Crystis blood ȝaf me bapteme,
Bystreke I was *with* rede streme,
Whan Ie*su* bled vpon a beme,
Of cip*r*esse and Olyue.

Christ's blood christens man, and gives him soul's heal.

His blood baptized me with its red streams.

[leaf 129 *b*.]

XXXV.

¶ Ie*su* seyde to Nichodem*us*
But a barn be twies born,
Whan domesday schal blowe his bemys,
He schulde lye as man lorn,
First bore of wombe wher*e* rewþe remys,
Siþ *with* font synne is schorn:
And I was cros to mannys quemys,
I baar þe fruyt þou ber*e* aforn,
¶ For þi beryng alone;
But I had born hym efte,
Fro riche rest man had be refte
And in a lore logge lefte,
Ay to grucche and grone.

A man must be born twice if he will be saved on doomsday.

Thy fruit had to be born twice, by thee and me.

XXXVI.

¶ Þou wer*e* crowned heuene queen,
For þe birþen þat þou ber*e*,
Þi garlond is of g*ra*cious greene,
Of heƚƚ Emp*er*esse *and* heuene Emper*e*:

On account of thy Son, thou wast crowned queen of heaven.

I am þe relyk þat schyneþ schene,
Men wolde wyte where I were,
At þe pleyn parlement I schal been,
At domesday prestly to pere;
¶ Whan god schal seye riȝt þere,
'Trewly on þee rode tre,
Man, I dyed for loue of þe;
Man, what hast þou do for me
To be my frendly fere?'

I, a bright relic, shall appear at doomsday,

when God shall say,

'Man, I died for thee; what hast thou done for me?'

XXXVII.

¶ At parlement I wil put pleynyng,
How maydenes sone on me gan sterue,
Spere and spounge and hard naylyng,
Þe hard hede þe helme gan kerue:
And I schal crye riȝtful kyng,
Ilk man haue as þe serue,
Þe riȝt schul ryse to ryche reynynge,
Truyt *and* treget to helle schal terve:
¶ Mayde meke and mylde!
God took in þe hy[s] flessch trewe,
I bare þi fruyt lele and newe;
It is riȝt þe rode to Eue helpe schewe
Man, woman, and chylde".

At doomsday will I make my complaint,

Each man shall then be rewarded according to his deserts."

XXXVIII.

¶ Þe queen þus acorded *with* þe Cros,
Aȝens hym spak nomore speche;
Þe lady ȝaf þe cros a cosse,
Þe lady of love longe loue gan seche,
. . . . .
. . .
.
. . . . . .

[leaf 130.]
Mary became reconciled to the Cross, and gave it a kiss.

Mary and the Cross bare Christ to deliver men from hell.

¶ Þe queen and þe cros acord:
Þe queen bare first, þe cros aftirward,
To feeche folk fro helłward,
On holy steyres to styȝe vpward
And reigne wi*th* oure lord.

XXXIX.

A clerk made this story of Mary's sorrow.

¶ A clerk fou*r*med þis figo*ur*
Of Maries sorwe to seiȝe su*m*me,
As he had see in scharp schour,
How c*r*istes armes were rent *and* rune;

But the Cross was ever deaf and dumb.

Þe cros is a colde creatour
And euer ȝit was deef and dum,
Þis tale florissched wi*th* a faire flo*ur*,

This story is therefore apocryphal.

Þis poynt I p*r*oue apoc*r*ifum;
¶ Witnesse was neu*er* founden
Þat euere crystis cros spak,
Ne oure lady leyde hym no lak,
But forto dryue þe deuył a-bak,
Men speke of C*r*istes wounden.

¶ A clerk fou*r*med þis fantasye,
On c*r*istes steruyng stok to stere;
Þat bare þe body ał blody,
Whan deþes dent gan hy*m* dere,

It is by no means a foolish story.

Þis Apocrifum is no foly:
In swich a lay dar þe naȝt dere

It may help man to seek mercy.

Þat doþe man to seke m*er*cy,
Wikked werkes awey to were,
¶ In tixte ful weł is write:
A lombe[1] haþ larged ał þis glose,
Plenté speche þ*er*-In to prose,
Þe counseił of þe cros to vnclose
Of Maryes woo to wite.

[1] ? *clerk*.

XL.

356 ¶ In flesshly wede
God gan hym hede,
Of mylde may
Was born to blede,
360 As cristes crede
Soþely to say;
On stokky stede
He roode, men rede,
364 In rede aray.
Fro deuelis drede
Þat duk vs lede
At domesday,
368 ¶ Whan pepil schal parte and passe
To holy heuene and hell þe wode.
Now Cristes crosse and crystes blode
And Maries praier mylde and goode
372 Graunte vs þe lyfe of grace. Amen.

God clothed himself in mortal garb.

Of a virgin he was born.

He rode in red array on a stocklike steed.

[leaf 130 *b.*]

May we through Christ's Cross and Christ's blood with Mary's prayer gain the life of grace.

[Royal MS. 18 A x, leaf 130 *b*.]

FESTIVALS OF THE CHURCH.

¶ *Deo nostro iocunda sit laudacio.*

¶ Ioyeful preisyng to god oure lord
Þe sawter book bereþ record.

I.

The Lord is a householder; he feasts and clothes his folk.

The lord þat is a howsholder,
With faire festis folk he fat;
Ʒiueþ hem wedys hym self doþe were,
On bolstre bed her balys bat;
Tonge gyueþ talke and stere
To preysen hym men taken gat;
Oure lord to preise is no ler,

It's no loss to praise our Lord.

Þe same help man he byhat,
With hym on bedde, man, þou sat
¶ On þe bolstre of heuene blisse.
With hys fleisshe he fediþ þe, þou wost wel þis,

He feedeth thee with his flesh.

Þi sowle schal be clad as hys
In lyfe þat neuermore lat.

II.

¶ Malachie witnesse haþ gunne
In hys rewle, as it is rad;
He seiþ þat god is sooþfast sunne,

Jesus is the true Son of God.

And in þat same þi sowle is clad;
¶ Þi lordes wede þan hast þou wonne

Thou hast worn thy Lord's garments, and with his flesh thy body is fed.

And with hys fleisshe þi goost is fed;
He let atame hys pyement tunne

To make his gode gestis glad,
¶ *With* a spere of grounden gad;
Þan was founde a fett fawset,
In þe tric tunne it was sette,
In cristes hert was piȝt *and* pette,
Hys brest was al be-blad.

Our Lord shed his blood as wine for his guests.

His breast was broached like a wine-tun.

III.

¶ I haue ioye forto gest
Of þe lambe of love *with*-oute oþe;
Hys flessche is oure faire feest,
And curteisly he ȝeueþ vs cloþe.

The Lamb's flesh is our feast.

IV.

¶ Viij feestis oure lord gan dresse,
And att be newe eu*er*y ȝere.
Heuene quene and hett Emp*er*esse,
A blisful blosum þi bosum bere!
¶ His fleissħ fediþ more and lesse,
And fendiþ vs from feendis fere;
Þe kirnett sprang at Cristemasse
Þat now is crist in a cake clere,
¶ Þe preest drynkeþ blessyd bere,
Goddis blood in sacrament.
Almyȝty god om*n*ipotent,
Hys blessyd body haþ sent
To fede hys freendys here.

[leaf 131.] Our Lord ordained eight feasts.

His flesh feeds all, and defends us from the devil.

At Christmas Christ appears in a clean cake, and the priest drinks "blessed beer."

V.

¶ Cristemasse first is founde,
Whan god was borne *with* beest in bynne.
At newe ȝere cryst þoled wounde
And schadde hys blood for mann*us*[1] synne.
Þe Epiphanye is gret on grounde.
On estre day welþes we wynne.

Christmas is the first feast

Epiphany is great on earth.

[1] MS. *mainus*.

On holy þursday god stiȝe þ*at* stounde.
On Whitsunday God did think of mankind.
On witsoneday god gan mynne
¶ To þenke on mannys kynne,
He sent man þe holy goost.
The feast of the Trinity has most power.
Þe Trinité feest haþ myȝtes moost.
In Corpus *christi* wel þou woost,
Is ioyned oure Ioye *with* gynne.

VI.

At Christmas Mary's bird was born.
¶ At C*r*istemasse mayde Mary,
Þorowe helpe of þe holy goost*is* heste,
Þi brid was born and lay þe by,
Aboute boþe bynne and beeste.
Angels sang a clear note in the sky, and
Þe Aungels maden melody
For ioye of c*r*istis feeste;
A clere note þei sang in þe sky,
Whan kyng*is* sone bare fleisshly creste.
¶ Scheperdes meest and leest,
"Ioye to god full of love,"
proclaimed peace and salvation to man.
Herden þei Aungels synge above,
"Pes to man, þe deuyll is drove
Fro goddis trone in þe eest."

VII.

¶ Þan myȝt þe mylde may synge
ysaias propheta. Isaiah prophesied of Mary's child.
Ysaye þe woord of þee;
Þou seydest a ȝerd schulde sprynge
Oute of þe rote of Ientill Iesse,
[leaf 131, back.]
¶ And schulde floure *with* florisschyng,
With primeroses greet plenté;
In-to þe croppe schulde come a kyng,
Þat is a lord of power *and* pyté,
¶ My swete sone I see.
Mary is the rod, Jesus is the flower.
I am þe ȝerde, þou art þe flour,
My brid is borne by beest in boure,

My p*r*imerose my p*ar*amo*ur*,
84 Wit*h* love I lulle þee.

VIII.

The maiden might sing Hosea's song:

¶ ȝit myȝt þe mylde may among
Her cradel trille to and fro,
And syng, Osye, þi song!—

Osyas propheta.
"My son's flesh shall die, and slay death for ever.

88 "Deþe, my deþe schal þee slo."
Þe deþe of hell is full strong,
Where spirites bren i*n* blases blo;
Þe flesshe schal dye þ*at* my sone gan fong
92 *And* sle þ*at* deþe for eu*er*mo;
¶ To helle my child schal go.
As Osye bigan to speke,
Þou schalt musell helle cheke

Thou shalt muzzle hell's cheek."

96 And hell barre þi hand schal breke,
And fette frendes fro wo.

IX.

[Balaam.]
Balaam prophesied of a Star that should rise out of Jacob.

¶ Balaam tolde hys trewe entente,
Of sooþfastnesse he schewed a signe—
100 Of Iacob schulde a token be glente,
A sterre þ*at* schulde schewe *and* schyne.

X.

[Moyses.]
Moses spake of the spotless Lamb, not a bone of which should be broken.

¶ Moyses ffull well he spak
Of þe lambe þ*at* sprang of mayden clene,
104 A white lambe, wit*h* senn blak
Spotty myȝt he neu*ere* bene;
¶ He lyued wit*h*-oute lak,
Till a spere hys loue gan spene,
108 Whan lambes blood on breeste and bak,
No boon was broke wit*h* Iewes kene;
¶ Þe lambe schyned full schene,

Þat Mary lulled in louely place,
As sche was ful full of grace,
To loke in þe lambes face,
Þat si3t god leue vs sene.

May God grant that we may see the Lamb's face.

XI.

[leaf 132.]

St. John bade us live in charity, then would the Lamb of love dwell with us.

¶ Seint Iohan wroot wiþ penne,
3if þou lyuest in charyté,
Þe lombe of loue lyueþ with þe,
And in god þi goost schal be,
In welþe heuene to wynne.

XII.

Make a cradle for Christ in thy heart.

Put a shirt and woollen garments upon a poor beggar.

Visit the prisoners, and give to the poor.

With this sail sail into the bliss of heaven.

¶ Make cristys cradell of þi herte,
In bonde of love bynde hym fast,
On a poure begger put a scherte,
And wollen wedys þat warm will last,
To poure in prisoun þou schalt sterte,
And 3eue þe wrecches of þe good þou hast.
¶ Þis seyle sette on þi mast
And seyle in-to þe blisse of heuene;
At domesday god schal full euene
Monewe þe dedis of mersy seuene
To kaytyfes þat be cast.

XIII.

Rock thy cradle high and low; be mindful of prosperity and misfortune.

Wash thy soul as white as snow.

¶ Rokke þi cradell hi3e and lowe,
Mirþe and Mischeef haue in mynde,
In heuene is ioyned ioye Inow,
In hell fyre and filþe þou schalt fynde;
Whasshe þi sowle white as snowe,
And in þat bed þis barn schal þe bynde;
In a cote, with-oute slow,
Oure lady lolled þi leve frende.
¶ Man haue þis in mynde,

Rokke þi cradeƚƚ aboue þe skye,
Þenk on þe Madenys melodye,
Þenk on helle stynkyng stye,
  Wher*e* goostis bren in bynde.

Rock thy cradle above the sky.

Think of hell's stinking sty.

XIV.

¶ In vitas patrum, a fader booke,
  Swiche a tale þ*er* is tolde;
A sinfuƚƚ wom*m*an *crist* forsooke,
  Putte in dispeir *with* deuelys bolde,
Sche was hent on hard hoke,
  For hete of feiþ kepte sche colde,
Tiƚƚ a wyse p*re*est *with* hyr woke
  And seyde, "for þe Ie*su* was solde."

Think of the woman of cold faith, who was

[leaf 132 *b*.]

caught upon the devil's hook.

XV.

¶ Take ensaumple of a childe in towne,
  With myshap his croune is craked,
With brode lippys he bereþ boune,
  Þ*er* is wepyng *and* deel awaked.
¶ Þe Norys *with* þe childe doþe roune,
  A rede Appil sche haþ hym taked,
And he forsakeþ hys sobbyng soune,
  And mochel myrþe þ*er*e is maked.
¶   Now sette þi will styf stakede
In fruyte swett*er* þan any mayde,
Þow þi synne haue hym affrayede,
ȝyue hym þi hert *and* he is apayede
  Þat pere hys pees haþ makede.

Take example of a child who has "cracked his crown," and roars out lustily.

The nurse soothes the child, and gives him a rosy apple, and he is quieted.

Set thy desire upon a fruit sweeter than any that exists.

Make thy peace with Christ.

XVI.

¶ Was neu*er* childe so sone stille
  With pere ne *with* appil swete,
As Maydens sone þat dyed on hiƚƚ
  And for þi loue blood gan swete;

Was never a child so quiet with pear or apple as the Maiden's Son that died on Calvary.

ȝif hym þi herte, *with* good wiłł,
He wiłł neþ*er* grucche ne grete;

His spirit he yielded up with "shrieks shrill," because he was unwilling to forgo thy love.

Hys goost he ȝelde *with* schrikes schrylle,
So loþe he was þi love to lete.
¶ Oure lady her hede sche schette in a schete,

Our lady was dazed with grief for the death of her Son.

And ȝit lay stiłł doted and dased,
As a wo*m*man mapped and mased,
Fro riȝtfułł resou*n* robbed *and* rased,
Tiłł fele teres gan flete.

XVII.

God will be easily reconciled to thee.

¶ Þe boke seiþ god askeþ lyte
With þee to make a loveday;
Þi hert weyeþ not half a myte
Ageyn þe lyf þ*at* lastiþ ay.

He will put to flight all thy foes, and by charter give thee heaven's hall.

ȝif hym þat, he wiłł not flyte,
But flemon ałł þi foos away;
He wil þe make chartre and skryte
In heuen hałł to holde þi way.
¶ Vppon a blody bay

[leaf 133.]

God once made a charter of peace with a thief.

A chartre of pees god made to a þef,
To aske mercy he was leef;
God bad hym go *with*-oute greef,
Into p*ar*adys forto play.

XVIII.

At this feast the Maiden kissed Christ, and rocked him to sleep.

¶ Thys feest at freeste
Godlyche gladed geste,
Mayden cryst keste,
And rokked hym riȝt in her reste.

Circumcisio[1] *domini*.

[1] MS. *Circimcisio.*

XIX.

The tender flower in the new year was

¶ At neweȝere þe flour ful fressche,
In holy writte I vndirstode

Was corve in hys tendre flessche,
For mannys loue he bledde hys blode.

cut, and shed his blood for man's love.

¶ Þe blood droppyd as dew on rysshe
Fro þe mylde membre of þat swete fode;
Synne was harde, hys blood was nessche,
To defende folk fro feendys wode.

Sin was hard, his blood was soft.

¶ The Iewes aboute ȝode
The olde lawe to fulfille;
Þe childe suffride *and* lay stille
To bigge vs alł, and þat was skille,
Whyle þe olde lawe stode.

The child suffered, and the old law was fulfilled to redeem us all.

XX.

¶ Þat day his first blood he bledde,
Þat ȝaf man griþe grace to haue,
With a scharp flynt hys blood was schedde;
Þat kyng was corve as a knaue,
Þe briddes lymes were brode spradde.

By this first blood man obtained grace.

¶ On schort membre þe child was schaue,
In lowenes was þat brid lad to haue
To kepe men fro helle cave,
Mannys sowle to save.

His humility saved men from hell's cave.

¶ Lownesse lay byneþe þe sterres,
To bye hys chaffare þe child payed erres,
Dropes rede as ripe cherrees,
Þat fro his flesshe gan lave.

Wounds and blood he paid for man.

[leaf 133 *b.*]

XXI.

¶ God cam not to fordo þe lawe,
Ij lawes fulfilł he wolde;
Goddis sone was leyde ful lawe,
Whan he was maydenys childe on molde.

God came not to destroy, but to fulfil the law.

¶ Holy writte seiþ þis sawe,
For mannys goost he ȝaf no golde;

For man's spirit he gave no gold.

He shed his dear blood to help us to obtain heaven.

Hys dere blood was oute-drawe
  To helpe vs to hys heuenes holde.
¶ Þe childe lay flat vnfolde,
Þe riche prince was þere aprised,
He suffred to be circumcised ;
Euery man þat is well avised
  Þis feest preyse he scholde.

This feast ought to be praised by all.

XXII.

The blood shed by Christ feedeth us.

¶ Festyng vs fedde,
Þe bloode ri3t þat a brid bledde,
Lordys and ladde
Preyseþ þe lord þat vs ladde !

XXIII.

Epiphania domini.

The kings that visited Christ made their horses run ; they had no time to stand still.

¶ The Epiphanye I preyse in prees,
  Whan þe kyngis clenly come,
Þei made her hors rennen in rees,
  To stonde stille þei had no tome.
¶ With dromedaryes þei droue fro dees,
  Many a hundred myle fro home,
To seche a childe þat choisly chees
  In maydenes blode to blome.

Many a hundred miles from home they went to seek a choice child.

¶ Swych a rose roos neuere in Rome,
As þan was clad in flesshli cloke ;
Goddis sone a mayden soke,
Milk ran by þe childys choke,
  Swetter þan hony on gome.

A maiden gave suck to God's Son ; the milk, sweeter than honey, ran down the child's cheek.

XXIV.

[leaf 134.]

A threefold gift they brought the child—

¶ Gold and myrre and frank ensens,
  Þei brou3t to þe born brid,
Of riche gold one 3af hym pens,
  For richest kyng he scholde be kyd,
Þer clerkis synge her sequens.
  Frank ensens þer is sone hid,

rich gold, for a king ;

frankincense, for a priest.

Aȝens þe fende it is defens,
And dryueþ hym vnder daunger lyd.
¶ And after it betyd
Þat god was grettest preest,
Þan was frank ensens hym nest,
And bitter mirre bote is brest,
To deþe Iewes him chyd.

It is a defence against the devil.

Myrrh is a remedy against corruption.

XXV.

¶ At þe feest of Architriclyn
Þe lord þat bouȝt vs oute of bonde,
Turned water in-to wyn,
Þorowe blessyng of hys holy honde;
I hope þat blessyng schal be myn,
Whan I lete lyfe in londe;
And gode man it schal be þine,
To folwe god fast ȝif þou fonde.
¶ In writ I vndirstonde,
Foure feestis faire *and* fre,
Epiphanye be set on þe.
Epiphanye blessyd þou be,
Þou kepest man fro schonde!

At the marriage-feast Christ turned water into wine.

Four feasts are set in Epiphany.

XXVI.

¶ Of fyue loves of barley greyn,
And ij fyssches in rwle is rad,
God made a feest faire *and* pleyn.
V Mt folk þer-with he fad,
With v lovys and fysshes tweyn,
Greet cumpany þer-with was glad;
Þes woordys myȝt þou soþely seyn,
Þe lord of plenté þe pepil fad;
¶ Riche relef þei had,
Xij baskettis full of broke mete;
To preyse god we are deþe in dete,

God made a feast with five barley loaves and two small fishes.

Twelve baskets of fragments remained after the feast.

Forget not to praise God.

To preyse hym no man forȝete
With speches gode and glad.

XXVII.

¶ Foure festys in one be set,
By diuers dayes it fell;
But at þe feest of mesure met,
Wyn of water god wrouȝt well,
Neuer festour fedde better.
V Mt folk þan crist gan fede,
To flum Iordañ þe kyng gan fle,
And Iohan baþed hym in þat stede.
¶ Iohan weissch his faire fell
And crystened crist in water colde,
Whan crist was xxx wynter olde;
Thus iiij feestis to-gedir folde,
To stroye þe fende so fell.

[leaf 134 b.]

Never did a host give better entertainment.

John baptized Christ in the Jordan.

XXVIII.

Pascha.

Easter is our perfect food.

It is the best of all feasts.

¶ Estren is oure ful fode,
Whan cristis flesshe freendys schal fede;
All festis arn full gode,
But þat is douȝtiest at nede;
We ete þe duke þat died on rode,
Þat all deueles in helle drede;
Forsake ȝoure synnes wrecches wode,
Or mete of mercy ȝif ȝou no mede.
¶ God his blood gan schede,
His riche ribbes weren rent all rede,
For mannys love he þoled dede;
Now is hys body in forme of brede,
To stroye þe prince of pride.

Forsake your sins, or ye will not get the meat of mercy.

Christ's body is in form of bread to destroy the prince of pride.

XXIX.

The king hath sent four summonses,

¶ Þe kyng haþ sent foure somouns,
Est and west in euery ende,

For clerkis *with* clere corounes,
  Þe mete of m*er*cy haue in mynde;
Þe godspelleres *with* benysou*n*s,
  To fest þei bid eu*er*y freende,
As well beggers as barou*n*s;
  To goddis borde þei bid hem bende
¶ Ihesus holt vp his ende.
To defende vs *with* a fowle (egle) in flyȝt,
A dere oxe luk haþe diȝt.
Mark a lyou*n* fell in fiȝt,
  Mathew a man ful kende.

that is to say, the Evangelists, to bid all to his feast, both beggars and barons.

XXX.

¶ Þe Egle is frikest fowle in flye,
  Ou*er* all fowles to wawe hys wenge;
In þis ensau*m*ple Ioh*a*n say eslye,
  As he slombrid in slepynge,
In goddis godhed he say full hyȝe,
  Þe heyȝtes of hys hyȝe kynge.
With-oute any

The eagle is swiftest of all birds.

John in his sleep saw heavenly mysteries.

[*The rest is lacking.*]

II.

HORÆ DE CRUCE*.

[MS Miscell. Liturg. 104. (Bodl. Libr.) temp. Edw. III. or Edw. II. and Isabella (?).] [fol. 50.]

Hic incipiunt matutine de passione domini nostri ihesu cristi antiphona.

Patris sapiencia ueritas diuina deus [&c.]

Versiculus. Adoramus te criste [&c.]

[fol. 50 *b*.] DOmine ihesu criste filii dei uini pone passionem crucem et mortem tuam [&c.] Amen.

[fol. 51.] Swete ih*esu* cryst goddis sone of lyue.
Þin *passion þin croys þin ded þin wondes five.
Beelde us houre sinful soules *and* þin iugement.
Nou and in tyme of ded þat we ne be y-schent.
[D]eyne to ȝeue my[ȝ]t an[d] grace to hem þat moten lyuen.
And to dare reste here sinnes þou for ẏẏue.
Mo holi chirche and *kyndom loue and pes þou sende.
And to vs wreche sinful. lif wyt-outen ende.
Þat leuest kyng god and man wyt-outin endingg*e*.
Fader and sone and holy gost to þulk*e* bl[is]se us bringge.

Sweet Jesus, may thy passion, Cross, [*fol. 51 *b*.] and wounds preserve our souls now and in time of death.

[*fol. 52.]

Father, Son, and Holy Ghost, bring us to the bliss of heaven.

[fol. 52 *b*.] *Ad primam horam.* [&c.]

[fol. 61.] HOra prima dominum ducunt ad pilatum. [&c.] Adoramus te. Domine ihesu criste.

[*fol. 61 *b*.] At prime ih*esus* was y-lad pilatus by*fore.
Many false witnesse on hym were i bore.

At prime Jesus was led before Pilate.

* Only the *English* parts are here given, with the beginnings of the Latin prayers, &c. preceding them.

Hiis schines were y beten hiis honden weren y bonden. They beat him, spat upon him.
Hiis face hy gonne on spete lyt of heuene þey fonde.

Ad terciam horam. amen

[A leaf is wanting here.]

Crucifige clamitant hora terciarum [&c.] Adoramus [te]. [fol. 66.] [fol. 66 *b*.]
Domine ihesu criste.

At hondren day on wde þe giwes gonne grede. At the third hour they clothed him in a purple garment.
In schorn he was i.-wonden in purpil palle wede.
On his schulder he bar þe crois to þe pininggе
Sicut oculi ancille in manibus domine sue [&c.] [fol. 67.]

Hora sexta ihesus est cruce conclauatus [&c.] Adoramus [fol. 70 *b*.] [fol. 71.]
[te]. Domine ihesu criste filij.

At midday was ihes*us* crist y-nailed to þe rode. At mid-day he was nailed to the Cross.
Bitwixe tweye þeues he hongid for houre gode.
For þu*r*rst of stronge pine y-fuld he was wy[þ] galle. [fol. 71 *b*.]
Ye holi louird so god y-wrout þ*er* buiȝt houre sinnes
alle.

DEus in adiutorium [&c.]

Hora nona dominus ihesus expirauit [&c.] Adoramus. [fol. 76 *b*.]
Domine ihesu criste filij. [fol. 77.]

At none houre loue*r*d c*r*ist of þysse lif he wende. At noon he died.
He gradde hely þe holi gost to his fader he sende.
A knyt wit a kene spere þerlede his syde.
Þe herye qu*a*kede þe so*nn*e bi-com swart þat erer
*schon wel wide. Deus in adiutorium [&c.]. [fol. 77 *b*.]

De cruce deponitur hora uespertina fortitudo [&c.] [fol. 83.]
Adoramus te. Domine ihesu criste filij.

At euensong he was i-nome a dou*n* þat dere us hadde At evensong Jesus was taken from the Cross.
ibouȝt.
His mytte hys his stregþe lotede in heiȝe holi þout. [fol. 82 *b*.]
Swech deþ he under feng hele of alle wo.
Alas þe croune of worschepe to lowe hy leide þo.
COnuerte nos deus salutaris noster. [&c.]

[fol. 89 b.] HOra completorii. datur sepulture corpus [&c.] Ado-
[fol. 90.] ramus [te]. Domine ihesu criste.

At the last hour he was buried.

He was y-ȝeue to beryyng ate laste tyde.
Cristes body noble hope of liue to byde.
In oynt he was wyt aromat holi writ to fulle. 32
ȝoruful meynde of his deþ bee in myne wille. Amen.

[Then follows]

[fol. 91.] DOmine ne in furore tuo [&c.].

GLOSSARIAL INDEX.

Aten ende, Atte ende, at end, finally, 20, 21, 28.
Ath, oath, 125, 114.
Atwinne, in two, 131, 16.
Auonge, to receive, 22, 44.
Auote, on foot, 56, 467.
Aw, ought, 87, 5.
Awer, anywhere, 30, 150.
Awonderd, astonished, 72, 365.
Ayenst, against, 159.
Aysylle, vinegar, 185, 105.
Aȝeyn, against, 134, 86.
Aȝt, owed, 110, 76.
Aȝt, wealth, 110, 75.

Bad, bade, 81, 689.
Bald, bold, 81, 689.
Bale, Balwe, sorrow, grief, 67, 194.
Balk, beam, 79, 617.
Band, bound, 125, 114.
Baptem, baptism, 146, 443.
Baptim, Baptyme, baptism, 114, 215; 166.
Baptist, baptized, 126, 158.
Bar, bore, 24, 74.
Barn, a child, 70, 289.
Barreres, barriers, 139, 247.
Bat, amends, 210, 6.
Batail, battle, 36, 209.
Baundone, Baundun, power, subjection, 52, 53, 414.
Bayne, bath, 159.
Beaulté, beauty, 167.
Beblad, bedaubed with blood, 211, 28.
Bed, bade, 24, 63.
Bed, offered, 64, 69.
Bede, a prayer, 90, 114.
Bede, to entreat, beseech, 22, 44; to offer, 109, 38.
Beelde, protect, 222, 3.
Beerynge, roaring, 140, 285.
Begge, to build, 78, 575.
Behelet, covered, 194, 168.
Beie, ring, 28, 134.
Bek, beck, stream, 82, 742.
Belamy, good friend, 84, 804.
Beleue, to remain, 110, 86.
Belise, bellows, 84, 849.
Belwe, to bellow, 145, 409.
Beme, trumpet, 146, 449.
Bemoyled, bedaubed, 144, 376.
Beore, a bear, 140, 285.
Ber, did bear, 26, 107.
Bere, beer, 211, 41.
Bere, bier, 44, 310.
Bere, to roar, 215, 154.
Beri, to bury, 72, 371.
Beriing, Beryiing, burial, 79, 604; 95, 285.
Betaken, betoken, 118, 364.
Bete, to amend, 30, 141; 71, 324.
Beted, beaten, 140, 286.
Beten, bitten, 74, 434.
Beting, healing, 114, 273.
Biclupt, embraced, entwined, 24, 75.
Bicom, became, 20, 32.
Bidde, to entreat, 23, 44.
Bide, delay, 113, 204.
Bide, to abide, stop, 112, 166.
Bidene, forthwith, 63, 41; 75, 489; 92, 199.
Bigge, to buy, redeem, 217, 206.
Bigile, to beguile, 64, 71.
Bigon, began, 30, 143.
Biheold, Bihuld, behold, 24, 25, 63, 77.
Biheste, promise, 18, 12.
Bihet, promised, 20, 37.
Bihote, p.p. promised, 23, 60.
Biliue, quickly, 80, 641.
Billed, written, 138, 221.
Bimene, to signify, 91, 158.
Binne, Bynne, stall, 211, 47; 145, 409.
Bironne, besprinkled, 137, 173.
Bisening, sign, token, 118, 370.
Biset, surrounded, 34, 192.
Bispek, Byspeek, spoke of, 32, 33, 178.
Biswonk, toiled for, 27, 96.
Bisyden, beside, 43, 305.
Bitaken, to betoken, 70, 308.
Bite = biȝt, bent, 137, 192.
Bitid, happened, befallen, 80, 649.
Bitwix, betwixt, 90, 136.
Bialle, to befall, 54, 422.

Biþenche, to bethink, 18, 13.
Bleo, colour, 131, 8.
Bleþeli, blithely, 112, 160.
Blin, to cease, 68, 212.
Blo, blue, 134, 107.
Blok, a block, tomb, 141, 314.
Blome, to bloom, blossom, 135, 116.
Blyne, by line, 203, 189.
Blyue, quickly, 44. 313.
Bobbe, to mock, 178, 54.
Bode, bidding, 64, 76.
Bolstre, bolster, 210, 6.
Bon, bone, 134, 93.
Bond, bound, 28, 132.
Bone, petition, boon, 42, 291.
Bord, tablet, 137, 188.
Boruȝ, Borwh, city, 54, 55, 439.
Bot, did bite, 135, 123.
Bot, Bote, but, except, 34, 198; 63, 51.
Bote, medicine, remedy, 24, 68.
Bot-if, unless, 96, 318.
Boune, ready, prepared, obedient, 75, 466; 81, 689.
Bour, chamber, 135, 116.
Bousomly, Buxumli, obediently, 90, 114; 108, 5.
Brade, broad, 77, 552.
Brast, did burst, 109, 54.
Braþeli, fiercely, 109, 54.
Brede, (1) breadth, 93, 209; (2) a board, 137, 188; 138, 204.
Breid, attack, 132, 37.
Brenne, Brin, to burn, 40, 272; 81, 680.
Brere, briar, 90, 133.
Brid, young bird, 133, 74.
Brig, Brugge, bridge, 30, 157; 82, 741.
Brim, stream, 125, 108.
Brisse, to bruise, 204, 225.
Broche, spear, 133, 55.
Brod, Brode, broad, 24, 73.
Bud, behoved, 79, 617.
Buirde, woman, 144, 381.
Buiȝt, bought, paid for, 223, 21.
Bulde, built, 30, 146.
Bus, behoves, 65, 127.
By, to buy, redeem, 67, 194.
Byforen, before, 37, 216.
Byhat, promiseth, 210, 10.
Byleue, remain, 44, 324.
Bylyue, to believe, 157.
Bynome, p.p. taken away, 46, 331.
Byuore, before, 36, 216; 56, 472.
Byȝe, ring, 29, 134.

Care, sorrow, 74, 439.
Caroyne, corpse, 161.
Catel, wealth, property, 112, 142.
Chargeour, charger, dish, 136, 165.
Chese, to choose, 40, 270; pret. Chees, 218, 244.
Childer, children, 73, 398.
Chirchen, churches, 52, 434.
Chinere, to shiver, 144, 386.
Choisly, 218, 244.
Choke, cheek, 218, 249.
Chyd, chided, 219, 263.
Chyned, split, cracked, 142, 329.
Clanliche, wholly, 52, 432.
Clath, cloth, 74, 428; 81, 680.
Clepe, Clupe, to call, 20, 21, 35.
Clergy, learning, 89, 67.
Clething, clothing, 129, 265.
Cleynt, clenched, 138, 205.
Clifte, hole, 205, 258.
Cliht, clutched, seized, 145, 410, 427.
Cloddre, clot, 142, 326.
Clunge, clotted, 142, 326.
Confermen, Confermy, to confirm, 26, 27, 107.
Core, chosen, 195, 194.
Coriosly, curiously, 123, 38.
Corone, to crown, 79, 607.
Corown, a crown, 78, 601; 130, 281.
Cors, body, 72, 356; 95, 291.
Corve, carved, cut, 217, 197.
Cos, a kiss, 147, 488.
Couenand, covenant, 110, 79.
Crake, to crack, 144, 388.
Creatour, creature, 148, 503.
Creste, covering, 212, 66.
Cristeny, to christen, 42, 299.
Crois, Croys, a cross, 34, 35, 185.
Croise, to cross, 133, 79.
Cromp, paw, claw, 139, 242.

Crop, Croppe, top, summit, 69, 259.
Croune, crown (of head), 66, 168.
Cumand, to command, 122, 10.
Cumbert, troubled, 196, 222.
Cun, to know, 93, 216.
Curnel, kernel, 26, 88.
Cusse, to kiss (pret. Custe), 133, 79; 134, 101.

Dalf. (*See* Delve.)
Dalt, distributed, 143, 351.
Dare (?), 222, 6.
Darted, uttered, 143, 364.
Dased, 216, 174.
Daunt, a check, rebuff, 145, 428.
Dawes, days, 28, 118.
Day, to die, 125, 130.
Debruse, to bruise, 40, 264.
Ded, dead, 26, 93; death, 81, 697.
Deef, Def, Defe, deaf, 130, 300; 148, 504.
Deel, dole, 215, 155.
Dees, dais, 218, 242.
Defaute, error, 22, 53.
Defende, to forbid, 67, 208; 119, 416.
Defoyled, defiled, 143, 370.
Dele, to distribute, 115, 277.
Delit, delight, 24, 65.
Delve, to dig (pret. Dalf, Dalve, p.p. Dolven, Idoluen, Idolven), 113, 184.
Deme, to judge, 83, 764.
Dent. (*See* Dint.)
Deol, dole, sorrow, 20, 21.
Dep, Deop, deep, 32, 33, 172.
Departe, to share, 143, 368.
Derne, secret, 28, 123.
Derworth, dear, precious, 195, 198.
Dete, debt, 219, 287.
Deyt, death, 195, 180.
Deþ, does, 24, 72.
Dight, Dihte. (*See* Diȝte.)
Dille, to hide, 108, 17.
Dint, Dunt, Dent, blow, stroke, 141, 296; 204, 205.
Dispitous, cruel, 143, 371.
Diȝte (pret. Dihte, Diȝte), to set in order, dispose, set up, treat, 50, 51, 410; 88, 47; 123, 49; 126, 144.
Dom, Dome, judgment, justice, 40, 270; 110, 70.
Domesman, judge, 83, 764.
Donne, dun, 144, 383.
Doted, bereft of reason, 216, 174.
Doute, fear, 48, 370.
Dradde, dreaded, 54, 452.
Draf, refuse, 141, 298.
Dredi, afraid, 140, 258.
Dreint, drowned, 138, 201.
Dreuen, driven, 68, 217.
Driȝt, Driȝtine, lord, 109, 60; 111, 119.
Drof, drove, 18, 12; 141, 298.
Drogh, Drouȝ, drew, 58, 489; 62, 4.
Dros, dross, 147, 490.
Drouknyng, swoon, 141, 309.
Druiȝe, dry, 142, 328.
Druri, a love token, a precious gift, 108, 26.
Dubbe, to deck, adorn, 127, 177.
Dubbing, ornaments, 130, 282.
Dude, did, 30, 140.
Dum, Dom, dumb, 130, 300; 148, 504.
Dunted, Dinted, struck, 138, 209.
Duyk, leader, duke, 149, 522.
Duȝti, doughty, worthy, 109, 29.
Dwelful, doleful, piteous, 150, 7.

Efsone, Eftsone, again, 24, 25, 77.
Eft, afterward, 69, 252.
Egge, edge, 136, 150.
Eghen, eyes, 64, 82.
Ek, also, 24, 81.
Eld, Elde, old age, 22, 43.
Encheson, reason, 38, 238.
Ending, death, 120, 442.
Enioynet, enjoined, 132, 44.
Enqueri, to enquire, 38, 241.
Ensoynet, excused, 132, 46.
Entent, heed, 82, 708.
Enter, entire, 196, 229.
Eode, went, 26, 101.
Eorþe, Erþe, earth, 20, 21, 33.
Er, are, 67, 188.

Er, previously, before, ere, 28, 111.
Erer, before, 223, 25.
Ernde, errand, message, 22, 58.
Erres, scars, wounds, 217, 218. (*See* Gloss. to Hampole's Pricke of Conscience.)
Erþliche, earthly, 50, 404.
Escrie, to cry out, 169.
Escte, asked, 22, 57.
Etin, a giant, 118, 359.
Euerich, every, 22, 50.
Euerilka, every one, 82, 721.
Euill, sore, 85, 844.
Eysel, Eisil, vinegar, 133, 75.

Fa, foe, 63, 64.
Fad, fed, 219, 280.
Fade, faded, 66, 156.
Falow, Falwed, withered, faded, 66, 156; 132, 28.
Fand, found, 64, 65.
Fanding, temptation, 70, 288.
Far, fare, 62, 17.
Far, Fare, proceeding, welfare, 80, 637; 95, 283.
Fat, feedeth, 210, 4.
Faunt, a child, 145, 424.
Fawset, a faucet, 211, 25.
Faȝt, fought, 118, 359.
Fe, goods, 125, 112.
Feble, poor, mean, 54, 458.
Feere, fellow, companion, 147, 472.
Fel, fell, fierce, 117, 335.
Fele, to smell, 73, 421.
Fele, Feole, many, 216, 177; 132, 50.
Feond, enemy, 137, 185.
Feor, far, 139, 257.
Ferde, fearful, afraid, 121, 472.
Ferdnes, fear, 122, 26.
Fere, 'IN FERE,' together, 74, 431
Fere, whole, sound, 74, 436.
Fere, to frighten, 174, 38.
Ferlely, Ferly, marvellously, wonderfully, 119, 413; 85, 849.
Fers, demands, 110, 98.
Fest, feast, 220, 290.
Festour, one who makes a feast, 220, 294.
Fette, Fett, fetch, 75, 485.
Feynet, pierced (?), 132, 50.
Fise, fish, 32, 172.
Flapped, struck, 176, 48.
Fleeche, 137, 179.
Flemon, to banish, 216, 183.
Fleoten, Flete, to flow, float, 216, 177; 32, 33, 179.
Flesse, flesh, 110, 84.
Fletynge, Fleotynde, floating, 32, 33, 180.
Flitte, to remove, 73, 391.
Flomb, fell (?), 139, 246.
Flum, stream, 220, 296.
Flyte, to strive, 216, 182.
Fodder, 133, 77.
Fode, creature, 217, 200.
Folfille, to fulfil (pret. Folfuld), 19, 13; 140, 275, 278.
Folliche, fully, 31, 146.
Fon, foes, 36, 207.
Fond, found, 26, 93.
Fonge, to take, 137, 181.
Forbed, forbade, 63, 52.
Forbled, all covered over with blood, 191, 140.
Forbrende, burnt up, 23, 50.
Fordo, to put an end to, 70, 283.
Fordolled, very dull, 141, 309.
Forlete, forsake, give up, leave, 35, 203; 120, 429.
Forlore, forlorn, ruined, wholly lost, 21, 20.
Formast, first, 70, 288.
Formfader, first father, 62, 1.
Foroldet, very aged, 25, 74.
For-swong, scourged, flogged, 194, 169.
Forte, until, 29, 114.
Forward, covenant, 110, 80.
Fot, fetched, 119, 420.
Fouled, defiled, 132, 28.
Foundement, foundation, 119, 391.
Foundet, found (? tried), 148, 507.
Fourteþe, Fourteneþe, fourteenth, 30, 31, 144.
Foȝte, fought, 52, 412.
Fram, from, 18, 2.
Frandes, fraudulent, 134, 108.

Fray, fright, 192, 146.
Freo, free, gracious, 131, 1.
Freond, friend, 135, 130.
Frike, bold, 221, 329.
Fulde, filled, 29, 120.
Fulfilde, filled full of, 120, 426.
Fun, Funden, found, 87, 3; 95, 308.
Fund, ceased (?), 120, 432.
Fur, far, 32, 170.
Fur, Fuir, fire, 40, 41, 273.
Fylde, field, 139, 257.
Fyne, to cease, 91, 150.

Gaaf, gave, 154.
Gad, goad, 211, 24.
Gaf, gave, 168.
Galwed, put on the gallows or cross, 132, 29.
Galwes, gallows, 132, 31.
Gast, ghost, spirit, 71, 334.
Gastly, spiritual, 88, 48.
Gat, heed, 210, 8.
Gaudes, jests, tricks, 134, 104.
Gelte, guilt, 132, 30.
Ger (= Gar), cause, 72, 371.
Gerne, diligently, 119, 423.
Gerrard, the devil (? = Low Germ. *Gêr-ard*, a miser), 64, 71.
Gest, talk, 211, 29.
Gidi, giddy, foolish, 58, 495.
Ginne, begin, 135, 113.
Gladliche, gladly, 38, 234.
Godhed, Godhead, 221, 333.
Godspellere, evangelist, 221, 320.
Gome, Goome, heed, 34, 35, 192.
Gome, palate, gum, 218, 250.
Gost, spirit, 138, 201.
Graid, prepared, placed, arranged, arrayed, 70, 299; 71, 351; 83, 753; 109, 43.
Graithly, straight, direct, 128, 219.
Gramed, enraged, 132, 24.
Graue, to bury (pret. Groue, Grofe), 79, 603; 72, 364; 108, 14; 89, 84.
Grede, to roar, cry out, 223, 15; pret. Gradde, 223, 23.
Gredire, Gledeire, gridiron, 58, 59, 503.
Greiþe, to prepare, 132, 31.
Grete, to weep, 67, 184.
Greyd (*see* Graid), 198, 44.
Grise, to be terrified, 121, 476.
Groche, Grucche, to murmur, 74, 443; 216, 170.
Groued, grew, 66, 154.
Grubbe, to dig up, 94, 267, 268.
Grundin, ground, sharpened, 110, 91.
Guarysshe, to heal, 155.
Gude, good, 73, 421.
Gudely, goodly, 71, 351.
Gun (pl.), did, 91, 140.
Gunfanoun, banner, 118, 384.
Gylour, traitor, 139, 254.
Gyn, Gynne, craft, deceit, 46, 331; 96, 318.

Ha, Habbe, to have, 18, 1; 139, 238.
Hailse, to greet, salute, 113, 206.
Hald, to hold, 87, 26.
Hale, whole, 73, 403.
Halghed, hallowed, 114, 211.
Halwe, to hallow, 56, 486; 132, 27.
Haly, holy, 75, 481.
Ham, them, 108, 19.
Hame, home, 70, 297.
Hamward, homeward, 70, 314.
Hasteliche, Hastiliche, hastily, 42, 43, 299.
Hate, hot, 85, 850.
Hayle, to pour, 132, 39.
Heder, hither, 62, 15.
Heerde, a herdsman, 141, 294.
Heght, height, 69, 256.
Heie, Heiȝe, to hie, hasten, 28, 29, 115.
Hele, salvation, 87, 2.
Helm, crown (of head), 142, 321.
Hend, hands, 71, 334.
Henede, killed by stoning, 40, 263.
Heng, hung, 34, 187.
Henne, hence, 46, 335.
Herdes, hards, tow, 81, 681.
Herre, higher, 52, 428.
Herting, comfort, encouragement, 88, 40.

known (pret. Kend), 66, 140; 90, 107; 132, 51; 89, 74.
Kende, Kynde, kind, nature, natural disposition, 144, 390; 145, 405.
Kenyng, sign, 128, 237.
Kerue, to cut, 136, 151.
Kest, pret. cast, 66, 168; 89, 87.
Kinne, nature, 138, 224.
Kiþe, to show (pret. Kid, Kud), 80, 650; 89, 76; 121, 469.
Knape, boy, 136, 142.
Knaw, to know, 81, 706.
Kowth, knew, 71, 348.
Kned, evil one, devil, 196, 222.

Lad, Ladde, led, 28, 122; 139, 253.
Laghe, law, 116, 296, 297.
Lak, fault, blame, 148, 509.
Lakke, to blame, 145, 432.
Lang, long, length, 71, 342; 116, 316.
Langer, longer, 68, 218.
Lappe, to wrap, 69, 261.
Lar, Lare, lore, 64, 75.
Largely, freely, 74, 451.
Last, leads, 22, 48.
Lat, ceaseth, 210, 15.
Lat, let, 65, 104.
Lauedi, lady, 110, 71.
Lause, release, 108, 4.
Lave, to pour, 217, 220.
Lawe, law, 217, 221.
Lay, law, 42, 298.
Laþ, loth, 108, 12.
Laȝt, took, 120, 443.
Leche, physician, 138, 217.
Lede, people, folk, 109, 37.
Leef, dear, fain, 216, 188.
Leete, let, 142, 324.
Lef, leaf, 24, 74.
Legge, to lay, 26, 89.
Leir, lair, 200, 96.
Lely, loyally, faithfully, 87, 10; 89, 69.
Lend, to dwell, abide, 64, 80; 67, 174.
Leng, longer, 46, 333.
Lenkith, Lenth, length, 73, 393; 125, 103.
Leof (Leoue, def. and pl.), dear, 21, 36; 136, 147.
Leone, to lean, 134, 90, 93.
Leop, leapt, 144, 385.
Leorne, Lerny, to learn, 32, 33, 164.
Leoþi, weak, feeble, 147, 483.
Ler, loss, 210, 9.
Lerd, learned, 96, 347.
Lere, bare, 24, 73.
Lere, to teach, 26, 27, 102.
Let, delay, 66, 143.
Lete, forsake, give up, 216, 172.
Lett, delay, 122, 10.
Leude, lewd, unlearned, 96, 347.
Libbe, to live, 21, 39.
Lift, left, 50, 391, 392.
Ligge, to lie (*Liggen*, lięn; *Ligand*, lying), 32, 166; 62, 14; 89, 89.
Lihtynge, Liȝtinge, lightning, 46, 47, 352.
Like, to please, 123, 46.
Liking, pleasure, 67, 174; 79, 608.
Lim, Lym, limb, 20, 21, 32.
Lite, Lyte, little, 216, 178.
Lite, remission, 112, 137.
Lith, member (of body), 67, 197.
Loddere, knave, 146, 450.
Logge, lodging, dwelling, 146, 458.
Logh, laughed, 71, 329.
Loked, Looked, ordained, devised, 133, 57; 145, 423, 433.
Lolle, lull, 214, 138.
Lomb, lamb, 141, 288.
Loren, Lorne, lost, ruined, 118, 373; 146, 458.
Lotede, lay hidden, 223, 27.
Loud, openly, 122, 13.
Loue, Louing, Loueing, praise, 75, 459; 81, 701.
Louerd, lord, 54, 456 (margin).
Loute, to do obeisance to, to worship, 34, 198.
Loþe, harm, sin, 139, 231.
Lulle, 133, 80; 213, 84.
Lumpyng, heavy, 141, 311.
Lure, loss, 135, 115.
Lute, Luytel, little, 36, 219; 37, 219.
Luþer, vile. 35, 183.

Ma, to make, 63, 63; Mase, make, 95, 311.
Maister, Mayster, master, victor, 36, 37, 212.
Maistrie, victory, mastery, 36, 219; 125, 109.
Mankunde, mankind, 18, 2.
Manslauȝt, manslaughter, murder, 30, 138.
Mapped, terrified, mated, 216, 175.
Mar, Mare, more, 113, 195.
Mased, amazed, 216, 175.
Maste, greatest, 114, 210.
Maugrefe, curse, 111, 125.
Maumet, idol, 34, 197.
Maumetry, idolatry, 90, 122; 124, 72.
May, maid, 148, 514.
Me, one, 56, 482.
Med, mead, meadow, 24, 66.
Medle, to mix, 139, 233.
Melle, to mix, 204, 220.
Mende, amends, 119, 415.
Mene, to recollect, 92, 175; to signify, 63, 42.
Mene, to moan, 78, 566.
Mencing, remembrance, 78, 590.
Mensk, to honour, 114, 209, 212.
Mekell, great, 64, 98.
Menȝé, Meyné, retinue, attendants, 73, 400; 115, 264; 122, 4.
Meode, mead, 139, 233.
Merk, dark, 139, 230.
Merk, mark, 79, 633; to mark, 117, 350.
Messagere, messenger, 110, 68.
Meste, most, 136, 164, 168.
Met, measure, 79, 621; meet, 220, 292.
Mete, to measure, 30, 152.
Meynt, mingled, 151. 31.
Mid, with, 46, 331.
Mikil, great, much, 114, 229.
Milse, Milce, mercy, 18, 19, 11.
Minne, Min, Myn, Mynne, to recollect, bethink, 145, 411; 138, 222; 114, 218; to talk of, mention, 134, 91.
Mirknes, darkness, 93, 223.
Mis, missing, sin, wrong, 66, 150, 157.
Misfare, misfortune, 118, 366.
Missay, to slander, 111, 128, 130, 131.
Mistrowand, misbelieving, 74, 442.
Mo, more, 28, 113.
Mochel, much, 215, 159.
Mode, mind, 177, 43.
Moght, Muȝt, might, 71, 342; 110, 81.
Mon, man, 132, 34.
Mon, moan, 131, 3.
Mone, moon, 144, 384.
Monslauht, manslaughter, 31, 138.
More, a root, 18, 5.
Mot, may, 38, 240.
Moun, may, 182, 89.
Mouwe, mockery, jest, 134, 103.
Mow, may, 192, 145.
Muche, great, 36, 206.
Muchedel, a great part, 36, 207.
Mun, must, 95, 312.
Munde, mind, 18, 1.
Murie, pleasant, 24, 64.
Musell, to muzzle, 213, 95.
Mustraunce, manifestation, 120, 448.
Mysuarynge, misbehaving, 50, 398.

Na, no, 114, 257.
Nabbe, have not, 45, 321.
Namlich, especially, 170, 9.
Nan, Nane, none, 68, 242; 118, 368; Nanne *(a. m.)* 22, 45; Nanes, nonce, 127, 178; Na wiȝt, nought, 111, 131.
Nas, was not, 24, 82.
Naþeles, nevertheless, 44, 307.
Neddre, serpent, 24, 75; 117, 335.
Neght, to approach, 74, 435.
Neih, Neiȝ, Ney, near, nigh, 20, 21, 22.
Neise, nose, 111, 107.
Nele, Nule, will not, 20, 21, 22.
Nelyn, will not, 150, 20.
Nemil, nimble, 113, 182.
Nempne, Nempnen, to name, 20, 29; 43, 300.

Neoȝe, nine, 28, 118 (margin).
Ner, nearer, 22, 56.
Nesch, soft, 143, 353; 217, 201.
Neuening, naming, 81, 694.
Neuereft, never again, 22, 51.
Neuyn, to name, 81, 688.
Nimen, Nymen, to take, 31, 152; 32, 169; pret. Nom, 18, 7.
Nite, Nyte, to deny, 121, 473, 478.
Niþe, ninth, 29, 122.
Nobleie, nobility, splendour, 54, 459.
Noke, nook, notch, 119, 395.
Nolde, would not, 20, 25.
Nome, name, 21, 29.
Non, noon, 44, 309.
Norys, nurse, 215, 156.
Note, advantage, profit, 119, 424.
Noteful, useful, precious, 108, 23.
Noye, to annoy, 122, 22.
Noþer, Nowþer, neither, 24, 74; 67, 184.
Noȝt for-þi, nevertheless, 121, 473.
Nye, nine, 28, 118.
Nyend, Nyþe, ninth, 28, 122; 76, 517.
Nuyȝe, to annoy, 132, 34.
Nywe, new, 56, 472.

O, On, one, 28, 127, 128.
Oblist, obliged, 126, 146.
Obouen, above, 68, 239.
Obout, Obut, about, 63, 40; 127, 177.
Ocupide, filled, 64, 84.
Of-liued, = over-lived, too-long-lived, 21, 36.
Of-swonk, earned by toil, 26, 96.
Oftsiþes, ofttimes, 82, 724.
Ogain, again, 62, 19.
Omang, among, 72, 359.
Omell, among, 90, 103.
Onloft, aloft, 121, 466.
Or, ere, 62, 7.
Ord, point, 136, 149.
Ore, mercy, 20, 21.
Os, as, 192, 148.
Ous, us, 18, 5.
Outtoke, excepted, 63, 51.
Ouercom, overcame, 36, 218.
Ow, you, 19, 8.
Owe, own, 30, 138.
Owhere, everywhere, 31, 150.
Owþir, either, 125, 115.
Oþe, oath, 139, 229.

Pace, to pass away, 149, 524.
Painym, Paynym, pagan, 34, 35, 204.
Panne, skull, 150, 11.
Parates, = parts, 119, 397.
Parlesy, palsy, 130, 299.
Partie, part, 48, 373; pl. Partise, 114, 238.
Pay, to please, 71, 328.
Pensynnys, pincers, 189, 125.
Pette, placed, put, 211, 27.
Piningge, torment, 223, 17.
Pinne, to fasten, 131, 14.
Pite (= Piȝt), put, 137, 190.
Plater, platter, 137, 171.
Plete, to plead (?), 141, 290.
Plett, inserted, 123, 54.
Pleynyng, complaining, 147, 473.
Polist, polished, 79, 631.
Pouder, dust, 66, 168.
Pouer, poor, 110, 75.
Pouerly, poorly, 129, 266.
Powder, to cast dust on, 65, 117.
Powsté, power, 63, 55.
Prece, press, 56, 468.
Prees, Prese, press, 218, 238; 128, 228.
Presthede, priesthood, 117, 347.
Prestly, quickly, 147, 467.
Preue, Priue, secret, 123, 61; 92, 182.
Preuely, secretly, 129, 268.
Pried, prayed, 69, 275.
Pris, worth, value, 144, 399.
Prout, proud, 48, 375.
Prute, pride, 50, 386.
Puiten, to put, 147, 473.
Pulle, thrust, 60, 514.
Pulte, thrust, thrust out, put, 24, 63; 134, 100; 140, 283.
Puruay, to make ready, 92, 208.
Pyement, a kind of drink, 210, 22.

Pyne, Peyne, pain, torment, 24, 25, 87.
Pyscyne, a fish-pool, 155.

Qua, who, 118, 370.
Quare, where, 108, 16.
Quasum, whoso, 109, 31.
Quat, what, 110, 73; 121, 467.
Quatkin, of what kind, 114, 232.
Queinteliche, Qweynteliche, neatly, 30, 31, 151.
Quelle, to kill, 39, 230.
Queme, to please, satisfy, 110, 100.
Quemus, pleasure, satisfaction, 146, 453.
Quen, when, 108, 9.
Quere, where, 112, 154.
Quert, joy, 108, 8.
Queynt, quenched, 138, 203.
Queyntise, craft, 48, 381.
Queþer, whether, 120, 457.
Quiche, which, 115, 246.
Quiddersum, whitherso, 120, 437.
Quilk, which, 113, 188.
Quite, quit, 112, 140.
Quiþerwine, enemy, 121, 483.

Rad, read, 210, 17.
Rad, advised, 137, 174.
Rane, touched, 113, 201.
Rape, hasten, 135, 140.
Ras, Rase, rose, 88, 41; 109, 53.
Rathly, quickly, 84, 786.
Raunsoun, ransom, 118, 383.
Raþer, sooner, 30, 142.
Reall, royal, 128, 226.
Really, royally, 130, 293.
Reche, to stretch, 147, 491.
Red, advised, 64, 67.
Red, counsel, 32, 166, 178.
Rede, to advise, 131, 17.
Rede, to tell, 108, 1.
Rees, race, 218, 240.
Regne, to reign, 148, 498.
Reke, vapour, fume, 94, 249.
Relef, remainder, 218, 285.
Releue, relief, 96, 347.
Rem, gore, 146, 444.
Rembnand, remnant, 84, 789.
Remu, to remove, 77, 536.
Remus, cries, 146, 451.
Renne, Rinne, Ryn, to run, 135, 140; 132, 47; 111, 122.
Rere, to raise, 28, 129.
Resoun, account, 93, 221.
Reuþe, sorrow, ruth, 146, 451.
Rew, to rue, have pity, 81, 684.
Reyn, 48, 382.
Riallté, royalty, 124, 69.
Rihtful, just, 114, 389.
Risshe, Ryssche, rush, 110, 95; 217, 199.
Riȝtwisnes, righteousness, 116, 300.
Ro, peace, 143, 358.
Robbyng, robbery, 132, 32.
Rod, rode, 148, 519.
Rod, Rode, Rude, rood, cross, 42, 304; 93, 227; pl. Roden, 42, 303.
Rosten, Rosti, to roast, 58, 59, 504.
Roune, to whisper, speak gently, 215, 156.
Rout, company, crowd, 91, 164.
Routhe, grief, 131, 17.
Royame, realm, 155.
Rugge, back, 136, 152.
Ruit, destruction, 132, 42.
Ryf, rife, 132, 32.
Rynde, bark, rind, 21, 74.
Ryot, riot, 132, 42.

Sa, so, 112, 146.
Sacrynge, sacrifice, 138, 218.
Sad, firm, 137, 180.
Sagh, saw, 109, 49.
Saih, saw, 148, 501.
Saint, holy, 111, 119.
Sakles, innocent, 69, 271.
Sald, should, 89, 99.
Samin, Samyn, together, 73, 415; 128, 236.
Sand, message, word, 82, 720; 66, 137; messenger, 109, 62.
Sare, sore, 71, 320.
Sareness, soreness, 85, 826.
Saueliche, safely, 54, 454.
Saun, sown, 90, 101.
Sawded, soldered, 77, 553.

Sonne, sun, 144, 385.
Sooþfastnesse, truth, 213, 99.
Sorowand, sorrowing, 63, 29.
Sote, sweet, 194, 173.
Soyle, defile, 143, 363.
Soyned, excused, 199, 59.
Soþ, truth, true, 114, 230; 42, 288.
Soþfast, true, 133, 61.
Soþliche, Soþly, truly, 132, 35; 148, 517.
Spede, success, 108, 2.
Spene, ? stop, 213, 107.
Spille, to destroy, 44, 330.
Spir, to enquire, 91, 168.
Sponne, spun, 144, 387.
Spot, blemish, 131, 15.
Spotty, defiled, 213, 105.
Sprong, sprang, 32, 171.
Squa, so, 108, 16.
Squat, bumped, 142, 319.
Squete, sweet, 114, 223.
Squorde, sword, 118, 362.
Stad, placed, 118, 377.
Stalle, manger, 133, 77; seat, throne, 124, 67.
Stalwurthly, strong, 77, 543.
Standen, p.p. stood, 116, 290.
Stane, stone, 72, 371; to stone, 81, 692.
Stang, sting, 117, 342.
Stanged, stung, 117, 336.
Stap, step, 22, 52.
Stayer, Steir, step, stair, 148, 497; 134, 85.
Stene, to stone, 41, 263.
Step, stepped, 22, 50.
Stepmoder, stepmother, 133, 71.
Stere, correction, 210, 7.
Stern, star, 123, 56.
Sterre, star, 48, 378; pl. Sterren, 56, 473.
Sterte, to go to, visit, 214, 124.
Sterue, to die, 147, 474.
Steuyn, voice, 129, 249.
Stike, to stick, 134, 85.
Stipre, support, 135, 135.
Stiþe, stiff, strong, 109, 36.
Stiȝe, ascended, 212, 52.
Stokky, stock-like, 148, 518.
Stounde, time, 18, 4.
Stour, throe, agony, 148, 501.
Strang, strong, 71, 341.
Streiȝt, stretched, 134, 100.
Strenkit, strength, 87, 18.
Stroye, to destroy, 220, 315.
Stude, place, 24, 64.
Stye, sty, 215, 142.
Suld, should, 63, 44.
Sulf, self, 24, 62.
Sumdele, somewhat, 65, 123.
Sunne, sin, 18, 9.
Suote, sweet, 56, 469.
Suotnesse, sweetness, 28, 120.
Surded, defiled, 143, 374.
Suth, sooth, truth, 62, 22.
Suthfastnes, truth, 94, 256.
Suwen, to follow, 53, 415.
Swapped, struck, 142, 336.
Swapte, fell down, 142, 340.
Swarmes (?), 135, 128.
Swart, black, 223, 25.
Swech, such, 223, 28.
Swelte, died, 135, 119, 127.
Swemly, swooning, 135, 127; 201, 140.
Sweore, neck, 134, 100.
Swerd, sword, 142, 336.
Swinke, Swynke, to labour, toil, 20, 33.
Swith, Swiþe, very, 28, 135; quickly, 76, 516.
Swonge, scourged, 142, 327.
Swote, sweet, 24, 67.
Swotnesse, sweetness, 29, 120.
Swouh, faint, swoon, 135, 127.
Swow, a swoon, 201, 140.

Ta, to take, 80, 652.
Tacched, attached, 143, 356.
Tak, tack, 145, 419.
Taken, to betoken, 117, 325.
Takening, token, 93, 243.
Takin, token, 95, 311.
Tald, told, 64, 91.
Taȝt, gave, 117, 349.
Tee, to travel, 192, 144.
Telli, to tell, 38, 240.
Tend, to attend, 120, 455.

Tene, Teone, sorrow, grief, wrath, 18, 19, 16; 74, 444; 135, 125.
Tent, heed, 67, 187; to attend, 118, 370.
Tere, tear, 135, 113.
Terve (= Sterve), to die, 207, 311.
Tethe, tenth, 52, 430.
Teye, to tie, 133, 62.
Thar, need, 67, 184.
Thret, threatened, 85, 829.
Thrid, third, 84, 788.
Thurgh, through, 65, 110.
Tid, betides, 44, 329.
Tilde, extended, 24, 80.
Tine, Tyne, to lose, 111, 113; 85, 822.
Tirand, tyrant, 121, 479.
Tite, Tyte, quickly, 81, 690, 704.
Tiþinge, Tiþande, tidings, message, 23, 58; 88, 45; 112, 159.
To-bursten, burst asunder, 132, 37.
To-clef, To-cloue, did cleave asunder, 142, 329; 144, 375; pierced, 137, 172.
To-dachud, beaten, dashed about, 180, 65.
To-fore, before, 154.
Toknynge, sign, 20, 27.
To-lachud, severely lashed, 180, 66.
Tome, leisure, spare time, 218, 241.
Tone, taken, 93, 231.
Tore, torn, 143, 372.
To-riue, riven asunder, 138, 210.
Tow, two, 125, 125; 201, 138.
Toyled, rent, 143, 372.
Traist, Trayst, trust, 125, 104; 88, 35.
Trauþ, faith, 109, 53.
Treget, sin, trespass, 207, 311.
Trene (= Strene), race, 147, 482.
Treo, tree, 131, 2.
Trie, choice, 143, 372.
Trille, to rock, 213, 86.
Tripet, trespass, 132, 41; 147, 480.
Trone, throne, 122, 9.
Trowth, belief, 67, 208.
Truit, Truyt, wrong, 132, 41; 147, 480.
Twei, two, 20, 20.
Twin, two, 119, 402.
Twyȝes, twice, 146, 448.
Tyde, hour, 224, 30.
Tynde, tine, prong, 201, 138.

Þa (pl.), the, 94, 289.
Þam, them, 62, 7.
Þarmes, bowels (? the arms), 135, 126.
Þeder, thither, 48, 373.
Þei, Þeiȝ, though, 18, 19, 11.
Þen, than, 34, 188.
Þen (acc.), the, 18, 7.
Þeof, thief (pl. Þeoues, Þeues), 34, 35, 187.
Þeose, these, 142, 331.
Þerlede, pierced, 223, 24.
Þes, this, 36, 212.
Þethin, thence, 90, 119.
Þir, these, 64, 100.
Þis-kin, of this kind, 88, 33.
Þit, this, 172, 23.
Þo, when, 20, 31.
Þo (pl.), the, 93, 219.
Þolie, to suffer, 52, 423, 425.
Þonky, to thank, 44, 314.
Þorou, Þoru, through, 18, 3; 118, 388.
Þrali, boldly, 110, 90.
Þrin, three, 119, 395.
Þrist, thirst, 151, 34.
Þritti, thirty, 20, 31.
Þrowe, suffering, 150, 18.
Þuderward, thitherward, 22, 45.
Þulke, that same, 18, 4.

Vche, each, 141, 294.
Vmþink, to consider, 116, 294.
Under-feng, received, 223, 28.
Vnderon, undern, 82, 722.
Vnfaine, sorry, 80, 637.
Vnfere, sick, 115, 277.
Vnfolde, spread out, 218, 229.
Vnfuyled, undefiled, 131, 21.
Vnioynet, dislocated, 142, 323.
Vnkid, unknown, 92, 189.
Vneþis, scarcely, 116, 285.
Vnquit, unpaid, 110, 85.
Vnsely, unhappy, 116, 283.

Vntill, unto, 62, 5.
Vnworþe, unworthy, 54, 452.
Unwrest, bad, wicked, 195, 191.
Vp, upon, 54, 458.
Vpbraide, abuse, 111, 136.
Vtterest, uttermost, 69, 268.
Vuel, evil, sickness, 24, 68.

Vaile, to fail, 30, 149.
Vair, fair, 24, 71.
Valle, to fall, 48, 382.
Vanist, vanished, 96, 333.
Uan-wite, lack of wit, folly, 180, 72.
Uaste, fast, 28, 126.
Velde, filled, 28, 120.
Velle, to fell, 30, 151.
Uerey, true, 190, 137.
Versch, fresh, 59, 504.
Uerst, first, 18, 3.
Vernorþ, far, 48, 383.
Vet, feet, 32, 173.
Vette, fetched, 28, 117.
Vewe, few, 26. 97.
Vil, vile, 32, 181.
Vili, to defile, 34, 183.
Viue, five, 40, 258.
Uolueld, fulfilled, 18. 13.
Vond, found, 22, 55; 26, 108.
Vondi, to try, 46, 331.
Vor, for, 22, 56.
Uorbarnde, burnt up, 22, 50; 58, 506.
Uorbrend, burnt up, 26, 92.
Uorlet, left, 22, 49.
Uorlore, lost, ruined, 18, 3.
Uorolded, grown old, 24, 74.
Uorsake, to forsake, 42, 298.
Vorte, until, 26, 101.
Vorte, for to, 44, 330.
Vorward, covenant, 50, 411.
Uorwelwed, withered, 22, 55.
Uorþ, forth, 22, 54; 38, 234.
Uorȝeue, forgiven, 30, 142.
Vylté, vileness, 161.

Wa, woe, 64. 98.
Wake, to watch, 76, 525.
Wald, would, 94, 245.
Walde, power, 93, 237.
Walt, suffered, 143, 355.
Walter, to die, 201, 132.
Wan, Whom, which, 24, 25, 72.
Wand, rod, 70, 303.
Wane, quantity, 74, 447; 130, 299.
Warde, care, 117, 338.
Waried, cursed, 121, 483.
Warisht, healed, 117, 342.
Warlaghe, traitor, 121, 466.
Warnist, furnished, 117, 326.
Wate, know, 63, 42.
Water, river, 125, 101.
Wawe, to wave, 221, 330.
Wayloway, well-a-day, 95, 306.
Wde, 'on wde' = (?) madly, 223, 15.
Wede, Weod, weed, 20, 21, 33.
Weft, woven, enclosed, 116, 292.
Welk, walked, 117, 337.
Welkit, withered, 66, 163.
Wellande, boiling, 121, 486.
Wenge, wing, 221, 330.
Weolþe, wealth, 145, 415.
Weop, Wep, wept, 20, 21; 142, 324.
Weopyng, weeping, 143, 355.
Werde, world, 113, 180.
Were, doubt, 72, 385.
Were, to defend, 121, 490.
Wered, Werde, drove off, 141, 297; 141, 302.
Werre, Worre, to war on, harass, 34, 35, 194.
Wers, worse, 111, 120.
Wesch, Wusch, washed, 32, 33, 173; 82, 726.
Weterly, truly, 65, 134.
Weȝt, weight, 110, 83.
Wha, who, 78, 584.
Whatlikere, sooner, 30, 142 (margin).
Whilk, which, 65, 121.
Whon, trade, 27, 96.
Whonne, when, 21, 38.
Wight, active, 78, 578.
Wikke, wicked, 133, 68.
Wilde, would, 120, 425.
Wilne, Wilny, to desire, 20, 34; 20, 21, 36.
Wirschip, honour, 73, 418.
Wis, to direct, 71, 335.

Wisse, wise, 125, 100.
Wit, Wite, to know, 77, 555; 18, 18; to protect, 37, 213.
Witering, knowledge, 114, 235.
Withgane, displease, 66, 152.
Withouten, without, 66, 148.
Wiþerwine, enemy, 108, 4.
Wobigon, woe-begone, 131, 6.
Wod, mad, 38, 243.
Wogh, woe, grief, 71, 330; wrong, 116, 305.
Woke, week, 196, 228.
Won, to dwell, 66, 150.
Won, (?) habitation, abode, 143, 347.
Won, conquered, 36, 219.
Wond, wound, 26, 105.
Wonder, wonderful, 50, 395.
Wonderly, wonderfully, 144, 401.
Wonynge, dwelling, 153, 13.
Wordle, world, 56, 473.
Worm, serpent, 117, 323.
Worthly, worthy, 124, 81.
Worþ, are, 22, 52.
Wounden, woundes, 40, 258.
Wouȝ, Wouh, wrong, 58, 59, 490.
Wox, grew, 28, 133.
Wreeches, poor men, 214, 125.
Wreche, misery, 138, 219; vengeance, 30, 139.
Wright, carpenter, 79, 616.
Wringe, to squeeze, 138, 214.
Wuch, which, 44, 306.
Wun, to dwell, 96, 320.
Wurth, to be, 95, 313.
Wurthed, became, 90, 127.
Wyf, woman, 132, 34.
Wykke, 153, 15. (*See* Wikke.)
Wyled, wild, 132, 25.
Wyte, to blame, 134, 95.

Yate, gate, 154.
Yauf, gave, 195, 208.
Yknowe, to know, 150, 20.
Ymad, made, 50, 411.
Ysinwed, sinned, 176, 50.
Ywys, truly, 151, 32.
Y-ȝeue, given, 224, 30.

ȝaf, gave, 33, 165.
ȝare, ready, 30, 146.
ȝarke, to prepare, 36, 208; 151, 24.
ȝat, ȝate, gate, 54, 466; 63, 31.
ȝef, gave, 32, 165.
ȝeld, ȝilde, yield, pay, 140, 261; 110, 82.
ȝelp, greedy, 140, 281.
ȝeme, heed, attention, 28, 130.
ȝer, year, 20, 25.
ȝerd, ȝerde, rod, 117, 323; 212, 74; staff, 141, 295; pl. ȝerden, rods, 26, 98.
ȝerne, ȝeorne, eagerly, 18, 19, 11.
ȝerne, to desire, long for, 62, 26.
ȝeufe, gave, 186, 110.
ȝhe, she, 152, 56.
ȝode, went, 73, 409.
ȝollynge, yelling, 44, 315.
ȝorne, diligently, 120, 431.
ȝoruful. *Read* ȝornful, earnest, 224, 33.
ȝut, yet, 32, 167.
ȝymmes, gems, 46, 344.

CORRECTIONS.

Page 8, line 20, *for* their speech (counsel) *read* it.
Page 12, line 1, *for* redeemed *read* redeemedst.
Page 17, line 6 from bottom, *for* we *read* þe.

www.ingramcontent.com/pod-product-compliance
Lightning Source LLC
Chambersburg PA
CBHW020346030726
47496CB00007B/2014

* 9 7 8 3 3 3 7 1 5 3 7 2 4 *